To Virginia

Best Wishes

Jerry Cooksey

Lincoln In The Basement

Bedside Books
An imprint of American Book Publishing
P.O. Box 65624
Salt Lake City, UT 84165
www.american-book.com
Printed in the United States of America on acid-free paper.

Lincoln in the Basement

Designed by Karl Andrews, design@american-book.com

Publisher's Note: *This is a work of fiction. Names, characters, places, and incidents either are the product of the author's imagination, or are used fictitiously, and any resemblance to actual persons, living or dead, events, or locales is entirely coincidental.*

ISBN 1-58982-268-4

Cowling, Jerry, Lincoln in the Basement

Special Sales

Lincoln In The Basement

A Historical Novel

Jerry Cowling

To my family,
Son Joshua, my hero
Daughter Heather, my joy
Son-in-law Matt, my other hero
Wife Janet, my love

Preface

Lincoln in the Basement began as a dream in 1989. I often dream stories in which I am an observer. This particular one was from the point of view of the Executive Mansion janitor, who was in the basement of the Executive Mansion when President and Mrs. Lincoln were escorted in at gunpoint by Secretary of War Edwin Stanton. Because he had seen too much, he had to stay in the basement with the Lincolns, and, after a period of time, began to believe he was the president.

As I began writing the story, I realized the poor janitor could not be the main character because he was basically incapable of change. I instead focused on the plight of the young soldier given the task of holding the Lincolns captive. He, indeed, changes from a naïve, eager servant of Stanton's cause to an alcoholic disillusioned by the abuse of power.

As a caveat, I want to make clear that I have taken historical figures such as Secretary of War Stanton and LaFayette Baker and used them to create fictional characters with qualities of greed, lust, and corruption. While some historians have theorized that Stanton may have been a conspirator in Lincoln's assassination, others maintain his innocence. I concur with this conclusion, and have fictionalized his personality to portray the danger of believing oneself to be infallible.

Lincoln in the Basement is meant as entertainment and as fodder for intellectual debate on political power, not as a strict interpretation of history.

Chapter One

Lifting his Remington revolver, its deep blue finish catching the late afternoon sun over the Potomac River, the young man smiled confidently as he looked down the wide sight groove at the coarse, unruly black hair of Abraham Lincoln, convinced his actions would save his country.

"Mr. Lincoln," said Secretary of War Edwin Stanton, causing the president to glance up from a file of Justice Department papers.

A quick smile flickered across Lincoln's broad lips when he first focused on the short, thickset man with the pharaoh-like beard, but it faded when his shadowed, hollowed eyes noticed the slender, rusty-haired army private holding his .44 caliber cap-and-ball pistol.

"Mr. Stanton, I see you brought company with you today," Lincoln said.

"Please come with us, Mr. President," Stanton said.

"It's for the best, sir. You'll thank us eventually. Trust me." The young man grinned broadly.

"Please come with us, Mr. President." Stanton turned sharply. "Private Christy, shut up."

"Yes, sir." He quickly looked down at the worn carpet and shuffled his shiny new boots, which were partially covered by baggy dark trousers.

Putting a long, bony finger to his forehead, Lincoln surveyed the secretary of war. "For what will I thank you, eventually?"

"The boy spoke out of turn, sir."

"Well, then, Mr. Stanton, may I inquire as to where you are taking me?"

Stanton removed his glasses, squinted, and took a deep breath, but before he could speak, Mary Todd Lincoln, wearing a flowing black brocaded silk dress over a rustling crinoline, swept into the room, waving a swatch of blue flowered-print cotton. The private concealed his revolver in his tunic.

"Father, Mrs. Keckley says I should move to a blue print from black but—" She stopped abruptly when she saw Stanton. Her eyebrows arched, and her lips pursed. "Oh. Excuse me. I didn't know you were here."

Stanton bowed.

"I suppose we can make Mrs. Keckley wait." Mrs. Lincoln focused strictly on her husband, who was putting his personal effects aside, ready to rise.

"Please inform your dressmaker, Mrs. Lincoln, that she must return tomorrow."

"Tomorrow? I go to Anderson Cottage tonight," Mrs. Lincoln said, slapping the billowing folds of her dress with the blue cotton swatch. "This is totally unacceptable!"

"Now, Molly," Lincoln said, finally making it to his feet and going to his wife's side, his long, gangling arms around her soft shoulders. "I think it'd be best if you kindly suggest to Mrs. Keckley that it'd be more convenient for us if she visited you at the Soldiers' Home tomorrow."

"But, Mr. Lincoln—"

"Blame it on me, if you wish, Molly."

"I certainly will!"

"Tell her it's a matter of state, dear."

"It's a matter of foolishness." Mrs. Lincoln sniffed and nodded curtly.

After his wife swirled from the room and down the private hallway to the oval family room, Lincoln returned his gaze to Stanton. "As you were saying?"

"Oh yes." The secretary of war put his small pebble glasses back on his pocked nose. "The basement."

"Not to review the kitchen staff, I presume."

Stanton smiled and shook his head. "The billiards room."

"These are desperate measures to round up competition for a game of billiards," Lincoln said laconically.

Their eyes were drawn to the door as the sound of stomping female feet echoed through the hallway. Eventually Mrs. Lincoln emerged and placed her hands on her ample hips.

"Now Mr. Stanton," Mrs. Lincoln said, "will you explain yourself?"

Private Adam Christy noticed Lincoln stepping back, glancing up at two cords over his desk, and slowly moving his hand up to the cord on the left.

Adam asked Lincoln, "What are those cords?"

Stanton turned. "Don't involve Mr. Nicolay and Mr. Hay."

"Well," Lincoln replied with a shrug, "I thought they'd enjoy a nice game of billiards."

"Billiards!" Mrs. Lincoln shook her head and moaned in exasperation. "What depths of insanity is this?"

This is not insanity, Adam thought. Ending the war is not insanity. The good of the nation called for Lincoln's temporary removal, Stanton had told him, so the correct decisions could be made to win the war.

"It's time to go," Stanton announced.

"Go where?" Mrs. Lincoln asked, edging toward hysteria. "Will someone please explain what's happening?"

"To the basement, Molly." Lincoln put his arm around her shoulder again and whispered, "Mr. Stanton wants to talk to us in the billiards room."

"Why?" Mrs. Lincoln looked at the secretary with bemusement.

"Lack of interruptions, I assume," her husband said. "The office is hectic."

No talk, Adam thought, just sit down there until Stanton wins the war. He would have informed the president of that, but he did not want another withering rebuke.

"Mr. President, we must go," the war secretary said.

Lincoln nodded as he eyed Stanton, then guided his wife through the door into the office waiting room. When they entered the president's office vestibule, Stanton raised his hand.

"Wait." He motioned to Adam. "Check the hallway and grand staircase landing."

Adam hurried down the hall, noting every door was shut on each side of the broad corridor. He stopped in his tracks as a tall, dignified black woman, modestly well-dressed, came from a door on the left, carrying a large carpetbag. Making eye contact with the woman, Adam dropped his jaw before composing himself and nodding to her. She examined the young man and crossed the hall to the door leading to the service stairs. Continuing to the end of the hall, Adam looked down on the landing covered with Brussels carpeting. He saw no one and hurried back through the ground-glass doors to the office vestibule.

"The way is clear," he said, huffing with excitement.

Before Stanton could reply, a tousle-headed boy of ten with a strangely impish round face slammed a bedroom door on the right and ran through the glass doors, but stopped short when he saw Stanton and the private. His dark eyes appraised the soldier.

"I know a boodle of soldiers," the boy said. "You're only a private, ain't you?"

"I haven't been in the army long." Adam shuffled his feet.

Stanton cleared his throat. "We don't have much time, Mr. Lincoln."

"I used to play with a lieutenant," the boy said. "Lieutenant Elmer Ellsworth. Of course, he got killed."

Grabbing the boy's shoulders, Stanton turned the boy toward the president.

"You can't push me around!" Wrestling away from Stanton's grip, the boy spun around, yanked the pharaoh beard, and stuck out his tongue. "I'm the president's son!"

"Now, Tad," Lincoln said soothingly as he enveloped the boy in his arms, "you know we taught you better manners than that."

"I say some people get what they deserve," Mrs. Lincoln said with a sniff.

"Molly," Lincoln said, looking at his wife, "don't make this more difficult."

"Take the boy to Mr. Nicolay and Mr. Hay." Stanton leaned into Lincoln. "Tell them to take Tad out to supper and don't return for two hours." He nodded at Adam. "Private Christy will be just out of sight behind the door, so don't say anything more."

Tad looked up inquisitively at his father. "Papa, why do you let hin. talk to you like that?"

"Hush, Tad." Lincoln smiled. "Let's go talk to Mr. Nicolay and Mr. Hay." Taking him by the hand, Lincoln went into the waiting room.

Following, Adam watched as Lincoln first glanced to the last door on the left, the secretaries' bedroom, and found it empty. He then turned to the last door on the right, where both young men hovered around the desk. The private stole a quick look the president's two secretaries before stepping behind the door. He was not impressed. One was about his age, twenty-two, and the other was somewhat older, perhaps thirty. But they were probably Nancy-boys in their French *zouave* baggy and pegged pants, their dark hair neatly trimmed and contrasting starkly with their smooth, alabaster faces. Women were drawn to pretty men in high-fashion clothes with clear, bland complexions, but it was Adam's experience that the ladies were disappointed when the dandies were more interested in themselves.

"Mr. Nicolay, Mr. Hay," Lincoln announced as he presented his son to them, "I have a favor to ask of you."

"Yes, sir?" Nicolay replied with a slight Bavarian accent.

Not even American, but some intruder from Germany—a suspect nation at best, Adam thought as he listened to Lincoln explain his supper request for the boy. Absently he stroked his rough cheek, mottled by a minor case of small pox when he was twelve years old. His brow furrowed as he remembered how women rarely were drawn to his ruddy, irregular face, his thick, unruly red hair, and his homespun clothes.

"Take him to the Willard," Lincoln said. "I've an account there. Let him have anything he wants for supper."

"Even pie and cake and ice cream?" Tad asked. "No vegetables?"

"If you wish."

"Are you sure Madame will approve?" Hay asked, uncertainty tingeing his voice, which was moderately higher pitched than Nicolay's baritone.

"Mrs. Lincoln won't mind, I assure you."

Adam could not resist the temptation of seeing the young men's faces to judge their response to this unusual presidential request. If they seemed too concerned, the secretaries might prove to be trouble later.

He slightly cocked his head to peer through the door. Tad was giving Lincoln a bear hug.

"I love you, Papa."

"And I love you, Tad." Lincoln wrapped his long arms around the boy, tangling his fingers in the curly brown locks. "Don't forget. Your papa loves you very much."

"Papa?"

"Yes?"

"I can't breathe."

Laughing, Lincoln released Tad, turned him around, and pushed him toward the two secretaries who looked, in the private's estimation, less than enthusiastic with their chore of supervising the rambunctious child, now jumping up and down, giggling, and pulling at their silk cravats. Lincoln quickly excused himself and walked through the waiting room. He looked over his shoulder and smiled slightly. "Come, Private Christy, for I fear the daggers shooting from Mrs. Lincoln's eyes may have dealt a fatal blow in Mr. Stanton's breast."

When they entered the vestibule, Stanton sighed deeply and headed for the glass door to the hallway. "*Finally*. This has taken entirely too long."

The small group walked down the hall to a door on the right leading to the service stairs. As they descended the narrow stairs, Mrs. Lincoln leaned into her husband.

"I still don't know what this is about."

"I'm not certain myself." Lincoln placed his massive, bony hand on her rounded shoulder and said, "I think it has to do with General McClellan's reinstatement as Army of the Potomac commander."

"The stairs aren't a proper place to discuss national policy," Stanton said before directing his attention to the descending steps.

"Are they a proper place to carry out the abduction of an American president?" Mrs. Lincoln asked, her voice barely under control.

"Molly, I don't think it's proper to discuss anything on the back stairs."

As they reached the first floor landing, all conversation ended; the only noise was the crackling of their footsteps on the straw mats covering the stairwell steps. Adam, hating a void, had a violent urge to speak but, with a will he was unaware he possessed, remained silent.

Chapter One

His mind went back ten years to when he was twelve, to his family's dark, cramped dining room in Steubenville, Ohio. Slowly the sensations came back to him. He remembered feeling warm, almost uncomfortable, with small beads of perspiration forming on his brow. School was out, it struck him, because he was relieved he would not have to tell his friends at school why he was crying. It was June. Of course.

"Wait until the newspapers hear this," Mrs. Lincoln hissed.

"Hush," Lincoln whispered.

How could Adam have forgotten that? Two days after classes ended his mother had died of smallpox. Family members from Ohio and nearby areas of Indiana and Pennsylvania had gathered for a large breakfast before a noon funeral. Adam remembered not being hungry at all as he had stared at a full plate of fried eggs, pork sausage, and blueberry muffins.

"Mother's favorite," he had mumbled.

"What?" Cora, his mother's oldest sister, said.

"Blueberry muffins. Mother always said she could make a meal of blueberry muffins and fresh-churned butter."

His father had coughed nervously, Adam remembered.

Aunt Cora, much stouter than his fragile mother, sniffed and spoke in a loud, bold voice. "I think we should just eat our breakfast and not speak."

Adam felt his neck burn with embarrassment and guilt. After all, if he had not come down with smallpox, his mother would not have died. He looked around the table, first at his father, hoping he would tell Aunt Cora to be quiet, then at the others around the table, but found no comforting eyes meeting his. During the next half hour, he was intensely aware of muffled chewing, the soft slurping of coffee, and the muted clicking of cups and scratching of knives and forks against china plates. All of this now flooded his mind as the crackling of the straw mats broke the stillness. Adam's back muscles flexed in agony.

For, ever since he was twelve years old, silence had sounded like death.

Chapter Two

Large, rusty iron traps clanged against each other in Gabby Zook's big rough hands as he lumbered down the hall of the Executive Mansion basement, muttering to himself.

"Got to find the rats; can't have rats in the White House. Not around the president and his lady. No, that wouldn't be proper. No, it wouldn't be right to have rats in the White House, not when there's a war going on; not when *no* war's going on, either. Rats in the White House aren't proper any time."

Sticking his gray-haired head in the door of the main kitchen, Gabby asked, "Seen any rats in here, Miss Phebe?"

"No, sir, Mr. Gabby." A tall, dark brown young woman looked up from the massive cast-iron stove set into the left wall and flashed a toothy, friendly grin. "We keep those critters chased out of here."

"Yeah, we chop them up and feed them to the white folks upstairs," said a short, slender, caramel-colored man in his thirties as he walked up with a basket of carrots, tomatoes, and onions.

"The president eats rats?" Gabby's eyes widened.

"Oh, Neal, don't tease Mr. Gabby." Phebe lightly slapped the shoulder of her companion in the kitchen and laughed.

"What does rat taste like?" Gabby said, his eyes squinted in curiosity.

"Chicken." Neal smiled broadly.

"Mr. Gabby, Neal is pulling your leg." Phebe shook her head in amusement. "Now, you pay him no mind. No white folks eat rat in the White

House, or any other house." She glanced at Neal. "Tell him straight that folks don't eat rat."

"That's right, Mr. Gabby," Neal said. "Nobody eats rats, unless they're real hungry and don't have nothing else to eat."

"And there's plenty of good stuff to eat in the White House." Gabby nodded.

"Plenty of good stuff here, Mr. Gabby," Neal said, putting the basket filled with vegetables on a rough chopping block table next to the stove. He looked at Phebe. "Are they eating here before they return to the Soldiers' Home tonight?"

"Nope," she replied, pulling the bunch of carrots from the basket. "So we're just cooking for the staff. Mr. McManus has a taste for pork chops."

Neal is in love, Gabby told himself as he watched the black man look at Phebe. Yep, he had seen people fall in love many times in the close to fifty years he had been on this earth, and it was easy to tell when a man was smitten. Gabby prided himself on observing people's eyes, which told him much, and he recognized the extra attention Neal paid to Phebe's form, her hair, the way her slender hands moved quickly and efficiently to peel and dice the carrots. He knew the young man was trying to hide his infatuation, but the eyes never lie, especially when there was a smart brain behind them. Yes, young Neal was smart. Gabby could always tell a smart person because he himself was smart. Not too many people knew that, but deep in his heart, Gabby knew he was smart.

"Aw, don't I have time for a nice cup of hot, black coffee before I go get the white folks' chops?" Neal sat on the edge of the chopping block table.

"You keep talking like that, and Mrs. Lincoln's likely to chop your head off."

"Well, I wouldn't want the queen to order a beheading." Neal stood.

"Mrs. Lincoln is a queen?" Gabby's face scrunched up in befuddlement.

"She thinks she is," Neal said with a snigger.

"How can she be a queen if Mr. Lincoln is president?" Gabby tried to sort this out. "For Mrs. Lincoln to be a queen, Mr. Lincoln would have to be a king, and he's not a king because he was elected, and kings aren't elected, they're just born that way."

"That's right, Mr. Gabby," Neal agreed, "just like you're just born the way you are."

"Neal," Phebe said, shaking her head in mild rebuke.

"But you called her a queen…"

"Neal was joking." Phebe stopped chopping and turned to Gabby. "Mrs. Lincoln is not a queen. Nobody thinks she's a queen. And Mrs. Lincoln would be hopping mad if anybody was fool enough to call her a queen to her face."

"Oh," Gabby said, subdued because he felt he may have made her mad at him. He liked Phebe very much and would not do anything to keep her from being his friend.

"Neal likes to joke. He's a big joker. If he says something that doesn't sound right, like folks eating rats or Mrs. Lincoln being a queen, you have to tell yourself, why, that joker Neal is telling another one of his tales, and you just laugh at it."

"Yes, ma'am, Miss Phebe," Gabby said. "I'm sorry."

"You didn't do anything to be sorry for," Neal offered.

"And, land of Goshen, don't call me ma'am," Phebe said, a bit irritated. "I'm just a nigger who works in the kitchen."

"You're not on a plantation anymore." Neal wrinkled his brow. "You don't have to call yourself that name anymore."

"That's what I am." Phebe resumed her chopping, concentrating her gaze on the rough wood table.

"Mr. Gabby," Neal said with a smile. "You and me got to teach this young lady a lesson about herself, don't you think?"

"This isn't a joke, is it?" Gabby eyed him carefully. "You really want me to help?"

"No joke. I want your help."

"Well, I've done a lot of thinking about this all my life." Gabby cleared his throat and stepped forward hesitantly. "I think it's all kind of silly."

"What's kind of silly, Mr. Gabby?" Phebe looked up and forced a smile.

"That name. Nigger." Gabby spoke the dreaded epithet with so much innocence that the two young African-Americans standing before him relaxed, their eyes widening slightly, willing to take in what the man with the rat traps was about to say.

"It's a lazy way of saying Negro, which means black. I don't know why people have to be lazy in the way they say words, but they are, and there's nothing we can do about it, but it still doesn't make it right."

"No, it doesn't," Neal interjected.

"Even if they did say it right, it still wouldn't be right. No, it still wouldn't be right; do you want to know why it wouldn't be right? Well, I'll tell you why it still wouldn't be right. It still wouldn't be right because you're not black."

"Not black," Neal blankly repeated.

"Black is absence of all color, of all light. And you have color in your skin, so you can't be black." Gabby extended his hand to touch Neal's face. "Now you, Neal, you're more of—of coffee with a whole caboodle of milk in it." He squinted as he lightly poked the freckles on the young man's cheeks. "With little speckles of nutmeg floating on top. Although I don't know why there'd be speckles of nutmeg in coffee. You put nutmeg on eggnog, and you're definitely not eggnog."

"Yeah, I'd rather be coffee than eggnog any day of the week."

Gabby turned his attention to Phebe, who took a small step back, but that did not stop him from laying his full palm against her tender, smooth cheek.

"And you're deep, rich coffee without a drop of anything else in it. No milk, no nutmeg, nothing but pure, dark coffee." He slowly pulled his hand away, his eyes filled with child-like curiosity. "Your family doesn't have any white people in it, does it?"

"What?" Phebe shook her head.

"Oh, Mama told me and Cordie all about slavery. Cordie's my sister. Mama told us how bad slavery is."

"So you think you know all about it?" Cynicism licked the edges of Neal's question.

"Oh no." Gabby vigorously wagged his head. "I don't know everything about anything. Nobody knows everything about anything. The smart man is the man who knows he doesn't know everything. Socrates said that. Or was it Plato?"

"So what do you know about slavery?" Neal crossed his arms over his chest.

"Mama said plantation white people would make babies with slaves anytime they wanted, because they were the white people, and they thought they could make the black slaves do anything they want." Gabby looked at Phebe again. "It looks like no white people came into your family's cabin." He then studied Neal. "You got a whole bunch of white people in you."

"Now, there's no need to be nasty." Neal laughed.

"You're joking now, aren't you?" Gabby asked.

"Yeah, I'm joking."

"Mr. Gabby," Phebe said as she cleared her throat. "I think I saw some rats this morning across the hall in the furnace room."

"And there's rat shit in the billiards room," Neal added.

"That's very funny." Gabby laughed.

"What's funny about rat shit?" Neal asked.

"What a joker you are." Gabby laughed again.

"Mr. Gabby, Neal isn't joking this time. There really are rat droppings in the billiards room. That means there are rats in there."

"Oh." Gabby stopped laughing, turned abruptly, and left the kitchen, going directly to the furnace room.

"That old man gives me the willies," Neal said to Phebe in a soft voice, but Gabby , across the hall in the furnace room, heard him. He prided himself on his keen sense of hearing almost as much as he prided himself on his intuitive discernment of the human condition.

"He wouldn't hurt a fly," Phebe said as she continued to chop vegetables.

Gabby smiled as he bent over to place a rat trap near the furnace. He always knew Phebe was a kind soul. Mama, before she died, had told Gabby it was a sin to assume a black person was bad or mean or stupid. No, Gabby had decided soon after he arrived at the Executive Mansion that Phebe was not bad, mean, or stupid. Now as for Neal, on the other hand, Gabby had not made up his mind.

"Think he's always been like this?" he heard Neal ask Phebe.

"Most likely so," Phebe replied with a sigh, her chopping more intense.

Gabby hung his head as he retreated further into the furnace room, placing his rat traps along the way. Phebe's acceptance of Gabby's current condition as being congenital weighted his soul, because even now he knew things other people did not. For example, he knew the official name of this building was the Executive Mansion; White House was kind of a nickname. Because Phebe did not realize he knew things did not lessen her kindness or intelligence. It only made her, Gabby decided as he coughed back tears, like all the others who thought so lowly of him—and they were all wrong, oh, so very wrong.

As he walked out of the furnace room and entered the next door down the hall, Gabby recalled how his life had been so different in Brooklyn, New York, where he had lived with his father, his mother, and his older sister Cordie in a modest brownstone. His early years were filled with happy days of hiding in the corner of his father's law office on the first floor of their home. The clients were always common workers and immigrants who ill could afford a lawyer when circumstances found them up against local authorities. The Zooks were not wealthy, but they were held in high esteem by their lowly neighbors whose husbands and fathers Zook had saved from prison or financial disaster. It was then Gabby had developed his ability to be still, to fade into the woodwork and take in all that was being said, digesting it so that the information was his own. Gabby also liked to reach up to his father's bookshelves and randomly select thick texts on subjects ranging from the law to Romantic poetry to integral calculus. The calculus ran a little deep for the boy, but he always enjoyed the challenge. And it was a good thing Gabby did indeed like challenges, because it turned out his life was going to be one challenge after another.

His first came just before his thirteenth birthday, when his father died of influenza. He had contracted it from a family of Irish textile workers whose landlord had sued them to remove their loom from the parlor in which they eked out a living, creating elegant lace much sought after by the wealthy ladies whose estates lined the banks of the Hudson River north of the city. Before he died, however, father Zook won the Irish family's right to their livelihood. In gratitude, they created a lovely lace pillowcase on which Gabby's father's head was laid. Gabby's keenest memory of that day was the embrace of his father's brother Samuel, the true success of the Zook family, a top member of his graduating class from the United States Military Academy at West Point. Samuel Zook was already a major, and the family expected him to become a general. He was tall, straight, and very impressive in his pressed blue uniform, Gabby thought, as he looked up at his uncle and felt proud. His eyes scanned the room to see many poorly dressed men and women, including the Irish people, crying softly. Gabby was at once sad to see the tears and pleased his father had had so many friends. He was further saddened to see his mother collapsed on the divan, life seemingly drained from her haggard body. His sister Cordie, seven, sturdily built and plain to the eye, enveloped their mother in her strong arms. Gabby remembered smiling when his best friend Joe VanderPyle slowly entered the room, wary of seeing his first corpse in a coffin displayed in a family's parlor, but determined to comfort his chum.

Walking to Joe, Gabby tentatively stuck out his hand to shake with his friend, since that was what Uncle Sammy had been doing all afternoon, and with his left hand patted Joe's shoulder, replicating Uncle Sammy's other gesture.

"Hi," Gabby said, his eyes on the floor.

"Hi," Joe replied.

"Yeah."

After a moment of silence, Gabby said, "He's over there."

"Who? Your uncle?"

"No—I mean, yeah, he's here. In his uniform. He looks like a huckleberry above a persimmon. See?" Gabby stepped aside and pointed to Samuel.

"Yeah. I wish my uncle was a major."

"Yeah." Gabby looked down and then chose his words carefully. "No; what I meant was, my pa is over there." He nodded toward the plain coffin.

"Oh." Joe stiffened. "Have you looked at him?"

"Yeah. He doesn't look different than before. He just looks like he's asleep."

"Oh."

"Do you want to see him?"

"All right."

Gabby led his friend through the crowd. Just before reaching the casket, Joe stopped and gripped his sleeve.

"Gabby?"

"Yeah?"

"Were you scared? To look at him, I mean?"

"No. It's just pa."

"You're braver than me." Joe shook his head. "I ain't seen a dead body."

"You don't have to look if you don't want to."

"I'm your friend." Joe straightened his shoulders. "I should look because that's what friends do."

"Then you're braver than me."

"What?"

"To do something you're not afraid of isn't brave. Doing something that scares you, that's brave."

"Oh." Joe smiled. "Thanks." He glanced at the coffin again. "I want to look now."

Standing in the billiards room, gray-haired Gabby shook his head and laughed. He knew he had lied that day to his friend about being afraid. When the casket first arrived at the house that morning, Gabby's mother gently pushed him toward it to make him look at his father's corpse. It was only after an hour of gazing at the cold countenance that Gabby had become comfortable, but he did not want to tell Joe that. He wanted his friend to feel braver than him, and that helped him feel brave.

Looking around him, Gabby sighed. He bemoaned the fact that he had no need to be brave now, and no need to be brave when catching rats. Counting the traps thrown across his arm, Gabby saw he had three left, and placed one under the worn but elaborate billiards table and another in the fireplace before deciding to place the last behind a stack of barrels and crates in the far corner.

Bending over behind the barrels and crates, Gabby thought how his new life, living in a boardinghouse in the nation's capital with sister Cordie, was pleasant enough.

He heard, or thought he heard, a hushed voice out in the hall say, "Quickly."

Life was not as good as in New York, but not as bad as he had feared when Cordie said their father's money was gone, and they had had to sell the brownstone and move. Uncle Samuel, now a general, arranged a job for Gabby in the Executive Mansion. Cordie mended clothes at their boardinghouse and volunteered at the hospital. His teen-aged years had been good in Brooklyn, where he and Joe VanderPyle had laughed and played through their school years. Both enjoyed everything from mathematics and science to literature and music, but exulted in running, jumping, climbing, and swimming. Each was hoping to receive an appointment to West Point, each secretly confident both would make it.

On his knees, looking down at the trap and at his spreading belly, Gabby touched his cheeks, now sagging, his eyes now surrounded by wrinkles, and his mouth now jerking in constant, silent conversations, and wondered what had happened to his dreams. No, he knew what had happened to his dreams, but he did not want to think about those tragedies, for they had destroyed him and cast him into a frightening world of brief, precious moments of clarity and long, disturbing periods of confusion, anxiety, and fantasy.

Gabby was on the verge of tears, which he often was when he allowed himself to dwell upon what was and what could have been, when the billiards room door opened, causing him to jump and hover behind the barrels and crates, shivering over the iron trap, as though he were a rat himself.

Chapter Three

Opening the door, Adam deferentially stepped aside to allow President Lincoln, his wife, and Secretary of War Stanton to enter the room. Lincoln stopped by the billiards table and placed his hands on the edge, his head hanging. Mrs. Lincoln ran a finger across the table and looked at it with disdain. "What a filthy mess," she announced. "If I'd known matters had come to this, heads would've rolled."

"Dust is the least of our problems, Mother." Lincoln turned to Stanton. "Isn't that right, Mr. Secretary?"

"Shut the door." Stanton nodded to Adam.

He obeyed and stood guard in front of the door, his arms crossed over his chest, his thoughts going to the revolver in his tunic: whether he might use it, and what circumstances would warrant using it against the president of the United States.

"Mr. Stanton, will you finally explain this ultimate insult to my husband?" Mrs. Lincoln's eyes glistened with anger.

"Certainly." Stanton removed his small pebble glasses, placed them in an inside pocket of his gray suit, and looked directly at the president. "Simply put, your lack of understanding of military strategy has imperiled the lives of thousands of soldiers and has threatened to lengthen, unnecessarily, this war."

"Imperiled lives?" Mrs. Lincoln's plump jaw dropped and her eyes widened. "Why, sir, that's the most—"

"Mother, please." Lincoln raised a large hand and returned his attention to Stanton. "I assume, Mr. Secretary, you're referring to my reinstatement of General McClellan to command the Army of the Potomac."

"I thought after your visit with the general in July outside Richmond after the Seven-Day Battle you'd come to grips with this problem with McClellan. He will not fight."

"You're not telling me anything I haven't told you," Lincoln replied. "As I recall, you were one of the original supporters of Little Mac. In fact, I had quite a task convincing you of the general's shortcomings."

Stanton stiffened. "That was last year. This is 1862. A year of slaughter, lost opportunities, endless drills, gourmet dining on the field, waste of—"

"That's enough!" Mrs. Lincoln's voice was shrill.

Adam shuffled his feet, uncomfortable with the display of emotions erupting before him. After all, in his small Ohio community, such outbursts were unpardonable, as evidenced by the reproach given a boy's comment of the favorite breakfast of his deceased mother.

"Not to mention the fate of the slaves," Stanton continued. "You've created the Emancipation Proclamation, but you can't release it until a military victory, which is impossible with General McClellan in command."

"And I agree," Lincoln said. "I'm a slow walker, but I never walk backwards. That's why I ordered McClellan's troops to reinforce the troops of General John Pope."

"An admirable choice," Stanton asserted.

"General Pope is a liar and a braggart," Mrs. Lincoln interjected. "I knew the family in Illinois. The father was a judge known to take bribes, and his mother put on such airs as to make her insufferable."

"A mother's lack of social skills shouldn't disqualify the son from being a proper general," Stanton replied.

"Losing two major battles in less than two months would disqualify him, however," Lincoln said, putting his arm around his wife.

"Cedar Mountain and a second debacle at Manassas," she said, trying to maintain her dignity.

Adam felt sorry for them. Lincoln may be incompetent, but he was still president, and as such deserved respect.

"Anyone deserves more time than was accorded General Pope," Stanton said.

"Perhaps some would," Lincoln replied, "but General Pope didn't. You may not want to believe it, Mr. Stanton, but I too want to end the carnage. It's just that at this moment, I'm afraid that General McClellan is our best hope." He smiled. "General Pope is a fool. Even I, with just the friendly Black Hawk War as my only experience, knew Stonewall Jackson wouldn't retreat. Jackson advances, always advances, but Pope recklessly followed Jackson's retreat, only to be attacked by reinforcements by Lee and Longstreet. I couldn't allow Pope to commit another costly mistake."

"Well, there are other generals than McClellan," Stanton blustered.

"And I'm sure each one will have his chance before this mess ends," Lincoln said.

"We don't have time," Stanton replied. "That's why I must insist you and Mrs. Lincoln stay in the basement until I'm able to end the war."

"Stay in the basement! You must be insane!" Mrs. Lincoln turned to her husband. "This man is insane! They're expecting us at Anderson Cottage tonight!"

"A message is being delivered now saying you're spending the night in town."

She stormed toward Adam, furiously wagging a finger. "And you, young man, how dare you betray your country!"

"I'm trying to save my country, not betray it." Adam's eyes fluttered as he looked to Stanton for assurance.

"Any man who can't control his wife can't control a war," Stanton said in a pious tone, his eyebrows raised.

"Please, Molly, don't do this to yourself," Lincoln whispered, reaching out and holding her.

"*I'm* not doing this," she said, spittle flying. She twisted to escape his grip and, when she realized she was completely restrained, her face went bright red and her eyes filled with tears. "He's the one doing this to us—not just to us, but to the entire nation!" Looking from face to face, she finally dissolved into sobs, her head buried in Lincoln's shoulder.

"Don't you think I might be missed at the Cabinet meetings?"

"You'll be there." Stanton smiled, pausing to chuckle at the look of puzzlement on Lincoln's face. "Or at least, a man who looks remarkably similar to you."

"Poor fellow," Lincoln said with a trace of a grin. "I didn't think any man on earth was as ugly as I am."

"This is no time for your silly jokes." Mrs. Lincoln did not lift her head from his shoulder, but slapped him on the chest.

"Details aren't necessary," Stanton continued, "but needless to say, I found a gentleman who, for the appropriate compensation, will dress like Lincoln, talk like Lincoln, and look like Lincoln, but say exactly what I tell him."

"And that one fact makes him nothing at all like Mr. Lincoln." Pulling her head up and daubing her eyes, Mrs. Lincoln pursed her lips as she looked at Stanton. "He's enough like Mr. Lincoln to convince the Cabinet members?"

"And Mr. Nicolay and Mr. Hay?" Lincoln asked.

The mention of the two elegant men serving as personal secretaries of President Lincoln caused Adam to frown. He secretly hoped they would not be fooled and would need some forceful encouragement—and Adam gladly would provide that force.

"They'll be no problem." Stanton addressed Mrs. Lincoln. "I even found a suitable replacement for you, madam."

"For me?" Her eyes widened.

"There's only one person in Washington I couldn't fool or intimidate into believing my impostor is the president, and that person is his wife."

"Of course I could tell the difference."

"I know," Stanton said.

"And I'd scream to high heaven about it, too."

"That's why you're joining the president in the basement."

"You'll fail." Mrs. Lincoln smiled. "This plan is ludicrous."

"You're wrong, Mrs. Lincoln," Stanton said.

"Why, Mrs. Keckley knows the shape of my body..."

"A colored woman," Stanton said dismissively. "It'll be no problem to convince her she doesn't see what she sees."

Adam furrowed his brow, uncomfortable to hear this attitude being expressed by Stanton, the man who had brought him to Washington and taught him of holy crusades. They were supposed to be fighting to end slavery because black men and women were equal to white people. A belief in that equality was not detectable in Stanton's tone of voice. That tone, Adam had always been told, was characteristic of Southerners using black muscle to till their fields.

"And Taddie," Mrs. Lincoln continued. "Taddie'll know that woman isn't his mother."

"A child will believe whatever it's told," Stanton pronounced.

Again Adam shifted uneasily at Stanton's remarks. Children did not believe everything they were told. As wise as the secretary of war was, he should know that. Adam certainly knew it; he was closer to childhood than Stanton was, and therefore had a clearer memory of what it was like to be a boy than did the man with the pharaoh beard. Adam remembered exactly the emotions coursing through a boy's heart when an adult preached sermons his guts told him were wrong. He knew to bite his tongue, nod his head, and allow the adult to think he was having his way, while all along the child comforted himself in the knowledge that, in his own brain, he knew the truth.

"Now, let me see if I got this straight." Lincoln cleared his throat. "You got a fellow upstairs right now—"

"He's probably unpacking at this moment," Stanton interjected.

"And you're going to have him stand before the Cabinet and tell them General McClellan will no longer command the Army of the Potomac and replace him with…"

"General Burnsides," Stanton supplied.

"A good man," Lincoln said. "A bit of a dandy, but a good man."

"He's not afraid to fight."

"But can he win?"

"If he fights, he'll win."

"You do wrong to underestimate Bobby Lee." Lincoln raised an eyebrow.

"Fear never won battles," Stanton said. "That's McClellan's weakness. He overestimates the power of General Lee."

"Don't waste your words on him, Father," Mrs. Lincoln said with a sniff.

"You may be right, my dear." Lincoln patted his wife.

"He's a fool. Don't waste your wisdom on a fool."

"I do have just one other question. How long do you think it'll take General Burnsides to win the war?"

"I expect you'll be able to celebrate Christmas upstairs."

"And you expect us to be jolly for Christmas?" Mrs. Lincoln asked.

"You'll thank me—as Private Christy said earlier—for saving lives, the Union, and your place in history." Stanton smiled. "Oh, you're a bit peeved now, but that'll pass when you bask in the accolades justly earned by me."

"'A bit peeved'? 'Justly earned'?" Mrs. Lincoln rolled her eyes. "I swear to God, that man's a fool."

"Who else is part of this grand scheme?" Lincoln asked. "Mr. Seward, I presume?"

"No." Stanton shook his head. "Very few are involved. I decided it'd be better that way. And it'd be better for you to ask no more questions." He nodded to the young soldier. "Private Christy will be in the next room and will attend to your every need."

"I need to be with my son," Mrs. Lincoln said.

"Well, perhaps not *every* need."

"But his main duty will be to keep us locked away," Lincoln said, "while you run the country upstairs through this man who's unfortunate enough to look like me."

"Good; as long as we all understand the situation." Stanton pulled out his watch and squinted at it. "I'll be calling an emergency Cabinet meeting tonight."

A slight metallic jangling from behind the barrels and crates in the far corner caught Stanton's attention.

"What was that?"

"Who goes there?" Adam pulled his Remington revolver.

"Don't shoot." Gabby Zook stood, raising his hands.

"Who the hell are you?" Stanton asked, fuming.

"Father! That man cursed in front of me!"

"Molly, Mr. Stanton's language is the least of our problems." He patted her reassuringly.

"Come out slowly," Adam ordered.

"Rat traps." Gabby came forward, shuffling his feet and lowering his head. "Rats in the basement. Rats in the basement, and we can't have rats in the White House basement. I put out rat traps. Then you came in, and I was trapped. Like the rats in the basement, but I don't want to get trapped."

"Who the hell is this?" Stanton repeated, his face reddening.

"If I recall properly, this is the nephew of General Samuel Zook. He put in a good word for his dead brother's son."

"You know Uncle Sammy?" Gabby walked toward Lincoln. Mrs. Lincoln cringed and hid her face in her husband's shoulder. "I like Uncle Sammy. He was always the smart one in the family. Everyone said he'd be the successful one. Being a general is pretty good, so I guess he's the successful one in the family."

"General Zook said he had a few problems," Lincoln said.

"What the hell is he doing here?"

"Setting rat traps," Lincoln replied. "Weren't you listening?"

"Can I go now?" Gabby inched his way toward the door.

"No," Stanton said. "You know too much. You heard too much."

"How can I know too much?" Gabby's eyes filled with confusion. "They kicked me out of West Point before I could learn much."

"You must stay in this room with the Lincolns."

Mrs. Lincoln's mouth fell open. "First, you stick a gun in my face. You tell me I have to live in the basement. You use foul language in my presence, and *now* you tell me I must live with this person?"

"It wasn't planned," Stanton said.

"Most of life isn't what we plan, Mr. Stanton." Lincoln took two small steps toward the secretary. "Stop this now, before it's too late. This man has shown up. Who knows what other complications await you? You've good intentions. I know that. But the road to hell is paved with good intentions."

"The rat trapper can set up house behind the crates." Stanton's eyes dismissed Lincoln's plea. "You won't even know he's there, Mrs. Lincoln."

"No!" As Stanton left the room, Gabby rushed the door. "I got to get back to Cordie! Cordie needs me!"

"Please, sir, everything will be all right." Adam grabbed him. "Please calm down."

"But Cordie! What's going to happen to Cordie?"

"She'll be fine. I'll tell her." Adam paused. "I'll tell her something."

Chapter Four

September 1, 1862 was the most fortunate day in the life of Alethia Haliday, or least she thought so as she unpacked her personal items in the large bedroom next to the oval sitting room on the second floor of the president's home. Only days earlier the plump woman with dark hair and full cheeks had been in the Old Capitol federal military prison, waiting for what superintendent William Woods had called her destiny: death by hanging for espionage.

"Don't believe it," Rose Greenhow, her best friend from childhood, advised her in muted tones as they ate dinner in the yard. "Laugh at that skinny little man. Call it a farce, a perfect farce, and eventually he'll be forced to release you, and then he'll be revealed to all as the buffoon he is at the core of his being."

"Why, I couldn't say that." Alethia remembered widening her large, expressive brown eyes. "Farce? A buffoon? Rose, you go too far."

That, of course, was Rose Greenhow's charm, being brash and audacious, and Alethia, meek and subservient, envied it. She always wanted to be more like Wild Rose, as the young rakes of Bladensburg had called her, when they were girls in the sleepy town at the head of the Anacostia River which flowed south to join the Potomac near Washington. Bladensburg was undistinguished except by a War of 1812 battle in which the local militia fought and was vanquished by the British army, which then marched on to burn Washington. Since then Bladensburg had slipped into relative obscurity and would have been forgotten altogether, had it not been a minor stop on the Baltimore and Ohio railroad.

"Anybody who is anybody has had a tinkle in Bladensburg," Rose had quipped many times to the raucous laughter of her beaux and to the embarrassment of her dear, hopeless friend Alethia. "You are much too gentle," Rose lectured her as they took their Sunday promenade in their teen-aged years.

"But I thought goodness, kindness, and innocence were virtues devoutly sought by men in prospective wives."

Rose laughed at her friend. "Those qualities are desirable if you wish to be a saint preserved in stained glass in a church and ignored by any young man worth having as your lover, but such qualities possessed by an actual flesh-and-blood girl make her a milksop, and therefore eschewed by paramours of promise."

"You mean men truly don't want ladies?"

"Of course, they want ladies—that is, they want women who *pretend* to be ladies."

"Pretend?" Alethia shook her head.

"The pretense makes you both appealing and dangerous," Rose explained.

"I don't understand."

"I know you don't." Rose sympathetically patted her friend's shoulder. "You poor creature."

Perhaps that was why Alethia Haliday was still a virgin and unmarried at age forty-two, while Rose had married and was the mother of several children. In fact, Alethia had resigned herself to a quiet life in Bladensburg earning a modest income selling bread, cakes, and pies from the home inherited from her equally bland parents. Rose had left Bladensburg for an exciting life in the nation's capital, rarely remembering her old, dreary friend in their backwater Maryland town.

All of this changed in the spring of 1862 when a gallant-looking young man with flowing blond locks appeared in Alethia's kitchen. He spoke with that odd accent spoken by residents of the Richmond, Virginia, area, which almost sounded like the speech pattern of Boston natives. He informed her that Rose was in a Washington federal prison, on charges of spying for the Confederacy. That Rose was a spy did not surprise Alethia; her flamboyant friend had always had a talent for the devious. That she was a spy for the South also was not a shock, for almost everyone in Bladensburg, including Alethia, was a Democrat with rebel sympathies. What amazed her was that Rose had been caught. Alethia thought her friend would charm herself out of any situation.

"Can you help?" the young man with the golden mane said with pleading, soulful blue eyes.

Alethia felt breathless to have such a handsome man so close, so inviting—even if he were not inviting her in a romantic sense.

"Will you help?"

"Yes," she said, her heart beating faster.

The young man breathed deeply, and Alethia's eyes fluttered. He asked her to bake a cake with an escape plan in it and present it to Rose on a trip to the prison. Within days, Alethia sat in a car of the Baltimore and Ohio train with the cake—chocolate with vanilla icing—on her lap. Her cheeks flushed when she pecked her friend on the cheek in the Old Capitol yard and handed her the cake. Perhaps it was her trembling hands that had caused the guard to saunter forward and comment on the freshness of the cake and its sweet aroma. Perhaps it had been her cracking voice when she told him it was chocolate that had caused him to smile suspiciously and reply he could not remember the last time he had had a slice of homemade chocolate cake. Perhaps it was the terror sparkling in her eyes that had prompted him to take out his pocket knife and cut through the middle of the cake, snagging on the packet of escape plans. No matter, for then Alethia had found herself in a room next to her friend, also accused of spying and facing an unknown fate.

Those were the worst days of her life, Alethia told herself as she stood inconspicuously at the window covered with fancy, white cotton lace curtains. She turned her head to glance through the door to the president's bedroom where a tall, raw-boned man leaned over a suitcase. She caught her breath as she considered whether this tall, sinewy man would ask her to join him in his bed, to make the ruse complete. Alethia remembered Rose's words: a farce, simply a farce. That was what she was living now.

It had begun one day in July when a short, stout man with a pharaoh-like beard visited Rose in the yard of the Old Capitol. The man turned out to be Secretary of War Edwin Stanton, the latest in a long line of officials who tried to force Rose into revealing how she learned military secrets.

"If I have the information that you say I have," Rose said to Stanton, "I must have got it from sources that were in the confidence of the government. I don't intend to say any more. If Mr. Lincoln's friends will pour into my ear such information, am I to be held responsible for all that?"

Alethia noticed the grave look in Stanton's eyes when they wandered in her direction, and she sensed a distinct snap in his head as he focused his attention on her.

"And who is this?" Stanton paused, as though to control his low, musical voice. "Is she a member of your spy ring?"

"Oh, dear me, no." Rose laughed. "This is my dear old friend Alethia Haliday. Her imprisonment is a farce, a perfect farce. Some scoundrel talked the simple country mouse into presenting me with a cake which contained a packet of scandalous papers meant to incriminate us both, the poor, little innocent lambs we are. She'll be released any time now, I'm sure."

"Is that true, madam?" Stanton studied Alethia's clear, plain, twitching face.

"Yes, sir." She averted her eyes.

"Would you elaborate?" Stanton said, leaning in.

"I don't know what else to say."

"Where are you from?"

"She's from my hometown of Bladensburg, Maryland." Rose stepped between them.

"Let her speak."

"Rose is correct. We grew up in Bladensburg. I still live there—until recently."

"I swear I detect a hint of a Kentucky lilt." A smile slashed across Stanton's Cupid's bow lips.

"Mother was from Kentucky," Alethia said, becoming disarmed. "Her accent was quite thick, and I succumbed to its influence from the cradle."

"In these war times," Rose said after clearing her throat, "you ought to be involved in some more important business than holding an inquisition of women."

Stanton bowed and left. A week later, prison superintendent Woods visited Alethia's cell after midnight. After shaking her awake, Woods pulled down his trousers, exposing skinny, hairy legs.

"I was told you were a good-looking woman," he murmured as he pinned her body to the metal cot with his arms and legs.

"You're mistaken," Alethia said in a small voice. She attempted to push him away but finally failed, her arms being pressed against her ample bosom. "Mrs. Greenhow is in the next room."

"I don't want a woman with a fresh mouth on her," he said, continuing to force his body on her. "I want you. You got meat on your bones. My wife is too skinny." Forcing his mouth on hers, Woods pulled up her nightgown and spread her legs apart. "I like women who know their place—bound for the gallows."

Numb, Alethia was fixated on the irony: forty years' of virginity ended by a vulgar, frenetic little man who, even though she did not know from experience, Alethia was certain did not do it right. Every midnight, Superintendent Woods appeared, said she was doomed to hang, and raped her. When she told Rose, Alethia expected sympathy and compassion; instead, she received a hard glint and a wagging finger of instruction.

"Tell him he's wonderful," Rose said, taking both of Alethia's hands into her lap. "I know he must be dreadful—he looks like he'd be dreadful—but lie. Tell him you love him."

"But I couldn't lie." Alethia's eyes fluttered.

"Do you want to die?" Rose snapped. "Don't be foolish. Lead him on until you can report him and gain your freedom." Rose smiled and gently brushed her friend's hair. "Please don't crumble like you usually do. I could have hugged you and said, oh, you poor baby, but what good would that have done? Understand?"

"I think."

"Alethia, darling, you can be delicate in Bladensburg, but in Washington you must be tough."

Nodding, she forced a smile even though she did not really understand what her friend was saying. Or rather, she did not think Rose understood her. What came naturally for Rose was impossible for her. As it turned out, Alethia did not have to follow her friend's advice.

The next morning she was to be taken to the reception room of the War Department for a hearing before Secretary Stanton himself.

"Tell him you're a poor delicate woman who has been violated," was Rose's quickly whispered advice in her ear as she walked to a carriage.

Alethia remember standing in the back of the room watching Stanton at a high writing desk, looking over the rim of his pebble glasses with impatience at men wanting contract bids, jobs, and political favors. Most of them, greeted gruffly with monosyllabic replies, were escorted from the room efficiently. After all the petitioners left, Stanton lifted his gnome-like hand and waved her forward, his glare withering Alethia.

I'm a fragile, delicate woman. I'm a fragile, delicate woman...

Stanton motioned to the guard at the door to leave. As soon as the door had shut and they were alone, his eyes darted Alethia's way. "Do you know who you look like?"

"I'm a fragile, delicate woman," she mumbled.

"What?" Stanton's brows rose. "That made absolutely no sense. If you're going mad, then I'll send you to the insane asylum across the river."

"I'm not insane, just flustered." Alethia blushed.

"Then answer my question. Do you know who you look like?"

"I've always been told I look like my mother."

"An insipid answer, but at least not insane," Stanton said. "No, you look like the president's wife. Mary Todd Lincoln."

"Is that good?" Alethia fluttered her eyes.

"Very good for you." Stanton smiled. "No one has ever pointed this out to you?"

"No, sir."

"Are you certain?"

"Yes, sir."

"Very good. Come with me."

"Come with you?" She furrowed her brow. "I don't understand—and—and I have a complaint about Mr. Woods."

"Yes, yes, I know all about that," Stanton said.

"You know?" Alethia's mouth fell open. "You allowed him?"

"Wouldn't you rather come with me than be bothered with Mr. Woods anymore?"

For the next few weeks, Alethia stayed in a comfortable room, enlarging on her Kentucky accent, poring over minutiae on the life of Mary Todd Lincoln and memorizing everything about the Executive Mansion, Anderson Cottage, and the staff. For instance, she knew Anderson Cottage was the Lincolns' summer home in the Maryland foothills. She also knew her closest friend in Washington was Elizabeth Keckley, a freed black seamstress. Alethia knew she must not like Lincoln's secretaries, John Hay, who enjoyed partying with the Lincolns' son Robert, and John Nicolay, who was a native of Bavaria. Details stuck with Alethia easily, until she knew Mary Todd Lincoln as well as herself. She longed to hold Tad in her arms and make him believe she was his mother.

Storing the last of her personal items in the dark oak chest of drawers, Alethia thought of her job, that of an actress, her stage the grandest house in America, and her audience the most important people in America, who must not know they are an audience.

"Excuse me," the tall, angular man from the next room said shyly as he stood in the doorway.

Alethia jumped slightly as she turned to smile brightly at him.

"I didn't mean to scare you."

"You didn't. I tend to lose myself in thought."

He smiled. "I thought we might want to get to know each other before folks start popping up all over the place."

"Of course." She stepped forward and extended her hand. "I'm Alethia Haliday from Bladensburg, Maryland."

"Duff Read, Michigan. Nice to meet you, Miss Haliday."

He took her hand in his, and Alethia was unsettled by the huge, hammy rough paw that tenderly engulfed her fingers. His touch was different from Woods's touch. Funny, she thought, she never paid much attention to a man's touch before, and now it was all consuming. Duff chuckled awkwardly as he tried to pull his hand away.

"Alethia. Please call me Alethia."

"As much as I'd like to do that, Miss Alethia," Duff said in a distinct Midwestern twang, "don't you think it'd be best if we start calling each other by the Lincoln names? It wouldn't do if I called you Alethia in front of Mr. Seward or some other important person."

"I suppose so."

"So you can call me Abe—"

"Oh no," Alethia quickly corrected him. "Mrs. Lincoln always calls him Father or Mr. Lincoln."

"That's right. I forgot."

"And you call me Molly or Mother."

"I'm glad you're smart about things like this," Duff said. "I used to have a pretty good memory until I spent time in a rebel prison down in Virginia."

"How terrible for you." Alethia impulsively touched his long arm, ill-fitted in the dark suit coat—unfortunately, the same way Lincoln's arms dangled unfashionably from his sleeve. "Do you want to talk about it?"

"No, ma'am, I can't." He ducked his head. "I was a spy."

"So was I," she sadly said, "or at least that's what I am told." Glancing away, she added, "For the South."

"Oh."

"But I'm not really. While I may have some Southern sympathies, I'd never—"

"You don't have to explain."

"I see you made your introductions." Secretary of War Stanton entered, his Cupid's bow mouth turned up in a form of a smile.

"Yes, sir," Duff said.

"Very good. Work closely together. Get your stories straight. Don't contradict each other. Play your parts." Stanton pulled out his watch to look at the time. "You should prepare for a cozy dinner soon with Tad. He is a holy terror." He glanced at the unpacked bags. "You go to Anderson Cottage tomorrow." He looked at Duff. "I leave you to call a Cabinet meeting tonight so you, Mr. President, can dismiss General George McClellan as commander of the Army of the Potomac."

Chapter Five

For several moments Mary Lincoln lingered in her husband's embrace, drying her tears. Finally, she looked up at him with a question in her eyes. "Do you think he's just joking?"

"It'd require a surgical operation to get a joke into his head," Lincoln said, giving her a loving hug. "No, I believe he's quite serious."

"Then he's a damned fool," she replied.

"On the contrary, Molly; it is he who believes me to be the damned fool, and if Mr. Stanton says I am a damned fool, then I must be one, for he's nearly always right and generally means what he says."

Adam cleared his throat. "I don't think Secretary Stanton thinks you're a fool, sir. I think he just disagrees with your policy."

"My policy is to have no policy."

"Well, I think that's what he means."

"And you, young man," Mrs. Lincoln said as she looked at Adam with disdain, "are as big a fool as Mr. Stanton."

"No, ma'am. I have to respectfully disagree. If we could only explain our position better, I'm sure you'd agree. Perhaps over the next few days I can describe Mr. Stanton's vision." Adam smiled broadly, confidently.

"Young man," Lincoln said after his sad eyes considered the private for a long while, "it is better to remain silent and be thought a fool than to speak up and remove all doubt."

Adam's smile slowly faded as the impact of Lincoln's words sank in. He stepped back in front of the door to stand guard.

Lincoln turned to Gabby, whose mouth was still agape, his eyes filled with uncomprehending fear, and looked at him with sympathy. "Well, my dear friend, you must be frightened out of your wits. I know I am."

Gabby nodded feebly.

"Now, don't worry. We'll all get through this just fine."

"Cordie's going to be awfully worried when I don't make it home tonight."

"Maybe this young man can do something about that." Lincoln looked at Adam. "Mr. Stanton did say you were to attend to our needs, did he not?"

"Sir, I already said I would speak to the gentlemen's sister, sir," he replied in his best, crisp, detached military voice.

"Cordie comes by Lafayette Park every evening to take me home."

"Can't you tell her something?" Lincoln asked.

"I'm not really good at lies," Adam replied. "But I could make something up."

"Well, don't make up anything too fancy." Lincoln smiled. "No man has a good enough memory to make a successful liar."

"Yes, sir," Adam said.

"And how are we to sleep?" Mrs. Lincoln demanded.

"Mr. Stanton said there were extra cots in the next room where I'll be staying."

"There's not enough room for a cot back there, but that's all right with me." Gabby looked around at the space behind the crates and barrels. "I can sleep on the floor. It'll be like camping out. I like camping out. Joe and me, we used to go camping all the time on Long Island. It'll be just like all the good times camping, except Joe isn't here."

"He rambles," Mrs. Lincoln said, clutching her husband. "I don't think I can stand staying in a closed space with a man who rambles."

"Remember Christmas with Billy Herndon?" Lincoln said with a laugh. "The stories that man told, and you couldn't get him to shut up."

"Comparing this man to that despicable Billy Herndon doesn't help the situation."

Adam cleared his throat. "I can get the cots now, if you please."

"Yes," Lincoln said. "That'd be good."

"I have to lock the door." He pulled the key from his baggy blue trousers.

"That's quite all right, son."

"And chairs, we need chairs," Mrs. Lincoln said with a sniff. "And a chamber pot—three chamber pots—and a small chest for my clothes…"

"One thing at a time, Molly," Lincoln interrupted.

"I'll return shortly," Adam said, slipping from the room. After locking the door he looked around before going to the next room, where two cots leaned against the wall. Bedding for each sat on the floor beside it. Bending, Adam tried to lift a cot with each arm but found the cast-iron beds too cumbersome. He carried a cot and a bedding bundle, deposited them outside the locked door, and returned for the rest. When he reappeared, Adam stopped abruptly at the sight of Phebe Bartlett leaving the kitchen.

"You need some help?" Phebe said, an open smile gracing her handsome, dark brown face.

"Yes." Adam smiled, fumbling with the cot and bedding. "Oh." Suddenly his eyes widened. "I mean, no. No, I don't need any help."

"It won't be no bother." Phebe turned to the kitchen door. "Neal, the soldier boy needs help with some cots."

"No, really," Adam said. "I don't want any help."

"Good," Neal's voice boomed from the kitchen. "I didn't want to help no white boy do his work anyway."

"He was just kidding." Phebe frowned and looked at Adam. "He's a big kidder."

"That's all right." Adam paused, shifted from one foot to another. "Do you have someplace to go?"

"I was going upstairs to ask Mrs. Lincoln what soup she wants with supper."

"Oh, she's…" Adam glanced at the billiards room, stopped, then pointed to the stairs. "Yes, she's in her room, I think."

"For a new face, you sure know a caboodle about the Lincolns."

"I'm on special assignment." He coughed. "You better be on your way."

Shrugging good-naturedly, Phebe turned the corner and disappeared. Adam waited until he heard the crackling of the straw mats under her feet as she climbed the service stars. Quickly unlocking the door and pushing the cots and bedding into the room, he looked at the Lincolns. "Here they are. Where do you want them set up?"

"In the corner, of course," Mrs. Lincoln said. "And I insist on curtains. I don't want this person"—she nodded toward Gabby—"coming around the corner of the crates to see me dressing. That'd be totally unacceptable."

"Of course, madam." Adam nodded.

"Bring me the curtains in my bedroom. They're of French fabric with allows me to see out, but no one can see in."

"But won't that arouse suspicion, having the curtains removed from Mrs. Lincoln's bedroom?" Adam asked, furrowing his brow.

"Young man, I am Mrs. Lincoln." Her voice rose. "And no one is allowed in my private quarters except Mr. Lincoln and Mrs. Keckley. And when it comes to Mrs. Keckley, you'll have to explain more than the disappearance of mere curtains."

"Be sure to bring her bottle of paregoric." Lincoln put his hands on his wife's shoulders. "It's in the top drawer of the chest in her room."

"Also my underthings," Mrs. Lincoln said, her eyes widening. "You must bring them down here immediately. I don't think it's proper to have a young ruffian such as you handling my delicate items, but I suppose there's no way around it."

"I'll try to be respectful," Adam said earnestly as he left the room. Locking the door, he sighed, hoping he would remember everything Mrs. Lincoln had requested. This project was becoming more complicated than originally planned. Stanton had made it seem like such a noble endeavor, upholding the ideals of Union and abolition. Adam had not imagined wrestling with the logistics of chamber pots, paregoric, and French lace curtains.

As he began to climb the stairs, he looked up to see Phebe, stepping lightly and smiling openly at him. Adam could not remember meeting a young, attractive black woman in Steubenville, Ohio. He recalled old black men who cut his hair at the local barbershop. He recalled old black women chasing little white children around the park. He saw strong young black men digging ditches along the road, but he had never encountered a young black woman who smelled of soap and freshly cut vegetables and whose eyes met his as though they were equals. Wondering why this particular black woman knew they were equals made his heart race.

"Did you get everything in the room fine?"

"Yes, fine. Thanks." As Adam passed Phebe he felt breathless and feared his neighbors in Ohio would not understand or approve of his reaction. When he reached the second floor, Adam looked both ways before walking across the hall to Mrs. Lincoln's bedroom. As he opened the door and entered with a sigh of relief, he looked up and felt his heart jump into his throat as he saw Mrs. Keckley, hands on her hips, staring at him.

"Now why am I not surprised to see you here?" she said. "But I am curious why a private in the Army of the United States of America boldly walks into the boudoir of the wife of the president."

His throat constricted, Adam coughed before words came through his lips. "I'm acting on orders from the president," he said in a whisper.

"And what orders are those, young man?"

Before Adam could find an appropriate reply, Alethia stepped around the corner from Lincoln's bedroom and spoke. "That's quite all right, Mrs. Keckley. Mr. Lincoln is waiting for him."

"Mrs. Lincoln." Mrs. Keckley's mouth fell open as she spun around. "I didn't think you were here. I came back because I didn't feel right when you dismissed me, and then I saw this strange young man in the hall. There was something in the look of his eyes that—"

"Well, there's nothing for you to fret about, dear," Alethia interrupted, guiding her toward the door.

"But you never decided whether you wanted the blue material."

"That sounds lovely."

"You finally decided to come out of mourning?" Mrs. Keckley turned and beamed. "Praise the Lord."

"Oh," Alethia said, putting her hand to her breast. "I haven't decided that—yet. What I said was that the blue material was lovely for when I do decide to move from black."

"Talk to Mr. Lincoln about it, ma'am," Mrs. Keckley said. "And the Lord. Pray about it. The Lord knows best."

"Please don't press me about this, Mrs. Keckley." Alethia closed her eyes. "I think one of my headaches is coming on."

"I'm sorry, ma'am," she replied. "Not another word." She paused and looked at Alethia sympathetically. "You have your paregoric nearby, don't you, ma'am?"

"Please go now," Alethia said.

"If you say so, Mrs. Lincoln," the black seamstress said with uncertainty as she was being pushed out of the room.

After she closed the door, Alethia turned to smile sweetly at Adam. "That went well, don't you think?"

"Yes, ma'am. I'm sorry to blunder in like this, Mrs. Lincoln, but Mrs. Lincoln wanted some things." He stopped and involuntarily moved his hand to his mouth. "I mean, Mrs. Lincoln in the basement, the real Mrs. Lincoln; I mean, not to say you're fake—I guess you are, but I don't mean to be disrespectful to you..."

"There's no need to be flustered, young man." Alethia patted his hand. "I know it's going to be quite a curiosity to contend with two Mrs. Lincolns, but I feel we must deal with it, for I really don't believe it'd be conducive to our enterprise for you to know my real name."

"No, ma'am, you're right. I mean, I don't think it'd be right for me to know your name," Adam said, fumbling his words.

"But I can know your name," she said.

"Private Adam Christy from Steubenville, Ohio, ma'am." He grinned.

"We'll see this venture through, Private Christy," Alethia said, "and soon our lives will return to normal." She shook his hand.

"Molly," Duff called out from Lincoln's bedroom, "who's that you're talking to?"

"This is your new adjutant, dear, Private Adam Christy of Steubenville, Ohio." Guiding Adam by the hand, Alethia walked into the other bedroom.

"Good to be working with you, Private." Duff nodded as he finished putting his clothes in the dresser.

"Mrs. Lincoln—downstairs—wants a few things," Adam said.

"That sounds reasonable." Duff sat on the edge of the bed. "It seems to me, if we don't treat those folks in the basement with the best of consideration, they surely will treat us with no consideration when they're released."

Alethia stepped toward Duff. "But Mr. Stanton promised…"

"Mr. Stanton's promises could be empty if the real Mr. Lincoln decides he doesn't take kindly to this."

"He should be grateful," Adam said.

"Well, I'll be grateful if he's grateful." Duff smiled.

For a moment, Adam was taken by the similarities between the two Mr. Lincolns. Both were gaunt, tall, and innately sad. They talked almost the same, although Adam detected a rougher, less educated tone in this one; he did seem to share certain wisdom with the man in the basement, though he did not express it as cleverly. Adam also sensed the impersonator was younger, but older in his view that the world was a place to be feared.

"So." Duff slapped his hands on his thighs. "What do they want?"

"Oh. Well, Mrs. Lincoln wanted her—well…" Adam paused as he glanced nervously at Alethia.

"I think I know what you mean." Her eyes lowered, and she nodded. "Her…" Alethia's voice softened, "…unmentionables."

"Yes, ma'am." Adam smiled as Alethia padded from the room. He liked this Mrs. Lincoln very much. Not that he disliked the other Mrs. Lincoln; mostly, she scared him. Perhaps under the best of circumstances the real Mrs. Lincoln could be as sweet and charming as the lady returning with a bundle of clothing wrapped in a sheet.

"Looking in the drawers, I found this paregoric," Alethia said with a smile, holding up the bottle.

"Yes," Adam said, "she asked for it." He took it from her, and then smiled sheepishly. "You know, I don't think I know exactly what paregoric is."

"Oh, just a little bit of opium in a liquid that's touched with alcohol." Alethia shrugged, and her eyes twinkled. "It keeps the nerves calm, so I'm told. I've never really been the nervous type." She turned to Duff. "How about you, Mr. Lincoln? Are you the nervous type?"

"No, not at all," Duff said, "until—well, you know." He glanced at Adam. "They'll need chamber pots."

"Three," Adam said.

"Three?" Alethia repeated.

"There's been a complication. I don't know if I should tell you." Adam looked apprehensive.

"Then don't tell," Duff said. "The less we know, the better." He shook his head. "Remember, our main goal here is survival. Don't forget that."

"I thought our goal was to end the war." Adam furrowed his brow.

"No, that's Mr. Stanton's goal." Duff wagged a finger. "And he would strike us down to reach his goal." He nervously grinned. "I talk too much." Taking the bundle from Alethia, Duff added, "I'll help you carry this stuff down."

"Mrs. Lincoln also wants the lace curtains from the bedroom windows."

"The lace curtains?" Alethia said.

"For a drape across the room," Adam explained. "For privacy."

"Anything she wants," Duff said, putting down the bundle and walking to the window to take down the curtains. "Get the ones in your room, Molly."

"Will you help me, Private?" Alethia asked as she left the room.

As they took the last curtain down, Tad bounded through the door yelling, "Oh, Mama, Papa, I had the best dinner I ever had. Pie, ice cream, cake, three ciders—" He stopped abruptly when he saw Adam. "Oh. You're still here."

Alethia dropped the curtains on the floor and walked swiftly toward the boy. "Yes, Taddie, my dear. Private Adam Christy is our new adjutant."

Adam observed the gleam in her eyes as she patted his shoulders and ran her fingers through his unkempt locks.

"Our last aide was a lieutenant, Lieutenant Elmer Ellsworth," Tad said in a huff. "Don't we deserve a lieutenant?"

"We deserve the best man for the job," Duff said, entering with the clothing bundle under one arm and the curtains in the other. "And right now Private Christy is the best man for the job."

"Yes, Papa." Tad cocked his head. "Why are you taking down the curtains? I thought mama liked them."

"Well, you know your mother." Duff smiled as he picked up the curtains from the floor. "She always wants new curtains and such."

"Father, that isn't fair," Alethia said, trying to play her role. "The Executive Mansion must always have the best."

"Oh, Mama never changes." Tad laughed.

"No, I never change," Alethia said in a whisper.

Adam and Duff left and went down the service stairs. As their feet crunched on the straw mats, Adam cleared his throat, again feeling uneasy by the stifling silence engulfing them.

"All this is for the best. Don't you think so, sir?"

"What?" Duff looked around, aroused from deep thought.

"All this," Adam repeated earnestly. "All this is for the best. To end the war. Mr. Lincoln was going—"

"I am Mr. Lincoln, Private Christy," Duff interrupted sternly, stopping to look deeply into Adam's eyes and place his large hands on his thin shoulders. "Don't ever say otherwise. Don't think otherwise." His grip dissolved into a fatherly caress before they started walking again, the straw crunching once more underfoot.

After a few moments of silence, Adam said softly, "Yes, sir."

"You're a good man, Private Christy," Duff said evenly, with a sad glance at him. "Take some advice. Be careful. Watch what you say. This is a dangerous time for all of us."

"Dangerous?" Adam shook his head. "I don't understand."

"Don't try to understand." Duff smiled sagely. "Just be careful."

When they reached the bottom and entered the hallway, Duff nodded to the door to the left. "That's the kitchen, right?"

"Yes."

"I think I should put in an appearance," Duff said, stopping in front of the door. "Please open it, Private Christy."

Pushing the door aside, Adam smiled when he saw Phebe sitting at the rough table, one shoe off, massaging her toes.

"Oh." Phebe quickly slipped her shoe back on her foot and stood awkwardly. "Excuse me, Mr. President. I was just resting my feet."

"Phebe," Duff continued uneasily, looking down and shuffling his feet, "we're staying in town tonight, so you'll have to cook for us."

"Yes, sir; I know. Mr. Stanton told me."

"Also, I have to confide something in you."

Adam's eyes widened, not believing this man chosen to replace President Lincoln might confide his deepest secret to the kitchen help.

"I've asked three very important, very intelligent persons to help me conjure up some winning strategies for this war," Duff said, finding more assurance as he spoke, his eyes rising to meet hers. "Now, I'm not saying they're from England, but if the folks out there thought the president was being told what to do by some foreigners—well, you can see…"

"Yes, sir," Phebe murmured, nodding in agreement.

"We've already snuck them into the billiards room." Duff nodded down the hall. "If you'd be so kind, I'd appreciate it if you'd fix three of your best meals three times a day for these friends of mine."

"Of course, Mr. Lincoln." Phebe paused, and then looked at Adam. "That's why you needed the cots."

"Yes." Adam smiled. "Of course. I didn't think I should tell."

"I'll leave you to your work, Miss Phebe." Duff looked away, and then added, "Oh. You might want to have a pot of coffee brewing. We're having a Cabinet meeting later tonight."

"It'll be ready, Mr. President."

Adam shut the door, and they walked across the hall to the billiards room. Duff hesitated, then handed the bundles to Adam.

"It might be best if you go in alone."

"I think you're right." Nodding, Adam loaded his arms with the bundles and smiled. "You're going to do just fine, Mr. President. All of us will do just fine."

Duff shook his head sadly, stared at him, and said, "Don't forget the chamber pots."

Chapter Six

"Thank you, Miss Jessie," a wounded soldier murmured as he looked up at a tall red-haired young woman with a beautiful smile who was mopping his brow with a cloth as he lay in a cot in the main ward of Armory Square Hospital, several blocks south of the Executive Mansion.

"You're quite welcome, sergeant, darlin'," she replied in a thick Scottish brogue.

"You come early in the morning and stay late at night, all without pay. You must be blessed with a good family who supports you."

"Aye, a good family they were." A cloud passed over her face. "Both me mother and father have passed away, but," she paused searching for a word and then continued, "me dear pa left a wee inheritance." Her eyes wandered. "I'm sorry, darlin', but I have to walk Miss Cordie home. She's so nervous about the dark."

"She's a sweet soul," the sergeant said. He grabbed Jessie's arm. "And you're a sweet soul."

Jessie smiled and walked toward Cordie who was putting away her mop and pail. She hoped the sergeant was unaware she was rushing away from him—actually not him, but painful memories of her parents. Her mother died before the family was to set sail for America. Visiting neighbors along the rugged, barren Scottish coast, she caught a chill, which developed into pneumonia. Her father's plan, to go to New York City, where all three of them could find jobs, went awry, but he did not mourn the ruined plans as he knelt by his dying wife's bed. He mourned the only love of his life. She gathered the last of her strength to reach for her daughter.

"Ye have to take care of the lad now, Jessie." Her eyes were moist with tears. "I robbed the cradle when I married your pa, but I couldn't help it. His bright red hair, his smooth handsome face, so I forgot he was ten years younger than me." She gasped for air. "Take care of him. His strong body deceives the eye. He's had more than his share of ills." A wracking cough shuddered through her. "Please, take care of him."

Shaking her head, Jessie did not want to dwell on that day. The pain of losing her mother paled against the sight of her father's heaving and moaning while clinging to his wife's corpse. When she reached Cordie, Jessie put on her biggest smile.

"Time to go, Miss Cordie," she said.

"Dear me, it's getting dark," Cordie replied, her watery blue eyes lit up. "Thank you, Miss Jessie, for walking with me. A big city can be dangerous."

Again Jessie's brow wrinkled in revisiting a traumatic past, although she fought the impulse. It was impossible. She found herself walking the streets of New York, remembering every detail; after all, it was only six months ago. A lunch basket on her arm, she walked to the construction site where her father worked, making good money. With her salary cleaning fancy homes on Park Avenue, the family actually was building a nest egg. Every night after work, she and her father sat at their kitchen table, discussing where they wanted to live when they could afford to move, because New York City was too big and loud for their country background. Jessie focused on a crowd gathering in front of her father's construction site. Instinct or intuition caused her to run toward the mass of people, pushing her way through. Stopping short when she reached the center, Jessie saw her father, lying on the ground, a vacant gaze in his eyes and bit of foam on his blue lips.

"My God!" She knelt beside him and then looked up frantically at the crowd. "Someone, please, call for help!"

Finally, an ambulance rattled up behind a team of clopping horses. The medics knelt by Jessie in front of her father's dead body. After a routine check of vital signs, they shook their heads.

"Are you family?" one of them asked.

"He's me father."

"I'm sorry. We're too late."

"I know." Jessie looked down at her father. "I've seen people die before."

"We can take him straight to the morgue where the coroner will fill out the death certificate, you sign an indigence form, and it will cost you nothing."

"What's an indigence form?"

"It says you're out of money and releases the city to dispose of your father's body as it sees fit."

Jessie paused to comprehend his meaning. Usually she had no problem understanding exactly what a person said. Being from a village in the isolated highlands of Scotland, Jessie was even adept at reading between the lines of slyly phrased gossip from wrinkled old women who had nothing better to do with their time. The cold, official language the medic used belied the awful reality behind it. She blinked her eyes.

"You mean a potter's field?"

"So to speak." He looked down. "Don't dwell on it, miss. You have enough sorrow to deal with as it is."

A touch on the shoulder from Cordie brought her back to the ward where several wounded soldiers were calling out good evening to her.

"All the men love you, you know," Cordie whispered.

"God bless you, miss; and you too, ma'am." An older man, stripped to the waist exposing bandages over flabby skin, reached out to touch Jessie.

As they reached the door, Cordie leaned into Jessie to say, "That's why they love you. You treat the old, ugly men the same as you treat the young ones." She paused. "Gabby was handsome when he was young."

Jessie's eyes focused on the long expanse of the Mall. Cordie's comments on men's bodies brought back even more painful memories of her father's death. Now her thoughts turned to the evening after he died. She was in the morgue, saying good-bye and explaining to him why she signed the indigence form. The burial would have taken all their money, and none would be left to pursue the dreams her father had for her. Gazing at his body after she lifted the white sheet, she thought what a fine looking Scotsman he was. No one would ever guess he had a weak heart. Her mother tried to tell Jessie with her last breath, but in sorrow she forgot the admonition.

"Miss, are you done?" a man said.

She jumped slightly as she saw a man in his thirties, fairly nondescript except for an aloof look in his eyes. Blinking, she did not know how to respond, still in grief.

"I've a family waiting supper on me," he informed her. "I want to lock up."

"It's me father," she replied in a whisper.

"Well, I'm a father, too, and my children want to see me." His face remained blank.

"Very well." She looked back at her father's body. "When will the funeral be?"

"Funeral? What funeral?"

"I know it's just a potter's field, but there's going to be a burial and I want to be there."

"There ain't going to be a funeral, miss. This is an indigence case."

"Funeral, burial, whatever ye call it, I want to be there." She was beginning to be impatient.

"I told you," he repeated harshly, "this is an indigence case, no funeral, no burial, no nothing."

"No burial. Ye have to put him in the ground somewhere."

"This is New York City, miss. Land is scarce, and it can't be wasted on indigence cases."

"I don't know what you mean." Her brow furrowed as she tried not to lose her temper.

"Didn't they tell you? We toss indigent bodies into the Hudson River."

"What?" A moment passed before she could collect her thoughts. "Ye can't do that."

"Oh yes we can. You signed the form."

"But I didn't know what I was signing!"

"Fine. Have your funeral parlor pick the body up tomorrow morning. We can't keep it around here."

"I don't have a funeral parlor."

"Then you better get one fast."

"I certainly will." She turned to leave as she thought of something. Looking around she asked, "And how much will a funeral parlor be costing me?"

"I don't know. Now will you leave?"

"Yes, I will, and tomorrow morning I'll be here with the most proper funeral parlor man ye ever did see."

Jessie went to several parlors the next day, each more expensive than the next, and visited a couple cemeteries, finding the cost of a plot even more. She could buy a farm in Scotland, she told them, and they told her to go back to Scotland and buy one. Giving her father a fitting funeral and final resting place would take all the money they had saved and put her in debt for another year. What would her parents do, she fretted, walking down the street, absently in the direction of the morgue. Such questions were foolishness, she told herself, because both of them were dead and could not give her advice.

Turning a corner, she repeated the thought that they were dead and incapable to help her, unaware fish would tear at his flesh and unable to rebuke her for putting her own future first. Entering the morgue, she went to the office to tell the man her decision.

"Very well. It makes no difference to me."

"May I see him one last time?"

"Don't take too long."

Jessie stared at her father's face, touching his cold cheek, not knowing whether to apologize or to tell him she made a good deal for herself; instead, she walked away. Soon she arrived at a mansion on Park Avenue to begin a day of cleaning. Within a few minutes she broke down in tears.

"What's wrong, darling?" the cook asked.

"I can't stay here," she replied softly. Without giving details, she told the woman her father had died and she could not stand the thought of living in the horrible city that took his life.

"Go to Washington. There are plenty of jobs there. You can make good money."

"Good money," she repeated absently. The thought of money repelled her now. She did not want more money now. She had enough on which to live simply for some time. Jessie thought this was the time to do penance for her awful deeds.

"They have soldier hospitals in Washington, don't they?"

"Oh, but they don't pay nothing," the cook replied. "They only take volunteers."

"Good, then I'll work for nothing. The poor wounded boys need me."

The cook must have thought her a fool, Jessie thought as she walked with Cordie, but her atonement made her feel better, and she hoped her parents, looking down from above, forgave her.

"The fog is thick tonight," Cordie said as they crossed the iron bridge over the old city canal, now a cesspool.

Her comment brought Jessie gratefully back to the present, not wanting to dwell on the fate to which she condemned her father's corpse.

"We're finally getting there," Cordie said. "I hope Gabby hasn't had to wait too long."

Jessie smiled and nodded at her, even though she was still recovering from her traumatic memories. As they approached the last block to the Executive Mansion, Jessie saw a slender male figure in the haze. Her heart began to beat faster, for the approaching man looked like her father—the same size, red hair glinting in the street lamp light. As she walked closer, her heart relaxed; this man, though similar in shape, did not have her father's strength. She sighed. It would be nice to have a beau who almost looked like her father.

Chapter Seven

Dusk fell over Lafayette Square as Private Adam Christy stopped at the Executive Mansion door to tell the Washington policeman, dressed as a doorman in a frock coat and baggy trousers, that he would be right back after meeting someone for a moment in the park. The guard narrowed his eyes.

"And who are you?"

"Didn't Mr. Stanton tell you? I'm the president's new adjutant." Adam cleared his throat. "And who are you?"

"John Parker."

John Parker...it struck a chord with Adam, who remembered Stanton telling him to be wary of a certain guard at the front door who tended to stay drunk. The metropolitan police had brought him up on charges of going to whorehouses, being drunk, and sleeping on duty.

"The president's last adjutant was a lieutenant," the guard said after carefully eyeing the single stripe on Adam's rumpled blue sleeve.

"Um, I'm from Mr. Stanton's hometown," Adam whispered as he looked down.

"Oh. So that's how it is." A grunt gurgled from Parker's lips.

"Yes." Adam glanced across Pennsylvania Avenue into Lafayette Square to see if Gabby's sister Cordie was there. "I'll be back soon."

"Of course, boss," Parker said, his voice tinged with irony and his breath reeked of whiskey.

As Adam walked down the steps, across the driveway, and into the street, he felt the back of his neck burn, though he kept telling himself there was no shame in taking advantage of a family acquaintance to get a leg up, as his father would say. How else would a young man from a small town on the banks of the Ohio River find himself in the center of his nation's government? Steubenville's only link to political importance was in its name, homage to Baron Von Steuben who had trained General George Washington's troops at Valley Forge, turning them into a viable fighting force. The Prussian native was well rewarded with land and money, but he spent his remaining years in New York, not in the back country of Ohio. So Steubenville itself was known for its manufacture of plates and cups and bolts of cloth, not its political influence. Therefore, when young Adam Christy announced as a child that he wanted to be a general, his father laughed. To be a general, his father explained as he stroked Adam's red hair, he would have to go to West Point; and to go to West Point, he needed to be appointed by a congressman. And congressmen only came to Steubenville once every two years before an election. Perhaps one day he could be a sergeant, he had tried to encourage himself. Then his father burst through the door on a bright day in June of 1862, grinning broadly.

"Boy, you might make general after all," he said, grabbing Adam's shoulders.

"What do you mean, Pa?" Adam's heartbeat quickened.

"I saw something in the newspaper back at the first of the year," the elder Christy began. "I didn't want to tell you because I didn't want to get your hopes up." He paused, smiling, to catch his breath. "You know how I've always said it's not what you know but who you know, and my problem was that I never knew anybody. Well, what I saw in the newspaper let me realize I finally know somebody."

"Who, Pa, who?"

"Well, I used to laugh and tell how I caught this fellow at the graveyard digging up your aunt. He'd taken a shine to her and wanted to make sure she was dead. But I caught him. I laughed at him and told everybody in town so they laughed at him until he finally got his back up. He blustered up to me, but dog-tailed it real fast when I said, 'Yeah, so what? What are you going to do about it?'"

"Pa, what does that have to do with—"

"Just this. That fellow is now secretary of war for Abraham Lincoln."

"But wouldn't he hate your guts?" Adam frowned.

"Son, he's a grown man," his father said. "Grown men don't hold grudges. Only boys do that."

"So you wrote him about me?" Adam smiled.

"Sure did. Took a few months for a reply, but I got it today." His father squeezed his shoulder. "He said for you to get on the next train headed for Washington. He has a special duty for you, and if you do a good job, he promised a commission."

The next few weeks went by quickly for Adam, who mounted the train in Steubenville, crossed the Ohio River, passed Pittsburgh and the Pennsylvania countryside, entered Maryland, and stepped off the train into the different world of Washington, D.C. A nameless man in a rumpled blue uniform met him at the station and took him to an induction center where he was sworn in as a member of the Army of the Potomac, but instead of being led away to one of the training camps around the capital, Adam was taken to the War Department, where he met Edwin Stanton and his destiny.

Nothing wrong with using connections to receive a special assignment, he told himself as he looked back at the Executive Mansion from Lafayette Park. The guard at the door was only jealous. Then he looked up at the statues around him. A smile found its way to his lips as his eyes adjusted to the failing light to recognize a monument to General Frederick William Von Steuben, his hometown's namesake. A portent of good fortune. Now that he had put his personal doubts behind him for the moment, Adam's attention focused on his promise to Gabby Zook to tell his sister Cordie that he would not be coming home with her for some time. Looking around, Adam could see that few elderly women walked in the park at twilight, so spotting Gabby's sister would be no problem. After a few minutes of shifting from one foot to another, however, he worried he had been wrong, until two female figures appeared far down Pennsylvania Avenue. One was short and had rounded shoulders. That one must be Cordie Zook. But he did not know who the second person might be, a tall, straight silhouette with a quick gait and lively waving of hands and bobbing of her head during conversation. He smiled, wondering what the young woman was saying. Adam already liked her.

When the two women drew closer, Adam stepped up and said, "Excuse me, are you Miss Cordie Zook?"

"Oh my goodness." Her eyes widened in apprehension. "Has something happened to Gabby?" She looked in desperation at the tall young woman with red hair. "I was afraid this was going to happen. I should have never let—"

"No, ma'am; your brother is all right. He didn't do anything wrong. He's fine."

"Then where is he?" Cordie's large, liquid blue eyes searched Adam's face intently. "Why isn't he here?"

"He's in the White House—" Adam stopped abruptly. "Um, he's in the White House, and he's fine, but he can't come home. Right now, at least."

"I don't understand," Cordie said.

The tall young woman with the red hair stepped forward and smiled confidently at Adam as she observed his uniform. "I hate to tell ye, Private, but you're not makin' yourself very clear at all." She spoke with a distinct Scottish brogue. "Perhaps it'd be better if ye introduced yourself and explain how ye have all this wonderful knowledge of comin's and goin's at the president's house?"

This woman was the most beautiful and intriguing female Adam had ever seen. It took him several seconds to find his voice.

"I'm Private Adam Christy, personal adjutant to President Abraham Lincoln. President Lincoln has ordered Mr. Gabby Zook to remain in the White House for an indeterminate amount of time—for security reasons."

"For security reasons?" The young woman almost broke into laughter.

Cordie shook her head in bewilderment. "What does indeterminate mean?"

"It means he doesn't know when your brother will come home." The young woman put her arm around Cordie's shoulders. "Isn't that the truth, Private Christy?"

"Yes, miss," he said. "It is."

"But Gabby needs me," Cordie replied, shaking her head. She looked at Adam. "You seen my brother, ain't you?"

He nodded.

"Then you know. Gabby needs me. He can't take care of himself. You know. You've seen him. I can't—he needs me..." Her voice trailed off as her eyes went from Adam to the young woman.

"He's fine, Miss Zook. We're taking care of him," he said. "I mean, I'm taking care of him. I mean, he's being taken care of. You don't have to worry."

"But I have to worry about Gabby," Cordie insisted. "On mama's deathbed she made me promise to always worry about Gabby."

"You don't have to worry," he repeated, trying to comfort her.

"Gabby was the smart one when we was young," she continued, ignoring Adam. "He was like Uncle Sammy. He went to West Point. Then something happened." Cordie shook her head. "Then he needed me. Nobody ever needed me as much as Gabby."

"Now, I'm sure this nice young man will be very happy to meet us here every evenin' to let ye know how brother Gabby is doin'." She hugged Cordie. "Won't ye be pleased to do just that, Private Christy?" She looked Adam squarely in the eyes.

"I don't know." He shuffled his feet and looked down. "I might be busy." Finding his gumption, Adam turned up his face and returned her gaze. "After all, I am President Lincoln's aide."

"Really?" She laughed and tossed her head. "Ye can't take a few minutes of your busy day for a dear sweet lady concerned about her beloved brother?"

"Please." Cordie impulsively grabbed his hands and squeezed. "I must know how Gabby is. I won't be able to sleep at night if I don't know how he's doing. I don't think *he* could sleep at night, if he didn't know I knew how he was doing."

"Surely a handsome young man like yourself couldn't ignore such a plea." She touched his pocked cheek.

"Not handsome." Adam mumbled, pulling his head back.

"Such a lovely head." Not to be deterred, the young woman reached and touched his thick, red hair. "Ye must be of me blood. Scottish blood. No man is more handsome than a highlander."

"Pa has red hair." He shook his head to rid it of her soft, warm caress. "I really don't know where mother's folks came from."

"These bother ye, don't they?" She gently put her fingertips on the larger pock marks on his cheeks. "They shouldn't, ye know. If ye didn't have them, ye would be altogether too pretty. The scars make ye manly, ever so attractive for a lass like me."

Adam opened his mouth to reply, but nothing came out at first, so choked with emotion at the warm touch of her palm. His eyes went from Cordie, whose face was contorted with worry, to the Scottish girl and her sweet smile.

"Will you come with her? Each day?"

"But of course, Private Christy." She hugged Cordie again. "Miss Dorothea Dix would have it no other way."

"Who?" Adam wrinkled his brow.

"Miss Dorothea Dix," she repeated. "Superintendent of Women Nurses. Faith, I thought everyone in Washington knew of the great pious lady of healing."

"I'm new to the city." Adam could not keep his eyes away from her.

"So you'll meet us here each evening with news from Gabby?" Cordie ventured a smile.

"I guess it wouldn't hurt anything." Adam caught his breath and added, "But don't tell anyone."

"Who, pray tell, would care to know what two unattached ladies do on their way home from a day of honest labor at Armory Square Hospital?" The girl laughed.

"That Miss Nix," Adam said.

"No, Dix. Dorothea Dix." She corrected him with an impish grin. "And, no, she won't ask. She may think she wants to know the comin's and goin's of all the nurses under her command, but she knows better now about tellin' me how to live me life."

"Don't boast too much, dear." Cordie touched her arm. "Miss Dix is a mighty important person. I'd not risk your words getting back to her."

"And what if they did?" She looked at Adam again. "Ye wouldn't tell her, would ye, Private Christy?"

"Oh no," he said. "I don't want her to know anything about me."

"Don't worry. I know how to handle her." She held her head high. "The first day I saw her at Armory Square Hospital, I knew all about her. An elderly lady, fragile, with a thin neck but a huge bun of hair pulled so tight she must have an eternal headache. And there she sat on the edge of an injured boy's cot, readin' the Holy Scriptures. Faith, if there weren't tears in both their eyes. I suppose it was because he felt he didn't have long to live, with both legs chopped off at the knees. I walked up to her and said I was fresh off the boat from Scotland where I had tended to me mother as she died of pneumonia. I wanted to volunteer as a nurse.

"Now, when those blue-gray eyes looked me over, she smiled and said, 'No, thank ye, dear, we won't be needin' ye.' Well, I put my hands on my hips and said, 'Now, ma'am, I've heard nothin' but how the Union needs nurses.' She pursed her lips a bit as she closed the Bible, stood, and looked me in the face. 'I don't want these young men's hearts broken along with their bodies. I can't take a chance on a pretty young woman.'"

She paused to smile ironically.

"I wasn't about to let that stop me. So I said, 'Is it pretty I am, Miss Dix?' And she said in a voice that sounded like it didn't want to pick a fight but was ready to stand tough, she said, 'Of course, me dear, ye are pretty, young, and, from what I have observed in the last few moments, ye are on the cusp of flirtatiousness which definitely is dangerous to weakened young men.' Then I asked her, 'If ye had your way—and evidently ye do—no pretty girls will work at Armory Square Hospital?' Without blinkin' her blue-gray eyes, she simply said yes."

Adam merely smiled, completely infatuated.

"I said, 'Then ye must leave this hospital, Miss Dix, post haste.' Her little mouth opened, and a bigger sound than I'd have expected exploded from her thin lips. 'I beg your pardon!?' Without a word I walked past her and sat on the edge of the cot of the poor unfortunate lad to whom she had just been readin'. He had drifted off to sleep apparently, but at the touch of my hand on his shoulder his eyes opened. 'Who's the most beautiful woman ye have seen today?' I asked him."

"He said you, didn't he?" Adam said.

"Ye don't know men as well as I do, Private Christy," she replied. "I knew he'd look up and smile at Miss Dix and say, 'She is.' I told her, 'Miss Dix, to these men your kindness, gentleness, your unconditional love, make ye beautiful, and, therefore, according to your rules, an extreme threat to the fragile emotional health of our soldiers.' For a wee moment I thought I may have overstepped me bounds, but then Miss Dix smiled and said, 'Ye may start tomorrow.'"

"I don't understand." Adam shook his head.

"Private Christy, beauty is not here," she said, touching his cheek, "but here." Her hand moved to his chest.

"If we can't see Gabby," Cordie said as she tugged at the girl's sleeve, "we better go. It's getting late."

"I'll tell your brother I talked to you and everything is all right," Adam said, trying to be soothing. "And I'll meet you here this same time tomorrow."

"He'll need a quilt." Cordie nodded as she turned to leave. "Tell Gabby I'm making him a quilt."

"Good." The girl put her arm around Cordie. "Then it's all settled." She looked over her shoulder and smiled. "See ye tomorrow. And don't be late. Miss Cordie gets mighty frightful to be out after dusk, even with a chaperone."

"I promise." After a pause, Adam jumped and waved his hand at the receding figures. "What's your name?"

"Jessie Home. Ye know what they say. There's no place like home."

Adam continued waving as they disappeared into the dark, one hand touching his face where her fingers had caressed his pock-marked cheek.

Chapter Eight

Opening the large cherry wood armoire in Mrs. Lincoln's bedroom, Alethia smiled with the excitement of a child entering a candy store as she gently stroked the gowns hanging close together on the rack. She wondered if she would fit into the beautiful clothing as well as Mrs. Lincoln did. Would she look pretty? Alethia hoped against hope that she would, and for once be the woman everyone in the room noticed and admired. In all years in Bladensburg, she had never been considered beautiful, not even pretty, not even considered alive. She pulled out a navy blue brocade trimmed with ivory lace on the collar and sleeves with small pearl buttons down the front. Clutching it to her ample bosom, Alethia bit her lower lip and smiled mischievously.

"Mr. Lincoln—Father—I need your advice," she said, walking to the door of the president's bedroom. "Would you please advise me on what to wear to dinner tonight?"

"It doesn't make much difference," Duff said as he pulled on his coat. He stopped as he turned to see the fancy blue dress Alethia held out. "Except…"

"Except what?" Alethia's face briefly clouded.

"Mrs. Lincoln—you—are still in mourning," he said.

"Oh, the little boy. Willie," she said in a whisper. "I forgot." Her fingers toyed with the fabric in her hands. "I'm so terrible. My heart sank when I realized I won't get to wear her beautiful clothes for a while. Then I thought of the baby…"

"He was a little boy."

"Oh no, they're always your babies, no matter how old they are." Alethia's eyes fluttered, specks of tears glistening in her lashes. "She lost her baby in February. Of course, she'd still be wearing black."

"Well, I don't think anyone would mind a nice blue dress at a family supper in the private dining room downstairs," Duff said.

"Tad would know." She shook her head. "We must try to keep all this from him."

The door to her bedroom flew open, and Tad charged in. "They said we're eating in town tonight, but I already had my dinner, my pie dinner, at the Willard. Don't you remember?"

"You could at least sit at the table and sip a glass of milk, couldn't you?" Alethia ran her fingers through Tad's tousled hair.

"I guess. I wanted to get back to the cottage tonight." Tad's eyes darted to the doorway where Nicolay and Hay stood. "So they're wrong. I don't have to eat again."

"We're terribly sorry, madam." Nicolay took a slight step forward.

"Don't worry about it, Mr. Nicolay," she said graciously, pausing awkwardly as she noticed Nicolay and Hay exchange confused glances. She hardened her voice. "But don't let it happen again."

"Yes, madam."

"The president and I are the only ones who determine what and when Tad eats." Alethia's face flushed as she attempted an imperious pose.

"Now, Molly, don't be hard on the boys." Duff put his arm around her.

She flushed again at his touch, a massive, strong hand gently squeezing her soft shoulder. Resisting a shudder growing from the bottom of her spine, Alethia stepped forward and smiled.

"Well, thank you, gentlemen."

"Thank you, madam." Nicolay bowed. "We're going to the Willard for dinner and will return in about an hour."

"And I was planning to visit some friends," Hay interjected nervously, his eyes darting to Nicolay.

"I hate to dash your social plans, Mr. Hay," Duff said, "but a late Cabinet meeting has been called. That's why we're here tonight. You and Mr. Nicolay will be needed."

"Yes, sir." Hay's head dipped.

"There, there, Mr. Hay." Duff walked to the two young men, put his long arms around them, and continued, "You'll have many nights to spend with your friends." He headed for the door.

"Let's go to dinner, Tad." Alethia looked down at the dress in her hands. "Oh." Smiling at the boy, she put the dress on a chair. "I'll put it away when we return."

"You never let nothing stay on a chair before," he said. "You always hang everything up."

Running her fingers through his hair, Alethia fought to remain calm. "Never let *anything*. Watch your grammar." She pushed him through the door. "Your father is already halfway downstairs. If you must know, I'll give Mr. Lincoln a tongue-lashing for forcing me to leave this dress out to wrinkle."

"Well," Tad said with a sigh, "don't yell too loud. I want to sleep."

"You scamp." Alethia gave him a tight hug around his shoulders as they began walking down the steps, her eyes wandering around the grand stairway as they descended slowly. Her lashes fluttered when she saw the half-moon window over the landing, and her fingers caressed the mahogany handrail.

"Mama, you're acting like you ain't never walked down these stairs before," Tad said bluntly, his brow furrowed.

"Please don't say ain't," Alethia said, averting her eyes from the ornate staircase. "Remember, you're the son of the president of the United States of America. It's important for you to use proper grammar at all times."

"Yes, Mama." He hung his head.

Alethia breathed deeply, praying for the self-restraint needed to mask her child-like wonder at her new surroundings.

"Sometimes I forget how beautiful this house is, Tad," she tried to explain with humor. "There are moments—well, the way the lights hit the windows or paintings, it just takes my breath away." She laughed. "It's the Kentucky girl in me, I suppose."

When Tad did not respond, Alethia sighed, because she could not describe her feelings. Garments made of rich fabrics she had seen only on fine ladies who stretched their legs during short layovers at the Bladensburg train depot were now within her touch. The most famous mansion in the nation, at one time home to Dolley Madison, was now her home. And, most important of all, a family—a warm, strong man and a beautiful, lively boy—was now hers to hold, love, and caress. All would be ripped from her bosom if she could not act as though these new joys were merely ordinary. At the bottom of the stairs she saw Duff wave good-bye to Hay and Nicolay as they left through the front door. He turned to smile at them and point to the small dining room off to a quiet corner. When Alethia walked in, she breathed a sigh of relief because, in this room, she did not feel overwhelmed but warmly welcomed. It was not imperious, but reminiscent of her aunt's dining room where she had eaten every Christmas dinner since childhood. Her eyes caught sight of white vases on each end of the buffet, which overflowed with fresh-cut camellias. The striking view of white flowers against the antique white of the vases, accented by a few camellia leaves, made Alethia breathe deeply. What exquisite taste Mrs. Lincoln must have, she marveled, becoming fearful she could not imitate such sophistication. She resisted the urge to rush over to smell the strong scent of the camellias, to touch lightly their petals and gently caress the vases; instead, she ignored them and invited her new family to sit. Phebe entered with a tray of soup bowls.

"Thank you, Phebe," she said, pleased she remembered her name. "You may serve the soup."

"Tomato bisque, as you requested," Phebe said.

"It looks delicious," Alethia said.

Looking at Alethia, Tad whined. "But you said I didn't have to eat this junk." He frowned as Phebe put the bowl before him.

"Oh." Her eyes widened. "That's right. I forgot. I'm sorry, Phebe. Please take the bowl away."

"That's all right, Phebe." Reaching for the bowl, Duff said, "I'll take care of it."

"Very well, Mr. President. Neal will be up in a few minutes with the main course."

"Thank you, Phebe," Alethia called out as she lifted her tray and left.

"Well, this looks good," Duff said, surveying his two soup bowls. He stopped short of picking up a spoon when his eye caught Alethia's.

She was frowning, thinking suddenly that she did not know if the Lincolns practiced the custom of saying grace before every meal. She had read speeches by Lincoln in which he referred to Divine Providence, but even a spinster from a country village knew politicians often said anything to win votes with no intention of living the words they said.

"Mama," Tad said. "Are you thinking about Willie again?"

'What, dear?" Alethia turned to him, rousing from her dilemma about the prayer and whether Tad would notice; for it was this young man, not members of the Cabinet or Congress, that Alethia feared most in keeping her identity a secret.

"You were awful quiet there," he continued.

"It's hard not to think of your brother." She smiled.

"What do you think would help, Taddie?" Duff asked, glancing at Alethia. "Mentioning him in our prayers?"

"All right. Mama and I can talk to him at our bedtime prayers."

"Maybe eating this good soup would make her feel better too," Duff offered.

"Yeah, Mama; go ahead and eat." Tad looked at Alethia and smiled.

"Let's go ahead and eat our soup." Duff smiled and picked up his spoon.

"It's delicious," Alethia murmured as she sipped, trying to hide the pleasure on her face at Duff's clever way of solving the blessing problem.

A few minutes later, Neal appeared with a tray holding three plates of pork chops, potatoes, and black-eyed peas. While Alethia's family ties made her lean toward the cause of the South, she held no personal prejudice against black men, although she had never had any personal encounters with any, other than to pay the porter at the train station and to tell the old fellow sweeping the wooden sidewalk downtown to be careful not to get dust on her Sunday dress. This young black man did not scare Alethia as some did, those large, muscular laborers, black as midnight and with brooding eyes. Neal was slightly built, with light skin and freckles, which made him appear less ominous. He did have brooding eyes, though.

"Thank you, Neal," she said.

"Neal, no." Phebe arrived breathlessly in the doorway. "I forgot to tell you to take only two plates. Master Tad isn't…"

"That's all right," Duff said, interrupting her and reaching for the tray. "Put two of those plates in front of me, Neal. I can handle them."

"Yes, sir," Neal said and gave a side glance to Phebe.

Was something wrong? Alethia worried. Had they noticed something already that made them suspicious? Only a few hours into their masquerade, she fretted, and found out so soon.

"Don't look at me like that, Neal. I know it was my mistake," she heard Phebe murmur.

Her eyes fluttering, Alethia realized they were not discovered. She sipped more tomato bisque to calm herself, thinking she should not assume every furrowed brow and every pregnant pause meant that someone had detected they were not the real Lincolns. Please, God, let this war be over soon, she prayed, for she could not take this stress very long.

"Neal, what kind of pie do you have down there?" Tad asked.

"You've already had your dessert," Duff said.

"But I'm still hungry."

"Then you should have eaten your soup."

Good, Alethia said to herself, family squabbling is good.

"Well, Neal, what kind do you have?"

"I don't know, Master Tad." He pinched his lips together.

"It's rhubarb," Phebe offered.

"Yuck, I hate rhubarb."

"Then it's just as well, as you weren't getting any in the first place," Duff said as smoothly as the authentic Lincoln would have said.

As Phebe and Neal left, Tad looked over at their dinner. "I like pork chops."

"You can have part of mine," Alethia said and sliced a wedge off the thick, pan-fried chop on her plate.

"You're going to spoil that boy," Duff said.

"I'm not going to have any more boys." Alethia touched his hair as he took the sliver of meat and stuffed it into his mouth. "He's my last one." She pulled away her hand and put it to her cheek, trying not to cry.

"Papa!" Licking his fingers, Tad's eyes widened, and his mouth dropped open as he watched Duff finish one plate of food and reach hungrily for the second. "You're eating like a pig!"

"Tad!" Alethia exclaimed. "What a way to talk to your father!"

Duff looked up, his eyes innocent and questioning and his mouth filled with potatoes. He swallowed hard.

"It's just that Papa always eats just a bit at supper. And just an apple for lunch," he said apologetically. "You're always after him 'cause he eats so little. That's all. I didn't mean nothing."

"Well, Taddie," Alethia said with a laugh, "it seems you're putting your father in a difficult situation. I fuss at him for eating too little, and when he tries to please me, you fuss at him for eating too much."

"I didn't mean to fuss." Tad scrunched up his face.

"Go ahead, Father, and enjoy your supper," Alethia said.

"I filled up." Duff looked as though he had been caught doing something much worse than eating more than his share. He pushed the plate away.

"Are you sure?" Alethia furrowed her brow.

"Yes," he replied. "Tad's right. I guess my eyes were bigger than my stomach." His eyes, however, gave him away as they stared longingly at the second pork chop from which he had taken only one bite.

"Then you must have a slice of that delightful rhubarb pie," Alethia said.

"No, all filled up." Glancing at Tad, Duff shook his head.

"Very well," Alethia said. She dipped her fork into the potatoes and tasted them.

The rest of the meal went quietly, until Secretary of War Stanton appeared in the door and loudly cleared his throat. The three at the dining table looked up to see his disapproving glare through his pebble glasses.

"The Cabinet members will be here soon," he said dourly. "We must prepare."

"Yes, of course." Duff looked up with wide eyes and wiped his mouth with the cloth napkin.

As the four of them left the small family dining room and walked down the hall, Stanton took Duff by the elbow to lead him to the service stairs. Alethia was alarmed that Duff looked confused.

"This way, Mr. President," Stanton said.

Looking at the grand staircase at the end of the hall, Duff muttered, "But I thought…"

"The president doesn't need to be prancing up and down the formal staircase all the time," Stanton said, hardly hiding the reprimand in his voice. "He needs to protect his privacy by using the service stairs."

"Of course," Duff said as he followed Stanton.

Tad tugged on Alethia's dress sleeve, and she bent down. "I don't know why Papa doesn't haul off and knock him down when he talks to him like that," he whispered.

"Well," Alethia replied, trying not to smile, "you know your father is very good at dealing with difficult people."

They began climbing the service stairs, well behind Duff and Stanton, who were almost the second floor door. Tad grunted.

"I'd rather kick him in the shins."

"Oh no; you mustn't do that."

"You said this afternoon that he got what he deserved when I pulled his beard." He turned to look at her quizzically.

"You know me," Alethia said with a desperate laugh. "Sometimes when I'm in a snit I say things I shouldn't." She playfully swiped at his shoulder with her hand. "As a young gentleman, you shouldn't remind a lady of when she didn't act like a lady."

By the time they reached the top and entered the second floor hall, Duff and Stanton had disappeared through the glass panels into the president's office. Alethia and Tad turned the other way to Tad's bedroom. Alethia was pleased with herself that she remembered the correct door to open.

"And now it's time for you to go to bed," she sweetly announced.

As Tad went to his armoire to change into his pajamas, Alethia busied herself pouring water into a basin to wipe some of the grime and perspiration from the boy's face and neck.

"I don't like that Mr. Stanton," Tad said as he crawled into bed. "He's too cross and bossy. Sometimes I think he wants to be president instead of papa."

"It's war, Tad." Alethia sat on the bed's edge and lovingly wiped Tad's troubled face. "That makes everybody a little cross. And men who want others to accept their ideas can look like they're a little bossy."

"Not a little, a whole bunch bossy."

"Oh, Tad, what are we going to do with you?" She laughed as she caressed his slender neck with the wet cloth, wiping around the nape and down the shoulders.

"I'm not that dirty, am I?"

"Of course not. Mothers just get carried away, that's all." Alethia pulled back and walked to the basin where she rinsed out the cloth. "And Mr. Stanton. Don't be too harsh on him, dear. I'm sure he has a wife and children and is quite gentle when he's with them. Remember, people aren't always as they appear." She suddenly felt the back of her neck turn red with embarrassment. She tried to smile. "What I mean is, while Mr. Stanton may appear mean to you, he actually is quite affectionate with his children."

"You already said that."

"Oh dear, I'm getting confused again, aren't I?" Alethia returned to the bed and sat close to Tad. She brushed the hair from his brow. "You'll forgive me, won't you?"

"I love you most when you're like this, Mama." Tad smiled and sat up.

"Like what?"

"You know, quiet and happy. Content and smiling. When you—now, don't get mad—when you admit you make mistakes and apologize."

"I don't do that enough," Alethia said. "I promise to try harder."

"I know you try." Tad leaned forward to hug her. "I love you, Mama."

Alethia held her breath in an attempt not to cry from the joy of having a beautiful young boy embrace her so tightly. Duff could worry about the danger of their situation; she was going to enjoy the moment. "And I love you."

Suddenly, Tad pulled away, his eyes wide with apprehension and confusion. He tried to talk, but no words came out. His little hand shook as it pointed at her bosom, and he held his other hand to his chest.

"What's wrong, Tad?"

He shook his head and pointed again to her breast. Her hand went to her full bosom and covered it.

"I don't understand, Tad. What's wrong?"

Not saying a word, only moaning pitifully, he lay back down and pulled the covers up to his face until only his eyes, filled with fear, were left showing.

Alethia continued to look down at her bosom and then at Tad several times, until her mouth flew open and both arms went to her chest as though to hide it.

"Oh."

Tad responded by sinking his head completely beneath the covers.

Chapter Nine

As Duff and Stanton entered the president's office, Stanton looked around and quietly shut the door, then crossed the room to look through the door to Nicolay's office.

"He and Mr. Hay are still at supper," Duff said.

"They may have returned earlier," Stanton replied. "You must always be on the alert for people who aren't *supposed* to be there."

"Yes, sir."

"And call me Mr. Stanton," he continued. "'Sir' is much too severe a salutation and implies subservience. After all, you're the president, and I the mere secretary of war."

"Yes, Mr. Stanton."

"And stop acting like a beaten dog, for God's sake!"

Quietly, Private Christy entered, nodded, and hesitantly went to a corner to stand at attention.

"He's your adjutant," Stanton said at Duff's look of unease. "He needs to be here."

"I know he's my adjutant. We met this afternoon. I know he needs to be here." Duff paused to pout. "I don't have to be told everything. I'm not stupid. I'm just nervous."

A knock at the door caused Duff to fidget.

"Then don't act so *nervous*. Relax! God, I hope you've a sense of humor." Stanton paused and then spat out a sigh. "Aren't you going to tell them to enter? It's your office, for God's sake."

"Come in," Duff called out as he sat behind the large wooden desk. When an older, balding man in servant uniform entered, he smiled. "Tom Pen, my friend."

"The members of the Cabinet are beginning to arrive downstairs." The servant smiled warmly and stepped just inside the door. "Shall I send them up?"

"Of course," Duff replied. "The lamb is ready for the slaughter."

As the old man laughed, Stanton caught the glimpse from Duff to acknowledge the fact that he indeed had a sense of humor. The war secretary told himself to calm down, because this man was going to be fine. He could see it in his eyes the day he met him in the War Department reception room. A bit stooped, defeated-looking, Duff spoke well and quickly, letting his intelligence shine through.

"That's quite enough, Mr. Pendel," Stanton said.

"Yes, sir." Pendel's eyes went to the floor.

"Mr. Pendel is my doorman, Mr. Stanton," Duff said quite aggressively. "I'll tell him when to leave."

A bit startled, Stanton stammered, "Yes, sir." His mouth pinched shut as he watched Duff relish his new authority.

Pendel smiled broadly.

"If you can't take time out of the day for a laugh, then you might as well be Edwin M. Stanton." He smiled as Pendel laughed again. When Stanton took his glasses off and tapped them on his palm, Duff coughed nervously. "I guess you better get along before those fellers start talking about taking over."

"Yes, sir, Mr. President." Pendel gave a side glance at Stanton and turned to leave.

"I promise to end this to-do at a decent hour," Duff said. "I know Taddie will have you up early tomorrow morning packing for the Soldiers' Home."

"Thank you; very kind of you, sir." Pendel smiled. The pleasant turn of mouth disappeared when he addressed Stanton. "Sir."

After the doorman left, Duff began to open drawers in the desk.

"What are you doing?"

"If someone asks for a sheet of paper, I got to know where to get it, don't I?"

"You're bordering on insolence."

"First you say I'm acting like a whupped dog, and then you say I'm insolent."

"Enough of that." Stanton waved his hand as he put his pebble glasses back on his nose. "Mr. Chase informed me this meeting was opportune, for he'd just written a letter of protest for Cabinet members to sign and present to you."

"So he's in on his?"

"No. While he has the right views, he lacks the imagination to understand the need for subterfuge."

Their heads turned as they began to hear footsteps and voices come up the stairs. As they came closer, Stanton took a seat at the long table covered with a green cloth in the middle of the room. Duff looked up at the portrait of President Andrew Jackson looming over the conference table.

"I wonder what he'd think about all this," Duff wondered aloud.

"Shh." Stanton furrowed his brow, leaned forward and whispered, "And don't acquiesce too easily."

"Is that Mr. Smith and Mr. Bates I hear plotting outside my door?" Duff stood.

Two ordinary-looking, elderly gentlemen entered the room with reserved smiles.

"Never plotting, Mr. President," Edward Bates, attorney general, said pleasantly as he extended his hand to greet Duff.

"Well, I'd plot against a man who roused me out of the house at a late hour like this," Duff said as he firmly shook Bates's hand.

"We're ever pleased to do our duty in serving the presidency," said Interior Secretary Caleb Smith with a slight lisp.

"My Lord, you should be in bed, Mr. Smith." Duff paused in the middle of his handshake to lean forward and examine Smith's prosaic, thin, pale face. "Forgive me, but you look worse than the puny turkey the poor relations turned down for Christmas."

Stanton stiffened at Duff's forwardness. If he had written a script for Duff to follow, it would not have included that observation on Smith's health.

"Exactly Mrs. Smith's sentiments as I dressed to come here," Smith replied. "She would've been frightfully upset with you, Mr. President, if you had not yesterday sent her a note concurring with her insistence that I see my physician."

Stanton relaxed in his chair as the light conversation continued between the men as they ambled to the conference table. Squinting at Bates, he surmised that the attorney general should not be a problem in agreeing with Chase's letter. Most of the time he was courteously quiet during Cabinet debate, except when a matter of Constitutional law arose, and then he spoke with authority.

"I know you can't expect to have the energy of a young man when you pass the age of fifty, but you'd think I could make it through the day without a nap," Smith said as he slid into the nearest chair.

He would be no problem, Stanton judged the Interior secretary, though he had expressed admiration for General McClellan's conservative approach to military strategy. Smith's health was failing, and he conceded arguments simply to end the stress.

"Mr. President," Gideon Welles said with a flinty New England accent, "I swear I'll join Jeff Davis if you don't stop calling these late meetings. I thought you were leaving for the Soldier's Home tonight."

The arrival of the secretary of the navy caused Stanton to stir uncomfortably in his seat. On one hand, he knew Welles was no supporter of McClellan and would welcome Chase's initiative; on the other hand, however, he could not abide the man.

"Good to see you, Mr. Welles," he said, smiling and stroking his pharaoh beard.

"Stanton." Welles nodded his way.

Welles may well have been a good administrator from his years of running a newspaper in Hartford, Connecticut, but he knew nothing about ships. When Stanton joined the Cabinet, replacing corrupt Simon Cameron, he recognized Welles's inadequacy immediately and could not conceal his contempt. Stanton showed no restraint in expressing disdain—his voice dripped with sneering reproof and his eyes glowed with incredulity until, to his surprise, Welles confronted him. It was then that Stanton had become alarmingly aware of how tall Welles was. His appearance may have invited scorn, with his flowing white beard and huge gray wig making him look like Saint Nicholas, but the gnome-like Stanton realized, as Welles loomed over him, Welles was not to be ridiculed. Since then, Stanton had forced himself to smile and be courteous, keeping his opinions of Welles to himself.

"So, Mr. President," Welles said, "what's the news?"

"Who else? General McClellan." Duff stole a glance at Stanton, who looked down at the table.

"Ah," Welles replied. "The man from West Point."

"The man from West Point?" A hatchet-faced man appeared in the door. "We must be discussing the esteemed commander of the Army of the Potomac."

"One and the same, Mr. Blair," Welles said. "Come, sit down."

"Good evening, Mr. President."

"Mr. Postmaster General," Duff said.

"Mr. Stanton." Montgomery Blair, tall and weedy, focused his intense eyes on Stanton, and nodded stiffly.

"Have a seat, gentlemen," Duff said, "we only lack two players, and we can start the game."

A mild chuckle rolled around the table as Blair sat next to Smith and leaned toward him to whisper. Stanton squinted as he tried to make out what he was saying, for he could not trust Blair. He was an abolitionist for sure; in fact, he had acted as defense attorney for the runaway slave Dred Scott before the Supreme Court, and urged hot action on Fort Sumter, but Stanton felt as though he could not control the man, and that made him dangerous. Radicals and moderates together hated Blair, because he always said what he thought, and true believers, Stanton knew, only wanted to hear what they believed.

"Ah," Duff said with light humor, "Mr. Seward and Mr. Chase. Now let the games begin."

Stanton looked to the door and saw the last two Cabinet members enter, each trying to force the other to go first to allow for a grand entrance, but they ended up looking like a pair of buffoons. Buffoons they were, Stanton told himself, trying to control a smirk as they came to the table.

"Mr. Seward," Duff said, "it's reassuring to see a man who knows so much and can still smile."

"Any occasion I can spend with you causes a smile, Mr. President," Seward said blandly as he sat in one of the remaining wooden captain chairs and slouched down.

"Mr. Seward," Duff said. "Pull the cord for Mr. Hay and Mr. Nicolay."

"Yes, sir."

Like Blair, Seward was a man Stanton could not trust. Not because of his bluntness, but because of his mystery and equivocating. The war secretary never knew where he stood with Seward, nor, indeed, where the former New York senator stood on anything. He hated the South, but loved Jefferson Davis. He could concede point after point in an argument until he won everything he wanted.

"Good evening, Mr. President," Chase said as he sat, looking a bit smug and satisfied, which made Stanton flush with anticipation.

Chase would take the initiative, leaving the war secretary out of any suspicion of conspiracy. Stanton liked everything about Chase—except his ambition.

"Sorry to interrupt your evening, Mr. Nicolay and Mr. Hay," Duff said as they entered, each with a pad and pen. "This shouldn't take long at all."

"That's quite all right, Mr. President," Nicolay said, sitting to the left of Duff.

Hay sat without a word to Duff's right. Stanton lowered his eyelids as he studied the secretaries. Hay would not be a problem. He cared only for drinking and whoring. Nicolay, on the other hand, was intelligent, and might put small clues together to guess the truth. Perhaps a trip out west could be arranged for him if this project took longer than expected, Stanton mused.

"May I introduce my new adjutant, Private Adam Christy," Duff said to an uninterested Cabinet.

Good, Stanton thought, he did not want the Cabinet to notice the change of guard.

"I have a letter for the Cabinet to consider." Chase pulled it from his coat pocket. "It's about the Army of the Potomac command problem."

"There is no command problem," Duff said, putting his hands to his face as if in prayer. "Only this week I reinstated General McClellan to that position, and expect him to perform to expectations."

This itinerant farmer from Michigan was good, Stanton thought. It was good for him to resist the idea at first; hopefully, he would not make too good an argument for keeping McClellan.

"He assured me this was his intention when he spoke with me earlier today on his way out of the Capitol," Welles said. "He said he was going forward. And I replied, 'Well, onward, General, is now the word, the country will expect you to go forward.'" Welles paused to sigh. "I don't think he detected the irony in my voice."

"So will you please read us your letter, Mr. Treasury Secretary?" Duff said to Chase.

"Of course."

Chase unfolded the sheet and began his recitation of objections to the general, who trained troops well but failed to engage them aggressively. Stanton nodded sagely at Chase's words, until he reached his conclusion.

"Therefore, we the undersigned call for permanent dismissal of General George McClellan and instatement as commander of the Army of the Potomac General Joseph Hooker."

Stanton's head jerked as he looked at Chase, who turned to smile at him. The decision, he thought, had been for General Ambrose Burnside. Was it a misunderstanding, or was Chase instigating his first move toward his campaign for the presidency?

"Any comments?" Duff asked amiably. "Please?"

Interior Secretary Smith cleared his throat and leaned forward. "I, for one, could not sign such a document," he said with a slight lisp. "Frankly, I appreciate General McClellan's conservative approach. Killing thousands of our young men from the North will not in itself free any slaves, nor convince any Southerner to stay in the Union."

"And I wonder about the legal repercussions of replacing generals so quickly," Attorney General Bates added. "While I agree civil authority outranks the military—"

"This is war, dammit," Stanton boomed, interrupting the gray-haired Bates, who pursed his lips and leaned back in his chair.

"Thank you, Mr. Stanton," Chase said. "Bringing back McClellan was equivalent to giving Washington to the rebels."

"That surprises me, gentlemen," Postmaster General Blair interjected, his face pinched with a hint of sarcasm. "I thought you and Mr. Stanton would have preferred the fall of the capital to the reinstatement of McClellan."

"Mr. Blair, please." Chase rolled his eyes.

"No," Duff interceded. "I'd like to hear more of what Mr. Blair has to say."

"I agree we can do better than General McClellan. But I blame Mr. Stanton for the general's defects, as much as McClellan himself."

"Now that's true." Welles shook a finger at Stanton. "The general has enough failings of his own to bear without the addition of your enmity."

"We've so many fine officers coming out of West Point," Blair continued, "jewels to be mined, so to speak."

"I don't know if I quite agree with you on that, Mr. Blair," Welles said.

"We all know your prejudices against West Point," Blair replied with a wry smile.

"No efficient, energetic, audacious fighting commanding general has yet appeared from the place," Welles said with a shrug.

This is foolishness, Stanton fumed. Why does not Duff end this banal debate?

"Another consideration, Mr. President, is political," Blair said, now leaning forward to make his point. "As you know, my father was an adviser to Andrew Jackson, and I grew up on politics. If you replace McClellan so soon after reinstating him, especially before he has a chance to prove himself on the battlefield, you'll look like a willy-nilly, not a quality to get you re-elected."

"And you must consider General McClellan's popularity with the troops," Smith added. "Recently I read how soldiers beat up a man in a bar who dared speak ill of their commander. 'Devil take the man who would say a word against McClellan,' the paper reported them saying."

"The military doesn't run this country," Bates said.

"You're absolutely right, Mr. Bates." Chase pushed the letter to the attorney general. "Sign this so we can end this war sometime this century."

"Well..."

"Then pass it to Mr. Stanton," Chase said. "I'm sure he has no reservations about signing it."

"Not in its present form." Stroking his pharaoh beard, Stanton wrinkled his brow.

"What?" Chase's eyes widened.

"I prefer General Burnside."

"He has declined the position twice," Chase said.

"He's a professional soldier. His campaigns have shown him to be capable."

"He himself said he wasn't fit for the job," Chase replied.

"And he's loyal," Stanton continued his argument. "Once, upon hearing the rash statement by other officers that the military would run the Republican Party out of Washington and take over the government, he said, 'I don't know what you fellows call this talk, but I call it flat treason!'"

"Hooker will fight!" Chase blustered.

"He's just like Pope, and he's a blowhard and a liar," Blair interjected.

Stanton sighed and wondered why Duff was allowing this meeting to get so out of control. But he knew why. This was not Lincoln, nor any other politician who had glided through the rough waters of government debate. Duff was drowning, and there was nothing Stanton could do without raising suspicions.

"What do you think, Mr. Seward?" Duff finally asked.

"There's some wisdom in everything that has been offered here." Seward smiled mysteriously. "If we just continue, we'll find the truth, somewhere."

Stanton made eye contact with Duff and could swear the man could read his thoughts—what the secretary of state had just said was rubbish. He watched Duff sigh with melancholy and stand, leaving the debate behind as he went back to his own desk.

"Mr. Stanton," Chase said gravely, "you've never expressed any criticism of General Hooker before."

Stanton hesitated before replying, watching out of the corner of his eye as Duff picked up a book left by Lincoln earlier in the day. No attention span, Stanton fretted, as he tried to find words to rebut Chase.

"I like Fremont myself," Smith offered.

"Fremont!" Chase responded with irritation. "Please, Mr. Smith!"

Duff exploded with laughter, causing everyone to turn to see him with his large feet on the desk and his dour face opened by a huge grin as he read from the book.

"I was just looking at this book by Artemus Ward," Duff said with a chuckle. "Listen to this: 'I showed my show in Utica when a big burly feller walked up to my wax figures of the Lord's Last Supper and seized Judas Iscariot by the feet and dragged him out on the ground. He then commenced to pound him as hard as he could, yelling, "Old man, that Judas Iscariot can't show himself in Utica with impunity by a darn sight!" with which observation he caved in Judas's head. The young man belonged to one of the first families in Utica. I sued him, and the jury brought in a verdict of arson in the third degree.'" Duff threw back his head and laughed loudly.

Stanton thought his worst fears had come true—Duff had succumbed to the stress and had gone out of his mind. Even this could be turned to his advantage if Stanton kept his head about him.

"Mr. President," Seward said, "you've broken the tension and made your point."

"And what, Mr. Seward, do you think this point is?" Duff finished his laughter.

"If we don't stop bashing General McClellan in the head, we'll surely be guilty of burning the future of our country."

Duff looked at Stanton to shake his head imperceptibly, which the war secretary took to mean that the effort to remove McClellan was defeated, unless they ham-handedly forced their opinion on the others, which would raise too many questions. Stanton nodded.

"You sure can read my mind, Mr. Seward," Duff said, standing. "I suggest we give General McClellan another chance to lead, until he fails so miserably even his most devoted followers would have to concede he must go."

Seward nodded. "Wisely said, Mr. President."

Chapter Ten

Gabby Zook, huddling behind the crates and boxes in the billiards room in the basement of the Executive Mansion, fought the hysteria growing inside him. He felt his reason, which was with him so little, fleeing him at this very moment. What was right became irrelevant since the strange, round man with the pharaoh beard and the young soldier had told him he could not go home to his sister Cordie. What was wrong with going home to Cordie? What was right about being forced at gunpoint to stay in the basement of the president's house? Of all the years he had spent fighting the confusion in his brain, this was the worst. No, he corrected himself: the worst was the time the confusion had begun, many years ago at West Point. What had happened that day was not logical, and Gabby knew logic. He was at the head of the class when it came to logic. If $a = b$, and $b = c$, then $a = c$. It was simple. But he had learned the world was not simple.

Keys jangling at the door caused Gabby to look up and remember he had not yet had his supper, and his stomach was rumbling.

"It's about time he arrived with our meal," Mrs. Lincoln said.

"Yes," Lincoln replied, "we must thank him for it."

"Thank him?" Her voice rose indignantly.

Before she could continue, the door opened and Adam entered with a large tray carrying soup bowls and plates of food. With his foot he shut the door and quickly went to the billiards table, put it down, and hurried back to the door to lock it.

"There's no need to rush to lock us in," Lincoln said. "We won't try to escape."

"Yes, sir. I'm sure you won't, sir. Mr. Stanton was very specific in his orders."

"He's cranky," Gabby offered as he walked to the billiards table to see what there was for him to eat. Tomato soup, a pork chop, and some potatoes. Not bad. "It's the beard. Beards make men cranky."

"Well, Mr. Gabby," Lincoln smiled, stroking his own whiskers as he replied, "I don't know about that."

"Can I take a bowl of soup?" Gabby asked.

"Of course," Adam said.

Gabby knew he was right, but he was not going to argue with the tall man with the black whiskers, because, after all, he had a beard and could become cranky, like the colonel at West Point.

He had needed a carriage driver to take him out to the field to observe artillery practice. Gabby had tried to tell him he was from New York City and had never learned to control a team of horses, but the bearded colonel would hear none of it.

"This is the army, Private," the colonel had said, scolding him. "I'm a colonel, and if I say you'll drive a carriage, you'll drive a carriage. No arguments."

"But—"

"No buts," he interrupted. "Do you want to receive your commission?"

"Yes, sir. Can I bring along my friend?"

"We have to go now," the colonel said.

"He's right here," Gabby replied, waving Joe over.

Gabby remembered his life perfectly to that point. He remembered his father's last words to him. He remembered swimming off Long Island with Joe. But after that day at West Point, Gabby could not remember anything. Confusion clouded his past and his present. He dared not consider the future.

"This soup is cold," Mrs. Lincoln said after sipping a spoonful.

Gabby admired her superior attitude, considering she looked like a child sitting at the adults' table as she tried eating at the high billiards table which almost came to her chest.

"Better cold soup than none at all," Lincoln interceded. He smiled at Adam. "Thank you, Private. You may retire. I'm sure you've had a long day."

"You will not," Mrs. Lincoln asserted. "You'll return in half an hour to retrieve the dishes. I'll not sleep in a room with filthy dishes. An hour later you'll remove the chamber pots, clean them thoroughly, then return them."

"That'll be awful late," Adam said, his eyes looking to Lincoln.

"I won't sleep in a room with filthy chamber pots!"

Lincoln nodded slightly, his eyes blinking apologetically.

"Yes, ma'am." Adam bowed his head.

"And what's in the pitcher?" Mrs. Lincoln asked.

"Water, ma'am," he replied.

She sniffed. "Very well."

"Private, sir?" Gabby said, his voice quavering. "Could you pour me a glass of water and carry it to my corner? My hands are full with this soup bowl."

"Of course." Adam smiled.

As Gabby settled on the floor behind the crates and barrels, crossing his legs and placing the soup bowl in his lap, Adam handed him the glass of water.

"Thank you," Gabby whispered. "I didn't want to eat at the billiards table with that woman. I'm afraid she'd have yelled at me if I spilled tomato soup on my shirt."

"She probably would have," Adam said.

"Did you see Cordie?" Gabby asked, looking up at Adam as he slurped a spoonful of soup.

Adam nodded. "Everything's fine. She's going to meet me every day at Lafayette Park to see how you're doing. I think she said she was making you a quilt."

"This soup isn't too hot." Gabby slurped again.

"Did you hear me? She's fine. She's making you a quilt."

"Cordie makes good quilts. She can make a quilt for you." He took another spoonful, dripping on his shirt. "It's got chunks of stuff in it. But it's still good."

"Well, good night." Adam turned to leave.

"You want to be an officer?"

"Yes."

"You going to West Point?"

"No, I'm earning my commission now. Mr. Stanton promised it."

"Don't go to West Point," Gabby said. "You can get confused at West Point."

"Oh. Good night."

"These chops are not the right size," Mrs. Lincoln piped up.

"They're fine, Private," Lincoln said.

"Thank you, sir."

Gabby heard the door shut and then a hand slap a shoulder.

"Mr. Lincoln, you big baboon. I'm ashamed I'm your wife."

His stomach tightening, Gabby hoped Mrs. Lincoln was not planning to fuss at her husband during every meal. It would not be good for his digestion. He may be confused on a great many things, but Gabby was sure arguments made the stomach tied up in knots and unable to process the food being chewed and swallowed.

"Why on earth have you allowed this to happen?"

"This is very fundamental, Molly," Lincoln said. "He who holds the gun can tell you what to do."

His gray head cocked, Gabby could hear slurping. Good, he told himself. Lincoln slurped his soup too. Did he dribble any on his clothes? It would be hard not to, sitting at a billiards table. Gabby was too afraid to peek around the crates to find out.

"What we have to do now is not overreact, to get along, just to live through this," Lincoln continued. "Try to act as normal as possible, Molly. Be yourself. Be cheerful and act courteously and grateful."

"Who could be themselves around a glum monstrosity?"

Am I a glum monstrosity? Gabby asked about himself. He knew he was confused and scared most of the time, but he did not think he was particularly glum.

"You long-legged awkward scarecrow!"

Oh, Gabby realized, she was talking about Lincoln being a glum monstrosity. This was getting hard for him to comprehend. All this emotion, talk, and activity swirled in his head, making it hard for him to keep it in straight, proper lines, like West Point would do it. But a hot feeling from the pit of his gut told him he did not want to do things the West Point way, even when it came to organizing thoughts in his brain.

"I wish I'd never laid eyes on you, you homely, uncouth brute!" Mrs. Lincoln said. "I wish I'd married in my circle! I wish I'd married Stephen Douglas!"

"I wish you had too," Lincoln replied. "But I said until death do we part. Maybe this is death. It's worse."

Gabby stared at his empty soup bowl. It was good, but now it was all gone, and he wanted more to eat. He wanted the pork chop on the other plate, but he was afraid to walk over to the billiards table to pick it up because that couple was in the middle of a big argument, and arguments always made him nervous. His mother and father never allowed anyone to raise his voice while in the apartment. If he and Cordie argued, they had to write notes. Gabby liked silence. Silence meant serenity.

"You hate me," Mrs. Lincoln said, choking back the tears. "You really hate me."

"No, I don't." Lincoln's voice sounded congenial and conciliatory. "Sometimes you make me wish I were dead, but I still love you."

As Mrs. Lincoln laughed and sniffed away her tears, Gabby decided this was a good time to come from around the stacks of crates and barrels to retrieve his pork chop. As he turned the corner, he saw Lincoln with his long, gangly arms around his wife, who was wiping her eyes. Her chin almost sat on the rim of the billiards table.

"Excuse me," he said. "May I get my pork chop now?"

"Of course, Mr. Gabby." Lincoln smiled. "In fact," he added as he leaned across the billiards table to spear his chop and place it on Gabby's plate, "you may have mine."

"Thank you, sir." Gabby grinned and hastened his step.

"You won't give away your portion." Mrs. Lincoln's voice cut through like a bullet.

Gabby stopped abruptly, the smile gone from his grizzled face.

"You know I don't eat that much of an evening," Lincoln said. He pushed the plate with the two chops on it toward Gabby. "Go ahead, Mr. Gabby."

"Maybe I shouldn't." He took a step back and bowed his head.

"Very well." Mrs. Lincoln sighed in resignation. "Take it."

"Thank you, ma'am." Gabby hesitantly walked to the table and lifted the plate. "You're very kind, ma'am."

She mumbled begrudgingly as Lincoln gave her a hug.

Gabby dared to look up and eye Mrs. Lincoln, her dark hair, plump cheeks, fair skin, and ample bosom—no, Gabby corrected himself as he stared at her bodice.

"You know, what they say about you, it's not true."

"What?" Mrs. Lincoln asked.

"What folks say about you."

"What do people say about me?"

"Mostly it's in the newspapers."

"The Washington newspapers are notorious in their vindictiveness towards me." Mrs. Lincoln arched her eyebrow. "They print nothing but lies."

"It's not what they say." Gabby stared at the two pork chops on his plate and wished he had kept his mouth shut, and maybe he could have been eating them by now.

"What on earth are you talking about?"

"It's the pictures."

"The pictures?" Mrs. Lincoln looked up at her husband. "I can't take this, Father. Do you know what he's talking about?"

"He's trying to tell us, Molly."

Gabby cleared his throat. "You're not as hefty a woman as the pictures in the newspapers make you look like."

"Oh." A smile flickered across her lips, and her eyes softened.

"It's your round cheeks," Gabby continued, encouraged by her response. "They make you look fat when you're really not."

"Why, thank you. That's very kind of you to say…"

"Yeah, you don't have any breasts at all," Gabby interrupted, nodding his head. "Now, Cordie, she's got a big bosom."

"What!" Mrs. Lincoln's hands instinctively went to her chest.

"I always liked putting my head on her bosom for a nap," Gabby said. "But I bet you're kind of bony."

Mrs. Lincoln looked around at her husband, her mouth agape. "Father?"

"Now you enjoy those pork chops, Mr. Gabby." Standing and walking around the billiards table, the president put his arm around

Gabby's shoulders and guided him back to the curtain across his little cubbyhole of crates and barrels.

"Thank you, sir. That's nice of you, sir." Gabby sat on the floor and picked up one of the chops and began to gnaw on it, trying not to listen to the conversation going on between the Lincolns.

"Father, I can't endure this," Mrs. Lincoln said, her voice shaking. "That man is not right in the head."

"I don't know many of us who are, Molly." Lincoln paused. "These taters look good."

"Please don't dismiss me, Mr. Lincoln," she said. "If I have to live in the same room with that man for any considerable period of time, I'm afraid I'll go mad."

"Now, Molly…"

"No, Mr. Lincoln," she interrupted. "Listen to me. I stared insanity in its frightening face when Willie died. It took all my strength to return. I don't think I have the power to do that again."

"Molly, I promise you that we'll be out of here within a week. I know how scared you are, and I'm terribly sorry. But it'll be over soon."

"You really think Mr. Stanton can end the war that soon?"

"No, I think Mr. Stanton will realize he doesn't know how to end this war any better than me, and that he'll be better off if he lets me out of here to take the blame."

"I should have let that strange little man have my chop as well. It's too tough for a reasonable stomach to digest."

Gabby shook his head and began chewing on the second chop. It did not seem that tough to him, but he had a strong jaw and things like that did not bother him much. He jumped a bit when he heard a key jangle in the lock, then he remembered the private was coming back.

"Excuse me, Mr. and Mrs. Lincoln," Adam said. "Are you finished?"

"Yes, we are," she replied airily.

"Yes, young man," Lincoln said. "And thank you for bringing dinner."

"Thank you, sir."

Gabby heard Adam's steps coming to his corner, and he began to chew faster.

"I need your plate," Adam said.

"But I haven't finished my pork chops." Gabby held the plate close to him.

"Very well." Adam sighed. "Don't get upset. I'll get it when I return for the chamber pots."

"Thank you."

"It'll be about an hour. I'll take your chamber pot, too."

"There won't be anything in it." Gabby lowered his head as he bit into the chop. "I'm too scared now to do anything."

Chapter Eleven

As Stanton sat back during his carriage ride to his home on Avenue K in Washington, D.C., he assessed how the day had gone, and decided to be quite pleased with himself. A few complications had arisen, like the janitor in the basement, and the fact he was unable to force the Cabinet to remove General McClellan, but perhaps such stumbling blocks made the situation he had created seem more real, less manipulated. Leaning his cheek on the back of the leather-padded carriage seat, he breathed the late night air and tried to relax. Quickly he pulled his head back, remembering he did not want to risk a new asthma attack. Stanton had not experienced one of his seizures for more than a year, and did not want a new episode at the beginning of the most challenging endeavor of his life, saving the Union from destruction.

His eyes closed, the war secretary could not help but think of the first time his lungs had refused to work, at age ten, in Steubenville, Ohio. His mother had held his slender little body as it was wracked by hacking coughs, while his father, a pious Methodist, prayed unceasingly over him. As the seizure subsided and his parents hugged him, he was aware of their moist cheeks pressed against his own, as though a baptism in tears. While the asthma regularly shadowed his early years, its effect was abated by the comforting knowledge that both of his parents loved him dearly. That assurance made the death of his father near Christmas when he was thirteen even more unbearable. Added to that trauma was the discovery that his father had left no money. With four children and generous donations to the church, Stanton's father had nothing in reserve to protect his family in the event of his death; therefore, being the oldest, Stanton was apprenticed to a bookseller, James Turnbell, who kindly filled in as a father figure and overlooked his bouts of asthma and his tendency to ignore customers while reading.

His Cupid's bow lips now turning up in a smile, he approached his Avenue K home, acknowledging that, while life had not been easy for him, there had been kind people along the way: Turnbell, his father's friend, had loaned him money to go to college and, when the money ran out, allowed him to come back to work in the bookstore; his mother's lawyer had tutored him on the bar exam, and a judge first took him into his practice and then turned it over to him upon being elected to the United States Senate. In a bit of irony, Stanton considered how Abraham Lincoln had favored him and named him secretary of war, a position he used to depose his patron, at least temporarily. He smiled to himself. Well, perhaps not temporarily.

The smile faded as he thought of the death of his first daughter and, three years later, of his first wife, followed two years later by the suicide of his brother and then the shattering blow of the death of his son by his second wife in February 1862. He had the boy cremated and kept the ashes in an urn on the fireplace mantel in his bedroom. Stanton knew he would have to dispose of the ashes sometime and move on with his life, but that deliberate action would be the permanent admission that two of his babies were gone. So until he could bring himself to that realization, the urn stayed in his bedroom, and his second wife dusted and polished it daily.

More than anything, Stanton's black heart could neither forget nor forgive the sins committed against him. No one lived the good Methodist life better than he—chaste, moral, crusading against the evils of slavery—so no one deserved the ridicule and harassment heaped upon him. His eyes opened and narrowed as he remembered his teen-aged years in Steubenville. Short and slight of build, he could not attract the prettiest girls because they always liked tall, robust boys who ran and played games better than he did. When the daughter of the owner of his family's boardinghouse paid him attention, he was enamored. At lunch one summer day in 1833, the girl's brother declared he would rather see his sister dead than in love with Stanton. She had slapped her brother, which pleased Stanton. That night, when he returned home from the bookstore, he learned the girl had died of a quick bout of cholera. Fearing contagion, her family had buried her immediately. In his delirium of sorrow, Stanton believed the brother had buried his sister when the cholera had placed her merely in a state of unconsciousness. He disinterred the girl's coffin to see for himself. As he stroked her cold cheek, Stanton had to admit she was dead.

In the carriage he clenched his fists as he remembered what had happened next. His ears still rung with the laughter above him when he looked up from the grave to see the brother.

"You have to rob graves to find girls?" the brother said, his face barely lit by the lantern in his hand, creating evil shadows across his face.

"I wanted to make sure," Stanton said.

"I should beat the tar out of you for desecrating my sister's grave, but you ain't worth it. Bury her back proper."

Even in the carriage in Washington, Stanton felt his neck burn with humiliation. But no longer. Besides winning the war, Stanton was avenging the most humiliating moment of his life, for the girl's brother who had treated him with such contempt was the father of Private Adam Christy. The father's letter had come fortuitously to complete Stanton's plan. Momentarily, Stanton saddened, because the private did resemble his aunt in the face, fresh and innocent, but he resolved that Adam's father had to pay for his insolence.

As the carriage arrived at the Stanton home on Avenue K, he saw two imposing figures waiting for him. This next meeting would be the linchpin to secure his plan's success. He had to convince Lincoln's personal bodyguard, Ward Hill Lamon, the taller of the two men standing in the dark outside his house, that the president suddenly had been whisked away before Lamon could be notified of new assassination reports.

Stanton leaned out of the carriage and called up to the driver, "If you could be so kind, let these two gentlemen join me in the carriage for a brief conversation before you return to the War Department."

The shorter of the two men, Stanton's private bodyguard, Lafayette C. Baker, entered the carriage first. Stanton took a deep breath as

Lamon plopped on the seat opposite him. A fellow Illinois lawyer and close Lincoln friend, he would not be easily deluded.

"What's this about the president?" Lamon said.

"Yes, you were out of pocket this afternoon..."

"That's because this man of yours had me out in the countryside looking for quinine in a young woman's skirt," Lamon said in a huff. "So what if a Southern belle wants to sneak a few bottles of quinine to Virginia?"

"That young woman was the niece of Postmaster General Montgomery Blair," Baker interjected. Stanton could see the resentment in Baker's eyes as he looked at Lamon, which delighted him. Baker had been a mechanic before the war, while Lamon had been a lawyer. Jealousy made Baker the perfect accomplice.

"Reports were intercepted indicating immediate danger to the president's life," Stanton continued. "He's in a safe place, along with his wife, until such time as the danger passes. To insure no public panic, we have placed a man and woman who look like the Lincolns in the White House."

"Where is the president, Anderson Cottage?"

"I can't tell."

"I'm his personal bodyguard, dammit!"

"Don't let your ego get in the way of national security," Baker said.

"I have no ego," Lamon said, sitting up stiffly.

"I'll communicate with the president, and transmit his orders to the impersonator, who'll inform the Cabinet of the decisions."

"This is damned foolishness."

Baker smiled. "Why? Because you didn't think of it first?"

Stanton held his breath as Lamon shuffled uncomfortably. This moment would make the scheme. If Lamon could be convinced, then all others would be easy to control.

"How long?"

Stanton shrugged. "Until the threat subsides."

"That could be to the end of the war."

"Exactly," Baker said.

"So I'm just district marshal now." Lamon blew out a long sigh.

"Oh no. You're still needed." Stanton tried to hide his relief in the shadows of the carriage. "The double still needs to be protected."

"Damn."

"Don't let him or the woman know you're aware they're not the real Lincolns." Stanton tapped his foot. "That's it. That's all you need to know."

"All I need to know?"

"That's what the secretary said," Baker replied.

"You may leave now."

Lamon exited the carriage, mumbling obscenities, and disappeared into the night. Stanton leaned back, pleased with his progress.

"So. Tell me how it went with Miss Buckner."

"Why, she's in the Old Capitol to spend the night." Baker brushed back his light brown hair and smiled.

"Very good."

"And her mother and—who else was in the party going to Virginia?"

"A minister, Buck Bailey."

"I can imagine the quality of sermon Buck Bailey would deliver." Stanton grunted with disdain. "Are they incarcerated as well?"

"No, sir. I tried, but Lamon stopped it. He said they looked too shocked when I found the quinine bottles sewn into Miss Buckner's dress to be part of the plot."

"What was her defense?"

"She showed her military governor's pass, signed by Major Doster, and a note from the president, and she said her uncle had supplied the money for the shopping trip."

Leaning forward, Stanton said, "Major Doster, huh? Well, rouse the provost marshal from bed and tell him I want to see the memorandum of Mr. Blair's recommendation first thing tomorrow morning."

"Shall I inform the postmaster general of his niece's unfortunate incarceration?"

"Of course." Stanton began to get out of the carriage, then paused. "Tonight. Mr. Blair has been a bit outspoken at Cabinet meetings lately. Perhaps this will dampen his spirit."

"Yes, sir." Baker followed him to the street curb.

Stanton tapped the seat of the carriage. "You may go."

"Your plan is going well, sir," Baker said as the carriage began to pull away.

"There have been a few developments I didn't foresee." He nodded thoughtfully. "But, yes, it's going well." He looked at Baker. "Be about your duties."

"Yes, sir." He disappeared in the shadows to pursue his dark missions.

Stanton entered his home, found the downstairs dark and empty, and proceeded upstairs to his bedroom, where he expected to see his wife, most likely polishing the urn. His steps slowed as he recalled how the death of his son James in February had not sparked the public sorrow and sympathy that did the death of Lincoln's spoiled boy Willie. His son was a saint compared to the Lincoln brat, but no one gave notice to their grief. Shaking his head to rid it of such feminine thoughts, Stanton tried to tell himself that such slights did not enter into his decision to take control of the government's executive branch. That would indicate a woman's emotional disposition in his character, and he would never accept that. When he reached his bedroom door he paused to look in to see his wife Ellen, still wearing black, standing by the fireplace, just staring at the urn. She was fifteen years younger than Stanton and still considered a fine-looking woman of child-bearing age, but in her eyes—her dark, soulful, heavy-lidded eyes—was a silent burden which aged her.

"You're home." She kept her gaze on the urn. "You must be hungry."

"I had a quick supper at the Willard."

"Very well."

"It was kind of you to wait up for me." He stepped into the room, went to her, and lightly touched her shoulder.

"Think nothing of it."

In the last few months, their conversations had been restricted to courtesies and pleasantries. She rarely smiled, and when she did it was at great emotional cost, as though betraying the memory of her son. This was, of course, all supposition on the part of Stanton, because he had never understood his second wife, unlike his first, Mary, who had been his promise of goodness and light. After Mary died in 1844, three years after their daughter's death, Stanton had refused the notion of remarriage. Twelve years of aggressively pursuing his law practice and political aspirations had passed before he noticed Ellen Hutchinson, stately, grand, and slightly taller than he. She was quiet, compliant, and sweet in a mysterious manner. Their son James had brought out the sparkle in her eyes, which Stanton had not taken time to appreciate because he had been busy seeking national political power. Now the sparkle was gone.

"Would you care for a cup of warm milk?" Ellen looked at him without emotion.

"No, thank you."

Could she suspect he was involved in an action that, if discovered, could ruin his career? Stanton wondered as he walked to his armoire, removing his coat. If she did know, would she approve? He softly grunted for worrying about what she would think. What he was doing was for the good of the nation, and he would not change his course now even if she did know and begged him to stop.

"What?" Ellen asked.

"What?"

"I thought I heard a laugh," she said.

"As Mr. Lincoln says, sometimes one must laugh to keep from crying."

"Oh."

Would she care her opinion did not matter to him? Perhaps that was the reason for Ellen's reserve. She knew her place was behind the deceased wife and children.

"Fine," Ellen said. "I'll prepare to retire as well."

Stanton sat in his large stuffed chair to remove his shoes. He watched her remove the white lace collar and the breast pin from her black silk dress. For all his sorrow and anger that aged him, he reminded himself that he still was only forty-seven years old.

"Did you see Mrs. Lincoln today?" she asked.

"Yes." Stanton stiffened.

"You don't like her, do you, Edwin?"

"What makes you think that?"

"The tone of your voice." She let down her shining hair. "Is she still suffering?"

"Suffering?"

"Mourning."

"Oh. Yes."

"I feel sorry for her."

Her compassion stirred him. The flickering lamp revealed her clear white cheeks to be too cold and stolid. Her pale lips never departed from their downward turn. Suddenly he was aware of his passion for her. Stanton, pulling the suspenders down from his trousers, walked to her.

"I think it's admirable you're able to be concerned about Mrs. Lincoln through your own grief." He paused, hoping for a response. "I don't want you to be unhappy."

"I know," she replied as she combed out her hair. "I don't want to be unhappy either."

"I want to make you happy." He tenderly touched her shoulder.

"You make me happy," she automatically said.

"Do I truly?"

"Of course."

Her emotionless tone drained his ardor, and he turned away. Stanton may force his will upon the nation, but not upon his wife.

Chapter Twelve

John Hay lay restlessly in his bed awaiting John Nicolay to finish ripping open letters in the office across the hall. As much as he tried, Hay was unable to go to sleep, because something odd struck him about the events of the afternoon and evening.

Hay had met Nicolay in Springfield, Illinois, and both of them met the gentleman who was a lawyer for the railroads. When Lincoln ran for president, he employed Nicolay to take care of his correspondence, and when he was elected, he took Nicolay's advice to hire Hay. Few secrets were held from the two men, and that was why Hay was he left his bed and slipped on his pants. Walking barefoot, Hay entered to see Nicolay in the dimly lit office, efficiently opening letters, scanning the contents, and assigning them to various piles. Flashing in the kerosene lamp was Nicolay's Bavarian wood-carving knife.

"Still busy?" Hay asked.

"*Ja*," Nicolay replied in a tired accent.

"I couldn't sleep. This afternoon and evening were so strange."

"In what way?"

"First of all," Hay began, while sitting on the edge of Nicolay's desk, "the whole idea of Mr. Lincoln's wanting both of us to take Tad to the Willard for pie and cake."

"It takes two men to contain the boy."

"I think he wanted both of us out of the building so we wouldn't witness what was going on." Hay's eyes searched his friend's face, hoping for an answer that would calm his fears.

"And what would that be?" Nicolay kept his eyes down as he continued opening and reading letters.

"Will you please look at me while I'm speaking?"

"I must have these letters ready for the president tomorrow morning. The unexpected trip to the Willard and the late Cabinet meeting put me behind in my correspondence."

"But didn't you think it was strange he'd call a Cabinet meeting so late, yet not come to any decision?" Hay's nerves were being unsettled by Nicolay's resistance to offer any solutions to his problems.

With a heavy sigh, Nicolay put down his Bavarian carving knife and placed his hands to his chin, narrowing his eyes on Hay, whose left eye was twitching a bit. "What is your job?"

"What do you mean?"

"I mean, what are you paid to do?"

"Take notes at meetings." Hay knew it would be folly to be esoteric. "Screen visitors to his office. Represent the president at events he doesn't wish to attend."

"Correct." Nicolay continued his duties. "At no time did you mention making unpopular observations."

"But it's our obligation—"

"My obligation is to open letters, read them, and assign them to various piles." He put the letter currently in his hand into the wastepaper basket. "That letter merited nothing. Others I pass on to you—social events and such. Some I pass on to Cabinet secretaries. And very few are forwarded to the president. That's my job."

"Are you saying," Hay said, wrinkling his brow, "you didn't notice anything?"

"I noticed the president was a half-inch taller," Nicolay replied. "He spoke in a dialect more likely found in Michigan than Illinois, and there were no stray black hairs peeking above his collar. But those observations are not part of my job."

"But that's not right." Hay shook his head.

"This is another letter from Mr. Herndon." He held up an envelope. "He's probably asking for another favor, obviously illegal or at least unethical, and which will certainly be approved by the president." Nicolay placed the letter unopened in the stack going directly to the president. "If I did the right thing, the ethical thing, I'd take it to the

Congress and report the president for impeachable behavior, but that's not my job, and I won't embarrass the president."

"But don't we have an obligation to the Constitution to reveal possible corruption?" Hay stood to lean over the desk toward Nicolay, who quickly rose and placed his knife to Hay's throat.

"You do know men have had their throats slit for trying to uphold the Constitution?"

"Yes, sir." Hay quavered, looking down at the knife.

"Don't worry, Johnny." Nicolay smiled, put his knife down, and patted Hay's pale cheek. "I wouldn't hurt you. And you're right—Mr. Lincoln has disappeared and been replaced by a poor substitute. But if you ask questions about the change, I'm afraid someone might use a knife across your neck to keep you quiet."

Chapter Thirteen

Gabby Zook awoke to disappointment again. Every morning for the last two months he had come from his night's sleep, forgetting he was on the floor in the basement of the Executive Mansion; he needed the comfort of his sister Cordie, who kept his world intact. With his head aching, Gabby wrestled with his identity, and longed for more mornings when he knew exactly who he was. Thinking back to his days at West Point, he tried to take comfort in memories of some of the courses in which he had excelled. He thought of his logic class, in which his teacher always said he was the best—and if Gabby ever needed logic it was now. Furrowing his brow Gabby fetched scattered bits and pieces from his fragmented brain: let's see, he mumbled, if $a = b$ and $b = c$, then $a = c$.

"That young man is late with our breakfast again, Father," Mrs. Lincoln said, just loud enough for Gabby to hear from his corner.

He shuddered, for this woman scared him with all her tantrums and orders. Gabby did not like being locked in the basement either, but common sense told him yelling, screaming, and throwing things would not change the situation—at least on those days he had common sense. While it was an elusive quality for him, he was certain he captured its essence more often than she did.

"The scandal of all this will rock the nation, Mr. Lincoln," she continued with her Southern lilt. "The audacity of holding the president of the United States captive in the White House basement…"

"Yes, I know, Molly," Lincoln said. Gabby smiled; he liked him. "I've heard your scenarios of trials before the Supreme Court every day for two months."

The president of the United Stats is being held in the basement. Gabby began using his pattern of logic. That was $a = b$. I am being held in the basement. That was $b = c$; so, he hypothesized, I am president of the United States. Gabby shook his head. That could not be right; he never remembered running for election. Jangling keys at the locked door started Gabby's salivary glands flowing. Breakfast had arrived. He stood to look around the stacks of crates and barrels to see Adam put a tray of breakfast foods on the billiards table.

"You're later and later every morning, young man," Mrs. Lincoln chided.

"Yes, ma'am," Adam mumbled. "I'm sorry, ma'am."

Lincoln ambled over. "Were you able to get me a pear?"

"Yes, sir. Right here, sir."

"I hope the coffee is still warm," Mrs. Lincoln said.

"Yes, ma'am. Just brewed, ma'am."

"Got some fried eggs?" Gabby ventured to the billiards table.

"Right here."

"And the morning newspaper," Lincoln added.

"Sorry, sir." Adam hung his head. "I'll get your newspaper right away."

Gabby watched the private go to the door. He did not have the same spring in his step as he had in September. Now, in November, Adam shuffled his feet and rarely made eye contact with anyone. On the off chance Gabby's exercise in logic was correct and he was, indeed, president of the United States, he decided he should do something presidential and comfort the downcast soldier. He walked up behind Adam as he unlocked the door to leave and patted him on the back.

"Everything is going to be fine, Private," he said.

"What?" Adam frowned at him.

"All this will be over soon," Gabby said.

"Oh."

"Things will get better."

Adam sadly smiled and left the room. Feeling satisfied that he had acted presidential, Gabby went back to the billiards table, took a plate, and proceeded to scoop two fried eggs on to it.

"He's a good boy," Gabby said.

"What?" Mrs. Lincoln asked.

"He said, Private Christy is a good boy," Lincoln said. "And Mr. Gabby's right. He's a good boy."

"He is not!" Mrs. Lincoln sputtered, almost choking on a blueberry muffin. "He's holding us here against our will! How on earth can you say that young man is a good boy?"

Gabby hunched his shoulders and wished he had kept his presidential opinions to himself. His hand shook as he poured himself a cup of coffee.

"Now, Molly, Mr. Gabby's trying to make the best of the situation," Lincoln said. "You should, too."

"He's out of his mind! It's plain as the mottled nose on his pitiful face that he's addled! And you're no better!"

"Let me know when the newspaper arrives." Lincoln looked at Gabby, shook his head, and retreated behind his curtain to his cot.

"I'm sorry, ma'am." Gabby turned to escape into his own corner.

"You're just like Cousin Fitzhugh on Mother's side of the family," Mrs. Lincoln began, her voice edged with faint contrition. "He wasn't a Todd. Heavens, no. I don't think he ever stepped a foot inside a Todd household. He wasn't even of Granddaddy's family. I don't even remember his surname. No one really wanted to claim him, and I only met him on sad occasions when one of Mother's elderly kin passed on. He was always there at the wake and the funeral. I just shuddered every time he walked into the laying-out room."

"We laid Papa out in the parlor," Gabby said. "We didn't have a special room for that. Our apartment wasn't that big, and we didn't have people die that often, so we didn't see any need for a special laying-out room."

"The parlor," Mrs. Lincoln said, sighing deeply, and nervously rattling her cup against the saucer, "*was* the laying out room."

"Oh."

"As I was saying, I just shuddered when Cousin Fitzhugh arrived. I've a naturally pleasant turn of mouth, which makes me look friendlier than I often wish to be, and he thought I wanted him to approach me and tell me all sorts of nonsensical things. Rambled, that's all he did. Rambled." Pausing to sip her coffee, Mrs. Lincoln wrinkled her nose. "Tepid. Just as I thought it would be." Her eyes darted to Gabby. "Just like you."

"I'm tepid?"

"Oh no." She giggled, and her eyes twinkled, creating for a split second the image that Gabby surmised was what her husband had fallen in love with many years ago. "No, ramble. You ramble just like Cousin Fitzhugh."

"Oh."

"Mama always said there was no reason to be afraid of Cousin Fitzhugh. He was gentle as a lamb." Mrs. Lincoln smiled and nodded to the chair across the billiards table from her. "Please have your breakfast out here. We may as well learn to be sociable. We're going to be here for a while, it seems."

"Thank you, ma'am."

Gabby sat in the chair and put his plate on the green top of the billiards table. After taking a bite of egg from the plate, which now sat uncomfortably near his chin, he looked over at her.

"I don't like that Mr. Stanton."

"You're certainly correct about that, Mr. Gabby."

Part of his presidential skills was being diplomatic. That was another class in which he excelled, diplomacy. He prided himself for finding ground for common interests.

"I sure miss my sister Cordie."

"I imagine you do." She paused. "She takes care of you, doesn't she?"

Gabby nodded.

"I miss my little boy," Mrs. Lincoln whispered.

"Of course, a mama would miss her child."

"People don't understand Tad." Mrs. Lincoln clasped her hands in front of her and looked off, as though in confession. "I know that they think he's wild and undisciplined, but he has a problem. His palate is malformed. Do you know what the palate is?"

"It's right here." Gabby nodded and pointed to his open mouth.

"Yes, Mr. Gabby." Mrs. Lincoln momentarily closed her eyes because Gabby still had semi-masticated egg on his tongue. "That's right." She smiled at him. "You're smarter than most people give you credit for."

"I went to West Point," he offered.

"Taddie is smarter than people think too. He speaks haltingly and baby-like sometimes, and that makes people think he's stupid. But he's not stupid." She chuckled. "The things that boy can think to say. You can't be stupid and come up with things like that to say."

They ate silently for a few minutes, with Gabby feeling quite proud that he was practicing his diplomacy well enough to keep Mrs. Lincoln from yelling at him. Maybe he was president, after all.

"Mr. Gabby," Mrs. Lincoln said, "may I be so bold as to ask what happened?"

"When?"

"At West Point."

"Oh."

"Something happened for you to be the way you are now."

"Yes, something happened." He pushed his plate away.

"Oh dear. I've upset you again. I shouldn't have asked."

"Oh no." Gabby shook his head. "I ate all my eggs. They were good."

"Was it absolutely dreadful?" Mrs. Lincoln asked. "What happened at West Point?"

In all these years, no one had asked him what happened that day. Many had, in a scolding tone, asked what was wrong with him, but no one put the question exactly that way. Cordie never said one thing or the other about why he came back to New York with the vacant look in his eyes. She just hugged him and took care of him, no questions at all. It was a relief for someone finally to ask.

"It was our second year there, Joe and me," Gabby began.

"And Joe was…"

"My best friend."

"Go on."

"This colonel—he had a beard and was cranky like Mr. Stanton—he told me to drive his carriage out to the field so he could watch artillery practice. I told him I was a city boy from New York City, and had never driven a team of horses before. But he said I was in the army now, and if he told me to drive a carriage, I was to drive a carriage, no questions asked. So I asked him a question. I asked if my friend Joe could go with us, ride with me up front and help me, and he said fine. So Joe and I got on the carriage seat and the colonel got in the back, and we were off.

"I used to think all men with beards were cranky, until I met Mr. Lincoln." Gabby's eyes wandered over to the corner, where Lincoln sat on the bed, eating his pear and reading a book.

"What happened, Mr. Gabby?" Mrs. Lincoln asked.

"Well, we were doing just fine," Gabby continued. "The colonel yelled up at us to go faster, so I did something—I don't remember what—to make the horses go faster. Then all of a sudden Joe yelled, 'There's a snake in the road!' I didn't know what to do, and the horses reared up, causing a big ruckus, and the next thing I knew, the carriage had turned over, and the colonel and I had blood coming out of our heads."

"And Joe?"

"He was under the carriage, ma'am," Gabby said. "He was dead."

"How dreadful."

Adam unlocked the door and entered with the newspaper. "Mr. President?"

Gabby sat up and was about to answer when Lincoln came through his curtain.

"Good. I wanted to check the congressional elections." The president smiled and reached out his hand.

"Yes, sir." Adam looked around at Gabby and Mrs. Lincoln. "Are you finished with your breakfast dishes?"

"Yes, thank you," Mrs. Lincoln said as she gathered the cups, saucers, and plates. "Bring me that pear stem, Father," she called out. "I won't have ants swarming around the room looking for your leftovers."

"Yes, Mother," he replied, plopping the pear stem on the tray.

"Anything else?" Adam's voice was vacant-sounding.

"No. That'll be all," Mrs. Lincoln said.

"Thank you, ma'am." Adam took the tray from the billiards table, bowed, and walked to the door.

"Oh, Private Christy," Mrs. Lincoln added.

He turned. "Yes?"

"Thank you."

"You're welcome." A moment passed before his eyes registered his first word of appreciation from Mrs. Lincoln. Rising from the corners of his mouth, a smile forced its way onto his face, but in the end lost the battle to the melancholy so apparently in control of his eyes. He left and locked the door.

"I used to like the military," Gabby said, watching Lincoln retreat behind the curtain with his newspaper. "Uncle Sammy went to West Point first. He was the smart one in the family. He's a general now."

"Yes," Mrs. Lincoln said in friendly agreement. "I've heard of General Samuel Zook. He may have his turn as commander of the Army of the Potomac before this war is over."

"Now I don't like the military anymore." He paused to look down and bite his lip. "They said I killed my best friend Joe."

"Oh no," she gasped.

"That colonel said the whole thing was my fault. He said I was the one driving the team. I was supposed to be in charge of the horses, and I didn't control the horses, and the colonel was hurt and Joe was killed."

"But he ordered you to drive the carriage over your objections."

"It didn't make any difference, they said." Gabby shook his head. "I was the one driving the team so I was the one responsible, they said. They said I was a murderer. They said they were doing me a favor by just throwing me out of West Point and not hanging me. They said—"

"Please, Mr. Gabby, no more," Mrs. Lincoln said, holding her handkerchief to her face. "I can't stand to hear anymore."

"They told Mama and Cordie I was no use to them and for them to take me home."

"That's dreadful," she said. "I'm sorry I had you tell me."

"That's all right." Gabby tried to smile as he wiped a tear from his eyes. "Most days, I don't even remember what happened. I just know I don't think as good as I used to." He shrugged. "I don't know why I remembered everything today."

"I'm so sorry for my behavior." Mrs. Lincoln reached across the billiards table to touch Gabby's hand. "If I'd known what caused your misery, I'd have been kinder."

"I know." He found the courage to squeeze her hand before withdrawing it. "I think—and please don't get mad at me—you're a little like me. Sometimes we can't help the way we act."

"Mr. Gabby, I do declare I think you're more perceptive than many of the intelligent men running this war at this very moment." She cocked her head coquettishly.

"Oh yes, I know I'm smart, except when I forget to be—smart, that is."

"You must spend more time out here in the room with us, Mr. Gabby." Mrs. Lincoln laughed as she stood. "You really must."

"Thank you," he said. "But I think that would make me too nervous."

"I know all about being nervous. Well, as you wish." She turned to go to her cot.

"Would you like a quilt?" Gabby asked.

"A what?" She turned to smile at him.

"A quilt," Gabby explained. "My sister Cordie makes them. She made me one. Just a minute, I'll show it to you." Quickly padding to his corner, Gabby grabbed the quilt and brought it out, proudly displaying a crudely sewn composition of rumpled squares of old cloth of different colors, textures, and patterns. "Cordie calls them Gabby quilts. She named them for me."

"How nice." Mrs. Lincoln smiled as she touched it.

"She cuts squares out of old dresses, shirts, and things she has around, and sews two of them together with an old sock in the middle, and then she sews the squares together, and you got a Gabby quilt."

"So each square is a memory of a loved one." Her eyes sparkled as she stroked it.

He pointed to a square of dark brown. "Mama wore this dress all the time. And this," he said, tapping a swatch of gabardine, "was part of Papa's best suit when he was a lawyer."

"How wonderful."

"Oh, they're really not worth much. Used to, Cordie would make fancy patterns with the squares. Now she just sews them up any old way. That way you can really use it. If you're sick and feel like you need to throw up, you can just let it go on a Gabby quilt. It doesn't make any difference."

Mrs. Lincoln withdrew her hand.

"I haven't been sick on this one."

"Oh."

"Cordie used to say Gabby quilts were like love. Love isn't something pretty to look at. Love is for everyday use. When you get sick you can wrap up in love—like an old Gabby quilt—and feel better."

Chapter Fourteen

A loud knock at the door broke the tender moment Gabby and Mrs. Lincoln were sharing. Gabby began to dart for his corner behind the crates, but she grabbed his arm.

"There's no reason for you to scurry off like a scared rat."

"We don't have any rats anymore. I caught them all. The traps going off in the middle of the night kept you awake, but I got rid of all the rats."

Mrs. Lincoln's grip on Gabby's arm tightened as the door opened, and Stanton briskly entered, turned to lock the door, and then walked to the billiards table.

"I've scheduled several important meetings today, so I don't have time to spend here." He looked up. "Where's Mr. Lincoln?"

"I'm reading election results, Mr. Stanton," Lincoln called out. "I'll be there as soon as I put on my shoes."

Stanton sighed with exasperation, but stopped short when he saw the quilt in Gabby's quivering hands. Gabby unsuccessfully tried to hide it behind his back.

"What's that?" Stanton said, stretching himself to his full height.

"It's—it's—"

"It's a lovely quilt made for him by his loving sister," Mrs. Lincoln interjected.

"By his sister?" Stanton pulled out his pebble glasses and placed them on his nose, peering at the quilt. "Who gave permission for anything to be transmitted between the outside world and this room?"

"It's just a quilt, Mr. Stanton," Mrs. Lincoln said.

"Give it here." Stanton snatched the quilt from Gabby.

"No, please." His face began to twitch and his eyes to tear.

"There's something in here." Stanton pulled a pocketknife out and opened it. His stubby fingers roughly punched several of the squares.

"Yes," Gabby said, trying to control his voice. "It's…"

"You and your sister will regret it if you're passing notes back and forth, sewn in quilts!"

"How ridiculous." Mrs. Lincoln furtively turned to look into the curtained area where her husband sat. "Mr. Lincoln, please hurry."

"No!" Gabby could not help the shriek in his voice as he watched Stanton rip through the material and pull out old, faded socks.

"I better not find any letters in here," Stanton muttered as he slipped his hand into the socks.

"You fool!" Mrs. Lincoln slapped Stanton full across the face, knocking off his pebble glasses. "It's just a quilt! Not everyone deals in evil plots, Mr. Stanton!"

"I'm sure Molly is sorry for striking you, Mr. Stanton." Pulling his coat over his broad, bony shoulders, Lincoln appeared through the curtains and swiftly placed his large body between his wife and the war secretary. "I wish I'd a dollar for every swat on the head she's given me." He looked down at the quilt. "What's this?"

"Part of some conspiracy cooked up by Mr. Gabby and his sister," Mrs. Lincoln said, Southern acid dripping from each syllable. "Fortunately for us, Mr. Stanton has foiled their evil plot."

"No, sir," Stanton said. "Just a quilt." He handed it back to Gabby.

"It's not just a quilt, Mr. Lincoln. It's a Gabby quilt." Gabby caressed it as he fingered the damaged squares. "With holes in it."

"Don't worry about that, Mr. Gabby," Mrs. Lincoln said. She looked imperiously at Stanton. "Will you be so kind as to provide me with thread and a needle so I can repair the damage you did to Mr. Gabby's personal heirloom?"

Stanton arched an eyebrow. "Of course, ma'am."

"Excuse me," she said, turning to her curtained corner. "This unfortunate incident has fatigued me." She disappeared behind the white French lace.

"So what do you wish to discuss today, Mr. Stanton?" Bending over to pick up Stanton's glasses, Lincoln smiled. "The election results?"

"Don't you want to withdraw to your corner also?" Stanton put his glasses back on his nose as he directed his attention to Gabby.

"No. I thought I'd sit out here for a while." He took a chair on the opposite side of the billiards table and folded the quilt. "You know, I don't get out much."

"That's absurd—"

"Mr. Stanton." Lincoln shook his head. "Let's proceed with our discussion."

"If I know my politics,"—Stanton sat, his chin barely clearing the top of the table, pulled out a notepad, and flipped it open—"the general victory of the Republican Party in the congressional elections give us—rather, you—the mandate to remove General McClellan."

"Which finally fulfills your wish that led to our detention in the basement," Lincoln said, staring at Stanton, who continued to read his notes. "Does this mean I may return to the world of the living, so to speak?"

"And give you the opportunity to reinstate him yet a third time?" Stanton kept his eyes down. "I think not."

"I assure you, that's a mistake I won't make again."

"And I'm going to make sure that you don't, by keeping you where you are." Stanton looked at Lincoln. "I'd hoped to have the war over by the end of the year, but getting rid of McClellan took longer than I thought."

Gabby did not understand Stanton's apparent disdain for Lincoln. Over the last two months, he had observed the man and found him to be quite capable. In fact, if Gabby were not president, Lincoln would make a good one. If he were president, Gabby corrected himself, because he was still not clear on that point.

Lincoln sighed. "So who is to replace General McClellan?"

"General Ambrose Burnside."

"He's turned it down before. Said he was not fit for the job." He chuckled. "Of course, that makes him smarter than McClellan right there."

"His excursion into North Carolina last year was commendable."

"But his actions at Antietam were questionable."

"We should be careful in our judgment of Antietam," Stanton said. "After all, our facts of the situation are taken from the report filed by General McClellan."

"Who feared Burnside as a pretender to his post," Lincoln continued, filling in the supposition. "It's not that I don't like the fellow personally. He's the first person I'd head toward to talk to at a party; unfortunately, we're not making out a party list, but an appointment to lead the Army of the Potomac."

"Whom would you select, then?" Stanton sat back and crossed his arms.

"Are you asking my opinion?" Lincoln smiled. "I didn't think my opinion counted for much."

"I'm wasting my time here." Sitting up, Stanton took off his glasses.

"Perhaps you're right." Lincoln stood and stretched.

"I merely came down here to keep you informed." Stanton stood, putting away his notepad. "Out of professional courtesy."

Was it very courteous to lock the man and his wife up in the basement? Gabby wanted to ask, but did not want to incur another round of Stanton's wrath. If he were indeed president, he thought distractedly, he would want to follow the diplomatic approach with the obstinate little man with the pharaoh beard.

"Where's the Army of the Potomac encamped at this moment?" Lincoln asked.

"Warrenton, Virginia."

"And its current troop strength?"

"I believe one hundred twenty thousand."

"I appreciate your professional courtesy." Lincoln smiled.

"I must be on my way." Stanton turned to leave.

"When you speak to General Burnside," Lincoln added, "you might suggest that he abandon McClellan's movement to the southwest down the peninsula, but instead take an aggressive advance on Fredericksburg."

"Fredericksburg?" Stanton pulled out his notepad.

"That'd position our troops on the road to Richmond and also protect our supply line to Washington."

"I'll pass on your ideas." Stanton wrote quickly. "As a professional courtesy."

"I'm grateful." Lincoln paused, then raised a bony finger to his forehead. "And he should attempt to move by the end of November."

As Stanton put away his pad again, Mrs. Lincoln stepped from behind the curtain.

"Mr. Stanton?"

"Now, Molly, Mr. Stanton is a busy man and must be on his way," Lincoln said.

Sighing, Stanton asked in his low musical voice, "What is it, Mrs. Lincoln?" He took out his pocket watch to check the time.

"I'm so sorry for slapping you," she said. "It's just that the quilt means so much to Mr. Gabby. Even so, ladies must express themselves in a proper manner."

"Apology accepted, and now I must—"

"You haven't told us how Taddie is doing," she said impulsively, her hand reaching for Stanton's sleeve but pulling back quickly.

"He's fine."

"Are his lessons going well? Is Mr. Williamson still his tutor? Has Tad learned to understand his Scottish accent better?"

"I really don't have time."

"Take time." Lincoln stepped forward. "This is our son. We've a right to know about him. Even you have to concede that."

"As far as I've observed, Master Tad's lessons are proceeding as usual in the oval family room with Alexander Williamson. Whether he understands Mr. Williamson's brogue is beyond my interest."

"Why don't you make it your interest?" Lincoln leaned forward, his hollowed eyes narrowing with contained anger.

He said that well, Gabby observed from his seat by the billiards table. If he ever returned to the president's office, he must remember to use that tone when giving orders to whomever the president gives orders. Under his breath he tried to sound imposing in an unthreatening way. It would take practice.

"Very well."

"Is he happy?" Mrs. Lincoln tried to smile. "Is Tom Pen keeping him amused?"

"Tom Pen?" Stanton asked.

"Thomas Pendel," Lincoln explained. "He's the doorman, and kind enough to play with Taddie."

"Oh yes, Pendel. I seem to remember seeing them running in the garden together. He's a bit old to be participating in such games."

"Some people put the feelings for others ahead of their own interests," Mrs. Lincoln said, with a hint of reproof in her voice. "Also Mr. Forbes. He's been Taddie's companion around town."

"The coachman," Lincoln offered.

"Between Mr. Williamson's Scottish and Mr. Forbes's Irish accent, it's no wonder the poor boy can't speak properly." Mrs. Lincoln giggled.

"Well, Molly, I think we should allow Mr. Stanton to go." Lincoln turned her shoulders away. "I'm sure he'll make a greater effort to keep us informed about Tad."

As the Lincolns walked away, Gabby noticed Stanton's gaze fixed on him, which caused his legs to twitch. That man made him nervous, and he wanted to escape to his little corner behind the crates and barrels. He stood, and was almost to his Promised Land when Stanton called out. Gabby clutched Cordie's quilt tightly.

"Mr. Zook. Come over here."

"Yes, sir?" Slowly Gabby turned and shuffled to him. "Yes, sir?"

"Will you swear your sister didn't sew a secret message into one of the squares?" Stanton tapped the quilt with his index finger.

"If she did, I haven't found it."

"Very well." Stanton sniffed in derision.

Gabby heard keys jangling at the door which opened suddenly, hitting Stanton in the back.

"Be careful when you open that door," Stanton said in a huff. "I always knock first."

Walking away, Gabby heard Stanton mutter to Adam, "Be sure to tell me everything—and I mean everything—that the sister wants you to tell her brother."

"Yes, sir."

"Good." Stanton left, shutting the door with more force than was necessary.

"Mr. Zook?" Adam asked.

Being called Mr. Zook was still unusual for Gabby. Mr. Zook was his father. General Zook was his uncle. It was good he had not finished West Point, or else he might be a general too.

"Call me Mr. Gabby, like the Lincolns do." He smiled at Adam, trying to make the troubled-looking soldier feel better.

"Um, your chamber pot. Does it need cleaning?"

"Not that I know of. Let me go look."

Going through the curtain, Gabby heard Adam walk across the room.

"Mr. Lincoln? Mrs. Lincoln?" he said.

"Yes?" Mrs. Lincoln replied.

"Chamber pots, ma'am?"

"Here they are," Lincoln said. "I'll carry them to the door for you."

"Oh. I don't think Mr. Stanton locked it," Adam said with a stammer.

"Young man, I don't think I'm going to bolt out the door after two months," Lincoln said. "It'd be too disconcerting for Mr. Stanton."

"Yes, sir."

"Private Christy," Mrs. Lincoln said.

"Yes, ma'am?"

"I want to apologize for my attitude," she said. "Mr. Gabby pointed out to me you're good at heart."

"Thank you, ma'am."

Gabby looked in his chamber pot to find it empty. He came around the curtain just as Adam opened the door and was scooting the pots out into the hall.

"Private, it's clean as a whistle. Sorry. Maybe I'll have something for you by lunchtime."

"Thank you, Mr. Gabby." Adam smiled.

Gabby was glad his presidential skills were working and lifting the young man's spirits. Adam was about to close the door when Gabby stuck his hand out.

"Will you tell Cordie to make another quilt? It's for Mrs. Lincoln. You know, a Gabby quilt is good for the soul."

Chapter Fifteen

One mid-afternoon, after two months of ruminations about his confrontation with Secretary of War Stanton and his henchman Lafayette Baker over the disappearance of Abraham Lincoln and the substitution of a double, Ward Lamon climbed the steps of the Executive Mansion. Entering the door, he nodded at guard John Parker, who, he noticed, was already glazed of eye from an early beer. Coming down the stairs was Stanton; Lamon quickened his step. Stopping abruptly when he saw Lamon, Stanton pursed his lips.

"Mr. Lamon, what are you doing here?"

"Remember, it was your idea I come back," Lamon replied. "After all, Abraham Lincoln is a personal friend of mine. He allowed me to pretend I was his law partner once. Even if I don't work for him anymore, I'm still his friend."

"Lamon…"

"And people might wonder why I never visit my old friend anymore."

Stanton puffed, stammered, but ultimately walked away. Lamon mounted the grand stairway, skipping every other step, eager to meet the impostor. Going down the hall, Lamon looked around and spotted the new Mrs. Lincoln, obviously a double because she had kinder eyes than the real Mary Lincoln. Opening the door, Tad smiled at Lamon.

"Mr. Lamon! I haven't seen you in a coon's age!"

"Good to see you, Tad." He patted the boy's shoulder. Despite the opinions of others, Lamon liked Lincoln's rambunctious son, because he reminded Lamon of himself as a child. If Tad survived his childhood, he would make a good bodyguard or policeman. "The marshal's office has kept me busy. I promise not to be a stranger anymore."

"Good." Tad ran down the hall. "Tom Pen! Tom Pen!"

Continuing the other way, Lamon was eager to see the double, wondering if he measured up to the original. He went through the glass panels and turned right into the first office. The bearded man at the desk looked up, momentarily went blank, then smiled in recognition.

"Mr. Lamon, so good to see you again."

Frowning, Lamon carefully shut the door, pulled a chair close to the president's desk, then sat and leaned close the double.

"You've never met me before in your life and you know it."

"I—I don't know what you mean."

"I know you're a fraud, supposedly because my Mr. Lincoln is hiding out somewhere. I don't believe it. Abraham Lincoln never hid from anybody." He paused to examine the man's eyes to detect what lurked behind them. "Where's Mr. Lincoln?"

"I can't tell you that."

"Why not?"

"Mr. Stanton wouldn't like it."

"I don't care what Mr. Stanton likes. What would Mr. Lincoln like?"

"I assume Mr. Lincoln wouldn't like it either. After all, this entire situation is Mr. Lincoln's idea. If he wanted Mr. Stanton to tell you, you'd know."

Fluttering eyelashes betrayed him. Lamon decided the double was afraid of Stanton and could not tell the truth. Standing, Lamon patted him on the shoulder.

"Well, we shall be friends then," he said. "Don't be bothered if I drop in from time to time for an aimless chat. I visited Mr. Lincoln often, and he enjoyed it."

"Then I shall enjoy your visits too."

Lamon left and went to the secretaries' office. He had known Nicolay and Hay since the carefree days in Illinois. Lingering at their door, he listened to their conversation.

"...and she's a senator's daughter, in addition to being attractive and extremely well-mannered," Hay said. "I think she's potential matrimonial material."

"*Ja*," Nicolay replied. "And the president can give you away."

They have not changed, Lamon thought, as he entered the room. Hay looked up from his desk where he was addressing envelopes, and smiled broadly.

"Hello, Ward."

"Ward, we haven't seen you in a while." Nicolay said as he looked up from his letter opening. He smiled only briefly, yet Lamon took it as a warm reception since it came from the cold, bland Bavarian.

Lamon sat near Hay, throwing his feet up on the desk, as was his wont during Lincoln's first year, when all was normal. He liked the secretaries immensely, Hay's boyish charm and Nicolay's reserved intelligence; still, Lamon had to learn what they knew about the president's disappearance.

"Marshal's office has been keeping me busy." He looked from one to the other. "You two look no worse for the wear."

"Thank you," Hay replied, "and same to you."

Taking a deep breath, Lamon continued, "I wish I could say the same about the old man." His observation was met with silence. Perhaps he was being too subtle, so he turned directly to Hay, whom he considered the weak link. "Johnny, haven't you noticed a difference in Mr. Lincoln?"

"Remember when we used to have booger-flicking contests?" Putting a finger up one nostril, Hay innocently returned Lamon's gaze. "You always won."

Lamon could not help but laugh, realizing, however, that Hay had not answered his question, deliberately or not, so he turned his attention to the inscrutable Nicolay.

"And you, John, have you noticed any changes in the president?"

"Mr. Lincoln hasn't changed since those days in Springfield when we all first met him." Ripping open a letter, Nicolay studiously read the contents.

"Those were the good old days with the president, weren't they?" Lamon asked.

"Yes, Mr. Lincoln smiled more then," Nicolay replied.

"Even the first year in the White House, the president made a few jokes," Lamon continued.

"That was when we all, including Mr. Lincoln, still had hopes of an early resolution to the war."

Narrowing his eyes at Nicolay, who kept his attention on the letters, Lamon then asked, "But since the time I saw him last, two months ago, Mr. Lincoln seems to have lost his spirit."

"The president has had good days this fall. You just haven't seen them."

"Well, I guess I've been lazy long enough," Lamon announced, putting his feet down and standing.

"Don't be a stranger," Hay cheerfully said.

"*Ja*, come back soon," Nicolay added, finally raising his eyes.

Lamon walked out, very proud of himself, feeling he had outfoxed Nicolay, who did not want to tell a lie, yet did not want to betray a confidence, but by playing his word games had revealed what Lamon wanted to know. In talking about Lincoln, Nicolay called him by his name; however, when Lamon referred to the man in the president's office as Mr. Lincoln, Nicolay followed up by calling the man Mr. President. That proved they knew the current president was not Mr. Lincoln; what Lamon still did not know was if they knew this was the plan of Mr. Lincoln, the man they called Mr. President, or, worst of all, Mr. Stanton.

Chapter Sixteen

Old Tom Pendel walked down the hall on the second floor, lighting the gas lamps as the last rays of the sun faded, creating vague, sad shadows lurking around the corners. Giggling, Tad ran in front of him, trying to trip him up. Alethia stood in the doorway of her bedroom and watched. Pendel was kind, patient, and understanding to the little boy with a lisp. She knew she should not, but she was falling in love with the Lincolns' son. She and Tad had come to a silent agreement: he knew she was not his mother, nor the man his father, but they both were kind and meant no harm to him, so he accepted them and went along with the "game."

"Taddie, it's time for supper," she said as the boy approached.

"Aww, do I have to?" Tad scrunched up his face.

"It's best that you eat, Master Tad," Pendel said as he continued down the hall lighting the lamps. "Or else you'll end up funny-looking like me when you grow up."

Tad giggled as Alethia ran her fingers through his hair. She could not help but think how wonderful it would have been if she were married and had children.

"You know, he's right. I don't know why you have to put up a fuss."

"But tonight I really don't feel good, honest." He looked up earnestly with his light brown eyes.

"Have you been into your father's licorice again?"

"No, honest."

"Very well." She felt his forehead, and he did seem a little warm. "But if you don't eat, you must go straight to bed."

"That's all right by me." And Tad scampered down the hall to his room, stopping only to pull on Pendel's coat one last time, which caused the old man to put up a comical protest, eliciting more giggles from the boy as he closed his door.

"So Tad isn't eating with us tonight?" Duff said as he stepped from his bedroom.

"No, Father, he says he's not feeling well." She smiled, and her eyes lit. Here was another person of whom she felt herself growing fond. When Duff stood close and towered over her, she imagined it was how the Virgin Mary felt when she was overcome by the Holy Spirit, and conceived.

"Then we'd best be on our way," Duff said with a smile.

Alethia took his arm, and they went down by the service stairs. She leaned into him as they crunched on the straw mats.

"Do you imagine I could get away with eating his dinner too?" he asked.

"I don't see why not." Alethia laughed, squeezed his hand, and chose to ignore his stiffening at her show of affection.

They settled into the dining room chairs and graciously thanked Phebe as she placed bowls of potato soup before them. Their sipping of the chunky broth and chatting about the day's events abruptly ended when the door opened and Stanton marched in.

"Stand up," he ordered.

Duff meekly put down his spoon and stood. Alethia watched as his eyes glazed over with acquiescence. Her heart ached to see him humiliated.

"Unbutton your coat."

Duff obeyed the order, and Stanton brusquely placed his small hand on the long expanse of Duff's abdomen. Alethia turned her head away, unable to watch the ritual the war secretary had been conducting for the past two months. Her eyes closed as she heard Stanton's low grunt.

"You're gaining too much weight." Stanton glanced at the bowl of soup. "You may finish the soup, but tell the cook you don't want the main course. The same tomorrow night also."

"Yes, sir."

"Sit down and resume eating." Stanton paused to smirk. "Enjoy it while you can." He pulled out his notepad and handed it to Duff. "This is what you'll say at the Cabinet meeting in the morning." Going to the door, he stopped and turned to look at Alethia. "Oh. How's the boy doing?"

"The boy?" Alethia looked up, a bit distracted.

"Yes, the Lincoln boy. Tad. Is he well?"

"Yes, he's fine." She paused. "His forehead was hot tonight, and he said he didn't feel well, so he went straight to bed."

"Oh."

"I'm so glad you cared to ask," she said, trying to smile at a man she both feared and loathed.

"I don't care."

"Oh."

"His mother asked." With that, Stanton left as quickly as he had appeared.

When Phebe arrived with a tray of fried chicken, potatoes, and collard greens, Duff put on a good show of not being hungry. Alethia noticed a glint in Phebe's dark eyes. Was it a recognition that something was wrong? Feeling panic rise from the pit of her stomach, Alethia tried to control her emotions while deciding what to do. Out of her chair she bustled to Phebe and placed an arm around her shoulders and squeezed.

"Dear Phebe," she said, "we work you to death, and for what? Willy-nilly appetites. We're so sorry."

"That's all right, Mrs. Lincoln."

Again seeing the cloud of doubt cover Phebe's eyes, Alethia pulled away.

"Of course, we do pay you well to accommodate our peccadilloes."

"Yes, ma'am." Phebe bit her lip and then looked at Alethia. "I hope you don't mind my being so bold, ma'am."

"What is it, Phebe?"

"I'm just glad to see you feeling better, since the passing of little Willie," she cautiously said.

Alethia was taken aback by Phebe's observation, knowing true mourning continued in the basement. Momentary shame crossed her mind for not grieving for Tad's brother.

"I didn't mean to upset you, Mrs. Lincoln," Phebe said. She turned to leave. "I probably shouldn't have said nothing at all."

"No, thank you." Alethia reached out to touch her. "Not too many people care how I feel anymore." She smiled. "No one much really likes me. Mrs. Keckley, and now you. I can count you as a friend, can't I?"

"Of course, ma'am." A grin flashed across her dark face.

After Phebe left, Alethia sat and looked across at Duff, who was staring at his empty soup bowl. "Did I do right?"

"What?"

"What I said to the cook. Did I blather on too long? I worry my own personality comes out instead of Mrs. Lincoln's."

"Oh. No. You were fine." His voice sounded hollow.

"What's wrong?" she asked.

Duff shook his head, refusing to look up. Before she knew what she was doing, Alethia was in the chair next to Duff, hesitantly touching his large, bony hands, becoming aware how sensitive they seemed, despite the calluses and scars.

"Please, tell me."

"I can't eat like this no more." He raised his head, his cheeks wet with tears. "It reminds me too much of Libby Prison. I can't go on. Mr. Lincoln may be able to live on vegetables and fruits, but I can't."

"Libby Prison?"

"In Richmond. I spent a year there before me and a handful of others escaped."

"That's where they sent you after you were caught as a spy?"

"Yes." Taking his napkin, Duff wiped his eyes, averting them from Alethia.

"I don't see why you can't eat what you want." Her fingers covered his hand, quivering at the hair across his knuckles and the warmth pulsating from his skin. "You're a big, robust man who needs his food."

"You should have seen me back in Michigan." He turned to smile at Alethia. "I was near three hundred pounds. Biggest man in town."

"Oh my." She fluttered her eyes.

"My body's used to having a heap of meat on it," he said, "not like Mr. Lincoln, who's always been a bag of bones."

118

"Prison must have been terrible," she consoled Duff. "To lose all that weight."

"I don't like to talk about that." He shifted uncomfortably in his chair, then stood and paced to the door. Pausing there, he hung his head. "Being here is like prison. Not getting to eat. Mr. Stanton's mighty close to being a prison warden."

"I thought the way he put his hand on your abdomen was disgraceful." Alethia stood and went to Duff. "It was so unseemly."

"I hate him," he whispered. "I hate being here." He turned to smile bashfully at her. "But not you. You make this bearable."

"Why, thank you." She touched his arm. "I feel the same." After Duff pulled his arm away, Alethia looked back at her plate filled with food. She said, "If you wish to leave while I finish my dinner, you may. It must be frustrating to watch someone else enjoying food you can't eat."

"That's very sweet of you, ma'am." Duff walked to her chair and pulled it out. "It wouldn't be proper for a husband to abandon his wife and let her eat alone." He smiled. "Please. Sit. Enjoy. It smells delicious."

Alethia gratefully sat and began to eat, thinking of his words—a husband and his wife. She wished that were true in the real world. Perhaps, after all this was over, she dreamed as she chewed on the collard greens. For the next half-hour they chatted and laughed, reminiscing about the pleasant times of the last two months, as though they were years of family memories—the irrepressible Tad, the lovely surroundings, the kind servants. In that suspended glow of romantic lies, Alethia felt happy, even loved. After she finished, she strolled to the stairs with Duff, who opened the door for her. She thought her heart would stop when he put his large arm around her shoulders. It was the first time Duff had ventured to make physical contact, and she held her breath, trying to keep from crying. They went into Lincoln's bedroom where Alethia hoped Duff would dare make the impertinent suggestion that they spend the night in the same bed as man and wife. He removed his coat, hung it up, and then turned to smile at her.

"Good night, Mrs. Lincoln."

"Good night, Father." She tried to hide her disappointment. As she went to her room, she decided it was for the best. They should not become intimate in the middle of their mission. She wiped a small tear from her cheek and thought Duff a very wise and wonderful man. Instead of undressing, Alethia quietly listened to Duff as he removed his shoes, slacks, and shirt. She clutched her bosom as she thought of him putting on his nightshirt and slipping into bed. Shaking her head, Alethia chastised herself for her silly thoughts. A knock at Lincoln's door caused her to jump.

"Mr. President?"

"Come in, Mr. Hay," Duff said.

"I wouldn't bother you so late, Mr. President," Hay said, "but I heard something tonight that I thought you needed to know immediately."

Alethia wrinkled her brow and went to the door to eavesdrop more efficiently.

"I was at a party…"

"Where was it?" Duff asked.

"At the home of Colonel Frederick W. Lander," Hay replied. "You know him. The civil engineer."

"Of course. Last I heard he was wrestling with a bout of influenza."

"He still is. He remained in his room the entire evening. The event was a fund-raiser hosted by his wife for the federal hospitals at Port Royal, South Carolina."

"She was an actress or something like that, wasn't she?" Duff said.

"An angel on stage," Hay gushed. "When I first came to Washington I was quite smitten with her. Along with many others. She had many suitors."

Not unlike Rose Greenhow, Alethia thought. Her mind often wandered to her childhood friend and wondered if she had ever escaped prison. She knew for certain Rose had not been executed, because she would have read about it in the newspapers.

"Even Mr. Stanton, before he remarried," Hay added, "if that can be imagined." After an embarrassing pause, he continued, "But that's not what I came to say. During the evening Mrs. Lander sat beside me on her davenport and told me of meeting a brash young actor at an opening-night party at Grover's Theater—a Virginian, I believe she said—who was trying to impress her with a story about some scandalous activity he was planning with friends that would make the front page of every newspaper in the nation."

"And what might that activity be?"

"She said he didn't elaborate, but from his tone and manner she drew distressing conclusions."

"Which were?"

"Kidnapping, sir, possibly assassination." Hay cleared his throat. "Of you, Mr. President."

The concept of losing Duff to assassins caused Alethia to lurch into the room. Thinking better of intruding into the conversation, she decided to be startled.

"Oh, Mr. Hay." She eyed him haughtily, as she thought Mrs. Lincoln would.

"He was telling me about a party," Duff said.

"And to give the president a gift. Going through the buffet line, I noticed a large bowl of licorice." He pulled a handful of the black candy from his pocket and placed it on the nightstand. "I thought he might like some."

"Oh." Alethia sniffed. That terrible stuff. He won't eat decent food but turns his teeth black with that disgusting candy."

"Now, Mother, you know it's my only vice." Duff looked at Hay and smiled. "Thank you, Mr. Hay. That was very kind of you."

Both Alethia and Duff noticed Hay staring at the top of Duff's open nightshirt.

"Is anything wrong?" Duff asked.

Hay paused, shook his head, and smiled, saying nothing. Alethia caught her breath, stepped forward, and then laughed.

"Oh, I know what you're thinking, seeing Mr. Lincoln shorn like a sheep," she said blithely. "But he has a cold coming on, and I absolutely refuse to rub ointment on that dreadful, hairy chest. So he must shave every time he feels under the weather."

"Yes." Duff coughed.

"You'll keep our little secret, won't you, Mr. Hay?" Alethia fluttered her eyes.

"Of course, ma'am." Turning a light pink, Hay backed up.

"We'll discuss that other matter tomorrow," Duff said.

"Yes, sir."

"I really don't think there's anything to it," Duff added. "Just chatter at a party."

"I hope so, sir." Hay backed to the door, fumbled with the knob, then left.

Listening for Hay's receding steps, Alethia and Duff smiled.

"At least you got the licorice." She nodded at the nightstand.

"Yes." Duff picked up a piece and looked at it. "It's the one thing I absolutely can't stand to eat, and I must."

Chapter Seventeen

Another day found Cordie Zook putting away her mop and broom in a small closet of Armory Square Hospital. The sun had already set beyond the Potomac River, which caused her to worry about walking home. If only Miss Dorothea Dix honored her original agreement to allow volunteers to leave before dusk, all would be fine; but as more war casualties filled the long, parallel sheds of the hospital, the volunteers were forced to work later and later. More than ever, Cordie wished she had never left New York City, sure she could have found a job as a maid in a Park Avenue mansion, and Gabby could have been a janitor on Wall Street. Her lip began to quiver, but she commanded herself not to cry. It would do no good. It helped no one, not Gabby, not herself, not these poor broken boys lying in neat rows of cots in front of her.

Gathering her wits, Cordie went to the nurses' cloak room, where she picked up her coat and hat and went down the line to get Jessie Home's smart little tam-o'-shanter and plaid jacket. Jessie had become a good friend, Cordie admitted as she left the cloak room and started wandering up and down the aisles of cots, even though the young Scottish woman tried her patience from time to time. For instance, Jessie was never ready to leave when Cordie was desperate to go to Lafayette Park to hear about Gabby from the nervous private. She stopped short in the middle of an aisle and found herself forced to smile as she watched Jessie competently pull a fresh nightshirt over the head of an embarrassed, thin, shockingly pale soldier, who still self-consciously tried to hide the reddish nub that once had been his left arm.

"Now there's no need for ye to be shamed in front of me," Jessie said cheerfully as she grabbed the recovering nub and stuffed it into the white, coarse cotton sleeve. "You're a national hero, and heroes should hold themselves proud."

"But—but my arm," the soldier stammered.

She smoothed the shirt down his chest and abdomen. "That's your badge of manhood," she replied smoothly. Smiling, she rubbed his white, gaunt cheek with her hand. "That shows you're no longer a boy. What woman worth being a wife wants to be yoked with a pretty boy when she could have a real man?"

Cordie watched a smile creep across his lips and forgot about her fear of crossing the Mall after dark. This was their purpose, to make the boys smile when other senses told them to cry. If they can do that, they can face the thieves and robbers who hid in the bushes surrounding the Smithsonian.

"It's time to leave, Jessie," Cordie said.

The young man looked up at Cordie, and then to Jessie. "You have to leave? You can't stay a little longer?"

"I'd love to, me hero," Jessie said, "but Miss Dix wouldn't hear of it. If she found out I stayed late to sit by ye, she'd think I was tryin' to romance ye, and then she'd fire me. Ye wouldn't want me fired, now would ye?"

"I guess not." His head fell a bit.

"Keep the faith, me hero." Jessie took her coat from Cordie and put it on. "I'll see ye again tomorrow."

"Thank you." His face brightened.

They walked away and put on their hats as several voices rang out.

"Good night, Miss Home."

"Thank you, Miss Home."

"God bless you, Miss Home."

"I suppose the old lady who mops the floors don't need a thank you," Cordie said with a smile, trying not to sound jealous.

"They appreciate ye," Jessie replied.

"Good night, Miss Zook," an older voice called out.

"See?" Jessie grinned and grabbed Cordie's arm. "It just takes maturity to recognize a true angel."

"You don't have to use your flowery words on me," Cordie said, giggling. "Don't forget. I'm a tough old Yankee."

They both laughed as they stepped out the front door of the hospital onto the Mall and into the rancid smell of the old city canal, broken into little cesspools of urine, rotting animal carcasses, and scum-covered water. Discreetly, they both pulled out handkerchiefs to cover their noses. Cordie tried to maintain her composure as they walked past the neatly landscaped grounds of the Smithsonian. Soon her eyes were searching the shadowy corners of the large, red, castle-like building. The many bushes around its walls provided perfect hiding places after dark for the roving gangs of thieves which preyed upon passersby foolish enough to come near.

"Are you sure we'll be safe?" Cordie whispered.

"Of course, me darlin'," Jessie replied with a laugh. "If anyone dared to jump from the dark to grab me, they'd better be ready for a swift kick and jab of me elbow. Scottish lasses are strong, and loud. I'd scream like a banshee and more help than we could imagine would appear in the twinklin' of an eye!"

"Are you sure?"

"As sure as I am of me red hair and Scottish brogue." Jessie put her arm around Cordie and firmly squeezed. "Ye worry too much, me love."

All the same, they increased their pace as they mounted the steps of the iron bridge over the stagnant canal, putting them out of harm's way from the Smithsonian gangs. Cordie tried to compose her thoughts and control her heavy breathing.

"I've never been one of the smart ones," she began slowly and humbly.

"Why, what a thing to say! You're sharp as a tack, ye are!" Jessie gently slapped at her shoulder.

"No, I'm not really that bright when it gets beyond cleaning a floor or washing clothes or sewing." Cordie shook her head. "Believe it or not, Gabby was the smart one. You wouldn't know it now. When we were young, he was so bright and smart. I pinned my hopes on him. I always saw myself taking care of Gabby's clothes and house, and he'd take care of me, always provide a roof over my head." She paused to laugh ruefully. "I knew I wasn't going to find a husband, the way I look."

"What's wrong with the way ye look?"

"Bless your sweet heart." Cordie patted Jessie's back. "You're so pretty and attract men so easily, you don't really understand how hard it is for plain women to find a husband."

"I'm not that pretty."

They stepped off the bridge and walked briskly up Thirteenth Street to escape the canal's stench. Turning west on F Street, they slowed their pace as the air cleared, and they put away their handkerchiefs.

"Now Gabby was a handsome boy, smart and handsome," Cordie continued. "Put him in a lieutenant's uniform, and I knew he's be irresistible to the young ladies. But I hoped he'd find one who wouldn't mind having his old-maid sister live with them as their maid and nanny to their children." She breathed deeply. "It was a good life I imagined. But it all ended when he went to West Point." Cordie paused, halfway expecting a question from Jessie, and was relieved when it did not come. Turning north on Fifteenth Street, she mustered the strength to finish her story. "When he came home," she said, "his mind was gone. I realized I would have to support him, to be the smart one."

She stopped talking to keep from crying. Looking ahead at the corner, Cordie saw Adam standing under the streetlight in Lafayette Square, his shoulders slumped and his head down. She noticed a change in him over the last two months—not as dramatic as the change in Gabby, but a change nonetheless—that scared her. Cordie did not want to witness another young man wasted by the insatiable needs of the war machine.

"There's me private," Jessie said with a chirp, quickening her step to reach the park.

Cordie practically had to run to keep up with her, but she did not mind. Watching young love bloom brightened her life and relieved her of the constant worry about Gabby and why he must stay in the Executive Mansion.

"Miss Zook, Miss Home," Adam said, straightening his shoulders as a grin covered his face. "I thought you had fallen into a bit of trouble, you were so late."

"Don't worry, me laddie," Jessie said. "I daresay I can defend meself and me friend better than ye could."

"Maybe so." He ducked his head and ran his fingers through his red hair. Looking up, Adam smiled again. "Did you have a good day at the hospital?"

"How is Gabby? Is he eating well?" Cordie chose to ignore his pleasantries.

"He's fine, Miss Zook," Adam replied. A cloud crossed his face. "Oh. There's one thing."

"Oh my Lord," Cordie whispered, putting her hand to her ample bosom.

"He's all right," he said, trying to reassure her. "His quilt got—cut up. He needs a new one."

"Cut up?" Jessie interjected. "Merciful heavens, what happened?"

"Someone cut it." Adam breathed in deeply, and then knitted his brow. "He—they thought something might be in it."

"There are only socks in it," Jessie said.

"Who could be so mean?" Cordie shook her head, unable to understand what was going on, why her brother was in the Executive Mansion in the first place, and now a perfectly good Gabby quilt ripped to shreds.

"Mr. Gabby would like another," Adam said.

"Of course," Cordie replied. "I don't want him to catch a chill, not with winter coming."

"Private Christy," Jessie said, "ye never answered the question. Who ripped the quilt?"

"I can't tell." His eyes pleaded with her. "Please don't ask anymore. We all could get into big trouble."

"The saints forbid ordinary people be privy to the goin's on in the White House," she said.

"Please don't be mad at me," Adam said, impulsively taking a step toward Jessie, who stood her ground. "It's not my fault. I didn't rip the quilt. I—I just can't tell who did. I agree with you. It was a mean thing for him—them—to do. But I can't do anything about it."

"Don't worry about it." Cordie patted his hand. "It's done and can't be undone. A Gabby quilt is easy enough to make. I'll start a new one tonight."

"Thank you, Miss Zook." He smiled at her and then glanced shyly at Jessie. "Do you forgive me, Miss Home?"

"Let me see, ye upset us dreadfully," she said slowly, a twinkle in her eyes.

"Don't tease the boy, Jessie," Cordie said, watching the agony in Adam's face. "I can't stand to see a young man as unhappy as he is." She smiled to herself over the skills Jessie used around men, skills she herself did not know how to use, nor did she possess the looks to make them effective. Cordie was too old to be jealous, so she just enjoyed watching men swoon at Jessie's feet.

"I'll tell ye true, laddie, if ye want to atone, ye may accompany us to our boardinghouses," Jessie said. "'Tis much too late for respectable ladies to walk the streets alone."

"Yes." Adam vigorously nodded. "I'll pay for omnibus fare, for all three of us."

"Faith, I didn't know the army paid so well," she said.

"Oh, it doesn't." He smiled. "But it would be well worth it." Adam hailed one of the lumbering omnibuses pulled by two large, bored horses and proudly paid the fares, stepping aside to allow the women to pass him and select seats.

"You can have the window seat, me dear," Jessie said to Cordie, who knew very well her young companion was more interested in sitting next to the private than allowing her to have the view of the dark streets of Washington. After Adam settled into the seat next to her, Jessie leaned into him. "So, from Ohio, ye are."

"Yes, Miss Home."

"Bein' from Scotland, I know nothin' about Ohio. I crave to learn, though."

Cordie turned her head to watch Adam's animated description of the land and rivers and trees and skies of Ohio, which did not interest her in the least. At her age, one place was as good as the next to her, but what did interest her was the sparkle in his eyes. She worried Jessie underestimated her charms. It would be a shame to see a nice young man disappointed. Wondering why she cared about Adam, she looked again into his wide, intelligent, excited eyes. Cordie smiled to herself, and tears came to her eyes. Pulling out a handkerchief and wiping her moist cheeks, she knew what she saw—the spirit of young Gabby living on in the image of Adam. The omnibus's grinding halt shook Cordie from her thoughts. Peering through the window, she nodded.

"It's my stop."

Her two companions did not hear her as they continued their enthusiastic conversation. Cordie looked fondly at them and regretted having to step past them to get out.

"Excuse me, my dears," she said softly, still not catching their attention. She walked down the aisle feeling strangely content, even though her world had been turned upside down.

"Good night, me darlin'," Jessie called out.

"Um, yes, good-bye, Miss Zook," Adam said.

"Good night, children." She turned and nodded.

Standing a moment at the curb on H Street to watch the omnibus clatter down the rough dirt road and disappear in the darkness, Cordie turned and walked up the steps to the front door of the three-story wooden clapboard boardinghouse occupied by a congenial older couple, Mr. and Mrs. John Edmonds. They leased it from a Maryland innkeeper who, the Edmondses said, rode in monthly to collect rent from boarders, mostly young men who needed mending done. That was where Cordie made her money.

As Cordie put her key in the lock, she heard Mrs. Edmonds's sweet, low voice being drowned out by a stern, demanding female voice. She slipped through the door and tried to make her way silently to the stairs.

"Just a minute!" The other woman, middle-aged, with dark hair parted down the middle and tied tight in the back, approached Cordie. "Is this the woman you're renting to?"

"Yes; Miss Zook," Mrs. Edmonds said, "a dear soul who tends to our wounded Union soldiers at the Armory Square Hospital."

The woman looked sharply at her, then at Cordie. "How long have you been living here and making a living off my boarders?"

"Not quite a year," she replied.

"From now on, I'm charging two dollars more for using my house as a place of business." Nodding curtly, she said, "Good night, Mrs. Edmonds." Without another word, she put on her coat and bonnet and left.

"Gracious me," Cordie said. "I hope I didn't get you into trouble."

"Don't worry about it, my dear." Mrs. Edmonds patted her hand. "I'm glad John had retired. Mrs. Surratt's tirade would have weakened his heart."

"Is she always like this?"

"No, for the longest she was a sweet soul, not very talkative, but nice." Mrs. Edmonds sighed. "Her husband drank too much. He died in August, and she hasn't been the same since."

Chapter Eighteen

Adam thought he was falling in love as he walked briskly from Jessie's boardinghouse. A few minutes with her each evening made cleaning chamber pots bearable. His eyes widened when he thought of chamber pots which should have been emptied already. Fear of another scolding from Mrs. Lincoln hastened him down H Street. He counted down the intersections—Tenth Street, Eleventh, Twelfth, Thirteenth, and then New York Avenue. By the time he headed toward the Executive Mansion, Adam was in full gait, and breathing heavily. He stopped at the bottom of the mansion steps to catch his breath. Nodding curtly to John Parker at the door, Adam went straight to the service stairs, trounced the straw mats as he raced down, passed the kitchen, and reached the billiards room door. Again he paused to catch his breath and fish the keys from his pocket. Steeling himself against Mrs. Lincoln's fury, he unlocked the door.

Inside, Mrs. Lincoln sat under the lamp which hung over the billiards table with the sewing kit and the ripped quilt. She looked up and smiled at Adam.

"Thank you so much for bringing the needle and thread. I'd forgotten how soothing mending can be."

"I'm sorry for being late to empty the chamber pots," he said.

"Oh, are you late? I hadn't noticed."

"I heard you come in," Lincoln said as he walked through the curtain carrying one of the pots, "so I thought I'd help out."

"Thank you, sir." Adam retrieved the second one and headed for the door as Gabby appeared from behind his curtain, carrying his chamber pot. Adam's hands were trembling as he unlocked the door.

"I finally had a bowel movement. It's been two weeks. I think I'm finally getting used to living down here, and my bowels are loosening." Gabby looked at Adam's hands. "Are you nervous about something? My hands shake sometimes when I'm nervous. I hope you don't get nervous like me, or the generals won't let you stay in the army anymore."

"It's nothing. I thought Mrs. Lincoln might be upset with me for being late."

"That's all right, young man," Lincoln said, patting him on the back. "She makes me nervous sometimes too."

Adam left one pot outside the billiards room door and carried the other two through the kitchen to the service entrance door. He wondered if the architect had ever thought full chamber pots would come so close to the food prepared for the president.

"Do you want me to get the third pot?" Phebe asked, looking up from the stove.

"No, thanks," he replied, quickening his step to the door to the driveway beneath the north portico. "I can get it."

"It won't kill you to accept help," she said with humor as she went into the hall to pick up the third pot. As she walked, Phebe looked down at its contents. "This man must have been constipated for weeks."

"You shouldn't talk about that," Adam muttered as he walked out the door and down the driveway to the deep gutter, where he emptied the two pots. Phebe joined him and dumped the third.

"I know they're top-secret helpers with the war, and I haven't said anything to anyone else, only to you."

"I'd feel better if we didn't talk about them at all."

"Why? Aren't they doing a good job? They never come out. Never get any fresh air."

"I said, I don't talk about it," he said sharply as he picked up the pots to carry them to the water trough.

"Suit yourself," Phebe said. She marched past Adam and plopped the third pot into the trough, splashing water on him.

Shaking his head, Adam washed out the pots and berated himself for not answering Phebe's questions any better, but every time he was around her he was in awe of her dark, smooth skin, her full lips and slender torso flaring into ample hips. Stacking the three pots, he carried them back through the kitchen to the hall.

"The boy is still bilious," Neal told Phebe outside her bedroom.

"Poor child," Phebe replied. "I suppose Mrs. Lincoln is fretting over him."

"Yes, but she's not as nervous about it as she used to be."

Adam's breath quickened as he realized what they were talking about, and he walked to them.

"Tad's not feeling well?" he asked.

"His mama's trying to make him puke," Neal replied.

"He was off his feed earlier today, and about an hour ago he started moaning with the bellyache," Phebe explained.

"He'll be all right, won't he?" Adam shifted his weight from one foot to the other, as it gradually dawned on him: a moral dilemma was about to loom over him.

"I don't know," Neal said. "I never heard such moaning in my life."

"I'm sure Mrs. Lincoln knows what to do," Phebe said.

Mrs. Lincoln would know what to do, he told himself, but she is not the woman tending to Tad right now.

"I suppose so," he muttered.

"I don't know," Neal said. "If it's his appendix, it could bust right soon, and he'd be dead before morning if nobody does anything about it."

"Neal." Phebe slapped his arm.

They walked off fussing at each other as Adam nervously unlocked the door. Could Tad die? he worried, as he entered with the three pots.

Gabby took his. "That Mr. Stanton, do you talk with him often?" He kept his eyes down.

"Yes."

"Please tell him—in a nice way, because I don't want to get him mad, since he's so hot-tempered in the first place—to be nice to Cordie."

"I will."

"She doesn't feel well."

"Oh."

"I think she has the family disease."

"What's that?"

"Sitters disease."

Gabby turned to scurry behind the boxes and crates. Mrs. Lincoln came from behind her curtain combing her hair out, and for the first time since Adam had known her, wore a look of quiet resignation instead of pent-up anger. She smiled at him.

"Back already? My, you're quick like a bunny rabbit."

"Yes, ma'am." Adam felt his face flush as he thought of Tad and his bilious condition. As had become the custom, he placed the chamber pots down outside the curtain and turned to go.

"Private Christy, is there anything wrong? You've the oddest expression on your face."

"No, ma'am." He turned back and felt his face turn redder. "There's nothing wrong."

"Nonsense." She clutched the comb in both hands. "Your face is as red as a beet."

"Well, I—I well…"

"Spit it out, boy," Mrs. Lincoln ordered.

Lincoln, his collar undone, exposing masses of black hair on a bony chest, stepped from his private corner and put an arm around his wife's waist and squeezed.

"It's—it's personal, and private."

"You're lying," she declared.

"No, I'm not!"

"Now, Molly, no need to harass the boy so late at night. He needs his rest, and you need yours. I definitely need mine."

"It's Tad," she whispered. "Something's wrong with Tad."

Adam's eyes went to the floor.

"It is." Her voice began to mount to its usual stridency. "I can tell. Oh, my God! Something's wrong with my baby."

"Come on, Private, we don't believe in killing the messenger of sad tidings," Lincoln said. "What is it?"

"The kitchen help said your son wasn't feeling well," he said. "They said he was bilious."

"Well, that's not so bad," Lincoln replied.

"Not so bad!" Mrs. Lincoln struggled to free herself from his grip. "What imbecility is that? Haven't you heard of appendicitis? Food poisoning? It could be any number of terrible, terrible things, and you say *not so bad*?"

Lincoln turned to Adam. "Why don't you go upstairs and do a little reconnaissance work for us?"

"Yes, sir." Adam left and went up the service stairs, his heart pounding so hard he could barely hear the straw mats crunching under his boots. On the second floor, he went straight to Tad's room, where he found Alethia wiping the boy's head with a wet cloth. To the side was a bucket filled with vomit.

"Poor child," Alethia said as she looked up at Adam, "he must have eaten green fruit again."

"No, I didn't," Tad protested.

"Is he going to be all right?"

"Oh, I think so." Alethia smiled and stroked his cheek. "I gave him a dose of subnitrate of bismuth."

"It tasted awful," Tad said.

"But you haven't thrown up since," Alethia said.

Adam breathed deeply "That's good."

"I want Mama." Tad looked from Alethia to Adam and back again. "My real mama."

"Why, I don't know what you're talking about," Alethia replied.

"I think you're a very nice lady who looks like Mama, but you're not her. And that man isn't Papa," Tad whispered conspiratorially. "It's part of a war plan. I got that part figured out." His bottom lip crinkled. "But I don't feel good, and I want Mama."

Adam stared at Alethia, not knowing what to do, and hoping she had some answer, but the scared look on her face revealed she knew as little as he did. He jumped a little as he suddenly became aware of Duff's presence in the room.

"What do you think?" he asked him, frowning.

"I think you should tell his parents that he's received medicine and is feeling some better, but wants to see them. They deserve to know that much." Duff looked at Tad and smiled. "I knew you were a smart boy. Thanks for keeping our secret."

"You're welcome," he said. "But I still want Mama."

"Of course, it's not my decision," Duff said to Adam, "but I think it'd behoove us to keep this child happy and willing to go along with our game. Isn't that right, Tad?"

"Yes, sir."

"I don't know." Adam shook his head. "I don't know what Mr. Stanton would say."

"What difference does it make what that old poop thinks?" Tad chimed. "My papa is in charge of this switch, ain't he?"

"Of course, he is," Duff said.

Adam and Alethia exchanged nervous glances.

"This young fellow here just likes to keep everybody involved in this caper happy," Duff continued, smiling at the boy and reaching to muss his hair.

"Hmph, I don't care if old Mr. Stanton is happy or not," Tad said in a pout.

"I'll see what Mr. Lincoln wants." Adam's stomach tightened as he lied to Tad. More and more, he feared the threads of Stanton's tapestry were unraveling—the war continued, the boy knew and could talk, and the kitchen help was curious, too curious.

"Yes." Alethia patted Tad's cheek. "Soon you'll get a hug from your mama. But you must promise not to tell anyone."

"Not even Robert?" he asked.

"Especially not your brother," Duff replied.

"Good." Tad smiled impishly. "I like keeping secrets from my brother."

In a few minutes, Adam was in the basement again, unlocking the door to the billiards room. Inside, Mrs. Lincoln rushed to him, grabbing his arm.

"How's Taddie? Is he all right?"

"He's fine. The lady thinks he has just a plain old bellyache. She gave him subnitrate of bismuth."

"How much?" Mrs. Lincoln's eyes widened. "Subnitrate is powerful medicine. If a child is overmedicated…"

"Now, Molly, I'm sure the lady upstairs knew the right amount to give him," Lincoln interrupted as he walked up.

Adam noticed the look in Lincoln's eyes did not match the moderation in his voice. Not even on the day he had brought the president to the basement did he see such anguish as he observed now. It made him nervous.

"Something else is wrong," Mrs. Lincoln said. "I can tell. Your emotions are written on your face like Mr. Dickens writes stories on a page. What is it?"

"Tad is all right," Adam repeated.

"What is it, son?" Lincoln asked ominously.

"It's nothing, really."

"Tell me!" she demanded, trying to control her hysteria, as Lincoln's big hands clutched her shoulders tightly.

"He wants to see his mother." Adam's eyes wandered around the room and spotted Gabby peeking from his corner. He must have courage, or else he would dissolve into another Gabby Zook.

"So he knows that woman is a fake." Mrs. Lincoln smiled with vindication.

"Of course he does," Lincoln said, relaxing a bit. "He's smart, just like his mama."

"Then bring him down here. It won't hurt. He already knows."

"He's kept the secret for two months now," Lincoln added. "He can be trusted."

"Oh, I know he can be trusted," Adam agreed. "It's just…"

"It's just what?" Lincoln's tone became ominous again.

"I don't know if Mr. Stanton will approve."

"Stanton! That evil man!" Mrs. Lincoln's hands began to flail about.

"Now, Molly," Lincoln said, forcing her hands down, "let me handle this." He solemnly looked at Adam. "Go get Mr. Stanton's approval right now."

"He doesn't like to be disturbed," he explained.

"This woman's already lost two babies." Lincoln suddenly grabbed the front of Adam's rumpled blue tunic, pulling him off his feet to eye level. "She gets fearful upset when another is ailing and she can't pet him," Lincoln stated softly, coldly. "So I suggest you get Mr. Stanton's permission to bring that boy down here."

Adam gasped in surprise as he nodded obediently. He quickly, painfully, became aware of Lincoln's strength and anger. Scrambling for the door and fumbling for the keys, he followed the orders of the president of the United States.

Chapter Nineteen

Adam collapsed into the omnibus seat, exhausted physically and emotionally, and watched the street signs appear. Avenue H, Avenue I…his mind stopped noticing for a moment as it tried to comprehend the explosion he had just witnessed. Never had he thought the soft-spoken, gently witty Lincoln would, *could* muster such rage so quickly. And what if Stanton said no? he fretted as Avenue K arrived. He waved at the driver to stop and stepped off the omnibus, which clanged its way up Fifteenth Street. Adam ran down the avenue several blocks until he reached Stanton's brick home. Coming down the steps as he leaped up, two at a time, was a strange, swarthy woman wearing dangling earrings and a peculiar scarf over her black curls. She nodded and smiled mysteriously at him and evaporated in to the night. He stood at the door, gathering courage to knock and fighting his doubts about Stanton's intentions.

Some nights, after cleaning and returning chamber pots to the billiards room, Adam sneaked out and wandered over to one of the taverns, where he was developing a taste for ale. Soldiers returning from battle swapped tall tales, but Adam stayed to himself, preferring not to explain why he had no wounds. He had learned quite a bit about the political scene in the capital and much of the gossip, including where the best whorehouses were, and who was taking graft in the government. For instance, he learned Edwin Stanton had become secretary of war by exposing the corruption of former secretary Simon Cameron, who was said to be willing to steal anything but a red-hot stove. Then one night, as Adam was nursing his second glass of ale, he overheard something disconcerting. During the summer of 1862, when Stanton was formulating his plan to move Lincoln to the basement, he had been the target of nasty rumors of failure to supply medical aid and armaments for the soldiers. There was even talk of forcing the president to remove him.

So, as Adam stood on the front step of Stanton's house, he could not help but wonder if Stanton's self-preservation was the actual reason for the grand scheme to save the republic, of which the private was an integral part. He finally knocked.

A maid opened the door, and Adam told her he wanted to see Stanton. He sat on a long bench in the hall while she disappeared through a door to the parlor. In a moment she returned.

"Mr. Stanton will join you in a few minutes."

She disappeared down the hall, and Adam, despite his better instincts, went to the door and listened.

"Ellen, who was that woman?"

"Mrs. Laury, from Georgetown."

"The name sounds familiar."

"She's a spiritualist."

"Ah, the one who told Mrs. Lincoln that all her husband's Cabinet members were his enemies." Sarcasm tinged his voice.

"It was Mrs. Lincoln who recommended her to me, since we share the sorrow of losing sons."

"Mrs. Lincoln? When?"

Adam noticed an urgency to the question.

"Last summer. Mrs. Laury's been ill with influenza until recently. Why do you ask?"

"No reason." Stanton paused. "Why do you need a spiritualist?"

Adam heard Mrs. Stanton sigh, but not reply.

"Well, I've someone waiting for me outside," Stanton said. "We can talk about this later." When he came out of the door, his eyes widened. "Oh. I didn't know it was you." He looked around nervously. "I told you not to come here."

"It's an emergency."

"Not here. Outside." Stanton pushed Adam out the front door. "What is it?" They stood on the porch and began to shiver in the November night.

"The boy—Tad—he's sick."

"So?" Stanton raised a cynical eyebrow.

"It's nothing serious, but he wants to see his mother."

"Isn't that woman there? She should be there."

"He knows."

"What do you mean he knows?"

"He thinks his father placed substitutes in the White House as part of a plan to end the war. That's why he hasn't told anyone—yet."

"Yet?"

"He says if he doesn't see his mother tonight, he might forget not to tell."

"Little brat tries to blackmail me, and he won't live until morning."

"Sir?"

"Hell." Stanton spat on the steps and scrunched his shoulders. "Fine. Take him to the basement. Just make sure no one sees you."

Within thirty minutes, Adam was back at the Executive Mansion and bounding up the service stairs. Entering Tad's bedroom, he found Alethia and Duff hovering over him.

Beaming brightly, Adam announced, "It's all right. It's been approved. Mr. Stanton said yes."

"Hear that?" Alethia brushed Tad's hair. "In a few minutes you'll see them."

"But only for a few minutes," Duff said. He looked up at Adam and back at the boy. "You don't want to endanger your father's plan."

"Oh no," Tad said. "I don't want to do anything to hurt Papa, but I do want to see Mama. I think it'll make me well faster."

"Of course it will." Alethia smiled.

"You're a nice lady." Tad looked up at her and then at Duff. "And you're a nice man. Papa picked good when he picked you."

"No one must see us," Adam said. "What about Nicolay and Hay?"

"They came in from a round of tavern visits while you were gone." Duff stood. "I think they're still awake."

"Oh." Adam's face clouded.

"I could go down to their rooms and discuss tomorrow's agenda," Duff offered.

"That's good," Adam said.

"They're good boys. Our late-night talks can last an hour, easy."

"That'll give us plenty of time," Adam said.

Duff left to walk down through the glass partition to the office reception area. The bedroom which Hay and Nicolay shared was in the corner across from their office.

"Oh, I'm so excited," Tad said with a bit of a giggle. "I bet Mama's going to cry."

"Of course she'll cry." Alethia hugged him. "I'm about to cry just thinking about it. Enjoy every minute of it."

"You can come with me," Tad offered as he sat up.

"I don't think that would be a good idea." Alethia cast a worried glance toward Adam. "You see, um, the fewer people going downstairs, the better. We don't want a grand parade to the basement, do we?"

"I guess not." Tad lowered his head in disappointment. He looked up at Adam. "We better go now."

Bending over to pick up Tad, Adam was surprised by how light the boy was. Hardly any meat on his bones, he thought, Just like me when I was that age. He held the child close to him.

"I'll open the door for you." Alethia pulled on the knob. "Wait a minute." She peeked out and looked both ways down the long, dark hallway, barely lit by flickering gas lamps. "Tom Pen makes his rounds soon to put out the lights." She smiled at Adam. "It's clear."

Tad lifted his head, which he had snuggled into Adam's shoulder, and smiled, waving his hand. "See you later."

"Yes, see you later, my darling."

Adam quickly crossed the hall to the service stairs, where he opened the door, looked back to see Alethia smiling through the crack of Tad's bedroom door, and then shut it and started down the straw-matted steps with the sickly, perspiration-drenched boy, scented by medicines and faint traces of urine, who snuggled and moaned.

"You're much nicer than I first thought," Tad murmured, not lifting his face but nuzzling in deeper. "You don't have to be a lieutenant."

"Thank you."

"Where did Papa find you?"

"Mr. Stanton recommended me," Adam replied after an awkward pause. "He's from my hometown."

"Oh." Tad wiped his running nose on Adam's rumpled blue tunic. "I don't like Mr. Stanton. He's mean."

"He's…" Adam stumbled over his words, trying to find the right one to describe the secretary of war. "He's professional."

"I don't know what that means." He turned his nose into Adam's armpit. "You smell like you ain't had a bath in a week."

"Oh."

"That's all right. I hate baths too."

"Do you want me to tell you what professional means?" Adam stopped at the basement door.

"No. It probably means he's mean but got a good reason to be."

"Close enough."

Adam opened the door and searched the vaulted basement hall. Finding no one around, he quickly entered, closed the door, and hastened his pace to the billiards room. Suddenly Phebe stepped from her room, fixed Adam in her gaze, and crossed her arms. Like a deer trapped by a poised hunter, he said nothing, did nothing, except to let his chin droop.

"Hello, Phebe," Tad said, with a chirp as he lifted his head and smiled. "I gotta go puke."

"You don't get sick in your room?" Her eyes widened.

"Stinks up the place, Mama says," he replied. "'Course, sometimes I don't know it's comin' up until it's too late. One time I got vomit over one of Mama's fancy dresses. Boy, did she get mad."

"I can imagine," Phebe said.

"Vomit won't hurt a uniform much," Tad informed her.

"So, Private Christy. You've been given puke patrol."

"Puke patrol." Tad laughed. "That's funny."

"Yes," Adam replied with a tight smile, "so if you'll excuse us, we've serious regurgitation business to tend to."

Phebe shook her head and waved them on, as she went back to her room.

"Reach down in my pocket and get the keys."

"All right." Tad retrieved them. "Here they are."

As Adam opened the door and carried Tad through, he noticed Phebe's door across the hall. It was slightly ajar. That might be a point of concern, but Adam dismissed it as he presented the boy to his parents.

"Oh, my Taddie! Oh, my baby! Oh, my baby!" Mrs. Lincoln grabbed her son from Adam, and immediately dropped to the floor, sobbing and clutching him to her bosom.

"See, I told you she'd cry," Tad said, his voice muffled.

"Thank you." Lincoln walked up and put a large hand on Adam's shoulder.

"You're welcome, Mr. President."

"I'm sorry I grabbed you. I should have never lost control."

"I understand, Mr. President."

"Have you had subnitrate of bismuth?" Mrs. Lincoln held Tad's face in her hands.

"It tastes awful."

"But it made you feel better, didn't it?"

"Yes, Mama."

"I suppose that woman isn't completely incompetent." Mrs. Lincoln held his head close to her breast.

"Oh no. She's a nice lady," Tad said, pulling away to look at his mother. "She looks just like you." He smiled. "'Course, I knew the very first day."

"You did? How bright of you," Lincoln said, kneeling down to his wife and son. "And how did you figure that out so fast?"

"She doesn't get mad like you do, Mama."

"Tad!" Mrs. Lincoln's mouth flew open. She looked at her husband. "Mr. Lincoln!"

Lincoln tried to be serious, but began to smile, which gave way to a chuckle. Mrs. Lincoln slapped at him, but could not help but join him. Tad, happy he had made his parents happy, giggled.

Adam smiled until he glanced over at the boxes and crates to see Gabby with his homemade quilt clutched tightly around his shoulders, and remembered this was not a happy ending, but merely a respite in their ordeal.

Chapter Twenty

For an hour, Phebe kept an eye to the slightly ajar door, watching comings and goings of the white people. At times she could swear she heard a woman screaming something about my baby, my baby, and other times she thought she heard laughter. When Adam reappeared in the hall carrying Tad she felt an impulse to confront them again, but decided to stay prudently hidden. After they entered the service stairs, Phebe went to the next door and knocked.

"Neal?"

She heard a soft moan, followed by grumbling and padding of stocking feet across the room. Phebe stepped back when she saw Neal's light coffee face speckled with nutmeg jut out the door and scowl.

"What do the white folk want now?" He paused before adding, "Tell them to get it for themselves. I'm off duty."

"It ain't the white folk."

A smile, slightly soured by the hint of a smirk, crossed his lips.

"It's about the white folks," Phebe said in clarification.

"Oh." The smile faded, replaced by a quizzical furrowing of his brow.

"Let me in."

Opening the door wide, Neal stepped aside, absently buttoning the top of his woolen long underwear.

"I hope you don't think this is anything improper, nothing romantic." Phebe stepped inside, turned sharply, her eyes widening.

"I know." Neal smiled and softened his gaze as he went to a small table to light a kerosene lamp.

"No," Phebe said. "Don't light the lamp."

"Well," Neal replied, "This room's pretty black without light."

"I don't want anyone to know we're talking."

"Oh."

"Shut the door."

"We won't be able to see each other."

"Shut the door."

He shrugged and closed the door, leaving them in complete darkness. "I feel foolish," he said after a moment.

"I do too," Phebe replied. "That's why I don't want you to see me." She paused and added timidly, "And I don't want to see the scorn in your eyes."

"I never look at you with scorn." A hurt tone clouded his voice.

"Yes, you have. But we don't have time to fight over it." She sucked in air. "There's something strange going on."

"Phebe…"

"And I don't want to hear no scorn in your voice neither," she said, interrupting him. "Please listen."

"All right."

Phebe closed her eyes to compose her thoughts. So many images raced through her mind that she had trouble deciding where to begin.

"The soldier boy—that Private Christy—carried Tad down here. They went into the billiards room. After a while they came back out, Private Christy looking around like he didn't want to be seen."

"So he didn't see you?"

"Coming down they did," Phebe said. "Tad said hello. The private turned red and looked away. On their way out, I just cracked the door."

"What do you think it means?"

"If I tell you, you'll laugh at me."

"I've laughed at you before."

"But those times you laughed because you thought I was funny. This time you'll laugh because you think I'm crazy."

"All right." Neal paused. "No laughing at you. Tell me what you think is going on."

"Well, I fixed the same meals for the Lincolns upstairs as I do for those important, secret people who stay locked away in the basement. Mr. Lincoln has peculiar eating habits, an apple and milk for lunch, just picking at a decent supper. Ever since September, when those mysterious important folks arrived, I never saw nobody go into that room."

"Sure, a whole mess of folks go in there," Neal said, "that soldier boy and Secretary Stanton."

"You see? Don't you think that's queer, only two visitors, ever?"

"I don't make it a practice to keep up with what the white folks do."

"The lunch being sent downstairs now comes back with nothing eaten but the apple and milk."

Neal remained silent. Phebe heard the cot creak as he sat. She had him interested, so she continued.

"About a month ago, the private came out of the billiards room with a laundry basket balanced on his hip as he tried to lock the door. Well, he lost his grip and dropped the basket."

Neal snorted. "I always thought he was clumsy."

"There was women's underthings in the basket—I mean, all over the floor. I came out to help him pick everything up. When it dawned on me what I held in my hand, he snatched it from me and gave me this look like he wished I'd never seen those panties. But I did see them and that meant only one thing."

"Which was?"

"There's a woman in that room."

"So?"

"So whoever heard of a woman advising men-folk about war?"

"Maybe she's the wife of some diplomat," he offered.

"No woman would stay in a locked basement room just to be with her husband, under her own free will, that is."

"So who do you think the woman is?"

Phebe hesitated.

"Stop playing games with me." Neal's voice sounded impatient.

"If you don't believe me, you'll laugh. If you do believe me, you'll get mad."

"Why would I get mad?"

"Because you're always mad, especially at the white folks," Phebe said. "I see it in your eyes. You really hate them, and I don't get it. I mean, you're born free—"

"Yes, I'm free, for what good that does me," he interrupted her angrily, spitting on the floor.

"I—I don't understand..."

"I was born the son of a freeman in the city of Boston. He was the son of a freeman, all in a long line of tutors, teaching French to Boston merchants who traded with Haiti and other points in the Caribbean."

"You speak French?"

"Yes. So what?" He paused. "My mother, as a child, came to Boston in the middle of the night in her mother's arms, a slave from a Virginia tobacco plantation."

"A runaway slave," Phebe murmured.

"She grew up cooking and sewing in wealthy New England homes. That's where she met my father, who tutored the master of the house. They married, found a comfortable apartment, and had me. I was supposed to be the one to climb the next rung on the racial equality ladder, perhaps the ministry, law, or medicine. But it was not to be. Ever heard of the Fugitive Slave Law?"

"Yes."

"Slave owners tracked down runaways in Free states, and local authorities and ordinary citizens had to help."

"So they came for your grandmother?" Phebe asked.

"No. She was dead. They came for my mother. My grandmother stole my mother from the farmer, who wanted her back." Neal paused. "And her offspring. Any child from her womb was his property too."

Phebe jumped when she realized he was talking about himself.

"I remember when they took my mother. Her cries woke me up. At first my father was angry, shouting at her. He didn't know he'd married a runaway. He stopped yelling when she said she didn't remember anything before life in Boston kitchens. White men banged at the door, demanding they come out. My father took me from my bed and pulled down the attic ladder. He told me to be quiet, and my mother kissed me, her lips still moist from her tears. He had just closed the attic ladder when the slave catchers broke through. I cried as I heard them drag her away. I never saw her again. "

"I haven't seen my mother in a long time either, but I still have hope." Immediately Phebe wished she had not spoken.

"You've been bought and freed, all legal. You got hope because you don't know no better. No, I don't have to worry about being taken South anymore. But I don't have a chance for a profession now." Neal sighed and mellowed. "When my father told me he'd arranged a job for me in Washington, I thought it might lead to something, but when I arrived at the White House, they sent me to the basement to be a butler."

"Butler is a good job," Phebe said, trying to be encouraging. "Why, on the plantation the butler was—"

"This ain't the plantation, girl," he interrupted. "This is the world. This is life. We may be free, but we ain't white."

"I know."

"Well, tell me," he said. "Who do you think the woman in the billiards room is?"

"I was talking to Mrs. Keckley. She's the lady who sews the Mrs. Lincoln's clothes. I said to her things had been odd for the last few months. She got real quiet, looked around, then pulled me closer and made me promise not to tell anyone."

"Not to tell what?"

"She said when she went to fit the Mrs. Lincoln for a new dress the middle of September she saw right off something was different. The Mrs. Lincoln was bigger, across her chest. The missus looked real flustered, Mrs. Keckley said, laughing and rambling on about gaining too much weight. When a woman gets fat, it goes on her butt or hips or belly first."

"Just what are you trying to tell me?"

"I'm still scared how you'll take it."

"You still think like a slave." Neal snorted.

"Well," Phebe said softly. "It's all I know."

Her owner was Pierce Butler, whose grandfather authored the fugitive slave clause in the United States Constitution. Her earliest memories were of being held by his beautiful wife, who was rumored to be a fancy actress from England. Then the master's wife had gone away. When Phebe asked about her, she was told to hush and mind her own business. The rest of her childhood was uneventful, though filled with hard work, until all the slaves on the plantation were loaded on a ship and taken down the Altama River to Savannah, where they were taken to the Kimbrough Race Track during a torrential downpour. Men prodded them, looked in their mouths, tested their muscles, and stood back, cocking their heads in judgment.

Earlier in the day she had watched her father being led away, and later her mother, her eyes filled with tears. Feeling all was lost, Phebe used all her willpower to keep from crying. Soon it was her turn to stand on the block, and a miracle happened. When the bidding was over, Phebe met her new owner, Mortimer Thompson, a reporter for the *New York Tribune,* who said she would be freed as soon as they arrived in New York City. But what will I do? Phebe had asked him; how will I support myself? He had taken her hand.

"I know an old friend of yours," he said.

Her old friend was Mrs. Butler, whose stage name, Fanny Kemble, was in large letters across a theater marquee.

"What a pretty face," Mrs. Butler said with a gush as she patted Phebe's cheeks.

"Thank you, ma'am," Phebe said shyly.

"I wish I could afford to employ another maid, but I can't." When Phebe's face fell, she added, "But don't give up hope. I've friends all over, here in New York, in London, and in Washington." She smiled at Phebe. "How would you like a job in the Republican administration? I've many contacts with abolitionists."

By the time the whirlwind had ended, Phebe lived in the basement of the Executive Mansion, cooking meals and witnessing the nation's business first hand. Which brought her back to Neal's question about who she thought was in the billiards room. Before she spoke, Phebe realized she risked not only Neal's ridicule, but also the loss of her job—a step backward toward slavery she did not want to take.

"I don't know." She walked to the door and opened it. "Now that I think about it, there's nothing wrong, nothing wrong at all."

Chapter Twenty-One

Heat, pervasive and stultifying, filled every corner of the billiards room in the Executive Mansion basement during the last half of May 1863. Gabby Zook sat on his pallet behind the barrels and crates, took off his shirt, unbuttoned his union suit, and pulled down the top, revealing a ghostly white, flabby, gray-haired belly. Before reaching for a washcloth in a nearby porcelain basin, he lightly stroked his abdomen and thought back to the days on Long Island, playing on the beach with his buddy Joe. If he closed his eyes as he dribbled water from the cloth onto his face, Gabby could swear he smelled the salt air and felt the sun's rays as he floated on the bobbing waves. Joe erupted through the water and landed across Gabby, sinking him below the surface. Gurgling, he came up and, laughing, pushed his friend's head down repeatedly. The boys, choking on salt water, rolled in the surf until they landed on the beach.

Then, Gabby remembered, they had heard the reeds rustle on the dunes. Joe had sat up suddenly and looked around.

"What's wrong?" Gabby asked.

"I think there's somebody watching us."

Gabby bolted up and turned to stare at the dune. Reeds rustled more rapidly. The boys scrambled for their pile of clothes, hurriedly slipping into their cotton undersuits which quickly soaked up the seawater and clung to their trim, tight bodies.

"Hello?" Gabby called out.

"I love to watch young men laughing and playing." A tall, odd-looking man in his early twenties, wearing a wide-brim straw hat, stood nonchalantly among the reeds. He began to saunter toward them.

"Who are you?" Joe asked.

"Poet."

"You shouldn't be watching us, Mr. Poet," Joe said.

"Poet is who I am," he explained. "Words flow from my belly to my fingers."

"Huh?" Joe knitted his brow.

"My friend meant your name," Gabby said.

"My name is Legion."

"What the hell does that mean?" Joe growled.

"It's from the Bible." Gabby turned to his friend confidentially.

"The ocean waves teach me always to see beyond the things on hand, as the ocean always points beyond the waves of the moment." The man in the hat looked beyond the boys to gaze at the ocean.

"What the hell does that mean?" Joe muttered again, this time to Gabby.

"You two are so young and strong." The eyes of the poet who called himself Legion returned to the soaked, lean white bodies before him. "You should serve your country. The army needs young men like you."

"We're going to West Point this fall," Gabby said.

"Good." He nodded as his hand reached out to touch Joe's stomach, which showed through the unbuttoned undersuit. "Such strong, lean, white bellies."

Joe stepped back, his eyes widening and his mouth dropping.

"Your nation needs you." Suddenly, the man cocked an ear toward the reeds on the dune. "More raucous laughter. There's nothing more alive than male laughter."

Without further word, the odd-looking man walked away toward the laughter and disappeared behind the dune.

"Gabby, I know what that guy's name is. Nancy."

Gabby laughed, hitting Joe on the arm as he bent over to pick up his trousers and shirt.

"But what the hell did he mean," Joe had continued, "with all that talk about ocean waves and pointing and things on hand?"

Sitting now in his suffocatingly hot corner of the billiards room in the basement of the Executive Mansion, Gabby pulled up the top of his union suit as he tried to remember what he had told Joe that day on the beach. "Ocean waves taught him always to see beyond the things on hand as the ocean always points beyond the waves of the moment."

Now if Gabby could just remember what that meant…

Jangling keys and the turning of a lock jarred his thoughts from the past to his empty stomach and his full chamber pot. Gabby carried it carefully around the crates and barrels, depositing it by the door and looking for Adam and the breakfast tray.

"Private Christy," Mrs. Lincoln said graciously as she emerged from her French lace curtains. "Good morning."

Adam kept his eyes down as he put the tray on the billiards table. Gabby could tell he was sinking into melancholia, a place Gabby himself visited many times and for extended periods. If the boy tarried there too long, he might find it hard to return, Gabby knew, and frantically tried to figure how to throw Adam a lifeline.

"Is it going to be another sweltering day, Private?" Mrs. Lincoln persisted in her pleasantries. "It's been absolutely stifling. I've been glowing, absolutely glowing."

"Yes, ma'am," Adam said in muted tones. "Another warm day." He avoided eye contact and went to the door.

"I appreciate your kindness, Private. Really I do."

"Thank you, ma'am." Adam turned to her and managed a weak smile.

"Father?" Mrs. Lincoln called out after Adam had left, and she had heard the lock clank shut.

The tall, bearded man—who Gabby sometimes thought was president of the United States when he was not certain he himself held that title—walked out of his makeshift bedroom, brushing his shaggy hair away from his brow.

"Now what, Molly?" he asked in a tired voice, nearing the sad, muted tones in Adam's voice.

Gabby frowned as he realized the similarities between Adam and Mr. Lincoln—the long, unruly locks and vacant stares. This was time for him to keep his wits about him, Gabby told himself as he subconsciously brushed his own hair out of his eyes.

"I want you to talk to Private Christy," Mrs. Lincoln said.

"What about?"

"He seems to be suffering from some malaise," she replied, walking to the billiards table to look at the tray. "Fried eggs again." She looked up. "Mr. Gabby, come get your breakfast."

"Fried eggs again?" His head down, Gabby shuffled toward the table. "I like fried eggs. Eggs taste good. Rooster eggs are best. Once the roosters jump on the back of the hens and pump them then the eggs can become chicks, if we don't eat them first. Wonder what it is about the rooster's stuff that makes the eggs taste better?"

"I have no idea, Mr. Gabby," she replied with reserved disgust. "This isn't actually a proper topic for conversation."

"Do you know if these are rooster eggs?" he asked, ignoring her comment. "I guess you don't since you haven't been out of this room for almost a year. I haven't been out of this room for almost a year, almost a year without Cordie. Cordie doesn't like fried eggs. She doesn't like the runny part—"

"Mr. Gabby." Closing her eyes, Mrs. Lincoln firmly grasped his hands. Her voice was frantic, but soft and fragile. After inhaling deeply, she continued. "I'm so glad you like fried eggs."

"You can have mine," Lincoln said.

"No, thank you, sir." Gabby examined Lincoln's loose-fitting suit. "You need to eat all you can get your hands on. You're a bag of bones. I haven't seen a bag of bones like yours since my father died." Responding to the sudden squeeze on his hands from Mrs. Lincoln, he stopped. After looking at each of the Lincolns, he took his plate. "I think I better eat my breakfast now."

Settling on the floor behind the crates and barrels, Gabby began to eat, his head slightly cocked to hear the conversation between the Lincolns.

"I wish he'd taken the fried eggs," Lincoln said, a hint of humor shading his voice. "Do you want them?"

"Heavens no!" Mrs. Lincoln replied. "I keep telling Private Christy I prefer poached eggs, but I suppose my poached eggs go to that woman upstairs." She paused to sip her coffee. "Mr. Gabby's right, you know. You're too thin. You should eat more."

Gabby smiled with pride as he wiped dribbled egg yolk from the corner of his mouth. Mrs. Lincoln knew he was smart. That colonel at West Point was wrong. He had said Gabby was stupid after the accident. He had said

West Point was right. Stupid people get people killed, the colonel had said. But Mrs. Lincoln did not think he was stupid.

"Father," Mrs. Lincoln said. "I was wrong when I said this was the worst thing that could happen to a human being."

Her remark shook Gabby up. He did not want her to be wrong about something. Mrs. Lincoln thought he was smart, and he did not want her to think she made mistakes.

"I've concluded it's much worse to be the guard at the door," she continued. "At least we've the peace of mind of knowing we're sinned against. How horrible to live knowing you are the sinner."

"Mother," Lincoln said, "you're too profound for this early hour of the morning."

"It's Private Christy, Mr. Lincoln," she said with persistence. "His appearance, his demeanor. He knows he's a sinner—an innocent sinner compared to that devil Stanton, but a sinner all the same—and that terrible knowledge is killing his soul."

"You expect me to save his soul?" Lincoln muttered, "My dear, I'm not divine."

Gabby's head turned as he heard the door unlock. Adam, sooner and sooner every day for the breakfast plates, Gabby grumbled. He stuffed an entire bran muffin in his mouth. Fretting that soon he would not have time even to finish his eggs, he stood to take his plate to the billiards table. Adam gathered the others, accepted Gabby's plate, mumbled thank you, and turned away. Gabby noticed Mrs. Lincoln nudging her husband.

"Say something," she whispered.

Lincoln scowled at her, then turned and forced a smile on his face. "Son, do you like licorice?"

"What?" Adam stopped on his way to the door, startled.

"Licorice. Do you like to suck on it?"

"Licorice?" Mrs. Lincoln said, hissing at her husband under her breath.

"I suppose. I ain't had much."

"Well, then, let me give you some." Lincoln walked toward him, patting his pockets. When he pulled out a white paper wrapping the licorice, a small framed picture fell to the floor.

"Thank you, sir," Adam said, taking the candy and leaving.

Lingering at the corner of the crates and barrels, Gabby watched Mrs. Lincoln pick up the frame, focus her small brown eyes on it, and turn a bright scarlet, her cheeks puffing out. Lincoln stopped when he saw his wife staring at the picture. The knowledge that an extremely private and explosive moment was about to occur transfixed Gabby, leaving him partially covered by the first stack of crates.

"Oh," was the only word Lincoln could say.

"I thought you left this photograph in Springfield," Mrs. Lincoln said softly, but with intensity.

"Looking at it makes me forget for a few minutes about this awful war and being held in this room," Lincoln awkwardly explained.

"Looking at me is supposed to do that." Her eyes welled with tears.

What kind of picture would provoke Mrs. Lincoln to such anger, Gabby wondered as he peered around the crates. The frame was small, perhaps three by five inches, not ornate but plain. Could it be a photograph of their first child who died? Shaking his head, Gabby decided that was not it. He would be very happy to have picture of his father, a face slowly fading from Gabby's memory.

"You promised me you wouldn't bring it." After a cold moment of silence, Mrs. Lincoln flung the picture across the room.

Gabby's eyes widened as Lincoln scrambled to pick up the frame, running his long bony fingers over it, to check to see if the glass had broken. Lincoln returned it to his coat pocket and walked slowly to his wife.

"She was only a child. And now she's dead," Lincoln intoned. "She's not a threat to you."

"Not a threat!" Mrs. Lincoln's face twisted. "That trollop has tormented me through my entire marriage!"

"Don't call her that." Lincoln's hand impulsively reached to the pocket holding the photograph. "She was a sweet, innocent child who encouraged my dreams."

"I didn't encourage your dreams?" Mrs. Lincoln's hysteria grew.

"I've told you; it isn't even her in the photograph."

"But it looks like her. That's why you bought it." Mrs. Lincoln's eyes narrowed.

Gabby wondered who the girl in the picture was to create such a torrent of emotions between the Lincolns. She must have been a former girlfriend of Lincoln. She supported his dreams, Gabby sighed. Joe had encouraged his dreams, and he had supported Joe's dreams. Joe had died, and all their dreams vanished with him.

"You've never loved me." Tears rolled down her cheeks. "Ann Rutledge won your heart, and she has it still."

Lincoln took a deep breath, and Gabby expected a reasoned reply from him, but the door opened, and Stanton strode in, breaking the tension. Mrs. Lincoln, wiping her tears away, turned to disappear behind her French lace curtains, barely acknowledging the secretary of war. Shuddering, Gabby retreated further into his corner out of fear of Stanton. He cocked his head to eavesdrop.

"Have a seat, Mr. Secretary," Lincoln said. Scratching of chairs covered another comment, which was followed by a Lincoln's deep chuckle and a sullen harrumph.

"The information from Chancellorsville was late yesterday afternoon. There was a surprise attack led by General Jackson."

"How bad was it?"

"Hooker was caught off-guard and…"

"More lives lost." Lincoln sighed. "More lives will be lost."

"Meade acquitted himself well, but it was not enough."

"Meade's a good man."

"Hooker must be replaced," Stanton said.

Gabby became aware of an awkward pause.

"Or perhaps he should be given another opportunity," Stanton offered.

He wanted Lincoln to decide, Gabby thought, but he did not want to say so. He wanted the president to say what he would say upstairs, except he was still locked in the basement. The president, Gabby repeated in his mind. If he were actually president, then perhaps Stanton was waiting for him to step from behind the crates and barrels to tell him what to do. Gabby moved a foot slightly before two other thoughts entered his mind: he did not know what to do, and if he were indeed president, he would follow the adage that the leader who leads least, leads best.

"And if Hooker were replaced," Stanton continued after another long silence, "who'd replace him?"

Again, stinging silence controlled the room.

"You've nothing to say?" Stanton asked.

"Oh. You expected a response," Lincoln ingeniously replied. "I presumed you were merely thinking out loud."

"You know very well I wasn't," Stanton said resentfully. "If I wish to think aloud I needn't come here."

Gabby heard Lincoln's sigh and respected his remarkable restraint.

"Where will you put me if I'm wrong this time, Old Capitol Prison?"

Stanton began to gurgle in indignation.

"I apologize," Lincoln said. Gabby thought he should not have. "Try to forget what I said. I seem to be in the middle of a malaise. Why I should be melancholy I don't know—once again I slide into irony. It's the Union's future that's important, and not me."

"Thank you, sir," Stanton whispered.

"Replace Hooker with Meade. With whom we shall eventually replace Meade can be discussed another day."

Very wise that I stepped back to allow Lincoln to decide, Gabby thought. He did well. Chairs shuffled about, indicating Stanton was leaving.

"Mr. Stanton?" Mrs. Lincoln's voice was subdued.

"Yes?" he wearily replied.

"I'm worried about Private Christy. His clothes are disheveled and his hair…"

"His appearance is his own business."

"I'm not complaining about his appearance," Mrs. Lincoln persisted. "It's the reason for his appearance. He's not happy."

"We're at war," he brusquely said. "No one's happy."

Before she could reply, the door opened. Gabby could see that it was Adam returning the chamber pots. Stanton left, and Lincoln disappeared behind his curtain. Mrs. Lincoln just stood there, eyeing Adam with sympathy. Gabby wanted to help. After Adam put the pots in their respective places, Gabby remembered what the strange man in the straw hat said to him.

"'Ocean waves taught me always to see beyond the things on hand as the ocean always points beyond the waves of the moment.'"

"Huh?"

Gabby followed Adam to the door.

"Young men are meant to laugh and play."

"All right." Adam wrinkled his brow as he unlocked the door to leave.

"Do you have a strong, lean, white belly?" Gabby reached out to touch his midsection, but Adam opened the door and stepped out into the hall.

As he heard the key locking the door, Gabby earnestly added, "Your nation needs you."

Chapter Twenty-Two

Leaning back in his chair, Duff relaxed, confident of handling the Cabinet meeting. He was learning to deal with the egos of all the self-important men around the table. He liked some more than others. Attorney General Edward Bates reminded him of himself, little formal education and even less pretension. Duff still mourned the death of Interior Secretary Caleb Smith, a Midwesterner as he was. His replacement, John Usher, was a mystery to him and, since his name had been offered by Stanton, not to be trusted.

"Mr. President, the gallant men of Maine should receive special commendation for their defense of Little Round Top yesterday," Stanton said. "They saved Gettysburg from falling to the rebels."

Duff nodded wisely, having learned this was the safest response to any comment during a Cabinet meeting.

"The latest telegraph reports indicate today's events should be the most pivotal since the second Manassas."

"Ah, fireworks for the Fourth of July," Duff dryly replied.

Laughter filled the room and boosted his self-esteem. Among the others around the table, only one merited Duff's respect: Secretary of the Navy Gideon Welles. He had to be careful not to be too friendly, because the real Lincoln did not admire Welles, finding him senile and altogether ludicrous in his large, ill-fitting white wig. Duff, on the other hand, found Welles to be profoundly wise.

"Have we received any wires from Gettysburg today?" Seward asked.

Duff did not trust Seward, whom he found hard to decipher; in other words, he could not tell if Seward believed him to be Lincoln.

"Preliminary wires indicated Lee's forces appear ready to advance on the center of General Meade's line," Stanton replied.

Absolute loathing covered Duff like a cold, wet wool blanket, and he remembered that sensation from his days prior to the first battle of Manassas. As much as he was choked with fear at the battle and as much as he was smothered by terror when he was captured, Duff felt even stronger emotions toward Stanton, who was adjusting his pebble glasses on his little nose.

"Is this necessarily a bad thing?" Chase intoned.

Chase evoked mere disdain from Duff, who saw him as a sanctimonious fool. He did not worry if Chase realized he was not Lincoln, because Chase never looked him in the eye or listened to what he said, as though Duff were inconsequential.

"We don't know at this time," Stanton said.

Duff did not like the contemptuous attitude Stanton had for Alethia, whom he had grown to love over the past year. He hesitated to tell her, because then he would have to tell her his secrets, and if she learned of all the horrible sins he had committed, she would surely hate him.

"Will you keep us informed?" Welles asked.

"Of course." Stanton smiled with condescension.

"I was talking to Mr. Lincoln," Welles said.

"Everyone at this table has access to the telegraph wires at the War Department," Duff said, noticing the grimace on Stanton's face.

"I know that." Welles nodded. "I just wanted to hear it from you. Sometimes it becomes a bit weary, learning official war news from Mr. Stanton."

"Mr. Welles, may I remind you I'm the secretary of war; therefore, by definition, all information concerning the war should come through me."

"Forgive me, Mr. Stanton, but as attorney general," Bates interjected, "it's my obligation to remind you that the Constitution names the president as commander in chief of the armed forces, therefore superseding you as the ultimate authority on releasing war news."

"I stand corrected." Stanton pursed his Cupid's bow lips.

Duff could hardly restrain the smile creeping across his lips; instead, he surveyed the room, trying to look wise. Not a person seriously doubted he was president, he decided, except Stanton.

On his staff, the only person who might suspect something was Nicolay, so Duff had sent him on a special mission to Colorado. With any luck, the war would end by the time he had returned. While Duff never thought he was particularly bright, he prided himself on detecting intelligence in others, and he deemed Nicolay one of the smartest men in Washington, which made him dangerous.

"Mr. Hay, do you have all this commotion on paper?" Duff asked.

"Yes, sir."

"And it was all clear as mud, correct?"

Hay laughed and nodded his head.

He was a good boy, Hay was, but not as bright as Nicolay, Duff thought. Perhaps he was as smart as Nicolay, but he was so preoccupied with pretty women and strong liquor that his keener senses were unnaturally blunted. Hay did not consider it strange that Duff sent him to a bookstore to buy a copy of Rose Greenhow's prison memoirs, *My Imprisonment and First Year of Abolitionist Rule in Washington*, not questioning why President Lincoln would be interested in a book written by a rebel spy.

"Is there any other business?" He looked pointedly into the eyes of each Cabinet member. When no one spoke, Duff sighed. "Then, let us adjourn to prepare for Independence Day."

As the Cabinet members left, Welles turned to Duff.

"Mr. President, would you walk with me to the gate?"

"No," Stanton interjected. "He's much too preoccupied."

"I'm not preoccupied at all."

"Good," Welles replied, taking Duff by the crook of his arm and leading him down the hall. "How's Mrs. Lincoln after her carriage accident?"

"Very well," Duff said, ignoring the exasperated grunts from Stanton behind them. "Doctors at the Soldiers' Home said her head injuries were minor. It'll be good for her to recuperate in the cool Maryland foothills."

"Yes, it can be quite sweltering in Washington during the summer months."

They began down the grand staircase.

"You know, Mrs. Welles always inquires about Mrs. Lincoln. She's quite fond of her. Often she has protested the unfair attacks on her in the newspapers."

When they reached the foyer, Welles gave a wary glance up the stairs and then at the front door guard, John Parker, who was already red in the face from drinking.

"Good morning, Mr. Parker," Duff said. "I'm escorting Mr. Welles to the gate. I won't be long."

"Very well, sir." Parker's voice was thick with whiskey.

As they walked down the steps, Welles leaned into Duff.

"I wanted a private word with you, Mr. President," Welles said in a hushed voice. "It seems Mr. Stanton has been omnipresent the last few months."

"Really? I hadn't noticed." Duff raised an ingenuous eyebrow.

"Mr. President, I wish I had your gentle wit." Welles chuckled and shook his bewigged head.

They took a sharp turn to stroll through the garden to the turnstile gate.

"What's on your mind, Mr. Secretary?"

"I was less than forthcoming during the Cabinet meeting," he whispered. He stopped to examine a rose bush. "I wish I still had my sense of smell. Roses have a marvelous bouquet." Again Welles looked up, this time at the second-story window, where Stanton stood glaring at them.

"I assume you weren't forthcoming because of Mr. Stanton."

"I don't trust him." Welles straightened and looked at Duff. "He exudes the aura of frustrated ambition. Put quite bluntly, Mr. President, he covets your job."

"So do Mr. Chase and Mr. Seward."

"But not as much as Mr. Stanton."

"So what do you want to tell me?"

"I've my sources at Gettysburg," he whispered as he gripped the top of the turnstile gate. "On both sides. I don't want Mr. Stanton to know."

"What is it?"

"On the Confederate side, my sources say General Lee isn't well."

Chapter Twenty-Two

"I'm sorry to hear that."

"It's his heart," Welles said, leaning into Duff. "His appearance indicated a heart attack. If that's so, his judgment's impaired. He'll make mistakes. His decision to attack Little Round Top was disastrous. There's no question his decision to charge the center of the Union line today will be an unequivocal failure."

"So that's good for us, correct?"

"Not necessarily. My sources on our side tell me General Meade errs on the side of caution to the extent he won't pursue Lee when he retreats."

"That wouldn't be good."

"Your understatement is amusing," Welles said wryly. "You—we—will need a replacement for General Meade."

"Of course."

"Before Mr. Stanton makes his suggestion, I'd like to recommend General Grant."

"But he's mired in the Mississippi mud outside Vicksburg," Duff said. "And my sources tell me he's disappeared in the bottle."

"My sources," Welles said, shaking his head, "which I assure you are faster and more accurate, say Mrs. Grant arrived in camp, and the drinking stopped." His mouth went close to Duff's ear. "They also say he's close to a great victory. Vicksburg's capitulation may come as soon as tomorrow."

"Thank you for your information," Duff said, glancing over his shoulder to the second-story window, where Stanton still glared down upon them. "I'll consider your recommendation of General Grant most seriously—as I'll consider nominations from other Cabinet members."

"Don't let Stanton sway you." Welles grabbed Duff's arm. "He's one of that breed who believes it's impossible that he could be wrong, therefore any action he takes is justified."

"We all, at one time or another, have to fight such delusions," Duff said with a slight smile.

"If, sir, you're implying I'm suffering from that delusion," Welles said, pulling away from Duff, "you're wrong."

Deciding to allow prudence to prevail, Duff nodded and extended his hand. A moment passed before Welles took it. He turned abruptly, went through the turnstile, and walked down the path to the War

Department. Duff paused to look at the second-story window. Finding Stanton gone, he feared what waited for him back in his office. He climbed the service stairs, trying to compose his thoughts, and as he entered the second-floor hallway and passed through the etched glass panel into the office area, Duff heard Stanton instructing Hay.

"You may have your dinner hour now."

"But I've a couple of questions about my notes," Hay replied.

"I've a private appointment with the president which may last hours."

"Would you like for me to stay to take notes?"

"I said I want you to leave the building. I've been quite clear."

Duff detected a pause.

"Oh. Yes, sir."

Entering the office with all the casualness as he could feign, Duff smiled at them. "Ah, Mr. Stanton, you remembered my order to stay for a couple of hours." Taking pleasure from Stanton's pinched Cupid's bow lips, Duff winked at Hay and laughed. "I shouldn't be too hard on the old man."

Stanton's cheeks burned bright red, and Duff flung one of his long, gangling arms around Hay's shoulders. "I hope Secretary Stanton didn't try to boss you into forgoing your dinner to take notes on our strategy session."

"No, sir."

"That's good. I've noticed Mr. Stanton oversteps his authority by ordering around my personal staff." Duff laughed again. "You know, he reminds me of the barnyard cock who strutted around the hens, thinking his crowing made the sun rise."

As Hay chuckled, Duff pushed him out the door, firmly shutting it behind him.

"That," Stanton said in an angry whisper, "was totally uncalled for."

"Oh, I don't know," Duff replied. "I thought it sounded like something Mr. Lincoln would say." He sat behind the large oaken desk, hoping to hide his shaking leg.

"Yes, and you know where his arrogance got him."

"Mr. Stanton, a day doesn't go by that I don't think about Lincoln in the basement." He looked grave. "What do you want?"

"You know very well." Stanton walked to the desk, planting both fists on it. "What did Mr. Welles say to you?"

"That bewigged, doddering old fool? Merely gossip."

"Gossip? What kind of gossip?"

"The campaign in Vicksburg will end successfully, possibly today."

"And?"

"He wants Grant to replace Meade."

"Why replace the victor of Gettysburg?"

"Circumstances change quickly. Our record of changing generals suggests that trend will continue."

"You see-it's futile to keep a secret from me." He cocked his head to eye Duff. "You've another secret."

"Nothing serious." Duff stalled Stanton, thinking of some crumb to toss him, something to appease him, something somewhat related to the war—but not connected to Alethia.

"It's foolish to defy me. Spit it out."

"It's something Mr. Hay said. Don't blame him. He thought he was reporting it to the proper authority."

"What?"

"He came to my bedroom several months ago…"

"You waited to tell me?"

"I had my reasons. One being concern for your personal life."

Stanton took a step back.

"As I was saying, he visits me often late at night to share stories he's heard at some party. I didn't know social gossip interested you. Besides, it involves someone you know."

"Who?"

"Jean H. Davenport Lander."

"Don't believe gossip." He shuffled his feet. "I was between marriages when Jean and I—enjoyed each other's company. This was before she married Colonel Lander."

Duff gained confidence; for once, he held the upper hand. Smiling at Stanton, Duff was certain he saw beads of perspiration across his brow.

"Mr. Hay, it seems, talked to her at this party."

"Go on."

"She seemed concerned, he said, about a young Virginian she had met who boasted of a great, daredevil thing."

"A daredevil thing?"

"What if he were planning an assassination?"

"That's highly unlikely."

"I thought, how ironic if I were killed instead of Mr. Lincoln."

"Did she mention his name?"

"I don't know."

"If Mr. Hay mentions it again, tell me."

Before Duff responded, office messenger Tom Cross rapped softly at the door and opened it. He timidly stepped in, his eyes wide with apprehension.

"Yes, Tom. What is it?" Duff asked.

"We just received a message from the Soldiers' Home." He paused to swallow hard. "They want you to come immediately. Mrs. Lincoln's condition, it's worse. She's got a fever and is in and out of consciousness."

Chapter Twenty-Three

His pounding heart drowned out the horses' hooves as Duff's carriage bumped and clanged along the rocky path into the Maryland foothills to the Soldiers' Home. He sensed a cool breeze in his face, yet not cool enough to relieve the burning on the back of his neck. Alethia's gentle voice, the touch of her loving fingers, and her soft bosom on which he had laid his head and cried himself to sleep—they all were important to him now. The clopping slowed, and his eyes focused on Scott Dormitory, a large building filled with wounded and ill soldiers, and Anderson Cottage on the right. A smile flickered across Duff's broad, thick lips when he saw Tad waiting for him on Anderson Cottage's large, covered porch, outlined in white gingerbread trim.

"Is she going to be all right?" Tad whispered.

"I haven't seen her yet."

"I want her to be all right." He hugged Duff tightly around his waist. "I like her very much." His hands slid down Duff's backside. "Your butt's fatter than Papa's." Tad's eyes softened. "But it's a nice butt."

"Thank you, Tad."

"You better check up on her. Tell her I love her." Tad lowered his eyes and backed away.

Duff walked through Scott Dormitory's front door into a long ward of cots along each wall under wide, tall windows opened to allow the cool air of the foothills to filter in. Within seconds, soldiers struggled from their cots to stand or at least sit up to applaud as Duff ducked his head, trying to hide his cheeks flushed with embarrassment. A doctor rushed to him.

"Don't worry, Mr. President," he said pumping Duff's hand. "There have been complications, but I felt the wording of the telegraph was overly dramatic."

"Where is she?"

"In that small room." He pointed to a door at the end of the ward.

"Thank you." Duff stopped to talk to the men, patting their thin backs as he walked to the rear. One particular man with an arm missing lowered his head when Duff approached.

"I know I ain't the best lookin' man in the world," said Duff, "but it can't hurt your eyes too much to look at me."

"It ain't that, Mr. President. I'm ashamed."

"Ashamed of what? That you gave only one arm for your country?"

"We ran away." He rolled over.

"What?" Duff walked to the other side. "I didn't catch what you said."

"We ran. All of us. Like scared rabbits."

"Hmm." Duff thought of his own experience, and then touched the soldier's shuddering shoulder. "That reminds me of a story I heard back in New Salem. This boy and his girl were caught in an embarrassing situation by her father, who took umbrage—and a gun—to the boy. Well, he lit out down the road. As luck would have it, a rabbit was runnin' down the road. 'Git out of the road, old hare,' the boy says, 'and let somebody run that knows how.'"

Others laughed, and the soldier smiled and wiped tears from his eyes.

"We all run faster than the rabbit at one time or another," Duff said.

He rose and was about to enter the small room, when another soldier, older and more grizzled, intercepted him.

"I hope the missus is all right, Mr. President."

"The doc says she's on the mend."

"Don't take no offense, Mr. Lincoln, but if this accident had happened a year ago, no one would've much cared. But she's changed in her ways, and we noticed it. I mean no offense…"

"No offense taken," Duff said, trying to hide his pleasure that they cared more for the woman he loved than the woman she pretended to be. "You know, Mrs. Lincoln led a sheltered life before she married me. It took her awhile to get used to my backwoods ways."

"I knew you'd understand." He flashed a grin interrupted by large gaps between the brown teeth. "You're one of us. We're all praying for her."

"Thank you, sir." Duff liked talking with honest, rough men who were what he wished he had been.

Entering the small room, he was taken aback by how small Alethia looked in the bed, how fragile, with gauze wrapping the side of her head. She appeared asleep, but when he closed the door, she opened her eyes and smiled, her cheeks moist with perspiration.

"How's Tad? Was he upset he couldn't see me?"

"First words out of his mouth were about you. He's calm. He told me to say he loved you."

"He's such a dear boy." Her head relaxed on the damp pillow. "Even though he knows I'm not his mother, he loves me."

"He says I've a fat butt, but that's all right."

"Don't make me laugh. I've this frightful headache." She closed her eyes. "Is Mr. Forbes all right? They haven't told me anything since he wrecked the carriage. I overheard someone say the bolts had been loosened on the driver's seat." She sighed. "Someone's trying to kill you, Father."

"Can I get you anything?" Duff sat on the edge of the bed and patted her hand.

"Send Mrs. Keckley up here tomorrow. I hate to take the nurses away from the men. I know she won't mind waiting on me." Alethia paused. "She's so kind. I think she knows who I am—or rather, who I'm not—but she doesn't care."

"I thought you might like to read this," he said, pulling from his pocket Rose Greenhow's book and handing it to her. "*My Imprisonment and the First Year of Abolitionist Rule at Washington.*"

"Rose wrote a book!" Her eyes widened. "I didn't know she was out of prison."

"The book says she was released last fall to the Confederates. She went to London, found a publisher, and wrote her memoirs."

"I knew she could talk her way out of anything." Alethia opened the front page and squinted at the dedication. "To Alethia Haliday, our unknown hero who disappeared in Old Capitol Prison while in service to the Confederacy." Her mouth flew open. "There's my name!"

"Shush. Don't tell anyone." Duff smiled as he squeezed her hand.

"At least I know Rose is alive and well." Alethia smiled and squeezed his hand back, lifting it to her lips to kiss.

"Are you sure you're all right?"

"I'm sure." She paused. "Does Robert know?"

"I sent him a wire."

Touching her head, Alethia moaned.

"Let me get the doctor."

"No, not yet. I'm enjoying your company."

"Then I won't return to Washington tonight."

"With the nation celebrating a victory? You have to be there for the candlelight parade."

"You would've have been a wonderful politician's wife."

"Besides, Tom Pen wouldn't get to light the oval room window as you stand waving to the crowd. He'd be so disappointed." Her smile faded as she moaned again.

"I must get the doctor." Duff left the room and grabbed the first doctor he saw to have him attend to Alethia's head wound.

Back at Anderson Cottage, Tad waited, sitting on the floor, meticulously unraveling the rug, strand by strand. When he saw Duff, he jumped up and opened the screen door.

"Is she all right? Does she still have a fever?"

"Yes, the fever's returned, but it'll pass. She asked about you."

"She did? I'm glad."

"Do you want to go back to town with me? There's going to be a candlelight parade tonight."

"With bonfires?"

"I suppose."

"And Tom Pen's going to light the window with candles, and you and me can stand there waving to all the people?"

"Of course."

"Gee, I ain't stood in the lighted window with Papa—I mean, with—I ain't stood in the window since last July Fourth. There ain't been no big battles won since—in a long time."

"Yes, it's been a long time."

"She still ain't feeling good, is she?" Tad looked off at the long white barracks where Alethia lay, wracked with aches and fever.

"No, she isn't."

"It'd make her feel good if I stayed here and sat with her tonight, wouldn't it?"

"Yes, it would."

"There'll be other candlelight parades." He narrowed his eyes in deep thought and sighed. "The lady needs me right now."

"You're a good boy, Tad." Duff hugged him and bent down to whisper in his ear, "I'd be proud to have you as my own son."

"You better go now." Tad stepped back and rubbed his nose across his arm. "The people need you."

As Duff rode back, he thought about Alethia and Tad. His heart raced as he remembered the touch of her soft skin. The tenderness in her eyes raised hopes that she loved him as much as he loved her. But there were secrets, secrets, secrets—even the clanging of the carriage wheels pounded out the secrets, secrets, secrets. Duff smiled as he thought of how much Tad had matured in the last year. He had been inconsiderate, brash, and irresponsible, never thinking of others' feelings; now, he put aside his enjoyment of the street parade to comfort a woman he knew was not his mother.

Back at the Executive Mansion, with the sun already setting beyond the Potomac River, Duff listened for the impending march, pounding of drums, and crackling of torches down Pennsylvania Avenue. He looked forward to the parade, an event yet to be experienced, even though those around him thought he had experienced it before.

"The parade's turning the corner," Tom Pendel said. "The window's all prepared, sir. All the candles are lit."

Smiling at the white-haired doorman, he tried to find a stance that Lincoln would take. Duff breathed in deeply as Pendel pulled open the curtains, and breathed out in relief as he heard the roar of the crowd on the street. Feeling the warmth of the tall candle Pendel held just out of view at window's edge, Duff was briefly imbued with confidence, until he realized the candlelight lit his neck and chin, not his full face. Glancing down, he saw Pendel looking at the floor, his arm raised routinely high enough to illuminate Lincoln's face. Evidently, Duff realized in horror, he was slightly taller than the president. An awful moment of revelation passed slowly when Pendel's eyes moved up and he became aware the candlelight was in the wrong place. Quickly he raised the candle, but his eyes stayed fixed on Duff's face. Duff was flushed with terror. What would Pendel say? Several minutes passed with Duff waving to the crowd before it went down the street and turned toward the Mall, where a stack of old wood and trash waited to become a bonfire. As the lights dimmed from sight and the bonfire lit the evening sky, Duff turned to Pendel and forced a smile.

"Too bad Tad decided to stay at Anderson Cottage. He always liked the candlelight parades and bonfires."

"Yes, sir." Pendel kept his head down as he blew out the long candle.

Duff excused him and fled to his bedroom, where he threw off his clothes and put on his nightshirt. He did something he had not done in years. He fell on his knees, clasped his fingers together, and emitted moans from his heart only God could hear.

"Forgive me," Duff said in guttural tones from the bottom of his belly. "Forgive me for my sin, my secrets, and my many offenses."

"Father?"

Recognizing Robert Lincoln's voice, Duff stood, buttoned the top of his nightshirt, and turned, hoping Robert had not heard him.

"I heard what you were praying." Robert sounded uncertain.

"Robert, I thought you weren't coming home." Duff stood, grabbed the bedpost, and smiled. "Your mother's fine."

"No, she's worse. The train stopped at Anderson Cottage long enough for me to see her. She got worse after you left. Tad's there." He paused. "I know I haven't been as cooperative as I should." Robert's eyes went to the floor. "When I saw those bandages on Mother's head, I realized parents don't live forever."

"It's not all your fault, son. Sometimes, I'm sure, you feel I don't trust you enough to tell you the truth."

"You don't have to apologize, Father," Robert said. "I know you have to keep secrets from me, and I know you feel responsible for all the deaths in the war. God forgives you." He scrunched his face in pain. "But I need you to forgive me. Please forgive me." He stumbled toward Duff with his arms outstretched, pleading. As Duff hugged him, he burst into tears.

"I forgive you," Duff whispered, even though his mind wandered to Alethia and if she would forgive him if she knew his secrets, his deep, horrible secrets.

Chapter Twenty-Four

Gabby finished his supper with one ear tuned to the noise of the crowd on the street outside. Something mighty wonderful must have happened at Gettysburg. The first day's news brought by Stanton was not good. The rebels had gained ground outside of town. The second day went well, thanks to the boys from Maine. Gabby tried to remember if any of his West Point friends were from Maine, but his mind was clouded, and the only friend he could remember was Joe, and he was from New York, and he was dead. Gabby could not do anything about it, just as he could not do anything about the soldiers dying at Gettysburg. His eyes strayed to his shirt front, and now he cared more about the stray drops of gravy there; that way, his heart did not hurt so much.

The door opened, and Gabby hoped it was Adam. Maybe today would be the day he would think of the right things to say to make Adam stop being so gloomy all the time.

"I've the latest news from Gettysburg," Stanton said.

Gabby sagged and stared at his plate; he did not want to see Stanton. He did not like the man; more than that, he was scared of him.

"What is it?" Lincoln asked, scooting a chair from the billiards table and plopping down.

"Please say it's a victory," Mrs. Lincoln said.

"Total victory," Stanton replied. "The rebels attempted a foolhardy charge up a hill strongly manned by our forces, and they were decimated."

"Yes! Yes!" Lincoln said.

"Oh," Mrs. Lincoln murmured.

Gabby detected the compassion in her voice. Perhaps some of her Kentucky relatives were in the charge, but you cannot worry about relatives at war, he told himself. Uncle Sammy was fighting, but Gabby could not think about losing someone else close to him—first had been his kind father and second his friend Joe. Losing Uncle Sammy was too painful to comprehend.

"Bobby Lee's slipping," Lincoln said. "In his prime he would've never made such a strategic blunder."

"I know the Lees very well," Mrs. Lincoln added. "They're fine and genteel folk."

"Now, Mother, we're not talking about hosting a party, at which I'm sure they excel. We're talking about military tactics."

"Still, I can't glory in the death of any young man, be he from north or south."

"Yes, yes, of course, Mother," Lincoln replied. "War's terrible, but terrible battles end a war fast so no more men die."

Adam unlocked the door and entered.

"What are you doing here?" Stanton said in a huff.

"I—I came to get the dishes."

"Oh," Stanton said. "Get on with it."

Gabby heard the clattering of china against the wooden tray. Adam turned the corner into his little corner of the world.

"I'm sorry I didn't bring my plate out to you, but that man scares me," Gabby whispered.

"He scares me too."

"Don't be scared," Gabby said. "Don't be sad. Keep yourself cleaned up. You don't want to end up like me."

Adam patted Gabby's shoulder and then turned to leave. He shut the door quietly and locked it.

"So," Lincoln said. "Do we have General Lee in custody?"

"Um, no. They retreated across the border. General Meade said his men were tired, and so he felt it was enough to force the enemy from our soil."

A giant slap against the felt covering of the billiards table made Gabby jump.

"Father," Mrs. Lincoln said with a gentle gasp.

"Excuse me, Mother, but my patience is at an end. He has the audacity to hold us in the White House basement because I'm incompetent, but he lets Bobby Lee escape!"

"Sir, I share your anger that General Meade didn't pursue Lee, but it was his mistake and not mine."

"If I were still in control, this would have never happened!"

Lincoln's outburst was not very presidential, Gabby told himself. Squinting, once again he wrestled with the question of whether he was the president or not.

"On another front," Stanton continued, "General Grant will successfully conclude his siege of Vicksburg tomorrow."

"And who will Grant let slip through his fingers?" Lincoln sighed.

"No one, sir," Stanton replied.

"So. We do have a general who knows how to win battles the right way."

Stanton grunted.

"I want…" Lincoln paused. "I *recommend* you send for General Grant as soon as possible. He should take on Bobby Lee."

"He drinks too much," Stanton said.

"And you think too much of yourself, but that hasn't stopped you."

"Father."

Gabby heard the fear in Mrs. Lincoln's voice. She was right. Lincoln was out of control, but Gabby could not be harsh with him. Melancholia made people act queerly. Gabby should know. He had been acting queerly for years.

"You must forgive me." Lincoln sighed again. "Cabin fever, that's what it is. Did you ever have cabin fever, Mr. Stanton?"

"No, sir, I don't think I have."

"How about you, Mother, have you ever had cabin fever?"

"I'm having it right now."

After a pause, Lincoln spoke, now more composed.

"Do as you like, but I believe General Grant would head the Army of the Potomac effectively."

"Gideon Welles agrees with you."

"He told you that?"

"Not me. The man upstairs."

"God? When did you find time to speak to God?"

"The man upstairs, meaning your replacement." Stanton paused a moment. "You know what I meant."

"Of course, but I need a good laugh to get through the day, and if it can be at your expense, so much the better."

"I've had enough of this," Stanton replied, hardly containing his temper. "I'll take under consideration your opinion."

He walked to the door, stopped, taking a few steps to the side so he could see inside Gabby's little nook behind the crates and barrels. Gabby shuddered when he saw Stanton's beady eyes trained on him.

"By the way," he said to the Lincolns, "I regret to report we lost several generals at Gettysburg. Among them was General Samuel Zook."

Quickly leaving, Stanton locked the door.

A groan escaped Gabby's lips, and he sank to the floor. Mrs. Lincoln swept around the corner, dropped beside Gabby, and held his head in her arms.

"That wicked, wicked man," she said. "He did that on purpose to hurt you."

"Not Uncle Sammy. He was the successful one in the family. He was going to take care of us all. Who's going to take care of us now?"

"Evil, evil. Why would he treat you like that? You dear, sweet, gentle man. What did you do to him to be treated so shamefully?"

"First, Papa died, then Joe, and now Uncle Sammy. What's going to happen to me and Cordie? We can hardly take care of ourselves."

"When this awful war's over," Mrs. Lincoln continued, patting his head, "and Mr. Lincoln is in office again, things will change. That Mr. Stanton will pay for his evil ways. He cannot crush people and go unpunished."

"I wish Cordie was here." His soulful eyes, glistening with tears, looked up at Mrs. Lincoln. "Her bosom is nice and big and soft. I could sink my head into her bosom and be comforted. The Bible says a rod and staff is supposed to comfort you, but I don't think anything can comfort you better than a big, soft bosom."

Her eyes widening and her jaw falling, Mrs. Lincoln stuttered, "I—I think Mr. Lincoln could comfort you better than I. He always knows the right thing to say."

Standing, she bustled away. Gabby heard them fussing at each other for a few moments. Lincoln ambled around the crates and barrels, taking his time to sink to the floor and managing to cross his ungainly legs. He reached into his pocket and drew out a packet.

"Licorice?"

"Cordie says it makes my teeth look dirty."

"Mother says the same thing." Lincoln took a big chaw of it. "That's why I like to eat it. It gives us something to talk about. If you want to talk about something, we can." More silence ensued, punctuated by loud smacks and chews. "I don't have any appointments in my book for tonight."

"I thought the whole idea of sticking you in this room was to keep you from having appointments."

"It was a joke."

"Oh."

"I'm sorry you got involved in all this." Lincoln finished his licorice, took out his handkerchief, and wiped his mouth. "If you had laid your rat traps earlier, you'd have missed getting caught."

"Do you think the rebels killed Uncle Sammy?" Gabby asked as he looked into Lincoln's deep-set eyes. "Or did Mr. Stanton kill him because he thought me or Cordie might write him? If he did, then Cordie and me killed Uncle Sammy." Gabby's eyes filled to overflowing. "Honest, Mr. Lincoln, I never tried to write Uncle Sammy. I couldn't kill Uncle Sammy. I needed him to take care of me."

"Mr. Zook, you could hardly kill rats. You couldn't kill anybody. No. You didn't kill your uncle. War killed Samuel Zook. It's war, not you, nor I, nor Mr. Stanton. It's war's fault."

Gabby could not hold his tears back any longer. He flung his head into Lincoln's chest. He did not mind that it was bony. It was comforting, and that was all he needed.

Chapter Twenty-Five

Her large, watery blue eyes followed the flight of stairs, so far up, so steep, so forbidding. A deep sigh made its way through Cordie's pale, wrinkled lips. Too many dying boys, too much moaning, she fretted, as she took her first step to ascend the boardinghouse stairs. The day was not over yet, because Cordie had agreed to join Jessie and Adam at the candlelight parade.

Finally reaching the top floor, Cordie breathed deeply before opening her bedroom door. And those trousers, she thought to herself, they had to be mended. Adam brought her a pair from Gabby, and they had to be fixed so he would have something proper to wear. In the room, the bed beckoned to her, but Cordie resisted; her duty to Gabby came first, so she sat, turned on her kerosene lamp, and proceeded to stitch the crotch of her brother's worn blue pants.

Downstairs the front door opened, and Cordie heard Mrs. Surratt's strident voice pierce the silence. After a few harsh words with Mrs. Edwards, the landlady stomped up the stairs. Cordie steeled herself as the steps neared her door.

"I'm here for the rent. It's past due." Mrs. Surratt swung open the door after sharply knocking once. She stopped and glared at the trousers on Cordie's lap. "Those pants. Who do they belong to?"

"Gabby."

"Gabby? Who's Gabby?"

"My brother. He lives with me."

"He lives here?" Mrs. Surratt went to the armoire to open it to see a rack of men's rough shirts, a jacket, and another pair of slacks. "You mean he's been living here all this time, and you haven't paid his rent?"

"He hasn't been sleeping here for almost a year."

"Well, does he live here or not?"

"I guess not. But I always think of him and me living together. We help each other get by."

"Then where is he living?"

"I—I don't think I'm allowed to say." Her eyes fluttered.

"When it comes to cheating me out of rent money you have to tell."

"As long as it doesn't go any further…"

"Get on with it."

"The White House," she whispered. "He—he's the janitor."

"Those Republicans make him work day and night?"

"Yes." Cordie's eyes went down.

"Those Republicans make everyone's life miserable." Mrs. Surratt's face softened as she sat on the edge of the bed by Cordie's chair. "Where are you from, dear?"

"New York City."

"Ah, the gallant Irish. You know, they're rioting this very moment against the infamous draft." She smiled. "Were your parents from Ireland?"

"No," Cordie replied. "They were born here. My parents never talked about where their folks were from." She looked at Mrs. Surratt with curiosity. "Is Zook an Irish name?"

"I really don't know what kind of name Zook is. It could be Irish."

"Why do you care if I was Irish or not?" Cordie did not know why Mrs. Surratt's questions irritated. Perhaps it was because climbing all those stairs wore her out.

"Oh, I don't care, really. It's just I like the Irish, that's all."

"Why?" Cordie told herself not be so impatient with the woman. After all, she was making an attempt to be friendly.

"I suppose it's their religion," Mrs. Surratt replied in a flat tone.

"We weren't much of anything particular."

"Oh. We in Maryland follow the true faith, Roman Catholic. As do the Irish. The Irish in New York don't want to be forced to fight against the South. The Pope sees this as a holy war against the Roman Catholic church. The Northerners have no respect for the Pope."

"Papa was a lawyer. He defended all kinds of poor people, Irish Catholics, German Jews, Gypsies. He even defended a man who didn't believe in God at all."

"But your father did believe in God?"

"Yes."

"You're confusing me. What side are you on?"

"We're for the Union. Papa said slavery was wrong."

"Oh."

"My uncle, Samuel Zook, is a Union general."

"You know, my dear, this war isn't about slavery, but states' rights."

"Papa said states don't have rights; people have rights."

"As I was saying, this war's about freedom, about the right to worship as you please."

"Catholics get to go to church like anybody else," Cordie firmly said.

"It's obvious you've led a sheltered life. Religious intolerance surrounds us. You've only to open your eyes to see it." She looked away, noticing the half-finished Gabby quilt on the bed. "What's this?"

"A Gabby quilt. I used to make pretty ones, wedding ring, starbursts…"

"I loved to make starburst quilts. They sold well at the inn."

"Good quilts sell for good money. These old things don't go for much. The boys living here buy them. They don't know better."

"When my husband died, I didn't have time to make quilts anymore."

"Old age caught up with me. Then I started making these out of any old material I had around. These swatches are the last of Mama's dresses. Then you sew old socks into the squares and sew the squares together in no particular pattern. I call them Gabby quilts because Gabby likes them."

"I'm sorry I've been harsh with you." Mrs. Surratt looked fondly at her.

"Then you're not going to charge me for having Gabby's clothes here?"

"Of course not." She paused. "While your loyalty to your father and his Union sympathies is worthy, you must admit Mr. Lincoln does nothing to ease your financial woes."

"Gabby and I take care of ourselves."

"You know, the awful northern press paints a terribly unfair picture of the South and its sympathizers. We don't want to see any citizen suffer. A lady like you shouldn't have to worry about where the rent money is coming from each month."

"Between selling quilts and mending socks I can pay our bills." Cordie was becoming irritated by Mrs. Surratt's comments on money. It was not her business.

"But you must have enough for emergencies."

"What emergencies?" Cordie tried to sound pleasant.

"Why," Mrs. Surratt said, with a twinkle in her eyes, "when a daft old woman like me demands more money than she should."

"Oh." That did not make sense to Cordie, but she did not want to be rude and tell Mrs. Surratt that.

"I shouldn't tell you this, but I do so want to help you—in the spirit of the Confederacy, of course." Mrs. Surratt put her arm around Cordie's rounded shoulders. "My son John has very close contacts with the Confederate government, and therefore access to the Confederate treasury. I think I could intercede on your behalf to my son for money."

"I don't want charity." Cordie was becoming angry.

"Bless you, my dear. Of course you don't want charity. That's what's so wonderful about the Confederacy. It's willing to examine your situation to find out what you have that it could buy."

"What on earth would they want to buy from me?" Cordie narrowed her eyes.

"Information."

"I don't know anything." Cordie felt extremely uncomfortable with Mrs. Surratt's arm around her shoulders.

"You're so modest. How sweet. Your brother works at the White House. He sees things. He hears things. The Confederacy pays to learn those things."

"We won't be spies." Cordie stood; she had had enough.

"You're so innocent." Mrs. Surratt laughed. "It's quite appealing. They're playing word games with you. If they send people to

Richmond, they call it surveillance, but when we southerners seek the truth, they call us spies."

"It's still spying." Cordie turned her back to her. "I don't even talk to Gabby."

"Then how does he get his mending?"

"A White House soldier takes it," she said grudgingly.

"Is he young?"

"He's a private."

"Appeal to his maternal needs. He can tell you—"

"I'm not his mother." Cordie turned to look at her with steely eyes. "I'm not good at being devious."

"You disappoint me." Mrs. Surratt stiffened and stood. "On second thought, maybe I should charge you for your brother. After all, we're saving space for him here, aren't we? Space I could be renting to someone else."

"Charge more?" Cordie held her breath. Gabby was not bringing in his salary, so there was not enough to pay more rent.

"And you're selling these quilts. I didn't know that. You're making quite a living under my roof. I should charge more for that."

"I can't pay more," she whispered.

"Then you'll have to find another place to live, won't you?"

Washington boardinghouses were filled; no rooms were available. Everybody knew that. What would she do? Cordie worried, as tears filled her eyes.

"Of course, if you were a friend of the Confederacy and asked your soldier friend a few questions about the White House, perhaps I could reconsider."

"Very well." Cordie wiped her tear-stained cheeks. "I'll try."

"Bless you, my dear." Mrs. Surratt kissed Cordie's forehead. "You'll save many, many lives." Walking to the door, she turned to smile. "When will you see that dear young private?"

"Tonight. We're going to watch the parade. I'll give him Gabby's trousers."

"Good. Like I said, ask him a few questions."

"Yes, ma'am." Cordie hung her head as blankness covered her face.

"Thank you, my dear." Mrs. Surratt reached for her change purse. "You look exhausted. Here's money for the omnibus." She dropped a few coins in Cordie's hand. "There's more where that came from, if you do your job well."

As the door shut quietly, Cordie looked at the coins and sighed. Mrs. Surratt gave her only enough for the ride to the Executive Mansion and not back. Gathering her things together, Cordie left and, with apprehension, climbed on board the omnibus.

Chapter Twenty-Six

Walking down the Executive Mansion steps to Pennsylvania Avenue, Adam inhaled and exhaled deeply, thinking of Jessie. In the beginning, just the mention of her name had been enough to make his heart race and his spirits lift. Now he had to rely on a few gulps of whiskey. Pulling a flask from the pocket of his blue jacket, he popped the cap and lifted it to his mouth. The clanging of an omnibus caused him to jump and quickly cap the flask and return it to his pocket. Perhaps Jessie was on the bus, and he did not want her to see him drinking. She did not like it. He brushed aside his unruly red hair and smoothed out the wrinkles in his uniform. Standing on one foot, then the other, Adam eagerly waited for the omnibus doors to open. His heart sank when he saw Cordie appear. He wanted an evening alone with Jessie, but he forced a smile as Cordie walked toward him.

"I mended these pants for Gabby."

Her hands were trembling, Adam noticed. Perhaps she was tired. His spirits rose when he decided to suggest that she go back home to rest. He wanted time alone with Jessie.

"Of course, I'll give them to Mr. Gabby. You look very tired."

"I'm fine. Jessie wanted me here tonight."

"Oh."

"And how are you? Did you have a hard day?"

"It wasn't bad." Adam glanced down the avenue, hoping Jessie would appear.

"How's Gabby?"

"Very good. He's always eager to get his food."

"That's good. At least he's eating well." Her eyes went down. "I hope the war's over soon, then Gabby and I can be together."

"Yeah, I hope it's over soon," he said, distracted. He looked at Cordie. "Do you know why she's so late?"

"Don't ask me." Cordie laughed. "I don't know anything. You're the one in the White House. You must know more than me."

"Hmm." His attention was down the dark avenue.

"I bet you even know what happened at Gettysburg today."

"What?"

"I bet you know how many soldiers got killed; where the army's going next."

"Troop movement?" Adam shook off his distraction to focus on her. "Casualty numbers? Why would you want to know that?"

"I don't want to know." Her eyes fluttered. "I was just saying you must know."

"You've never asked questions like this before."

"I was just making conversation."

Her hands trembled more, making Adam think something was wrong.

"People don't make casual conversation about troop movements," Adam said.

"I don't know what you're talking about. I didn't even say that. I only asked about your day."

"No. You asked where the Union army was going next."

"I didn't ask anything. I never asked a question." Cordie's voice rose to a high pitch. "I said I bet you knew where the Union soldiers were going next. That's all."

"Don't try to play games with me. I like you, Miss Zook, but I think you're up to something bad." Adam heard his voice, but did not recognize it, which frightened him. "Who put you up to this? I know you. You wouldn't do anything like this on your own."

"No one put me up to it!"

"Was it a Confederate spy?"

"She's not a spy."

"She? Who's she?"

"Nobody! I—I didn't say anything about a woman." Her voice began to crack.

"Don't lie to me." Adam stared into Cordie's watery eyes until she looked down at the hard dirt street. "Who is she?" He took her chin and lifted her face.

"My landlady." She averted her eyes again. "She forced me to tell her about Gabby. And she wanted more information."

"Did she give you money?"

"Enough for the omnibus," she whispered.

"More to come later?"

"Only if I could find things out."

"Are you that bad off?" Adam softened the tone of his voice. "If you needed money, I could have gotten some for you."

"She was going to raise my rent." Cordie took a handkerchief from her pocket to daub her cheeks. "She was going to put me out on the street."

"You didn't want to tell her anything?"

"No. But she scared me, just like you're scaring me now."

"I'm sorry."

"Could you make something up for me to tell her, so she won't raise my rent?"

"I don't know enough to make up a good lie." Adam ran his hand through his coarse red hair. "Tell her I'm a mean cuss who won't tell you anything. Tell her it might take months to soften me up. By then, maybe the war will be over."

"Thank you." Her eyes focused on the trousers stuck under his arm. "Make sure Gabby gets his pants." She sighed. "I'm tired, but I don't want to disappoint Jessie."

"You don't have to stay," Adam said hoarsely.

"Are you sure?"

"Yes," he whispered. "Here's omnibus fare." He held coins out to her.

Cordie looked as though she were about to decline his offer, but instead smiled and took the money.

"Thank you. Tell Jessie I'll see her tomorrow." She walked toward an approaching omnibus.

Adam's heart raced as he watched Cordie's iron trolley disappear into the night. He jumped when he felt fingers tapping his shoulder.

"What are ye lookin' for, me pretty soldier boy? Jessie asked.

"I was looking for you, Miss Home." Adam turned and grinned.

"Ye was lookin' down the wrong lane, me darlin'." Jessie squinted and rubbed her gloved fingers along his unshorn cheek. "And what kind of military mission are ye on, Adam Christy, that ye can go days with shavin' that wonderful face?"

"They don't seem to care much."

"And ye don't seem to care much, either."

Looking away, Adam could not find answer to her observation.

"I wonder where Miss Cordie is," Jessie said. "She's late for the parade."

"She's already been here." Adam held up the folded trousers. "She gave me these pants for her brother. When she said how tired she was, I told her to go home to rest. I told her you would understand."

"Hmm." Jessie narrowed her eyes. "How lucky for ye, me laddie. Now we don't have a chaperone, do we?"

"Pretty soon," Adam said, smiling nervously, "we'll have ten thousand chaperones, all around us."

"Oh. Well." Jessie laughed. "As long as you put it like that." She pointed to the trousers. "Shouldn't ye take those pants inside to Mr. Gabby?"

"Oh." Adam glanced toward the Executive Mansion. "I think I hear the parade coming. I wouldn't have time. Mr. Gabby always wants to talk. It'd take too much time." He shuffled his feet and ran his fingers through his red hair. "Gosh darn it, I don't want to lose any time with you."

"A cursin' man, are ye?" She laughed. "Well, we wouldn't want to provoke another such outburst."

Before Adam could reply, the crowd arrived. Many carried torches; others had drums, and a few banged pots and kettles with wooden spoons. He looked up to a second-story window and pointed. "The president stands in that window—see, the one that's lit with candles."

As the crowds jostled them, the curtains opened, revealing Duff.

"See there," Jessie said, pointing. "Look, the light is on his Adam's apple."

Adam looked up to see the candle move from the neck to Duff's face.

"Isn't it glorious, Miss Home?" a voice behind them asked.

Chapter Twenty-Six

Adam turned to see a middle-aged man wearing a wide-brimmed hat.

"A monumental movement of humanity, jointed by joy and patriotism."

"Yes, Mr. Whitman," Jessie said. "'Tis good to see people happy. Too much sadness surrounds us today."

"Well, aren't you a handsome, strapping soldier?" He appraised Adam and then turned to Jessie. "Are you two courting? I hope so. Your progeny would be beautiful, red-haired demigods, worthy of loud huzzahs."

"No, we're just good friends." Jessie's eyes fluttered.

"Where are you going now?" he asked. "I'm going to follow the crowd, wherever it may go. Perhaps I'll find myself drinking and singing with a group of soldiers as dashing as your friend."

"We're going to supper," Adam impulsively said.

"Very well. Enjoy." He disappeared in the crowd which was fading into the darkness.

"Who was that?"

"A poet and a nurse. One of the noblest creatures I've ever seen. He's the first one there in the mornin', checkin' for the dead, to remove them to make room for the newly wounded. I've seen him obey young men about to die, tellin' him to pin their socks together and crossin' their arms across their thin chests, all the while tears rollin' down his cheeks."

"And he's very smart," Adam added as he and Jessie turned to walk down the street. "He said we should be courting. Maybe while we eat we could talk about that some more."

"Ye think so, do ye?" Jessie laughed. Rubbing his cheek, she added, "If I'm to be your girlfriend, ye have to look your best. Ye want to look your best for me, don't ye?"

The world cannot be all bad if red-haired angels are here, Adam decided; he smiled and nodded.

Chapter Twenty-Seven

Duff's mouth went dry as Stanton told him he was to deliver a short address at the dedication of the cemetery at Gettysburg. Four months after the battle, the war dead were being memorialized. Duff Read, private citizen, had never spoken in public; as Abraham Lincoln, he must speak as a seasoned orator.

"Do I have to do this?"

"Yes," Stanton replied. "Don't blame me. I don't want you talking in front of reporters."

"Then why do I have to go?"

"Because David Wells of the Gettysburg Cemetery Association asked. Ward Lamon suggested it and managed to have himself named procession grand marshal."

"What will I say?"

"Lincoln will write the speech."

The day arrived, and riding the train to Gettysburg with Duff were Hay and Nicolay, Lamon, and Cabinet members Seward, Blair, and Usher. The new treasurer, Francis E. Spinner, refused to attend, saying, "Let the dead bury the dead." Stanton also declined to go. Reading the speech as he sat in the rail car, Duff noticed it was short, and smiled. When they arrived at the Gettysburg station, Seward spoke to the crowd. The next morning they proceeded, with Lamon, exuberantly waving to the people on the roadside, leading the way to the new cemetery, where Duff waited through Edward Everett's two-hour oration. When time came for Duff to speak, he stood on wobbly legs and tried to find his voice as he stared out on the assembly. A photographer set up his camera.

The words were good, sturdy, Anglo-Saxon words with depth and meaning, yet when he tried to give them voice, Duff choked. Taking a sip of water, he began Lincoln's speech, though softly and without much projection, so that when he had finished, half of those attending did not know he had begun. A photographer's flash caught him just as he returned to his seat.

Afterwards, most of the reporters seemed interested in getting a copy of Edward Everett's speech; however, a few did request Lincoln's address, which Duff obliged by handing out copies Stanton had provided. Stanton insisted he tell them the original had been composed on the back of an envelope. If this were true, Duff did not know; but Stanton swore the shred of information was the stuff that history was made of.

On the train back the next morning, Duff sat alone watching Seward, Blair, and Usher dictating letters to their secretaries. His secretaries were laughing at Lamon, who was singing and dancing.

"All the grand ladies who live in big cities…"

Hay laughed out loud at the rhyming end of the next line, while Nicolay smiled and shook his head.

"Mr. Lincoln did well on his speech, didn't he, John?" Lamon asked, huffing after his dance.

"*Ja*," Nicolay said. "The president did quite well."

With that reply, Lamon laughed and danced a few more irregular steps before concentrating on Hay.

"Johnny, how would you compare today's speech to those Mr. Lincoln made on the campaign stump back in Illinois?"

"I haven't noticed." Hay looked up, wide-eyed.

Again Lamon laughed and jigged his way to sit next to Duff. Lamon slapped him on the knee.

"Well, Mr. Lincoln," Lamon loudly said, "you did yourself proud, sir."

"I don't know," Duff replied in a mumble. "No one seemed much impressed."

"They will." Lamon leaned into him to whisper, "Modesty is a good touch. My friend would have been reticent, too."

Duff's eyes roamed out the train window to see crowds gathered by the tracks.

"You should let the people see you," Lamon said loudly. "Wave to them. They love you."

Standing, Duff leaned out the window to wave with his right hand, while resting his left hand on the sill. Soon he was aware Lamon's hand was on top his.

"Say nothing," he advised under his breath, "and continue to wave. I'll ask you questions, and you'll respond by making a fist under my palm for yes. If the answer is no, flatten it."

Duff quaked inside: one of his terrible secrets was that he was innately a coward.

"Is this plan really the idea of Mr. Stanton?"

He could not make his hand move. Lamon lifted his weight from it, making it easy for Duff to make a fist if he wanted to.

"Is Mr. Stanton acting on the orders of Mr. Lincoln?"

His fingers quickly went to a fist, as though if he hesitated he would not have the ability to lie.

"So Mr. Lincoln is not being held against his will?"

Duff's hand went flat, and he hated himself for it.

"Are you afraid?"

His hand stayed flat, but it shook. Lamon patted it.

"Wave to the people, Mr. President."

Chapter Twenty-Eight

Cordie awoke early, went downstairs to the kitchen to have a cup of coffee and a muffin with Mrs. Edmonds, solicited sewing jobs from other boarders, and asked if anyone wanted a nice, sturdy, plain quilt, cheap. After gathering several pairs of socks to darn, Cordie slowly climbed the steps. She had to finish her mending by noon, so she could volunteer at Armory Square Hospital. Every morning was similar: busy, hectic, and tense. She never knew when Mrs. Surratt would appear and demand information from the Executive Mansion. Her chest was beginning to hurt, but she decided it was just a bellyache and chose to ignore it. Settling in her chair by the window, she jumped when she heard a forceful knock at the door. Only Mrs. Surratt knocked that hard.

"Miss Cordie? Are you there?"

"Yes, Mrs. Surratt," Cordie replied. "Come in."

She shuddered as the door opened and the landlady came in, her hands cupped together, a smile cemented to her face and her eyes hardened with determination.

"Isn't it a beautiful November morning, Miss Cordie?"

"Yes, ma'am, very nice." She kept her eyes on her darning.

"May I sit on your bed?"

"Of course, ma'am."

"Thank you." Mrs. Surratt sat primly on the edge of the mattress, her back stiff. "Have you heard from your brother lately, dear?"

"Yes. He's doing quite well, thank you."

"And the young man, the private. How is he?"

"Very well, too, ma'am." Before she knew it, she was blathering. "He has a new spring to his step. Keeping himself groomed, clothes washed."

"It's very rude not to look at people when they talk to you, dear."

"Yes, ma'am. I'm sorry, ma'am." Cordie looked up, her eyes beginning to well with tears.

"You mustn't sound so contrite," Mrs. Surratt said. "After all, we are comrades in the good fight." She looked into Cordie's eyes. "And there's no need to cry. You start to cry every time I visit you."

"I—I don't have anything to say," Cordie whispered. "I don't want to be put out in the street."

"That young man is still being uncooperative? After all these months?"

"Yes, ma'am." She fought the urge to return her eyes to her darning.

"That's a Yankee for you. Never thinking of others."

"He's very considerate. He's nice to me. And to his lady friend, Miss Home. But then we're nice to him. I mean, I don't mean you're not nice, ma'am."

"I swear, if you call me ma'am one more time…" she said lightly, then paused to laugh. "I shouldn't say such things. You take them so seriously. So what are we going to do about this situation?"

"I don't know, Mrs. Surratt," Cordie said. "He doesn't seem like he's going to change. Maybe he doesn't know anything to tell."

"Hmm." Mrs. Surratt opened her hands, revealing several gold coins. "I think I have another way the Confederacy can help you."

Looking over, Cordie saw the coins, and her eyes widened.

"What do I have to do for that?" she asked, thinking she could never do anything wicked enough to earn that much money.

"Oh, dear me." Mrs. Surratt laughed. "This isn't for you. Your reward is staying here. These coins are for our gallant men in Virginia."

"I—I don't understand."

"Downstairs I have two dresses, and you will sew the coins into the hems," she explained. "Tightly, so no one can hear them as the ladies move around."

"I'm busy with my darning."

Mrs. Surratt took the torn socks.

"What do we have here? Oh. These can wait," she said, tossing them to the floor.

"But the boy needs them..."

"I don't care what the boy needs." She stood and put the coins in Cordie's lap. "I'll bring the dresses right up."

"This doesn't sound right."

"Some terribly sweet lady friends of mine wish to wear these skirts when they take a leisurely carriage ride through the Virginia countryside tomorrow morning. What is wrong with that?"

Cordie sighed deeply, causing Mrs. Surratt to put her hands on her hips.

"Now what?"

"It's just that..." Cordie searched for the right words. "I feel guilty."

"You feel guilty?" Mrs. Surratt took a deep breath. "It's the damnyankees who should feel guilty!"

"I wish you wouldn't use that word," Cordie said softly, looking down. "I'm a Yankee."

"Haven't I told you how they've burned whole towns?"

"Yes, ma'am."

"Taken livestock, food, left our people to starve?"

"Yes, you've told me."

"Do you think I'm lying?" Mrs. Surratt's eyes narrowed. "Am I not a woman of honor? Am I not letting you stay in my boardinghouse?"

"You said I can stay in your boardinghouse only if I sew the coins in the dresses."

"I didn't put it that crudely," Mrs. Surratt said with a sniff, "but it's a reason for you not to feel guilty then, isn't it?"

Chapter Twenty-Nine

Late April found the capital drenched in an eternal cold, tingling drizzle. Duff, well into the second year of pretending to be Abraham Lincoln, stared out of his office window at the people running through the rain, trying to jump around mud holes. In many ways, he felt content with his life as husband to Alethia, though he had not found the courage to consummate their love, fearing the intimacy would require that he reveal his secrets to her. He liked Tad better each day, and enjoyed his contact with the Cabinet members. On the other hand, Duff hated himself for lying to Lamon, for fearing Stanton, and for allowing the Lincolns to waste away in the basement.

"Mr. President, Mr. Stanton is here to see you." Hay broke Duff's trance with his announcement.

"Very well."

Hay stepped aside to allow Stanton, wheezing and coughing, to enter. After Hay closed the door, Stanton sat and wiped his mouth with a handkerchief.

"Have you seen your doctor?"

"Yes, this morning." A hacking cough erupted. "Damn asthma. Damn nuisance."

"You should take to your bed."

"That's what my doctor said." He looked up at Duff. "You'd like that, wouldn't you? You'd have Ward Lamon here and tell him the whole story."

"How do you know I haven't already told him?"

"Because Lamon hasn't stormed the building." Stanton coughed. "And because you know if Lincoln's freed now, you'll return to prison to hang."

"Maybe not."

"I don't think you're willing to take the chance."

"In any case, you're not willing to give me the chance."

Stanton laughed and coughed at the same time. Putting his head in his hands, he continued, "The newspapers are responding well to the news that General Grant has been named head of the Army of the Potomac. He's taken control of the troops, and they seem to be responding favorably to him. In the next few days, you should send a series of letters to him, reiterating your support."

"Anything else?"

"I'll let you know." Stanton stood. "I'm going home, but I've instructed Private Christy to spend more time with you in the office. After all, he is your adjutant."

"Yes, sir."

"He'll be here in a few minutes." Stanton turned for the door. "I'll return this evening, with news from the telegraph room."

How he loathed the man, Duff thought as he returned his gaze to the rain outside his window.

"Mr. President?" Hay hesitantly asked as he stepped into the office. "May I have a word with you?"

Duff nodded. Hay looked back before he closed the door.

"I think I should mention something, but you may not want to hear it."

Stiffening, Duff remained silent but motioned for Hay to sit.

"Mr. President," Hay began with his eyes down, "as you know, I enjoy my night life, going to bars late into the evening. Often I hear gossip, and I dismiss it as gossip, but recently soldiers, many of them recently released from army hospitals, were complaining about lack of medical supplies."

"We're funding the military as well as we can," Duff replied.

"They aren't blaming you or Congress. It's Mr. Stanton."

"It's gossip."

"They say you were going to fire him—back in sixty-two." Hay stressed the year, cocking his head.

"Have you heard the one that Mrs. Lincoln's a Southern spy? Not only that, she stole my State of the Union address and sold it to the newspapers. Best of all is the story that I'm totally insane."

"You haven't been yourself for almost two years," Hay whispered. He looked startled and then dropped his head. "I'm sorry. I shouldn't have said that."

Duff did not know whether to be relieved or threatened. Hay knew. If he knew, Nicolay knew, yet they had said nothing all this time. Wondering why Hay had chosen this time to approach, Duff put his hand to his mouth; perhaps, he thought, the asthma outbreak had weakened Stanton's position. Maybe it had. Maybe this was the time. Duff leaned forward in his chair. A knock interrupted him.

"Yes?"

"It's me, sir, Private Christy." Adam paused at the door. "Mr. Stanton told me you needed me."

For a moment Duff made eye contact with Hay, then decided the opportunity had passed.

"Come in, Private."

Adam entered, and Duff was impressed. He looked sharp in his uniform. Maybe he was filling it out, too. His eyes no longer looked glazed over.

"What do you need, Mr. President?"

"A letter delivered to the War Department," Duff said, watching Hay slump back in his chair. "For General Grant. Ready for dictation, Mr. Hay?"

"Yes, sir." Hay pulled a pad and pencil from his pocket.

"Dear General Grant…"

Duff leaned back in his chair and tried to think of the right words to say while he watched Adam's eyes wander out the window and a smile land softly on his lips.

"I want to take this occasion to express my confidence…"

Adam was in love, Duff decided. He had been young once. He remembered how it felt. He knew how it felt even now when Alethia walked into the room. Did love make his intolerable job tolerable? Duff wondered. Perhaps, because love gave hope, and hope meant there was going to be a tomorrow.

"Reports say the troops are responding well to your leadership…"

And what kept Hay going? Duff thought, as he switched his attention to his secretary. He did not believe Hay was in love, except for his love of life. Maybe that is what gave him the courage to speak the unspeakable and the hope for something better.

"Please feel free to correspond with me any time…"

And what kept him going? Duff asked himself. Was it love, hope, or pure, simple fear that he would be discovered; his cowardice and his evil desperation, all of it exposed to the world for condemnation. As long as he lied and walked the tightrope of deception, his world would continue.

"Best wishes, A. Lincoln."

Duff turned to look out of the window.

"That will be all, gentlemen."

Hay and Adam left, and after they shut the door, Duff choked back tears. This was torture, but he was afraid the torture would end.

The torture did not end. Days extended into weeks. May arrived, the rain continued, and Duff again heard Stanton coughing.

"The news is not good from Chancellorsville," Stanton said, wiping spit from his chin.

"What is it?"

"Grant has engaged Lee in a forest called the Wilderness."

"That's what we wanted, isn't it?"

"Heavy losses." Stanton coughed again.

"So you're going to replace Grant?"

"I don't know." He leaned back in the chair and moaned. "I haven't seen Lincoln yet."

"What?"

Stanton sat up and coughed. "I haven't given it much thought yet."

"You talk to…" Duff paused to look at the door behind Stanton. "You go to the basement?"

"It's not your concern." Stanton straightened his shoulders. "You will be informed of our—my decision eventually."

"Oh." Duff tried not to smile.

The next morning Stanton announced to him that he had decided to stay the course with General Grant.

"Grant's determination will prevail in the end, like the little dog hanging on to the traveling salesman's trouser leg," Stanton said, acting a little delirious. "We'll stay out of Grant's way."

"Very astute," Duff replied.

In another few days, Stanton relayed news of a devastating defeat at Spotsylvania.

"Perhaps I should write a letter of encouragement to General Grant," Duff said.

"Yes," Stanton replied, pursing his Cupid's bow lips.

On the last day of May 1864, the rain finally stopped, and Duff walked out of the Executive Mansion to the turnstile on his way to the War Department, wanting to find out details on the battle at Cold Harbor. Stanton was suffering from another hacking asthma attack in Duff's office. Deep in his heart, Duff wished Stanton would stop coughing and just die. Looking up, Duff found Lamon blocking the turnstile.

"Mr. President."

"I was on my way to the War Department telegraph office."

"Yes. It doesn't look good."

"We're staying the course." Duff's eyes went to the ground. "With Grant."

"I can see you're staying the course." Lamon paused. "Where's Stanton?"

"In my office. Wrestling with his asthma."

"He's still sick?"

"Yes."

"Maybe he'll die."

"Maybe." Duff looked up.

Lamon laughed as he stepped out of the way to let Duff go through the turnstile.

"I'm here when you need me, Mr. President."

"Thank you."

Lamon stopped the turnstile, blocking Duff in the gate. He looked deep into Duff's eyes for a long moment and then leaned in close.

"I can't help if you lie to me."

Chapter Thirty

Ward Lamon knew the double was lying; Abraham Lincoln never hid from his enemies. Edwin Stanton had put the president somewhere and replaced him with this fellow who was a very bad liar. Nicolay and Hay knew Lincoln was gone, but he did not think they knew where he was. The private was the linchpin, but Lamon could not get to him. He was everywhere, yet nowhere, and no one would help.

Once or twice, while in the president's office, he saw the red-haired private walk by.

"Who's that?" he had asked the double.

"My adjutant, Private Adam Christy."

"Where is he going?"

"About his duties."

Questioning Nicolay and Hay had not been any more helpful; once Lamon had talked to Tad about him.

"He's only a private. We used to have a lieutenant."

"Yeah. Too bad. Where does he come from?"

"He told me, but I forgot."

"Does he know where your papa is?"

Tad looked at him quizzically. "Are you in on it?"

"In on what?"

"If you have to ask, then you're not."

"Oh, you mean 'it,'" Lamon said, trying to trick the boy.

"You're pulling my leg now."

"No, I'm not." Lamon became flustered.

"I gotta go." Tad ran down the hall and down the stairs.

Skulking away from the Executive Mansion garden after blocking the double at the turnstile, Lamon tried to figure out why Tad did not want to tell him if Private Adam Christy knew the whereabouts of his parents. The "it" was the switch of presidents, which Tad was in on, but obviously the boy thought his father was in charge. Throughout the afternoon, as he sat in his office reading, as district marshal, reports of spies in the capital, Lamon's mind dwelled on the almost two years that had passed since Lincoln had disappeared, and felt stupid, first for having just accepted what Stanton had told him, and second, for not figuring out why Lincoln was missing and where he was.

As evening approached, he sighed and went to a small restaurant to eat. As he was seated and began sipping a beer, his eyes focused across the room on a young couple, both red-haired, the man in a blue, rumpled private's uniform. His back was to Lamon, who could not decide if this was the elusive presidential adjutant. When the waiter came up, the private turned his head, and Lamon saw that it was Adam. After the waiter left, he went to the table. The girl, young and vivacious, saw him first and smiled, but when Adam looked up, his face sobered.

"Mr. Lamon," Adam said as he stood and extended his hand. "We've yet to meet. Always just missing each other." He turned to the girl. "Jessie, this is Mr. Lincoln's personal bodyguard, Ward Lamon. He's also the district marshal."

"Pleased to meet ye, Mr. Lamon."

"Nice meeting you, Miss…"

"Home," Adam supplied.

"Miss Home." Lamon smiled. "Do you work in the White House too?"

"No," Adam interrupted. "She volunteers at Armory Square Hospital." He looked at Lamon. "Is there a problem with the president?"

"I don't know," he replied, his smile disappearing. "I was hoping you could tell me."

"I have to go powder me nose, gentlemen," Jessie said, standing. "I'll let ye talk business in private." Before they could reply, she had disappeared into the crowd.

"Sit," Adam told him as he took his own seat.

"Very pretty young lady," Lamon remarked, sitting. "How did you meet?"

"Through mutual friends."

"Oh, might I know them?"

"What do you want to ask about Mr. Lincoln?" Adam asked, sipping his coffee.

"Where is he?"

"Retired to his bedroom, I suppose."

"No, I mean the real Mr. Lincoln."

"I only know of one Mr. Lincoln." Adam stared into Lamon's eyes.

"When did you start working at the White House?"

"September of sixty-two; why?"

"It was about that time that Mr. Lincoln grew half an inch."

"I wouldn't know anything about that." Adam sipped his coffee again. "I just do what I'm told to do."

"You stay busy, don't you?"

"Yes, I do."

"But not always on the second floor."

"That's true." Again Adam stared at Lamon. "The Lincolns have me doing chores all over the place." After a pause, he asked, "Mr. Lamon, what do you want?"

"Well," Lamon replied with a small laugh, "I think it's like finding out if you know the same secret I do without telling the secret, if that makes any sense."

"What secret?"

Lamon looked deep into Adam's face, his eyes, his mouth, trying to detect some nervous tic which would let him know if the boy was lying to him.

"That's a pretty good job for a private to get, presidential adjutant," Lamon said, deciding to go in another direction. "How did you get it?"

"Mr. Stanton." Adam looked down at his plate and pushed string beans around with his fork. "He's from my home town. My father grew up with him." He looked up with a smile. "Sometime, when we can spare a few hours, I'll have to tell you some funny stories about him."

"Well, I don't care for Mr. Stanton much."

"Neither do I." He speared some beans and put them in his mouth.

"Do you know why Mr. Stanton picked you for such an important job?"

"Like I said, he knows my family."

"Hmm. Tad's a handful, isn't he?"

"Yes, sir."

"Does he ever tell you things?"

"Mr. Pendel is his main playmate." Adam sipped his coffee. "He doesn't like the fact I'm only a private and not a lieutenant."

"So you must really like your job."

Adam stopped and swallowed hard. Lamon thought he detected a tic in his left eye, and then Adam smiled and stood. "Jessie."

Looking around to see her walking back, a twinkle in her eyes for Adam.

"So, did me darlin' tell you what you needed to know about Mr. Lincoln?"

"I don't know." Lamon stared at Adam's face. The tic vanished, if it had been there in the first place.

Chapter Thirty-One

A miracle occurred one early August morning, 1864, in a corner of the billiards room in the basement of the Executive Mansion. Gabby awoke refreshed and clear-minded. This day, reality embraced his brain like an old friend. To maintain emotional stability, he knew he had to stay busy, sweeping floors, dusting, anything to keep his mind occupied. Standing, Gabby subconsciously straightened his shoulders and walked out to the billiards table, where Mrs. Lincoln sat brushing her hair. When her eyes caught sight of him, she stopped in mid-stroke.

"Mr. Gabby, you seem different somehow."

"Thank you, ma'am." He bowed. "I feel particularly refreshed."

"I pray you remain refreshed." She smiled.

"I appreciate your concern." Gabby glanced at the curtained corner where Lincoln still slept. "If you wish, I could move your chamber pots to the door. It'd be much more pleasant for you that way."

Mrs. Lincoln appeared to ready to say something, but her mouth stayed agape with no words coming out. Keys rattling broke the silence, and Adam entered. This situation would not end well for the boy, Gabby reflected. Stanton could not be trusted to keep promises. His impulse was to tell Adam to leave, this very hour, to go out west where the government could not find him, but he knew the boy would ignore him.

"Breakfast!" He walked to Adam to help him with the tray.

"Here, Private Christy, I can help too," Mrs. Lincoln said.

"Thank you, Mr. Gabby; Mrs. Lincoln," he replied with a smile. Taking the chamber pots, he left.

"Mr. Lincoln will want his usual apple and milk. I somehow don't feel like a double helping of eggs."

"Yes, Mr.—Zook—I think you're right." She took the tray and placed it on the billiards table. "You may have your breakfast at the table if you like."

"I'd appreciate that."

As they began to eat, Gabby noticed he was sitting aright, his left hand in his lap and his right hand delivering proper amounts of egg to his mouth.

"I apologize for anything I've done or said that was improper."

"Why, thank you." She sighed. "And I apologize for my behavior."

Gabby slowly chewed, swallowed, and smiled. "Thank you."

They ate in silence.

"Mr. Zook," Mrs. Lincoln said, "do you think this—this clarity will last?"

"I don't know," Gabby whispered. "I hope so." He paused. "I fear it won't." He looked into her eyes. "I don't want to go back to thinking I'm president."

"At times you thought you were president?" Mrs. Lincoln leaned forward.

"Unfortunately, yes." Gabby looked at the remnants of egg. "Mrs. Lincoln, if at any time I express that delusion, please pity me and ignore it."

Before she could reply, Adam returned with cleaned chamber pots. Gabby stood and took the pots from him. Lincoln came out, stretched, went to the tray, and picked up the apple and bit into it.

"Good morning, Private Christy; Mr. Gabby."

"It's Mr. Zook," Mrs. Lincoln said, correcting him.

"Mr. Zook." Lincoln looked at Gabby's posture and clear eyes. He cocked his head. "Yes; Mr. Zook."

Gabby took the pots and placed them in their respective places. Stacking the plates on the tray, he turned to Adam.

"Is there anything else I can do for you this morning?"

"No, thank you," he replied. "Anything I can bring you, Mr. Lincoln?"

"Nothing, Private," Lincoln said. "Thank you."

Gabby enjoyed the structured line of conversation he had initiated. Efficiency, courtesy, flourished in routine, a lesson Gabby had learned at West Point. He frowned; he did not what to think about West Point. Negative emotions sapped his mental energy.

Everyone looked to the door as it was unlocked. Stanton entered. Adam lowered his head, took the tray, and left quickly. Mrs. Lincoln stiffened and went behind her French lace curtains, and Lincoln stopped eating his apple. Gabby could feel the tension rise in the room. He found the broom to begin sweeping.

"I thought you might be interested in General Grant's latest plans," Stanton said as he sat, motioning to Lincoln to do the same. "General Grant's in favor of multiple large attacks on the Confederacy to destroy rail lines." He pulled out a notepad, put on his glasses, and began to read. "Banks's forces at New Orleans will move east to Mobile, then on to Georgia; Sherman will advance on Atlanta and then to the coast; and Grant's army to Suffolk, Virginia, and then to Raleigh, North Carolina." He paused to glare at Gabby, who was at his shoulder. "Must he be hovering?"

"He's not hovering; he's sweeping."

"As I was saying, Grant thinks the enemy would be forced to evacuate Virginia and East Tennessee."

"What do you think, Mr. Zook?"

"I think if General Grant moves to North Carolina," Gabby said, keeping his eyes on the floor, "he'll leave the capital unprotected."

"Thank you, Mr. Zook," Lincoln said. "I agree."

"I'm not defending the proposal; I'm merely relaying it to you."

Stanton stared at him.

"Very well," he said slowly. He turned to Lincoln, crossing his arms across his chest. "What's your opinion?"

"Mind you, I don't think his entire plan is without merit." Lincoln leaned forward. "Just not properly focused."

"What does that mean?"

"He means General Grant is spreading his forces too thin," Gabby mumbled

"For instance, General Bates attacking Mobile is good," Lincoln continued, "but he should not march on Georgia too. General Sherman will do that. But General Sigel should attack the Shenandoah, and

General Butler should move against Petersburg and then Richmond. Leave Grant's Army of the Potomac where it is."

Shutting his notebook, Stanton stood, grumbling to himself. Lincoln reached to touch his sleeve.

"I'm concerned about Mr. Nicolay. The trip out West kept him occupied, but now..." Lincoln paused to collect his thoughts. "He's a good man. I don't want him hurt if he figures out what's going on."

Gabby had not thought about what danger awaited those who knew about Stanton's plan. He might be killed; and because of him, Cordie might be killed. His mind began to feel a dull pain.

"I've kept him busy," Stanton curtly replied. "I sent him to New York to talk to Thurlow Weed, who was not pleased with the appointment of Chase's friend John Hogeboom as appraiser in the New York Customs House. Nicolay tried to appease him and shore up support for your re-nomination. He went to the Republican convention, and now he's busy with plans for the fall campaign."

"Good." Lincoln stood and disappeared behind his curtain.

Stanton grabbed Gabby's arm and shook at finger at him.

"And don't you ever speak like that again."

Gabby wanted to reply, but became aware his mind could not compose thoughts. His shoulders slumped.

"Yes, sir."

As Stanton left, Gabby's eyes felt heavy, and he walked to his corner to rest. Mrs. Lincoln stepped from behind her curtain and gasped.

"Mr. Zook, are you all right?"

"Just fine, ma'am." His eyes went to the floor. "Just fine."

Lying on his pallet, Gabby thought about what had just taken place. As president, he should have that man, Stanton, punished for his insolence. That is—Gabby's mind clouded, and he closed his eyes in pain—*if* he were president.

Chapter Thirty-Two

Lighting the last of a dozen candles around Tad's room, Alethia settled next to him on his bed at Anderson Cottage and cuddled.

"The candles look nice," Tad murmured, resting his head on her full bosom. "Mama always said candles were romantic."

"They can be." Alethia caressed his brow. "But they can also be comforting, soothing, nurturing for the soul."

"Could you sing me that Gloria song? It's nice."

Softly and off-key, Alethia sang, and Tad hummed along.

"I don't know what language that is, but it's pretty. I like this. It makes me feel good and calm. I sleep better. I'm gonna miss it when Mama comes back."

"I'm glad."

"I mean, there's nothing wrong with the way Mama puts me to bed. I still want her back. But I'll miss you…"

"Hush, Taddie, my baby." Wrapping her arms around his head, she continued, "I know what you mean."

Moments went by without a word, and Alethia relished the intimacy.

"I'm glad you're feeling better," Tad whispered. "I got worried about you last summer. Your head was all bloody. I thought you were going to die."

"No need to worry."

"I don't think we could find another lady who looked like Mama and who was so nice." He paused. "I liked going to the White Mountains with you and Robert."

"It was so cool there," Alethia said. "The wind gently blowing against my brow made my head feel better."

"I'm sorry you couldn't go hiking with Bob and me. It was fun." He looked at her. "But you would have got a headache. I don't want you to have headaches like Mama. They're awful."

"Thank you." She smiled. "I loved watching you two from the veranda. I could tell by the way Bob put his hand on your shoulder he loves you very much."

"I know," he said with a chirp. His face clouded. "He thinks I'm a spoiled brat, but he still loves me."

"And I love both of you."

"Mama does too," Tad said. "It's just that…"

"What?"

"What Mama calls love, some folks might call bossing people around."

"I don't understand."

"You love up on me, but Mama fusses at me about brushing my teeth and combing my hair."

"She means well," Alethia said. "She loves both of you." She smiled. "I'm sure she was as proud as I was when Bob graduated from college in June."

"He wants to join the army, but Mama's scared he'll get killed. She's lost two sons already, and she doesn't want to lose another. I can sound like Mama when she's fussing at Bob. Do you want to hear it?"

"No, thank you." Alethia paused to take all this information in. "So should I keep him out of the army?"

"If you don't want him to find out you're not Mama. I don't think he'd play along with it like I do." Tad frowned. "There's something else Bob told me as a secret. I don't know if I should tell."

"Please."

"He's afraid you'll make him go to law school next month."

"I see. Thank you for the help."

The candles began to wane.

"There's something else about Bob."

"What?"

"Bob's got a girlfriend."

"How sweet." Alethia smiled. "What should my reaction be?"

"Fight it at first—Mama would, until you find out who the girl is. She's a doozy."

"Really? Who is she?"

"A senator's daughter. A big shot with the Republicans. Mama will love that." Tad smiled. "Do you want me to show you how she'll yell when Bob tells her?"

"No, thank you," she replied. "I can imagine."

"The candles are just about out." Yawning, Tad settled down into bed.

"Then that means it's time to go to sleep." She hugged him again. "Let me pray for you." She mumbled sweet words and then kissed him on the forehead. "Good night, my love."

Standing to leave, Alethia went to each candle to make sure it was out and then walked to the door.

"Thank you, Mrs. Mama. When the war's over, and Mama and Papa come back, and you go, I hope you have a happy life."

"Thank you, my love."

Alethia closed the door and walked to her room. Closing her eyes, she enjoyed the cool breeze. The cottage in the Maryland foothills was charming and romantic. Before going in, she looked into Duff's bedroom and found him sitting on the edge of the bed, drinking from a flask.

"Father? Are you all right?"

"Molly, come in. Sit next to me." He turned around, and his face was wet with tears.

"You look troubled."

"Demons." Duff sipped his whiskey. "Old demons. I've kept secrets from you, Molly." He paused. "No, I've kept secrets from Alethia. Molly knows everything she needs to know, but I want Alethia to know everything."

"Don't be afraid to tell me." Her heart pounded so hard she feared she would faint.

"I wasn't just captured at the first Manassas," he said. "The Confederates caught me and a bunch of pals as we were deserting."

"You still spent time in prison," she offered.

"Libby Prison at Richmond. The worst time of my life. Rotten food, rotting flesh. The hunger." He looked at her. "I told you I was a big boy. I was always hungry. I'm still hungry."

"There's no shame in that. No one knows you were running away. Everyone was running away. Most of them were running back to the army, and some didn't know where they were running—just running. They can't prove anything. You got more punishment than you deserved."

"No," he whispered. "I deserved even more. Back in Michigan everyone thought I had courage to match my size. Many men challenged me to fight so they could brag they whupped the biggest man in the county. I ran away. I always ran away. I always was a coward. That's what they called me. Big Yeller. When the war broke out, my friends told me if I wanted to shake that Big Yeller name I'd better join up."

"Courage isn't beating men up. Courage is admitting you can't handle things. You're smart, cautious, and brave."

"After awhile in prison, when a cell mate would die, I wouldn't tell the guards for a few days. They never came in, just pushed the plates through the slot. I didn't tell so I could eat the dead man's food."

"This is war." Her eyes fluttered. "You do what you have to do to survive."

"Soon," he continued, with his head down, "I think they caught on to what I was doing. So they started putting healthier men in with me. I suffocated them in the middle of the night so I could get their food."

"Oh." Alethia could not help but be shocked. Only a monster could do that, but Duff was not a monster. War made monsters; prisons made monsters; a normal life made him normal again.

"Next they put a man as big as me in the cell. We figured a way to get out."

"Did he know what you had done?"

"No. But the men in the cell block knew. When we all broke out and made it back to the Union lines, the others told. My last cell mate spit in my face when he found out. They court-martialed me and sent me to Old Capitol to be hanged. At least the food was good. Stanton found me, said I looked like Mr. Lincoln, and gave me a chance to escape hanging." His eyes narrowed with intensity. "I hate him." He looked at Alethia. "You hate me now, don't you?"

"Do you want me to hate you?"

"No."

"Good," she replied. "I love you too much to hate you."

Chapter Thirty-Three

Phebe washed and dried the last of the pots and pans, rubbing hard as she thought about the past two years and Adam's lies. The door opened and he entered with the evening tray. She had not lit the whale oil lamp yet, so deep shadows fell across his face.

"I'm sorry the dishes are so late."

He was on his way out the door when Phebe said, "I hope Mr. Gabby enjoyed his meal."

Adam stopped and turned. Wiping his red locks off his forehead, he opened his mouth, but nothing came out.

"Mr. Gabby's in there, ain't he? When those people moved into the billiards room, Mr. Gabby disappeared. Nobody would fire him. From what he said, he got his job because his uncle was a general."

"General Zook died at Gettysburg. Then he could be fired." Adam looked down. "Mr. Stanton didn't like him."

"Mr. Gabby disappeared almost a full year before Gettysburg."

"Your memory isn't that good."

"My memory is just fine."

"I'm tired tonight," he said. "I could explain all this real good, but my mind's fuzzy."

"What about Master Tad?"

"What about him?"

"You carried him down here."

"I don't even remember that."

"Don't remember?" Phebe grunted. "You're too big of a coward to tell the truth."

"I'm not a coward." Adam stepped toward her. "Don't call me that." He sank into a chair. "Don't press me on this. You don't understand. If I say too much," he said, choosing each word carefully, "Tad could die. I could die." He looked up. "You could die."

"I'm sorry." She bit her lip, fearing she had been too hard on him; after all, she did not dislike him. If anything, she liked him more than she wanted to admit. "I didn't mean anything by it."

"You don't know how hard this is." Adam put his head in his hands. "I'd never been out of Steubenville until I came here."

Phebe had never been off the plantation until she was sold, so she knew those feelings of isolation and fear.

"My mother is dead—she died when I was young. She was the one who always solved problems for me," he said.

Her mother had been sold before her eyes. She had been Phebe's protector, her hope, her salvation, and her key to all knowledge—language, arithmetic, religion.

"I've said too much." Adam sniffed and looked at Phebe. "I'm sorry I've been mean. From the first time I saw you, I liked you very much." He paused as she looked away. "I like the way you smell like soap."

"Thank you." She tried not to smile. "It's late. I have to wash those dishes." Phebe went to the sink.

"Let me help you." Adam came up behind her. "To make up for me being such a fumble-mouth."

"That's all right—" Phebe turned and was startled by his closeness. She looked into his open, naïve blue eyes, and could not complete her sentence.

"I…" Adam could not finish his sentence either.

Slowly they came closer, until he impulsively kissed her. Phebe's eyes widened, startled. Her hand frantically reached for the sink; she grabbed a plate and shattered it against his head.

"I'm sorry." Adam staggered back, fingering his temple to find blood.

Phebe wanted to lash out indignantly, but the words were not there; perhaps she felt sorry for him, and maybe she was angry at herself for hitting him.

"Pardon me." Adam stumbled toward the door. "I should have never…" Then he was gone.

Phebe knelt to pick up the shards of plate from the floor, berating herself. Mama would be wagging her finger if she were here. There was no excuse. After putting the bits of broken plate in the trash barrel, she returned to the sink and vigorously scrubbed the rest of the dishes.

Walking into the room and removing his butler's jacket, Neal asked, "Do you want me to dry?" After she nodded, he joined her at the sink and started wiping. "Those white folks get later and later finishing their supper, don't they?"

"Will you please stop it about the white folks?" Phebe said, tensing her back.

"All right," he replied, glancing over at her. After a few moments, he asked, "What's wrong, Phebe?"

"Nothing."

"I don't believe that."

"You're a good man, Neal." Looking at him, she smiled.

Neal was not big; Adam was taller than him by a head, and Adam was only average size. Neal's face was very pale for a Negro and covered with light brown freckles. Her mother had told her if one of the light-skinned servants in the big house wanted to marry her, she should let him; but when Phebe looked at Neal, who, by her mother's standards, measured up to be the perfect husband, all she saw was a feisty, friendly, constantly barking dog.

"What happened?" he repeated.

"It was my fault." She concentrated on the last of the dishes, wanting to finish her chores, disappear into her room, and forget what had happened.

"Who touched you, girl?" Neal took her arm and turned her toward him. He looked into her eyes.

"No one." Phebe pulled away from him. "Forget it. I've got to finish the dishes. It's late."

"No." Neal positioned himself between her and the sink. "It was the soldier boy, wasn't it?"

"I handled it. I hit him upside the head with a plate."

"What did he do?"

"He kissed me."

"I'm gonna whip his ass!" Spinning around, Neal rushed to the door.

"No, you're not," she said, following him. "You're a Negro. He's white. You're a butler. He's a soldier." Phebe now stood between him and the door. "Whose side do you think the law is gonna come down on?"

"Damn the law!"

"No! The law will damn you!" She sighed in guilt, having yelled at Neal. "Please," she said, "we're Negroes in a white man's town. There are things going on in this house. Evil things." Phebe stepped closer. "He told me something's bad's going on. He said if word got out, Tad could die. He said he could die. He even said I could die."

"Did he threaten you?"

"He didn't threaten me. He warned me. Neal, if I could die, you could die."

He was quiet a long time. Then, staring at her intently, he asked, "Did you like it?"

"Like what?"

"Did you like the kiss?"

"No. If I had, I wouldn't have broken a perfectly good plate."

"Have you ever had a good kiss?" Neal stepped closer.

"Yes." It was a lie. She did not want him to kiss her.

"I know how to kiss." He pulled in his broad lips, moistening them so they shined in the whale oil light.

"So find somebody who cares," Phebe said as she pushed past him to return to the sink. Washing the last glass, she dropped her head. "I'm sorry, Neal. I like you. But I don't want to kiss you any more than I want to kiss Private Christy."

"Why?"

"Because I hope for a better life." She turned to look at him, drying her hands nervously on a ragged cloth. "If I kiss you—or any man—I might relent and allow you to have me. Then, alone with a baby, I'd have no chance for a better life."

"I wouldn't do that. If you let me kiss you, I know you'd love me. I want to marry you." He paused. "I'm not a common dog."

"I know, Neal." What an unfortunate choice of words. Phebe restrained herself, not wanting to hurt him any more.

"I love you, Phebe, but you'll never love me, will you?"

"I'm sorry."

A long sigh escaped Neal's lips as he turned to leave, softly adding, "I lied about kissing. No girl ever let me kiss her."

Chapter Thirty-Four

Gabby's head turned sharply when he thought he heard the crash of a plate. Something was happening out there, he could sense it, and his body shook with fear. Since that morning in August when he had been able to think again, Gabby had become increasingly nervous, never knowing when his mind would clear and when it would cloud, when the people in the basement with him would be nice and when they would be mean, and when he would see Cordie again.

Mrs. Lincoln came to the edge of Gabby's crates and barrels. He shuddered, wondering if he had done something wrong again.

"Mr. Gabby," she said, "may I come in for a visit?"

"That's all right, ma'am." He stood. "I'll come out."

"No, I don't mind." She swept around the corner and stood just inside his curtain and smiled. "Sit, so we can chat."

Chatting with her husband, that is what she should be doing, Gabby thought. It was not right for her to be chatting with him. Cordie should be chatting with him, but she could not, because he had to be in the basement and she had to be at the hospital tending sick soldiers.

"Please sit."

"All right." Gabby sat on the far end of his pallet.

"Mr. Gabby, do you remember the things you told me?"

"What things?"

"Sweet things." She sat on his pallet.

"Did you hear a crash or something?"

"No. You're right about Mr. Stanton."

"I thought I heard a crash. I'm not sure of anything anymore."

"He's evil."

"I don't even know what month this is." He looked at her. "What month is this?"

"It's the middle of October." She clenched her jaw. "Pay attention to me. You're right about Mr. Stanton being evil."

"Then it's been two months since..."

"Only an evil man would put good people in an awful place like this."

"There were rats here."

"Yes, you told me."

"I think I caught them all."

"Thank you." She sighed deeply and closed her eyes.

"You're welcome."

"Mr. Stanton's calling people by the wrong names. There's people upstairs he's calling Mr. and Mrs. Lincoln."

"I know."

"He's calling you Mr. Gabby..."

"He doesn't call me Mr. Gabby," he interrupted. "He doesn't call me anything."

"But you're Mr. Lincoln, my husband and president of the United States."

"What?" Could those thoughts lingering in the back of his mind be true?

"For reasons known only to himself, Mr. Stanton calls the White House janitor Mr. Lincoln, and you the janitor."

"Oh."

"But this has gone on too long. It can't continue. When Private Christy comes in with the clean chamber pots, jump him, wrestle him down, and get the keys so we can escape. You can do it."

"All right." Gabby knew he was strong. He remembered how he could wrestle Joe into submission every time they wrestled on Long Island beach. But if he were Lincoln, how would he know Joe? Maybe Joe had been Lincoln's friend, but that meant they had to be from Illinois. How could they have wrestled on Long Island beach? Gabby fretted. Maybe it had been on the shores of the Ohio River.

"So when Private Christy comes in," Mrs. Lincoln was saying, "I'll distract him, and you jump him and get the keys."

"You don't want me to kill him, do you?"

"No." A shadow crossed her face. "I don't want him dead. I just want to be free."

"Should we take Mr. Zook with us?" Gabby asked. "After all, he might have a sister or somebody waiting for him."

"Yes, we'll take Mr. Zook with us." Mrs. Lincoln smiled. "I wouldn't want to leave him behind."

"Good," he replied. "He needs to see his sister."

Adam unlocked the door, fumbling with the pots. Both Gabby and Mrs. Lincoln jerked their heads to the door.

"I've got to go." She stood. With a flourish of her billowing skirt, she disappeared through the curtains.

Gabby went to the edge of the crates and barrels to listen.

"Mrs. Lincoln," Adam said, "are you busy right now? I mean, there's something I need to talk to you about."

"Of course," she replied. Looking at him closely, she added, "Private Christy, you've a touch of blood at your temple."

"I know. That's what I want to talk to you about."

"Come over here, and I'll straighten everything out for you."

Gabby stepped out around the corner to see that Adam had left all three chamber pots by the door. He stood next to Mrs. Lincoln by the billiards table, his back to Gabby. Looking down at the chamber pots, he wondered if he should use one to bash Adam's head. No, that would kill him, and they just wanted to be free.

"I did a bad thing tonight," Adam said.

"Tell me what you did, and I'll tell you whether it was bad or not." Mrs. Lincoln looked over Adam's shoulder to make eye contact with Gabby. Get it over with, she seemed to be saying.

"I kissed Phebe."

"The colored cook?" Her eyebrow rose.

"Yes. I know it was wrong. She hit me with a plate."

Gabby knew he had heard something. He frowned. He liked Phebe. She was one of the few people he ever knew who treated him nice. Adam was right. He did a bad thing.

"Was it one of the good plates?" Mrs. Lincoln asked, holding her breath.

"No."

"That's good," she said in a murmur. "Did the girl do anything to provoke you, make you think she wanted you to kiss her?"

Gabby did not like that question. Phebe was a good girl. She would not do anything like that. She was too honest. Gabby was ready to hit somebody.

"No, not really, I guess," Adam replied.

Bellowing, Gabby jumped on Adam's back, causing his knees to buckle.

"Good!" Mrs. Lincoln screamed. "Force him to the floor! You've got him now! You've got him down!"

Gabby bounced on Adam's back, trying to break him and force him to his knees, and then to the ground.

"That's it! Ride him down! Break him!"

With a groan from the pit of his stomach, Adam regained his balance and allowed himself to fall backwards. Gabby landed flat on his back on the cold hard floor, heard a noticeable crack in his spine, and whimpered. Adam rolled off him and pounced on Gabby's chest, pinning his shoulders to the floor with his knees.

"What the hell are you doing?" Adam slapped Gabby's face several times.

"Stop it!" Mrs. Lincoln screamed as she tried to pull Adam off Gabby. "It's not his fault! I made him do it!"

"What the hell's going on?" Lincoln, in his nightshirt, appeared through the lace curtains.

"Quick, Father!" Mrs. Lincoln stopped pulling on Adam and ran to her husband. "Kill him! Get us out of here!"

"Molly! Shut up!" Lincoln yelled. He charged Adam, who was still on Gabby. "Get the hell off him!"

Before Adam could do anything, Lincoln grabbed him by his armpits and threw him across the room. After gasping for air, he reached for Gabby, who cringed and pulled away.

"No, Mr. Gabby, you're all right. Does anything hurt?"

"I don't think so." Gabby sat up carefully and reached around to feel his back. "I thought I heard something crack, but it must not have been important, because it doesn't hurt now."

"That's good."

"I guess it was bad to jump him like that."

"Try to forget it." Lincoln went down on his haunches to smile into Gabby's face. "Don't take seriously anything that Mrs. Lincoln says."

"Then I'm not president?"

"No."

"And you're president?"

"Yes."

"Good," Gabby said. "It works out better that way."

Lincoln stood and walked to Adam, offering him a hand to help him up.

"This is Mrs. Lincoln's fault. She's not stable. It's your responsibility as the military authority here to keep a handle on things."

"Yes, sir." Adam straightened his back.

"Good. Now go about your duties."

Adam looked down, avoiding looking at Gabby and Mrs. Lincoln, and left the room.

"You fool!" Mrs. Lincoln snarled, rushing her husband. "You could have killed him, and no one would have cared! One word from you, and Mr. Stanton would be off to the Old Capitol in chains!"

"And if the nation discovered someone had put the president in the White House basement for two years and no one knew, what confidence would the people have then to fight a war?"

"So you're on Mr. Stanton's side?"

"I'm on the Union's side," he replied. "Only the Union is important."

"Yes, sir." She pursed her lips.

"Don't do this again, Molly." Lincoln pointed at Gabby. "You could get him killed. You could get us all killed." He sighed deeply. "I think it's time to sleep." He disappeared behind the French lace curtains.

"So you're not my wife?" Gabby stared a long time into Mrs. Lincoln's face, expecting to detect a trace of remorse.

"No."

"I knew I kept having memories of New York and not Illinois." He paused to compose his thoughts as well as he could. "Why did you do it?"

"Because I want to get out of here."

"Well, that's all right. I'd rather have Cordie as a sister than you as a wife, anyway."

Chapter Thirty-Five

Adam hurried out the front door, past guard John Parker, catching a whiff of the whiskey on his breath, and deciding it smelled good. Kicking the dirt on Pennsylvania Avenue, he meandered several blocks before being drawn by the dim lights and noise of a small bar. He had been there several times. This was where he had both heard the rumors about Stanton and acquired his taste for alcohol. It was a good place to forget how stupid he was.

Inside, he sat on a stool, reached into his pockets for some change, and threw some coins on the counter.

"Your usual ale, buddy?" the bartender asked.

"No, whiskey."

"You got it."

He wanted to stop the arguments in his brain. In his heart of hearts, he knew he loved Jessie Home. She knew who he was, because that was who she was too. Jessie had seen his dark side and did not care. She was going to save his soul. When this hell with Stanton and the Lincolns and the basement ended, she would be there to help him forget it. If he knew this so deeply, he asked himself, why was he drawn to Phebe? It was not like she was a temptress, actively seducing him away from his beloved. Adam did not know if she even liked him. It was not that she was more beautiful than Jessie. Jessie was a light that drew life to her. Any man would gladly want her, and Adam did want her more than he had ever wanted any woman. So why had he kissed Phebe?

"Here you go, general."

Quickly downing the shot, Adam pushed the glass back toward the bartender.

"Another."

She smelled of soap, he thought. Adam could not recall what Jessie smelled of. He was too busy being engaged by her eyes, her smile, and her smart conversation. How stupid could one man be?

"Another."

The pain was not going away. He had to forget. For just this one night, he wanted to drink himself into oblivion, forgetting how stupid he was, how he had almost thrown away the love of his life.

"Another."

Cringing, he remembered how he had almost killed Gabby, the most innocent, defenseless man he had ever met. He did not want to remember that either.

"Isn't it late for you to be out, soldier?"

Adam looked up to see Lamon, another person he did not want to think about. He gulped another shot.

"Take it easy," Lamon said. "Most men sip their whiskey."

"I can handle it."

"Sure you can."

Adam wanted to retort with something smart, but his mind was becoming numb. All sorts of thoughts to put Lamon in his place crowded his brain, and Adam felt he was strong enough to beat the bigger man in a fist-fight too.

"Feel like talking about Mr. Lincoln?"

"No."

"Why not?"

"Because." He looked at the bartender. "Another."

"You better not," Lamon said. "Your face is as red as your hair."

"So?"

"When liquor hits a man like that, he'd better go home and go to bed."

"Mind your business."

"I am." Lamon smiled. "Tell me where Mr. Lincoln is."

Adam stared at the last shot glass of whiskey and fought the impulse to throw it in Lamon's face. His head swirled with all the anger he had kept trapped down inside his gut for the past two years. Life was not fair. He was a good boy. He had always done what his mother said, what his father said, what Stanton said, and he was still in the shit barrel.

"Well, when you get tired of being Mr. Stanton's stooge, talk to me." Lamon said. "I'm in the district marshal's office."

After Lamon walked away, Adam took the glass in his fist and squeezed it, finally throwing it across the room.

"Whoa, cowboy," the bartender said. "No more for you."

"Sorry," he said in a mumble, dropping more coins on the counter as he left.

Stumbling along the street back to the Executive Mansion, Adam became angrier, because all that whiskey had not made him forget a thing. It just made him think about Jessie, Phebe, Gabby, and Lamon more. What the hell, his clouded mind thought, what difference did it make? What difference did anything make? Putting Lincoln in the basement did not make a difference. The war was still going on. Being in love with Jessie did not make a difference. He still longed for someone different. Being good did not make a difference. People still thought he was bad.

Entering the basement hallway, another thought entered his mind. If nothing made a difference, then why the hell not go ahead and be bad? Adam thrust his head forward, pursed his lips, and went to Phebe's room, grabbed the knob and entered. As the door swung open, Adam saw, in the light of hallway whale oil lamp, Phebe lying in bed. Her smooth black skin, lithe figure, full lips, and large eyes—now wide open, startled by the sudden shaft of light—drew him into the dark room. Instinctively, he unbuttoned his shirt.

"What? What is it?" Phebe mumbled, putting up her hand to shield her eyes from the light.

"It's me."

"Oh." She sat up. "What was that noise? It sounded like yelling and banging about."

"It was nothing."

"Anything you say." She yawned and fell back. "Just let me sleep."

"You still smell of soap." Walking toward the bed, he paused at its edge, breathing deeply. "So clean."

"You're scaring me." Phebe sat up and pulled the covers up to her chin. "Please leave."

"You don't want me to leave. I know. Your eyes tell me you're happy when I walk in. You always have something to say." He sat at the bottom of the bed. "You want me as much as I want you."

"You're drunk."

Adam leaned forward to grab Phebe, but she rolled out of the cot onto the floor. Grappling with the sheets, he found them empty.

"Dammit! Come back here!"

Adam scrambled from the bed, and by the time he was on his feet, Phebe opened the door, allowing him to see exactly where she was. Lunging, he caught her by the crook of her elbow and swung her around.

"Help!" she yelled. "For God's sake, somebody, help!"

"Shut up!" Throwing her back on the cot, Adam put his hand over her mouth as he planted his sweaty body over her.

"Help! Help me!" Phebe bit his hand, causing him to pull it back in pain.

"What the hell is going on?" Neal stood in the doorway wearing his nightshirt.

"Neal!" Phebe frantically pulled her head away from Adam, her eyes searching for him. "Please stop him!"

"You sumbitch!" Neal raced to the cot and grabbed Adam's feet to drag him off onto the floor.

Adam's face bashed into the hard floor. The acrid taste of blood seeped onto his tongue, which only infuriated him. He jumped up, grabbed Neal by the armpits and threw him, just as Lincoln had manhandled him earlier, out the door. Turning his back to Neal so he could focus on Phebe, cowering on the cot, Adam walked toward her.

"Damn you!" Neal screamed as he jumped on Adam's back.

Instinctively, Adam did as he had done earlier when Gabby had attacked him; he fell backward with a great moan, trapping Neal under him. His head turned around when he heard pounding from the billiards room.

"Stop that!" Gabby yelled. "Stop that hollering! And stop hurting people!"

Adam rolled over and pinned Neal's shoulders with his knees. He struck Neal with his fists, his eyes wide and glassy from the alcohol and his anger.

"Stop hurting people!"

Adam felt a sheet fall across his face and settle around his neck. He saw Phebe twisting the sheet with all her strength.

"Let Neal go, or by God, I'll kill you!" she screamed.

"Stop hurting people!" Gabby repeated from behind the wall.

Adam jerked the sheet from her hands and knocked Phebe away. He tied a knot in the middle of the sheet, wrapped it around Neal's neck, and pulled hard.

"Stop hurting people!"

Adam strained his muscles, pulling the sheet tighter into Neal's neck. Neal's veins were bulging, his eyes popping out of his head.

"You'll never talk back to me again!"

"No, no," Phebe whimpered from the floor.

"Stop hurting people!"

Neal's tongue lolled out and spittle dripped from the corner of his mouth. Finally, Adam felt the body go limp.

Phebe crawled over to look at Neal's blank eyes staring at the ceiling.

"Oh my God! He's dead! You killed him!"

"Shh." Adam turned to put his hand over her mouth. Looking his hands he saw blood on his knuckles and he wiped them on his tunic. He glanced at Phebe who was shivering and crying. "Don't worry."

"Murderer," she said softly.

"Shh." He looked down and grabbed the sheet.

"Oh my God! No!"

"Shh. I'm going to stick this in your mouth to keep you quiet."

The knot went into her mouth. Adam pulled the lower sheet to tear it and tie her hands together. Slowly, methodically, he tore another strip from the sheet to tie her feet.

"Stop hurting people!"

Chapter Thirty-Six

Adam walked back to his room and collapsed on his cot, his mind racing. What to do? Collecting his thoughts, he decided to go directly to the metropolitan police station. Turning himself in to the police would be the right thing—but would it be what Stanton would want, he wondered. Going to Stanton for every decision was part of his nature now; he could not change. Adam went to the wash table to clean his flushed face and his sweaty arms and neck. On Pennsylvania Avenue he caught an omnibus to K Street. Night breezes cooled his heated face, but to no avail; his skin still burned from anxiety. Finally the omnibus stopped at the block of Stanton's house. As he walked down the street, Adam noticed how slowly he walked. He mounted the steps, imagining that this was how it would be when he went to the gallows.

"Yes?" the maid said, answering the door.

"I need to speak to Secretary Stanton."

"That's out of the question," she replied.

"This is an emergency."

"Can't it wait until morning?"

"Tell him Private Adam Christy is here."

"Very well." The maid pursed her lips as she surveyed Adam.

Within a few moments, Stanton appeared in his dressing gown, his eyes glaring.

"What are you doing here?"

"I've killed someone."

Stanton came out of the door, shut it, and hunched his shoulders against the cold night air. He stepped close to Adam.

"Say that again."

"I killed the butler. He tried to keep me from raping the cook."

"You're a damned fool," Stanton said. He shivered as he looked out at the fog. "Damn you." He paused. "Damn you." He looked at Adam. "Flag down a carriage while I get dressed."

In a few minutes, they were riding down the dirt street. Stanton barked an order to the carriage driver, who nodded and turned north at the next corner.

"Where are we going? The police station?"

"You're a damned fool."

Several minutes passed before the carriage stopped in front of a dark, two-story frame boardinghouse.

"Mr. Baker's room is the first one at the top of the stairs." Stanton narrowed his eyes. "Go get him." He put a hand to his mouth to muffle a cough.

Jumping from the carriage, Adam bounded up the steps, entered, climbed the stairs, and knocked at the first door.

"What?"

"Secretary Stanton wants you."

"Oh."

Adam could hear a female voice complain and Baker calming her. Baker came out, buttoning his coat, and descended the stairs with Adam following closely. In the carriage Baker leaned into Stanton, who whispered to him as the carriage went to the Executive Mansion. Once they had arrived at the service driveway, Stanton motioned to Adam to get off with him and waved on the carriage with Baker still aboard.

"Where is he going?"

"To get a War Department carriage."

They entered the service entrance and walked through the kitchen.

"Down there," Adam said, leading Stanton to Phebe's room.

Stanton walked in and examined Neal, ignoring Phebe, tied up on the floor. After a close study of the body, he crossed over to her.

"Young woman, if you keep your mouth shut, eyes closed to this, you'll live. If someone should ask you someday, whatever happened to…" He turned to Adam. "What was his name?"

"Neal."

"Whatever happened to Neal, you say you don't know anyone by that name. I'll have a new butler here tomorrow. He'll be the only butler you remember. If you don't, you die, and disappear as quickly as Neal. Do you understand? Nod if you understand."

Phebe slowly moved her head up and down, her eyes filled with tears.

As Adam pulled Neal's body into the hall, Baker bounded into the hall from the kitchen. Baker lifted the corpse, threw it over his shoulder, and left as quickly as he had come.

"Go to his room, wrap up all his possessions in a sheet, and take them out to Mr. Baker."

"Yes, sir."

Stanton coughed deeply, turned, and walked through the kitchen to the service entrance door. Adam went to Neal's room, lit a candle, pulled the sheet loose from the cot, and began tossing shoes, coats, shirts, pants, and underwear into it. He turned his attention a stack of books on the washtable. Holding them close to the candle flame, he read the titles—*Uncle Tom's Cabin, Constitution of the United States of America, On Civil Disobedience*. There was also a diary. Adam turned to the last entry.

"'I finally confessed to Phebe I loved her,'" Adam mumbled. "'She rejected me. I won't give up.'"

"No time for reading," Baker said, snatching the book from his hand. Placing the last of the items in the sheet, Baker pulled the corners together and tied a knot. Before leaving he turned. "Don't mess up again, or else I'll make you disappear too."

Chapter Thirty-Seven

John Hay raced up the service stairs, his wits shaken by the sight he had passed in the basement hall, and trying to compose his thoughts before waking up John Nicolay in their bedroom across from their second-floor office. Entering the room, he lit the lamp on the table between their beds, then shook Nicolay's shoulder until his eyes opened.

"Something terrible has happened."

"What?" Nicolay rubbed his eyes as he sat up.

"I just saw something horrible."

"What do you mean, something horrible?" Nicolay coughed and shook his head.

"I just came in through the basement. I heard an odd voice inside one of the rooms, saying, 'Stop hurting people.'"

"What people?"

"Neal, the butler." Hay paused to swallow hard. "He was on the floor of one of the bedrooms. The door was open, and the room was dark, but from the light of the hall lamp, I could see his body. His"—Hay shuddered—"dead body. Then I heard whimpering from the darkness behind him. I heard the service entrance door open. I hid in the stairwell."

"Slow down. Neal is dead. How?"

"From the stairwell I heard Christy talking Stanton—"

"Stanton?"

"—that Christy had killed the butler, Neal, when Neal had tried to keep the private from raping the cook. She was the one whimpering. Stanton went in and spoke to her. I didn't understand what he said. Then I heard Lafayette Baker."

"Why was he there?"

"He took out the body."

Nicolay leaned into him. "Was anyone aware you were there?"

"No." Hay shook his head. "Maybe the cook."

"She won't tell." He bit his lip. "Remember what I said about doing our jobs and ignoring everything else?"

"Yes."

"Well, we can't do that anymore." Nicolay stood, went to the door, and cracked it to look out, then shut it carefully.

"So what do we do?" Hay asked.

Extinguishing the lamp, Nicolay sat next to him.

"I've friends in the State Department who can get me a post overseas. I know the Paris consul is open. Once I get there, I'll find a job for you."

"But shouldn't we stay? Try to stop Stanton?"

"I never trained in the army. Did you?"

"No."

"Could you overpower Lafayette Baker?"

"We have the law on our side."

"Stanton and Baker are the law."

"Lamon suspects something. He'd be on our side."

"If they can abduct the president and keep it a secret for two years, they can make Ward Lamon disappear too."

"We should try to do something."

"Like the butler who tried to stop a rape? He's dead, and no one will know he ever existed. Do you think anyone would notice if you disappeared?"

"Oh." Hay put his hand to his neck. "Perhaps Paris would be good."

Chapter Thirty-Eight

Sitting at a small table covered by a red-and-white checkered cloth in the back of a small, busy café, Jessie tapped her fingers impatiently for Adam's arrival. He had broken their engagement the night before, and she was not happy. Jessie was in love, but sensed something terrible had happened. As much as she cared for Adam, she was bothered by his lack of honesty about what was going on at the Executive Mansion.

Her face lit when Adam first walked through the door, but it darkened as she watched him weave between the tables; he had not changed his clothes, shaved, or washed. When he plopped down in the chair next to her, Adam tried to kiss her, but she turned away, repulsed by his breath.

"Ye stink and look terrible."

"I'm a man, a soldier." Adam leaned back in his chair and looked ahead.

The waiter came up.

"What do ye crave for supper?"

"Whiskey."

After the waiter pulled out his pad, Jessie leaned to Adam and said, "I want a bowl of beef stew and a glass of milk."

When Adam did not respond, she looked up at the waiter who nodded.

"And for the gentleman?"

"Whiskey," Adam said sullenly.

"We don't serve hard liquor."

"Nothing, then."

"Very well, sir," the waiter said and turned away.

"Me darlin', what's wrong?"

"I've been given the awesome knowledge of life and death."

"What does that mean?"

"It's terrible to give a young man the awesome knowledge of life and death." Adam said nothing more because the waiter arrived with Jessie's bowl of soup and glass of milk.

"Ye need to talk to somebody," she said softly. "Somebody who can help ye."

"It's too late." Avoiding Jessie's eyes, he shook his head and replied, "The awesome knowledge of life and death changes a man forever. A woman will never know the awesome knowledge of life and death."

"Will ye stop that 'awesome knowledge of life and death'?" She pushed away her soup bowl. "I lost me hunger. Take me home."

Adam bolted for the door, leaving Jessie to pay the waiter and scurry out after him. He was already in his seat on the omnibus when she climbed on board and passed the fare slot.

"Sorry, miss, I need your coin," the driver said.

"I'm with the gentleman," she replied, motioning to Adam in the back.

"Oh. Him. He just paid for himself."

Searching her reticule in frustration, Jessie finally found the right coin, deposited it, and walked to the back, debating whether to sit next to Adam, who had left her humiliated in his wake. The bus started with a jerk, causing her to fall into the seat by him.

"Where were ye last night?"

Adam stared into the night.

"I think your actions were despicable," Jessie said in a low, intense voice. "And don't give me any more of that knowledge of life and death foolishness. Ye are a better man than this, me laddie."

Turning toward her, Adam smiled queerly, which unsettled Jessie to the point of making her shudder. When her street came up, Jessie stood to leave; Adam began to follow her.

"I don't need an escort."

Again he smiled queerly, which caused her to walk swiftly to the omnibus door, where she jumped to the road and trotted toward her boardinghouse. Not looking behind her, Jessie sensed Adam was staggering behind her. At the door, she rummaged through her reticule, trying to find the key, until she smelled foul breath over her shoulder.

"Adam, please go away before I tell ye to go away forever." She did not look at him, but spoke firmly and solemnly. "Now."

Spinning her around, Adam planted a moist, open-mouthed kiss on her lips. His teeth smashed her lips against her own teeth, causing an abrasion. The taste of his tongue was acrid and repellent. His body odor curled up her nostrils, making her gag. Her fists hit against his shoulders. Finally her hand, still fumbling through her reticule, found the key. Grasping it tightly, she swiftly brought up her hand, scraping the key on Adam's temple. Staggering backward, he moaned loudly, his hand going to the bleeding gash on the side of his head. Jessie unlocked the door and rushed in, locking it behind her. Adam lunged forward, banging his hand on the frame.

"Damn you!" he screamed. "Bitch!"

Chapter Thirty-Nine

Stanton confidently stood in the War Department telegraph room, awaiting the November presidential election results. Others around him paced nervously, because some states were late in reporting. In his gut he knew it was won for Abraham Lincoln and Andrew Johnson. Stanton laughed at the thought of Johnson, a known alcoholic who had been taught to read and write by his wife—he would be easily manipulated. That was why Stanton had influenced the Republican Party to drop Hannibal Hamlin as vice president and nominate Johnson.

"Don't worry, Mr. President." Lamon patted Duff on the back. "The country's behind you."

"Mr. Lincoln, we've the latest results," Noah Brooks said with a glint in his eyes. "You've won."

Brooks had replaced Nicolay, who in late October had resigned to go to Paris to become United States consul. Hay was taking time off to finish personal business before going to Paris as secretary to the legation. Stanton did not care, relegating Nicolay and Hay to the category of small potatoes, and he saw Brooks as just as innocuous. He had been a correspondent from the *Sacramento Union*. Some thought the young reporter was politically astute, but Stanton doubted it.

"These telegrams are from Andrew Johnson," Brooks said, handing one to Duff and one to Stanton.

Stanton read his message to himself:

Mr. Stanton,

My Washington sources tell me of your omnipresence around Mr. Lincoln

and of your reprehensible behavior toward him. Let me warn you I will be

Mr. Lincoln's champion in all matters. Your reputation is that of a bully and

a coward. Let me assure you that you shall not bully me and that I shall make

it my mission to reveal your craven cowardice to all.

Vice President-elect

Andrew Johnson

"What does Mr. Johnson say, Father?" Alethia asked, squeezing Duff's arm.

"'Dear Mr. President,'" Duff began. "'It is with great humility I acknowledge the will of the nation for you to proceed with the preservation of our Union and the task of healing. I do not understand why you chose me to be by your side, but I pledge to be your champion in all matters.'"

"Hear, hear," Brooks said.

"Sounds like my kind of man," Lamon said with a laugh.

Stanton could feel his neck burn red, yet he said nothing. He was not ready to return power to Lincoln, even though the end of the war was nearing.

"How nice," Alethia said. "I knew he was a Southern gentleman."

"And articulate," Duff said. "I hope he doesn't drink as much as they say he does."

Everyone chuckled, except Stanton, who wadded his telegram tightly in his fist.

"What did your telegram say, Mr. Stanton?" Lamon asked.

"Basically the same thing," he lied. "He said he looked forward to working with me for the next four years."

Chapter Forty

"I want my breakfast!" Gabby insisted, pounding on the door.

Stopping with the key in the lock, Adam shuddered at the tone of Gabby's voice, the same tone he had used in October to demand that Adam stop hurting people. It was now April, and Adam had stopped hurting people. He also had stopped having dreams, goals, love, pain, or anger. His spirit was dead; his body barely functioned. Steeling himself, he finished unlocking the door and entered.

"It's about time," Gabby said. "You're starving people in here."

"Be quiet," Mrs. Lincoln said, looking at Gabby with loathing. "Mr. Lincoln didn't sleep well last night. Nightmares."

"I have nightmares." Gabby took his plate and headed for his corner. "Every night I see Joe dead under that wagon. If Mr. Lincoln can't take nightmares, he shouldn't be president."

"Crazy old man," Mrs. Lincoln sneered.

"Liar," Gabby retorted. He looked at Adam. "Next time you beat up somebody, beat her up, the old liar." He continued to mumble as he rounded the corner of crates and barrels.

"My husband's nightmares are more important because he's still president, and still makes decisions." Mrs. Lincoln sat at the billiards table and began eating. "For several weeks he's dreamed that Tad and I were on a shopping trip to Philadelphia and Tad, for some reason, pulled out a gun and started shooting people. He kept mumbling, 'I didn't pay enough attention to the boy.' I know he's worried about how those people have treated Tad."

Tad was just fine, Adam thought, no longer running amok, tearing at things, and kicking people as he did before. Now he was kind and loving, respectful of everyone. Mrs. Lincoln will be pleased, he decided, if she can ever be pleased with anything again.

"Then last night he dreamed of being awakened by loud sobbing. He found a casket surrounded by soldiers in the East Room. He asked, 'Who has died in the White House?' The soldier replied, 'The president.'"

Not wanting to consider what Stanton had in mind for the president, Adam began to gather the chamber pots.

"Don't walk away while I'm talking to you," Mrs. Lincoln ordered. "What's that man doing in Richmond? He went down the same day the city fell, and he hasn't returned."

"I don't know, ma'am," Adam said. He hated answering her questions. "You'll have to ask Mr. Stanton."

"You always say that." Mrs. Lincoln took a long sip of coffee. "The last drop of coffee was cold." Putting down her cup, she turned to stare at him. "I want to know when this war will end. Since their capital fell, the rebels can't go on."

"Jefferson Davis said being relieved of defending a capital has left the army free to roam at large and stage preemptive attacks on the Union."

"So he thinks he can still win the war?"

"I don't know, ma'am."

"You don't know," she snidely replied. "Is there anything you do know?"

"Tad's having fun in Richmond."

"Tad's in Richmond?"

Closing his eyes, Adam wished he had not told her.

"Who allowed my child into a war zone?"

"I don't know."

"That woman," Mrs. Lincoln said. "She's ruined everything."

"The army made a thorough sweep of the city, making it safe for the president."

"But that man's not the president!" she blustered. She took a deep breath and returning her attention to the toast. "At least my other son is safe in law school."

"Robert joined the army in January." Adam did not know if he had slipped again, or if he had told her purposefully to hurt her and to allow her to hurt him. He wanted to be punished for his sins.

"Oh my God!"

"He's on General Grant's staff."

"That butcher!" She put her head in her hands. "If I could only write him. If only he could write me."

"I'm sure his fiancée has been writing him."

"Fiancée!" Her face reddened. "When did this happen? And who?"

"February. She's Mary Harlan, daughter of Senator James Harlan of Iowa."

"That little mouse." She rubbed her eyes. "At least her parents are respectable."

"I must go now, ma'am."

"Very well." Mrs. Lincoln sighed. "I'm not asking questions anymore."

"Yes, ma'am." As Adam turned, he found himself confronted by Gabby, whose eyes were wide with anger and his mouth smeared with egg yolk.

"I want to know about Cordie," he demanded. "I want to know how Cordie is."

"She's fine. I see her every day."

"Liar!" Gabby slapped Adam hard across the face.

"Now, now, Mr. Gabby," Lincoln said, walking through his curtain. "There's no need to hit Private Christy."

"He hit me!"

"That was last fall. It's time to forgive and forget. Isn't that right, Private Christy?"

"Yes, sir." He hung his head.

"Go about your duties." Lincoln looked at Gabby. "Why don't you finish your breakfast?"

"My coffee's cold."

"The coffee's always cold," Mrs. Lincoln added.

Adam took the chamber pots out the service entrance to clean them. He kept thinking of Lincoln's words, forgive and forget. How could he forgive himself? How could he forget? Cleaning the pots took longer each day, so that by the time he had finished and returned them to the billiards room, the breakfast tray was ready to return to the kitchen. He put them next to the sink where Phebe stood.

"Hello," he whispered.

Her face hardened as she continued to look down.

"I'm sorry," he added. This was not his first apology. He had lost count of the times he had tried to seek her forgiveness. Each time, stony silence met his offer.

After lunch, he left the Executive Mansion and walked down the street, where crowds were gathering to greet Duff upon his return from Richmond. Several men slapped Adam on the back and offered him mugs of beer, which he refused. Since October he had stopped drinking. Crossing the iron bridge over the slough, Adam headed for Armory Square Hospital. He had to apologize to Jessie again, hoping against hope she would finally forgive him. Standing just inside the door to the ward, he watched her wash a soldier's brow. She was about to stand, and he was ready to intercept her, when a shout arose from Pennsylvania Avenue. He knew he had to go. Quickly looking back into the ward, Adam made eye contact with Jessie. He smiled and waved, but she stared blankly.

Back at the Executive Mansion, he watched Duff pass down the hall, surrounded by enthusiastic admirers. Alethia rushed to give him a long embrace.

"Private Christy!" Tad called out.

Adam looked down to see Tad jumping in front of him.

"It was great! The ship went adrift, then we spent the rest of way on a barge rowed by sailors and when we landed they shouted, 'Glory hallelujah!' and I got to play in Jeff Davis's house and—"

"Come, Tad," Alethia called out.

Tad bounded toward her as she smiled at Adam. Looking out the window, he noticed the sun was lower in the sky, a sign it was time for another meal in the basement. He walked down the service stairs, crunching the straw mats, vaguely remembering how once he had thought silence sounded like death. Now everything sounded like death. When he entered the kitchen, he saw Phebe putting the plates on the tray.

"Hello, Phebe," he said, trying to put his hand on her shoulder. "Please say something. I'm so sorry."

Phebe pulled away sharply, grabbing a knife from the sink and pointing it at Adam, her eyes ablaze with hatred. A tall, older black man, the new butler brought in the day after Neal's death, entered the room. Cleotis was his name, and Adam found him affable, a quietly confident, educated, freeborn man from Rhode Island. He swept in between Adam and Phebe, taking the knife and putting his arm around her.

"The tray's ready," he said. "Here's a War Department wire for Mr. Stanton. Do you know where he is?"

Nodding, Adam's gaze remained fixed on Phebe, as he noticed for the first time, the slight swelling in her belly.

Chapter Forty-One

Riotous celebration lasted until the late afternoon, leaving Duff depleted and nervous. His office was filled with revelers opening bottles of wine and drinking with elation. Duff was trying to slip from the room when Brooks caught up with him.

"Where are you going, sir? Everyone wants to toast your return."

"War Department," Duff replied.

"You look drained, Mr. Lincoln. Why don't you stay here, and I'll go for you."

"No, thank you, Mr. Brooks." Retreating hastily, Duff replied, "I'd rather go myself."

Walking swiftly through the turnstile gate onto the War Department grounds, Duff went to the office of statistics and approached the front desk.

"Do you have fatality lists for Michigan from 1863?"

While he waited for the clerk to return, Duff breathed deeply, feeling his stomach tighten. On the *U.S.S. Malvern* returning from Richmond, a Union sailor had sneaked into his room as Duff slept, crouched by his bed and awakened him with a thump on the head.

"What are you doing pretending to be president, Duff Read?"

Duff's mouth had gone dry, his heart pounding.

"Who are you?"

"Grover Kenton."

Grover Kenton, Grover—then Duff had placed him; a boy from a neighboring farm who always liked to torment him.

"What are you going to do?"

"Nothing. You're already dead."

"What?" Duff sat up. "What do you mean?"

"You're dead." Kenton rose, turning away. "It was in the local newspaper. You died in some battle. I don't know which one."

"My family, how did they take it?"

"I don't know."

Duff's thoughts went to his elderly mother and father, and how they must have felt when they read his obituary. Perhaps his family was proud he had died a hero.

"You're not going to tell anyone, are you?"

"Why? You're dead." With that, Kenton had left.

The clerk plopped the fatality file for Michigan on the front desk, rousing Duff from his thoughts. He quickly flipped through the pages until he found his hometown. Sliding down the page, his hand stopped at his own name: killed in action at the Second Battle of Manassas, August 1862.

"Did you find what you wanted, Mr. President?" the clerk asked.

"Yes, thank you." Duff forced himself to smile, and then a thought crossed his mind. "Will you bring me the file for Ohio fatalities, please?"

As the clerk walked away, Duff wondered if from the beginning Stanton had planned to have him killed, and if Stanton also planted Adam's obituary early on; if so, all of them were to die, including Alethia.

"Here it is, sir." The clerk put the file in front of Duff.

Where was Adam from? Steubenville, he remembered. Duff thumbed through the pages until he came to Adam's hometown, then stopped abruptly. Adam Christy had been killed in action, Second Battle of Manassas, August 1862.

Chapter Forty-Two

Stanton unlocked the billiards room door, rousing Gabby from a restless afternoon nap. Gabby listened carefully to Stanton as he spoke to the Lincolns.

"The president has returned from Richmond."

"With Tad safe and sound," Mrs. Lincoln said.

"You have to learn the details of the trip," Stanton said, ignoring her. "When you return upstairs, you'll have to answer questions from the press."

"Our places upstairs?" She sounded surprised. "This will be over soon?"

"General Grant is pursuing General Lee through the heart of Virginia."

"I'll be back with my precious Taddie."

And I'll be back with my precious Cordie, Gabby thought. His heart raced as he thought about what he would do first once he was free to go to her.

"Calm down, Molly," Lincoln said. "Listen to Mr. Stanton."

"After Richmond fell," Stanton began, "the navy removed Confederate torpedoes in the James River. You were aboard the *U.S.S. Malvern* until it could no longer pass the line of enemy obstructions, then you transferred to a barge pulled by the tugboat *Glance*. You were recognized by a group of colored workmen who shouted, 'Bless the Lord, this is the great Messiah! Glory, hallelujah!' From there you, Mr. Lincoln, and Tad went to the Confederate White House where you sat in Jefferson Davis's chair." He paused to cough.

"You don't look well, Mr. Stanton," Lincoln said.

Good, Gabby thought. I hope he dies.

"You spent time reviewing troops, and left Richmond yesterday evening, and arrived at the capital this afternoon. You'll speak to the public tomorrow and meet with the Cabinet on Wednesday.

"About reconstruction of the South?" Lincoln asked.

"I'm sure the topic will come up. I've encouraged him to pursue your agenda. He's been so persistent he's alienated several sympathetic Cabinet members."

"When I return, I can soothe any hurt feelings," Lincoln said.

"Perhaps."

Gabby noticed a pause.

"Mr. Stanton," Lincoln said, "exactly what is your position?"

"On what?"

"Reconstruction."

"Undecided."

Stanton, as far as Gabby was concerned, did not want reconstruction. He wanted to keep the nation divided to make it easier for him to become king. Long ago, Gabby had decided Stanton was not interested in ending the war, but making himself all-powerful.

"The rebels must be punished," Stanton said.

"I believe they already have been," Lincoln replied.

"They certainly have," Mrs. Lincoln agreed.

Gabby heard the door open. It must be the private with supper.

"When you return to office, you may pursue any reconstruction policy you wish, but I doubt you'll succeed."

"Excuse me," Adam said.

Slowly rounding the corner, Gabby watched him place the tray on the billiards table.

"Here's a wire from the War Department." Adam handed Stanton the envelope and turned away. As he was about to pass Gabby, Adam lowered his eyes. Gabby noticed Lincoln watched intently as Stanton opened the wire and read it. He reached to his wife to squeeze her hand. Stanton cleared his throat, and Gabby saw Lincoln lean forward.

"This is the news we've been waiting for. General Lee surrendered at the Appomattox courthouse in Virginia. The war is over."

The war is over, Gabby repeated in his mind. At first he did not knew what to do or what to think. He finally would be reunited with Cordie. That was all that mattered. He was going to see Cordie.

Chapter Forty-Three

"Cordie will fix me a good supper once I get home tonight."

"It'll be end of the week before you can leave," Stanton said.

"That's fine." Lincoln put his arm around his wife. "We'll arise Easter Sunday."

His mind a blank, Adam unlocked the door. Not knowing where his feet would take him, he did not care; this was the first happy day for many months and he was unable to deal with it. He was out the door and in the hall, looking both ways. When he focused on the kitchen, he thought of Phebe. Even though he knew she would never forgive him, Adam felt an obligation to let her and Cleotis know the good news. He found Phebe sitting and rubbing her feet while the butler swept the floor.

"The war's over."

Phebe dropped her feet to the floor and slipped on her shoes.

"Thank you, Private," Cleotis replied in deep, solemn tones. "The struggle for freedom is at last over. Hallelujah."

"We can go home," Adam softly said.

"You may be going home, but, the Good Lord willing, we are home. Free and where we should be."

"Yes, sir." Looking at Phebe, he saw her reach for Cleotis's hand and smile. Adam left the kitchen, looked down at his clothes, and rubbed his chin. He needed to clean up, he decided, before he went to Jessie to beg for her forgiveness.

In his room, Adam removed his blue tunic, stained with bean soup and mustard. Looking in the mirror, he brushed his fingers through his unruly red hair. They would have beautiful red-haired children, and he would be a good father. His brush lathered soap onto his stubbly face. Perhaps he could get a job at one of the pottery factories in Steubenville. He did not want to be in the army anymore. Next he searched his room for a spare tunic, finding it under the cot, stained with vomit. Deciding the first tunic was better, Adam put it back on and took a wet hand cloth to wipe away the worst of the stains. When that failed, he told himself it did not look all that bad.

Making his way through the crowded streets, Adam crossed the iron bridge and ran to the Armory Square Hospital. Inside the ward, he looked furtively around, hoping to find Jessie, but could not see her. He did notice the odd-looking man who had approached them on the street the night of the Gettysburg celebration. Adam walked up to him, and he looked up from writing a letter for a soldier whose hands were covered with bandages.

"Where's Jessie?"

"She's in a back room with Miss Zook," the man said, "who's not feeling well. I'm afraid the war has not been kind to her."

"The war's over."

"I was expecting it." He looked down at the wounded soldier. "I have to finish this letter. He wants his mother to know he's coming home."

Adam walked down the long aisle, his stomach slightly turning from the mixture of smells—liniment, incontinence, alcohol. Opening the door at the end of the hall, he saw Jessie sitting on the edge of Cordie's cot, wiping her moist cheeks. Jessie turned to look at him, her eyes blank.

"The war's over," he said.

Jessie turned her attention to Cordie, who was delirious.

"I've got to get it done," she mumbled. "Gabby needs a quilt. I can't get it done just lying here. I got—I got…"

"Of course, me dear, get your strength back," Jessie said. "Be quiet, me love. Try to sleep now."

"Did you hear me?" Adam said.

"Yes."

"Gabby's got to get a quilt," Cordie insisted feverishly.

"Darlin', I'll finish the quilt meself."

"So tired." Cordie shook her head. "Can't finish the Gabby quilt." She looked up at Jessie and grabbed her arm. "Take care of Gabby. He used to be so smart, but he needs somebody to take care of him." Her eyes searched Jessie's face. "Take care of him."

"Of course, me darlin'. Try to sleep."

"Gabby's leaving the White House soon," Adam said. "He can help you get well."

"Gabby's coming home?" Cordie's eyes widened. "Good. Good." She focused on Adam. "Bring him here as soon as you can."

"I will."

"Gabby's coming home. That's good. I feel better now. Gabby's coming home." Cordie coughed, gasped, and stopped breathing. Her eyes gazed blankly over Jessie's shoulder.

"God bless ye, me darlin'," Jessie said as she closed Cordie's eyes.

"You were good to her." Adam put his hand on her shoulder. "We can take care of Gabby. He'll like it in Steubenville. It's a friendly little town."

"What do you mean?"

"Are you all right?" Adam realized how warm her body felt beneath his hand, and that her face was moist with perspiration. "You seem awfully hot."

"I'm fine." She coughed.

"How long have you been sick?"

"I don't know."

"Have you seen the doctor?"

"The doctors are for the soldiers."

"But you're important too," Adam said.

"I can take care of meself."

"But I want to take care of you," he replied in a whisper.

"Ye can't take care of yourself."

"You're right," Adam said, his mind racing to form the precise words to win her back. "I've behaved terribly, but all that is behind me. I've grown up."

"I have to make funeral arrangements," Jessie said, standing.

"What about Gabby?"

"I'll think of something."

"What about me?"

"You're grown up. Take care of yourself."

Adam followed her out the door, watching her cough as she disappeared into the crowded ward. The odd-looking man walked up.

"Miss Zook is dead, isn't she?"

"Yes."

"You love Miss Home, don't you?"

"She hates me."

"Love and hate are related; she could not be so deeply hurt if she did not love as deeply."

"No, she hates me."

"She loves you. Give her time."

"We don't have time."

Chapter Forty-Four

Alethia looked out of her bedroom window at the setting sun, thinking back to the late afternoon, two years ago now, when she unpacked her bag. She had been afraid until she met Duff. The last year had been the happiest in her life, and she had hopes it would continue. She was a little sad that she would never see Tad again. He had been so wild when they had first met, but now he was a kind, loving child. Perhaps she would have her own child soon, if Duff proposed taking her to Michigan and marrying her.

"Molly," Duff said at her bedroom door, "it's time for supper."

"I thought the crowds would never leave." Alethia rushed to him and hugged him tightly. Looking up, she kissed him. "I missed you so much while you were in Richmond."

"I missed you, too," Duff said. His face seemed to darken. "You know, the war will be over soon."

"Yes, I know," Alethia replied, taking Duff's large, rough hand in hers as she led him out the door. "I can hardly wait. We've so many plans to make, plans we were afraid to make before now."

"I thought you might be doing that."

"Of course. Don't tell me you haven't thought of the day when all of this would be over."

They entered the dining room, and Tad was already there. Cleotis appeared with their dinner of beefsteak, gravy, potatoes, and greens. Smiling graciously, he put the plates down and then poured milk for Tad and coffee for Alethia and Duff.

"Thank you, Cleotis," Alethia said.

"My pleasure, madam," he replied and left.

"I like Cleotis very much," Alethia said, sipping her coffee. "He's much friendlier than Neal—not that Neal was rude, but there was something aloof about him. Neal's departure was so sudden. Do you know why, Father?"

"No. Perhaps he finally crossed the line of proper behavior," Duff replied.

"Shouldn't you have been told why?" she asked.

"Sometimes it's best not being told."

"Anyway, I like Cleotis very much," Alethia said.

As they finished their meal, Stanton opened the door and sat in the empty chair at the end of the table, his face as somber as ever.

"General Lee surrendered today at the Appomattox courthouse in Virginia."

"The war's over!" Tad exclaimed. "Good! I can finally—"

"Tad dearest," Alethia sweetly said, "have you finished your supper?"

"Yes, Mama."

"Would you like to inform the staff the war's over?"

"Yes, Mama."

After Tad closed the door, Stanton listened for the little footsteps to fade. After what Alethia thought was an interminable pause, he put on his pebble glasses and pulled out a notepad, opened it, and read slowly.

"Your debts will be canceled Friday, and you both can leave after sunset."

"Thank God," Alethia said in a whisper.

"Thank me," Stanton said, "for both of you would have surely hanged if I hadn't intervened."

Alethia stiffened. Looking at Duff, she could not sense a direction to follow. In the last two years, she not only had fallen in love with Duff, but also had learned to lean on his judgment. At this moment, she found him indecipherable.

"So, it'll be as simple as that," Duff finally said. "We pack our bags, mount a carriage, and disappear in the night."

"As simple as that." An odd smile crossed Stanton's Cupid's bow lips.

His tone bothered Alethia, until she thought of her new life in Michigan. Once they were on the steamboat up the Potomac, they could forget all the lies, pretense, and, most of all, Edwin Stanton.

"Your duties aren't over yet," he continued. "There'll be a candlelight parade tomorrow evening, so you'll have to read a speech on the balcony."

"Will Lincoln write it?" Duff asked.

"Yes, like the others," Stanton replied. "And then the Cabinet meets on Wednesday and Friday."

Alethia concentrated on experiencing spring in Michigan; frankly, affairs of government no longer interested her.

"Enjoy your supper," Stanton said. "Take everything with you; we don't want any evidence that anyone except the Lincolns have lived upstairs."

No evidence left to show they were there, she repeated to herself; a disturbing notion. Shrugging, she decided not to dwell on that thought. After Stanton left, Alethia went to Duff, putting her arms around his neck. She chose to ignore the slight stiffening in his back.

"Isn't he a queer little man?"

"Yes, he is odd."

"The war's over." She plopped into the chair next to Duff, leaning toward him. "The war's finally over. I can hardly believe it. Can you?"

"No." Duff stared at his food.

"Eat, eat," she said. "You don't have to worry about being as bony as Mr. Lincoln anymore." Her giggles erupted. "I can't wait to see you at your full, glorious size."

He did not respond to her joke.

"You're still worried about your past?"

Duff nodded.

"Then you don't have to eat. Let's go upstairs." They stood and went to the door. "Your week has been so hectic. The long trip to Richmond, capped tonight with news of the end of the war—why, no wonder you're let down." She paused for a reply from him, but when none was forthcoming, Alethia continued, "You're tired, that's all. Why, after a good night's sleep, you'll be all rested and able to concentrate on our new life together."

Duff climbed the service stairs quickly, Alethia noticed. Maybe he was eager to return to their bedrooms where they could be alone, the thought of which made her heart beat faster. Once they entered Duff's bedroom, he went to the bed and slowly sat, his head sagging. Something was weighing on his mind, and Alethia did not know what it was. She joined him on the bed, her arm around his waist.

"I know I've said it before," Alethia said in a whisper, putting her head on his chest, "but now that we have all the uncertainties of the war behind us, I want to say it again…I love you."

Duff's sad eyes stared into Alethia's open face. She could feel his emotional intensity and leaned in to kiss him. He kissed back passionately for a second, then pulled away.

"No, I can't do this to you," he said.

"What do you mean?"

"I'm not worthy, Alethia."

"Don't judge yourself too harshly," she said, shaking her head. "You told me what you did. Yes, it was terrible, but war's devastating, forcing good men to do unspeakable things. I forgive you."

"You don't know everything."

"I know everything I want to know. We're all flawed human beings. You may have killed innocent men, but you saved my soul. All that kept me going was the promise of living with you in Michigan."

"You can't go to Michigan." Standing, he walked to the window and looked out onto Pennsylvania Avenue, where small groups of people were already gathering. Alethia held her breath when he turned to speak. "I've a wife and three children."

"You're married?" Alethia blinked in disbelief. "Oh." She felt her heart collapse. "Mr. Stanton knew about your family?"

"Yes."

How foolish she must have looked to Stanton, who had watched as she caressed Duff's hands and looked fondly at him as he spoke. Stanton must have been laughing at her. Alethia loathed him even more than before. Her eyes turned hard as she focused on Duff.

"Will you tell your wife you deserted, you killed men for food, and you had relations with a woman who thought you loved her?"

Duff remained silent.

"Does she know you're a coward?"

Chapter Forty-Four

"Leave tonight," he said softly. "Don't wait until Friday."

Alethia stood, straightening her back in an attempt to keep from crying.

Duff stood also. "I'm very fond of you, Alethia."

"You seduced me."

"I think we seduced each other."

"You're a coward." She slapped him hard across the face.

Walking through the bedroom door, she slammed it and sat on her bed. She swore she would never cry again. Perhaps returning to Bladensburg was best. She would never be a fool again. Tad bounded in, rousing Alethia from her thoughts.

"Everybody knows now!" he announced. "Old Tom Pen, Mr. Brooks, Tom Cross, Charles Forbes, Alexander Williamson, Phebe, and Cleotis." He came close to whisper, "I even talked to Mama through the billiards room door. She said she already knew. Ain't it wonderful?" He paused long enough to wipe the tears from her cheeks. "Oh. I didn't think about how sad you'd be. I'm really going to miss you, Mrs. Mama. I'll miss Mr. Papa too, but not as much as you."

"I'll miss you too, my love." Alethia hugged him around the neck. "You see, I never had a son of my own. So you're the only little boy I'll ever have." She pulled out a lace handkerchief to daub her eyes, then smiled and ran her fingers through Tad's tousled hair. "I'll keep up with you through the newspapers. I'm sure they'll report where you go to college, when you graduate, and whom you marry."

"That's right." His eyes widened. "We won't ever get to talk to each other again. Even if we saw each other on the street we couldn't even wave. You'll know about me from newspapers, but I won't know about you, unless you do something to get in the papers. Like marry somebody important."

"I don't think that'll happen."

"Do something big. What's your name, so I'll know it's you?"

"Alethia Haliday."

"That's a pretty name." He kissed her cheek. "I love you, Alethia Haliday."

Chapter Forty-Five

Lamon raced up the Executive Mansion steps, past the drunken guard, and up the grand staircase, eager to confront the man who pretended to be Lincoln. Less than an hour earlier, a deputy marshal had burst into his office with the news that Lee had surrendered to Grant, and Lamon wanted to find out the truth that Stanton had kept from him for more than two years. Opening the president's bedroom door, he saw the man stretched out on the bed, a gangling arm across his face.

"Sir?" Lamon said. "I just heard the war's over."

The man sat up, revealing red, moist eyes, and replied, "Yes, everything's over."

"No, sir. Everything won't be over until I see Mr. Lincoln again."

"Everything's over for me."

"You have to help me."

"What do you mean?"

Lamon shut the door and sat on the bed next to him and whispered, "You can tell me the truth. Mr. Stanton can't hurt you now."

"The truth." He bowed his head. "The truth doesn't solve anything."

"The truth will solve everything. Look. I know you were lying about all this business being Mr. Lincoln's idea." Lamon waited for a response. "Are you still scared?"

"No, not really."

"Then why not tell me where Mr. Lincoln is?"

"You don't know?" The man looked up.

"No. If I can rescue Mr. Lincoln, we can stop Mr. Stanton before he does anything else," Lamon said. "You want to help us, don't you?"

"We're beyond help." He sighed.

"All right." Lamon paused to control his emotions. He wanted to throttle the man, but knew that would do no good. "I know after two years it seems like everything's hopeless. That's what Mr. Stanton wanted you to think, but we can still help each other." He searched the man's face. "Mr. Lincoln could die if you don't help."

"What? How do you know this?"

"Know? I don't know anything. But my gut tells me if Stanton was crazy enough to do all this he's crazy enough to kill Mr. Lincoln."

"Then Mr. Lincoln is going to die despite what I can do. I'm already dead." He put his head in his hands for a moment and then looked up, his hands cupped in front of his mouth. "But we all don't have to die."

"That's right." Lamon's eyes widened as he leaned forward. "Nobody has to die."

"Baltimore."

"Mr. Lincoln is in Baltimore?"

"And Mrs. Lincoln," the man added.

"Where in Baltimore?'

The man blinked several times.

"Where in Baltimore?" Lamon repeated.

"Fort McHenry."

"They've known all along?"

"I don't know." The man turned to smile. "I'm only the double."

"I'll leave right now."

Lamon stood, but the man grabbed his arm.

"Take the woman with you."

"What woman?"

"Her." He nodded toward the other bedroom. "I want her out of here tonight. I don't trust Mr. Stanton."

"Very well." Lamon said. "Do you want to go too?"

"No." He let Lamon's arm go and looked down. "I have meetings to attend. There's a candlelight parade tomorrow night. The people still need to see the president."

"Good man." Lamon patted the man's back. "I'll make sure she's safe."

"Thank you."

Lamon left and went next door and knocked. The woman softly told him to enter, and he did. He found her sitting in a rocking chair, staring out the window.

"Mrs. Lincoln?"

"Yes?"

"May we speak?"

"Of course, Mr. Lamon."

Her voice sounded lifeless. Lamon walked over to her and went down on his haunches. Her face was expressionless.

"You can leave, miss," he said in a whisper.

"What?" She continued to look out the window.

"I know you're not Mrs. Lincoln," he said as kindly as he could, sensing she was emotionally fragile. "I know Mr. Stanton put you here."

She looked at Lamon.

"How long have you known?"

"Since the beginning. Mr. Stanton told me it was Mr. Lincoln's idea, but I didn't believe him." Lamon paused for her response. She was as forlorn as the man. "Miss, I know this has been very stressful for you."

"Not all of it." She smiled slightly. "Tad is a delightful child."

"I'm leaving for Baltimore tonight." He leaned toward her. "I can take you with me. There's no reason for you to stay any longer."

"I can leave now?" She straightened her back. "Mr. Stanton said I could leave tonight?"

"No, the man—Mr. Lincoln's double—suggested it. He's worried for your safety. Mr. Stanton knows nothing of this."

She fell back in the rocker, the air seemingly leaving her body, and looked back out the window.

"Miss?"

"I don't care what he wants," she said in a rueful whisper.

"I don't care what Mr. Stanton wants either," said Lamon. "He's had what he wanted for the last two years. Now it's what we want."

"No, I mean…" Her voice trailed off as her hand went to her cheek. Her eyes seemed to focus on a distant object. "I don't want Tad to be left alone."

"His parents will be back soon," Lamon said, "and the man is still here."

"The man is still here," she repeated blankly. "No, I don't want him to be left alone. He's been through so much, and he's come to depend on me. I can't let him down."

Sighing, Lamon stood and put his hand on the rocking chair.

"As you wish." He smiled. "I must say, miss, I've been wrong about you and the man."

"Wrong?" She looked up.

"I didn't think much of you for replacing the Lincolns," he explained. "But now I see both of you are fine people."

"Both of us?" She smiled queerly. "Fine people?" Her eyes returned to stare unseeingly out the window. "Thank you."

Chapter Forty-Six

As Adam balanced the breakfast tray the next morning to unlock the billiards room door, he heard Mary Lincoln fuss about packing.

"I know that woman ruined all my dresses," she said, "and I wouldn't be surprised if she's stolen all my finest toiletries and unmentionables."

"Excuse me," Adam said as he entered, keeping his head down and going to the billiards table.

"You would come in as I was talking about my unmentionables," she said with a sniff. After a pause she added, "Thank you for retrieving my items for me as I required them."

Adam watched out of the corner of his eye as Mrs. Lincoln plopped things into a box. She paused to consider the bottle of laudanum in her hand.

"How many bottles of this have I used since living in the basement?"

"I don't know, ma'am," he replied

"The partial bottle you brought down here the first day, and this one," she said, answering her own question. "It's close to empty now." Pausing, Mrs. Lincoln looked at Adam, her eyes seeming to soften. "A bottle used to last a month. One would think I'd need more than two bottles in two years." A smile flickered across her face. "Perhaps I'm stronger than I thought."

"Yes, ma'am." Adam hoped that was the proper response; with Mrs. Lincoln he rarely knew. It apparently was appropriate, because she nodded, sat, and sipped her coffee.

As he had for most of his time in the basement, Lincoln stayed behind the French lace curtain. Adam's routine was to leave his plate on the billiards table so Lincoln could retrieve it when he wanted. Yet on this morning, Adam felt the urge to speak to Lincoln, so he took the plate to the edge of the curtain.

"Mr. President," Adam said. "May I bring in your breakfast?"

"If you like," Lincoln replied.

Lincoln, dressed in a shirt and trousers, was sitting on the cot when Adam brought the plate in and placed it beside him.

"Thank you, Private Christy." He looked at Adam, who was standing on one foot and then the other. "Something on your mind?"

"Yes, sir." His eyes looked away.

"Sit down, please."

Settling on the edge of Lincoln's cot, Adam tried to compose his thoughts so that the president would not think he was a bigger fool than he already believed himself to be.

"Mr. President, I wish to take this opportunity to express my sincere apologies for carrying out Mr. Stanton's orders."

"Well said." Lincoln sipped his black coffee. "Please don't continue. Your innocence was as plain as the spots on a speckled pup the first day you pulled your revolver on me."

"Thank you, sir." He paused, trying to compose his thoughts further. "Life will be better now the war's over."

"Well," Lincoln said with a drawl, his eyes darting up with sad amusement, "don't expect too much." After chewing on a dry piece of toast, he swallowed and cleared his throat. "Let me give you some advice. Don't look outside yourself to find happiness."

"Yes, sir."

"Do you know what that means?"

"No, sir."

"Good. Your honesty is intact." Lincoln sighed in resignation. "The war's over, yes. The conflict continues. The Union will go on, yes; but we won't."

"I don't understand."

"Ah." Lincoln looked at Adam. "Don't give up your honesty. You know exactly what I mean; it's just that it's too awful to accept."

Adam's face flushed, and he could not speak.

"I've scared you," Lincoln said. "Don't be afraid. Why be afraid of things you can't change?"

"Yes, sir." Adam stood, nodded, and left through the curtains, where he faced Mrs. Lincoln quietly eating her eggs at the billiards table.

"I hope your breakfast is to your taste," Adam hesitantly said.

"It's fine." Mrs. Lincoln paused to chew daintily. "It was always fine." Patting her lips with her napkin, she put it down and pushed the plate away. "I complained to punish you. I focused my anger on you." She looked at him with compassion. "Mr. Stanton's the one I should have abused; but, unfortunately, he wasn't here and you were." Mrs. Lincoln reached out to pat his hand. "I'm wicked," she said in a whisper. "I knew very well your mother died when you were a child. I played upon your soft disposition to get what I wanted, and when that didn't work, I hurt you as your mother's death hurt you."

"Thank you, but I should have behaved more like a gentleman."

"Your sins are trivial compared to mine. Please let it go. We've the rest of our lives now to be good people."

Adam furrowed his brow.

"You frown?"

"Mr. Gabby's sister died last night at Armory Square Hospital. Her last words were for him."

"Oh." Mrs. Lincoln's hand went to her cheek. "How sad. I'd never seen such devotion between brother and sister." She looked into his eyes. "I could tell him for you."

"I thought he wasn't talking to you."

"We settled all that last night. Just as you and I have settled our differences now."

"I appreciate your offer," Adam said, "but I promised her I would tell him."

"I understand," she replied.

He smiled at Mrs. Lincoln, nodded, and turned to Gabby's cubicle behind the crates and barrels. He watched Gabby on his pallet, stirring restlessly and mumbling.

"Cord—cord—cordiecordiecordie," Gabby muttered. After twisting and moaning a few more moments, he suddenly sat up, shouting clearly, "Cordie!" His eyes were wide and blank; after batting them several times, he focused on Adam.

"I'm sorry to wake you up, Mr. Gabby," Adam said, setting the plate on a chair with dirty trousers and shirts strewn across the back of it.

"Cordie is dead, isn't she?" he whispered, staring at the plate.

"Yes. Last night." Love really did connect people, Adam decided, realizing Gabby already sensed his sister's death. He envied even the old man's grief.

"I'm not hungry anymore." He looked at the plate of fried eggs and toast and then glanced away indifferently. "They say we'll be out of here by the end of the week."

"Yes, sir. We can all go Friday night."

"It doesn't seem to matter anymore, does it? The rats are gone. Wish we hadn't killed all of them so fast; it gave me something to worry about. I mean, something of no account to worry about. I've enough honest-to-God worries as it is."

"You really don't have anything to worry about now." Adam tried to sound hopeful.

"Cordie's dead. There's plenty to worry about. Uncle Sammy's dead. Mama's dead. Papa's dead. Joe's dead. Everybody's dead except me."

"No, you don't have to worry. Cordie had a friend at the hospital. She was with her right to the last moment. Her name's Jessie Home."

"Is she a young woman?"

"Yes."

"Then I'll scare her away. Young women have always been scared of me. Well, not always, but that was a long time ago when I was someone else. I don't remember him very well, but I do remember young women were rather fond of him."

"Jessie's different than most young women," Adam said. "She doesn't care about what people seem like but what they are like."

"You love this girl, don't you?" Gabby looked at Adam. "I can tell by the way you talk about her. And your eyes. Say her name again."

"Jessie Home."

"See. When you say her name, your cheeks turn red. And you can't help but smile when you talk about her. If you can trust her, then I can trust her; after all, you can't love somebody you can't trust."

Adam darkened when he thought about how much he loved and trusted Jessie, and how little she must love and trust him.

"And don't worry. I forgive you."

"I hurt you the night you jumped me," Adam said quietly. "If Mr. Lincoln hadn't pulled me off, I might have hurt you real bad."

"You couldn't help it," Gabby said. "You just fought back like anyone would have. You know, it was all her fault." He nodded beyond the crates and barrels to Mrs. Lincoln. Leaning into Adam, he added in a whisper, "I don't think she's quite right in the head. When people are like that, there's nothing you can do but forgive them."

"Are you sure about breakfast?" Adam asked.

"Maybe I'll be hungry again sometime, but right now I don't think so."

Adam smiled and took the plate away. He stacked the dishes on the tray and left for the kitchen. Phebe kept her head down when he came in, and he did not say anything. Back in the hallway, Adam felt a tug at his elbow. It was Stanton, who pulled him into the stairwell.

"I've a new assignment for you."

"No." Adam moved away. "When the Lincolns are back upstairs, when the others leave, I want to go. I want to return to Steubenville. Forget the commission."

"I have," Stanton said. "You're guilty of kidnapping and holding hostage the president and his wife. I was aghast when I learned of your plot."

"Do you think people will believe that?"

"Do you think they will believe you?"

"Lincoln," Adam said with confidence. "Lincoln knows the truth." He paused and softened his voice. "Lincoln won't judge me. He won't judge you. He knows you did what you did to help the nation. The war's over."

"The war's never over. We now have to make the rebels suffer. They must obey the law."

"That war Mr. Lincoln can win. He won't punish us. He's a man of justice."

"It is exactly because he is a man of justice that we will be punished."

"I've already been punished." Adam turned somber.

"You don't know what punishment is." Stanton's beady eyes narrowed. "Do what I say. You murdered the butler. We hang murderers. If you cooperate, you can go home to Steubenville."

"What is it?" Adam said, hanging his head in defeat.

"The old woman, the sister of the janitor, the one who died this week. Did she ever say anything of interest?"

"No."

"Are you sure?"

"Yes."

"She's dead," Stanton said. "It makes no sense to protect her when your life's in danger."

"Oh." He looked off. "One time she asked about troop movements."

"Troop movements?" Stanton pursed his Cupid's bow lips.

"She said her landlady might turn her out if she couldn't get any information from her brother who worked in the White House."

"Do you know the name of the landlady?"

"No."

"Do you know where the boardinghouse is?"

"I escorted her home several times."

"Very good." Stanton paused to think. "Go to the boardinghouse to say you're collecting her personal effects to give to her brother. Then keep your ears open."

"What am I listening for?"

"Conspiracies, plots, assassins."

"Assassins?" Adam's eyes widened.

"What do you think we're talking about?" Stanton snapped. "Lincoln must die."

"But he's forgiven me."

"He's never mentioned forgiving me, and if I go to prison, you hang."

"I don't think I can help kill President Lincoln." Adam swallowed hard.

"You can, and you will." Stanton paused. "If you find anyone interested, tell them to meet you under Aqueduct Bridge at midnight."

"But I don't know—"

"Just tell them to be under the bridge at midnight."

Chapter Forty-Seven

Adam climbed the stairs to the second-story door of the white boardinghouse at 541 H Street, his stomach tied in knots. He had always admired Lincoln, even as a youth in Steubenville, reading stories about the Illinois lawyer. In the last two years, even though he had had to keep Lincoln hostage, he had known the president was right. Adam did not want to be part of his assassination—but neither did he want to hang for killing Neal. He forced himself to knock.

"Yes?" A tall, black-haired woman dressed in black opened the door and stared at Adam with blank eyes.

"Mr. Zook asked me to empty his sister's room and bring the items to him."

"She always talked of a brother." She raised an eyebrow. "But I never saw him."

"I assure you Gabby Zook exists," he said. "We work together at the Executive Mansion."

"And who are you?" Her mouth hardened at the mention of the Executive Mansion.

"I'm Private Adam Christy," he replied. "And what's your name?"

"I'm Mary Surratt, the owner of this boardinghouse, and as such have the right to deny entrance to anyone I consider suspicious."

"Are you saying you're going to deny Mr. Zook his rightful possessions?"

"That's not what I'm saying," she replied.

"Then what are you saying?"

"I just want to make sure Miss Zook's possessions won't be stolen." She fluttered her eyes in frustration.

"Are you accusing me, an agent of the White House, of stealing a deceased woman's property?"

"I did not say that."

Out of the corner of his eye, Adam noticed a young man, perhaps a few years older than he, standing in the parlor door. He had a fair complexion and curly, black hair. On his face was a bemused expression which Adam could not decipher.

Covertly watching the man, Adam said, "Just because Abraham Lincoln has no morals doesn't mean I'm a thief."

The curly-haired man smiled.

"I did not call you a thief," Mrs. Surratt said in irritation.

"Good," Adam said. "Where's her room?"

"Upstairs." She stepped aside to allow him in. "Follow me."

Adam watched the young man move into the hallway as they went up the stairs.

"This is her room," Mrs. Surratt said, opening the door.

"Thank you." Adam walked in to see a clutter of tattered clothes, sources of Gabby quilts that would never be made. "You may leave the door open."

"Of course I will." Mrs. Surratt glared at him and left.

Looking into a chest of drawers, he noticed neat stacks of worn clothing. On top of the chest was a framed photograph of Cordie and Gabby when they were younger and not beaten down by life. Gabby would like to have that picture now, Adam thought as he reached for it.

"I couldn't help but overhear your telling Mrs. Surratt you're assigned to the Executive Mansion."

Adam turned to see the young man who had been standing in the parlor door. He leaned against the wall in a nonchalant pose.

"Yes, I am," he replied.

"She often talked of her brother who couldn't leave the mansion."

"I'm gathering her things to give him."

"In my opinion," the man said, stretching to his full height, "the Republicans killed her, keeping her from her brother." His eyelids drooped but could not cover his intense emotion.

"I agree." Adam paused to appraise him further. "Who are you?"

"John Booth. Perhaps you've heard of me."

"No."

"My family is well known in the theater."

"I don't go to the theater."

"I've performed in several Shakespearean plays."

"I don't understand Shakespeare."

Booth blinked his dark eyes and ran his fingers through his curly, black hair. Adam was pleased; he seemed to unsettle Booth.

"So you think Lincoln has no morals?"

"Yes," he lied.

"Neither do I." Booth smiled, revealing white, even teeth underneath his full black mustache. "I'm from Maryland and have no taste for Union bullies."

Before Adam replied, he went to the door and closed it. He studied Booth's eyes. Was he the interested party for whom he was searching? Adam wondered.

"How were you assigned to the White House, Private Christy?"

"My father knows Edwin Stanton."

"He's another person with no morals."

"Yes," Adam said. "I hate him." He paused. "I hate them both."

Adam could see Booth's brain working through his etched, pallid brow. He hoped he had convinced him.

"And why do you hate Mr. Lincoln and Mr. Stanton?"

"I was supposed to get a commission," he replied. "They lied."

"I could have told you Republicans were liars."

"I hate them all," Adam lied.

"I'd have fought for the South," Booth confided, "but the reality of war is that it does eventually end, and life goes on, and my life is acting. I might have been scarred in battle, which would have ruined my career."

"Oh."

"I feel guilty," Booth added. "I want to do something. Now. To redeem myself."

"Why are you telling me this? We're not friends."

"I make friends easily." Booth smiled. "I've many friends here. You should meet them."

"Friends or conspirators?" Shivers roamed over Adam's body, but he forced a smile on his face.

"If they be conspirators, they must be friends first," Booth replied.

"Then if you consider me a friend you must want me as a conspirator." Adam had the strange feeling the conversation was going the same way as those he had had with prostitutes on street corners at midnight. What kind of good time do you want to show me, he remembered saying to painted women in cold shadows. "And what kind of conspiracy are you talking about?"

Before Booth could answer, a large, brutish young man opened the door and stuck his large head in. While this fellow was bigger and brawnier than he, and his facial features—chin, cheeks, nose—were more handsome than his, Adam felt superior because stupidity flowed through his eyes.

"Hey, Johnny," the man said, "this guy pickin' on ya?"

"No, Tommy," Booth replied. "I think we've a new friend here."

"Oh."

"Now please leave and shut the door."

"All right, Johnny." The large, stupid man left.

After a moment of listening to loud, thumping footsteps fade away, Booth smiled at Adam, a smile which made him nervous.

"What kind of conspiracy do you think I'm talking about?"

"Kill the bastards. All of them." Adam was tired of romancing about the subject. Stanton wanted it done by the end of the week, so he decided to be blunt.

"What do you bring to the table?" Booth asked.

"What?"

"What do you know that I don't already know about assassination?"

"I know a man who thinks like us." Adam narrowed his eyes. "Things like how to get close to the president."

"When can you arrange a meeting?"

"I don't know."

"Tonight."

"Too soon," Adam lied.

"It must be tonight."

"Very well. Tonight at midnight, under the Aqueduct Bridge."

"Do you think the man will show up on such short notice?"

"I don't know," Adam lied again. "I'll try."

"We'll be there."

"All right." Adam was more nervous knowing he was closer to killing Lincoln. Self-preservation made men do terrible things, he decided, and extended his hand.

"To success," Booth said as he shook Adam's hand.

"To redemption," he replied.

That afternoon he met Stanton at the turnstile gate between the grounds of the Executive Mansion and the War Department.

"I met someone," Adam said in a whisper. "He'll be at the bridge with friends."

"How many?"

"I don't know. I didn't want to ask too many questions."

"Very well. Mr. Baker will be there. What did you say?"

"I said I knew a man who knew how to get close to Lincoln."

"Good."

When Adam took the supper tray to the basement, Mrs. Lincoln hugged him and Gabby was still grinning at the old photograph Adam had given him in the afternoon. Adam could not help keeping his eyes down in front of Lincoln.

"Anything wrong, Private Christy?"

"Nothing, sir." He did not want to look the president in the face. A traitor, a lowly coward, that was all he was, all he would ever be. In Steubenville, he could have lived into old age without realizing what a despicable person he was. He could have been content to think he had admirable, manly qualities, but his life in Washington had stripped away his pretensions, leaving him with a person he neither liked nor wanted to be.

At midnight Adam stood under the Aqueduct Bridge waiting for the others to arrive. He decided not to be concerned with whether he was happy, sad, frightened, or disgusted. All he wanted was to endure the next few days. He heard footsteps behind him.

"Where's your man?" Booth asked.

Adam turned to see the actor, the hulking, dull-eyed man, and two other odd-looking fellows, a witless, clean-shaven youth, and a whiskered man whose irregular gait bespoke drunkenness.

"There he is." He nodded at a shadowy, short, stocky figure striding toward them.

"Is this it?" Baker asked in a clipped tone.

"This is—" Adam began.

"Don't tell me," Baker interrupted. "We're planning to kill the president of the United States, dammit. I don't want to know any of your names." He cleared his throat. "Now. Tell me something that convinces me you're smarter than you look."

"Sir," Booth said, pulling himself up to his full stature, "you're no gentleman, and not welcome to our noble endeavor."

"This noble endeavor is murder," Baker replied. "True gentlemen don't kill, so get that idea right out of your head." He paused to light a cigar. "So, what are your plans?"

Adam watched Booth pinch together his thin lips.

"In the last few weeks we've considered kidnapping Mr. Lincoln."

"What the hell for? The end of the war has been in sight since the first of the year."

"As leverage for release of prisoners."

Adam could sense Booth trying to maintain an air of confidence, but faltering.

"Are you so stupid that you think prisons will house and feed rebels any longer than they have to?"

"Of course not," Booth sputtered.

"Forget the Confederacy," Baker continued. "The Confederacy is dead. Cry your eyes out. Light some candles. Get over it." He puffed on his cigar. "But you can kill the bastards who killed the Confederacy."

"Hear, hear," the youth said.

"*Ja*," the bearded man added.

"Yeah, let's blow their heads off," the tall, stupid one mumbled.

"But the Confederacy—"

"To hell with the Confederacy!" Baker said, derisively. "Are you stupid? The Confederacy is dead. All we have left is revenge."

"Yeah," the stupid one repeated. "Let's get revenge."

"Very well," Booth acquiesced. "Revenge."

"Who do we hate the most?" Baker asked.

"Lincoln," Booth replied, spitting. "I hate the bastard."

"The Lincolns are going to Ford's Theater Friday night."

"I know that theater well," Booth offered.

"They will have only one guard, and he will be drunk."

"I can handle the details," Booth said.

"Good." Baker nodded curtly. "Now, what about Vice President Andrew Johnson?"

"We decided on Port Tobacco." Booth gestured to the bearded one.

"*Ja*, I rented a room in the Kirkwood House, directly above Johnson."

"Come here," Baker ordered.

Port Tobacco stepped forward, his head down. Baker leaned into him and sniffed.

"Just as I thought. You're a drunk." He looked at Booth. "He won't do. Johnson must die." He pulled his revolver and pointed it at Port Tobacco. "He must die. He knows too much."

"No! No!" Port Tobacco's eyes widened. "I stop drinking. I kill Johnson! On *mutter*'s grave! I stop! I kill Johnson!"

"For God's sake," Booth said with a hiss.

"Incentive." Baker put away his revolver.

"*Sheitze*." Port Tobacco stepped behind the others.

"Seward. He must go." Baker looked around for a volunteer.

"Who's that?" the stupid one asked.

"Secretary of State, Reverend Wood," Booth said.

"What's that?"

"You're a moron, aren't you?" Baker asked as he spat on the riverbank.

"I can't help it." Reverend Wood's eyes went down. "I got kicked in the head by a horse once."

"I'll help him," the youth offered.

Baker eyed him. "You look as dumb as he is."

"I work as a druggist's aide," the youth said. "And I know things. Secretary of State is a top aide to the president. He deals mostly with other countries." He looked at Booth. "Ain't that right?"

"Of course, you're right." Booth looked at Baker. "We can work together without all the insults."

"So you think you can lead him to the Seward house?" Baker asked.

"Yes, sir," the youth replied.

"That leaves Stanton," Booth said.

"Don't worry about Stanton," Baker said. "I'll kill him."

"You feel warmly about it?" Booth smiled.

"You hate Lincoln," Baker said. "I hate Stanton."

"Then it's settled," Booth announced with finality. "*Sic Semper Tyrannous.*"

"What's that?" Baker wrinkled his brow.

"It means, 'Thus ever to tyrants.' It's the motto of Virginia."

"Virginia," Baker mumbled.

Adam could see the wheels turning in his mind.

"Ah yes, Virginia. Do you know an actress called Jean M. Davenport?"

"Why, yes." Booth looked taken aback. "I've performed with her many times."

"You talked with her once at a party about accomplishing a great daredevil act, like kidnapping the president."

"How did you know that?"

"Now you know you can't keep secrets from me."

"We're united in a noble cause, sir," Booth said.

Baker puffed on his cigar and squinted at Booth through the smoke. "Get out of here."

Booth and his friends dispersed into the dark mist. Baker threw his burnt cigar onto the muddy shore.

"This is dirty business," Adam muttered.

"This is war," Baker retorted.

"The war's over."

"There's always a war."

Chapter Forty-Eight

The next morning when Adam delivered the breakfast tray, he kept his eyes down when serving the Lincolns. Hoping his face was not red from shame, Adam tried to move on to Gabby as quickly as possible.

"You're not still worried we're mad at you, are you?" Mrs. Lincoln asked with a note of concern in her voice, her hand touching his arm.

"No, ma'am," he replied. He knew she would be a widow on Friday. "I know. I appreciate it."

"Don't worry about it." Lincoln was behind the French lace curtain, sitting up on his cot, a place from which he had rarely stirred since the end of the war.

"That's all right, Mr. President." Adam went to the curtain, looked in, and tried to smile. "I know you don't hold any grudges."

"You know that's not what I meant." The deep shadows under Lincoln's sunken eyes frightened Adam. "I know what's going to happen. Don't bear the guilt. I know who's responsible."

Adam blinked and opened his mouth, but nothing came out. He turned toward Gabby's corner. He was already awake, his knees pulled up under his chin.

"Good morning, Mr. Gabby." Adam put the plate on the floor in front of him. "Fried eggs, just the way you like them."

"Private, what's going to happen to me, now that Cordie's dead?" His large eyes were filled with tears.

Squatting in front of Gabby, Adam began his explanation slowly, since he had no idea what would happen to Gabby, to himself, or to

Jessie. He did not want to lie to the old man again. No gloomy predictions of living on the streets, which possibly could happen, because Adam did not want to scare him any more than he already was; but he could not tell him he would have a warm place to live and plenty to eat, either.

"I wish I could assure you everything will be fine, but I can't," Adam said. "But I won't let you down. I'll do everything I can to help you."

"Promise?"

"I promise."

"Now I feel hungry."

"What do you want done with the rest of your sister's things?"

"I don't need them." Gabby's attention was drawn to the eggs. After a big swallow, he looked up. "Ask the ladies at the hospital. Maybe they need some clothes."

"Yes, Mr. Gabby." He smiled. It was another chance to try to change Jessie's mind. "That's a good idea."

After Adam retrieved the tray and cleaned the chamber pots, he caught an omnibus to the Surratt boardinghouse on H Street. Bounding up the stairs with a large burlap bag, he entered Cordie's room, gathered her clothing, and tossed it in the sack. He was about to leave when Reverend Wood blocked the door.

"I didn't like that feller last night."

"I don't like him, either. But we don't have to like him, as long as we get what we want."

"What's that?" he asked, nodding at the bundle under Adam's arm.

"The old woman's clothes."

"Mama could wear those. If only I could get them down to Florida."

"I'm taking them to the hospital. For the nurses."

"Oh."

Adam quickly left. Sighing with relief when another omnibus arrived, he ran down the boardinghouse steps to H Street. As the omnibus rattled down the street, Adam tried to think of a new way to win back Jessie. Hugging the burlap bag, he wanted a happy future. The omnibus turned south on Thirteenth Street. As he covered his nose when it crossed the open sewer by the Mall, Adam wondered if the most direct words would be best—I love you more than life itself. He had to think of the right thing to say. When the omnibus stopped at Independence Avenue, Adam stepped off to run down the street, past the red towers of the Smithsonian, to the rows of low barracks of the hospital.

Immediately upon entering the ward, Adam scoured it, trying to locate Jessie; instead, Dorothea Dix's pinched face was in front of him.

"You're the young man who's always around Miss Home."

"Yes." He gulped before continuing. "Miss Zook's brother wanted me to bring her clothing here for the ladies who need it."

She opened the burlap sack to examine the dresses.

"Very good. It was very kind of her brother. Miss Zook was a good person. I miss her." Miss Dix looked into Adam's eyes. "What are your intentions toward my Miss Home?"

"Most honorable, ma'am," he replied.

"I thought so. Go find her and take her home. She hasn't been well since Miss Zook died. I told her to rest, but she won't listen to me. She never listens to me." She paused. Adam thought she was about to cry. "I don't want to lose another dear one."

"Yes, ma'am."

Miss Dix turned away quickly and began fussing over a wounded soldier. Adam scanned the room for Jessie's red hair. Almost ready to give up, Adam heard a loud shout from a far corner. His throat constricted as his eyes focused on Jessie's frail body, on the floor in front of frightened young man on a cot. Adam ran to her, knelt by her side, and felt her moist, hot forehead.

"She was replacing my bandage when she fell over," the soldier said. "I hope she's all right."

Swooping her up into his arms, Adam walked to the back room where Cordie had died. Behind him was Miss Dix.

"I told her she should go home to rest. Now she can't be moved," she said. "Put her on the cot." She hovered over Jessie, feeling her forehead and taking her pulse. "This isn't good. I think it's influenza."

His eyes widening, Adam found he couldn't speak.

"Can I help?" the odd-looking man asked as he appeared in the door.

"Get me a bowl of water and a stack of cloths," Miss Dix replied.

"May I stay awhile?" Adam said.

"Yes, please. Wipe her brow. I have to attend to the wounded."

After she left, Adam sat on the edge of the cot, waiting for the odd-looking man to return with the bowl and cloths.

"Jessie? Can you hear me?" He paused. "I love you."

"What happened?" Her green eyes fluttered open and focused on him.

"You fainted. Miss Dix thinks you've got influenza." He took her moist white hand and squeezed it. "And I'm going to take care of you."

Once her bleary eyes saw Adam's hand over hers, Jessie pulled away and rolled onto her side. The odd-looking man entered with the bowl of water and cloths.

"How is she?"

He looked into the odd-looking man's clear blue eyes and saw intelligence. Stanton believed himself to be smart, but Adam did not see anything like that in his eyes. He saw imagination in Booth's eyes, but not intelligence. He sometimes sensed a deeper intelligence in Gabby's eyes, but it was blurred by terrible torture and bewilderment. Yet this man had pure intelligence.

"Awake but she doesn't feel like talking," he softly said.

Perhaps this man's pure intelligence could help him, Adam thought, but he did not want to tell him anything that could endanger his life. He had endangered too many lives as it was.

"I'll be back later. She's in good hands now." The man smiled and left.

Adam turned back to Jessie and touched her shoulder.

"Please go away," she said.

"Don't you know? You can't get rid of me that easily." He took a cloth, dunked it in a bowl, squeezed it, and wiped her brow. "Maybe if I sit here long enough, wipe away enough perspiration, you'll finally realize how much I love you."

"It's too late."

"It's never too late. I love you," he said in a whisper as he rested his head against her shoulder. "Please tell me you love me too."

"I'm so tired," Jessie said softly.

"Please tell me you love me."

Her hand weakly reached up to his and patted it, then went down to her side. Adam heard her breathing softly. He leaned over to kiss her cheek, then walked out of the ward at a pace so fast the nurses and patients could not notice his wet, red eyes. Instead of taking the omnibus, he trotted across the Mall and the iron bridge over the slough. His racing heart helped his mind to clear. Jessie was young and strong. She must survive.

He walked up the service drive to the Executive Mansion, went in to pick up the luncheon tray, and delivered it, hardly noticing the Lincolns and Gabby, instead concentrating on Jessie's pat on his hand. It had to mean she loved him, Adam told himself, as he went up to the second floor.

"Private!" Tad called out when he appeared in the hall. "I haven't seen you in the last few days! Richmond is a mess!" He hugged Adam. "Did you see the parade last night? It was great!"

Adam could not look at the boy who had his arms around him. He could not look into the eyes that in two days would be filled with tears because Adam had conspired to have his father assassinated, but he did return Tad's embrace.

"Yes, the parade, that was fun," Adam mumbled.

"You're gonna stay, ain't you?" Tad looked up at him. "After Friday, I mean?"

"I don't know," he lied. "I'm a soldier. I never know where the army will send me."

"I hope they let you stay here," he said with a big smile. Running down the hall to the grand staircase, he yelled for Tom Pen.

When Adam entered the president's office, he found the double in a pensive mood.

"Sir? Is there anything I can do for you?"

"No, thank you." Duff paused. "Are you staying after we leave?"

"No, sir."

"Then run away now. Go out West. Pan for gold. Don't finish their game."

"I can't."

"Why?"

"My girlfriend—my friend—is sick. I can't leave her."

"Very well." He looked at Adam. "Is she very ill?"

"We think it's influenza."

"Oh." He put his head in his hands. "Then maybe it's for the best."

Seeing Lincoln's double recede into his thoughts, Adam went down the hall to knock on Mrs. Lincoln's bedroom door.

"Who is it?"

"Private Christy, ma'am."

"Come in."

Opening the door, Adam found her in the same pensive mood as the president's double. She was more melancholy today than he had seen her since they had met. Of all the characters in Stanton's plan, she was the only one who was always optimistic, which had many times lifted his own spirits. He wished he could say something to make her feel better.

"Do you need anything, Mrs. Lincoln?"

"No, thank you."

"Do you need any help with your packing?"

"No. You're very kind."

"If you don't mind, I want to go to Armory Square Hospital this afternoon. I have a sick friend there."

"Of course."

Adam exited quietly and went downstairs to clean the chamber pots, which did not bother him as much as it usually did, because his mind was on Jessie, hoping they would have a future together. Walking through the kitchen with the pots, he ignored Phebe, which had become easier to do over the last few days. After the last pot had been washed and returned, Adam ran out the service entrance and down the street to the Mall, across the iron bridge to the Smithsonian and on to the hospital.

Huffing, Adam stopped inside the ward door as he saw a couple of orderlies carry a small body wrapped in a sheet from the back room. His mouth dropped when they passed, and he saw a tuft of red hair peeking from the top of the sheet. In the distance, Miss Dix daubed her eyes, and the strange man patted her shoulder. Adam walked to them.

"I knew she should have gone home," Miss Dix said in a small voice.

"A true American patriot." The strange man, his eyes welling with tears, looked at Adam. "An immigrant, fresh from Scotland, devoted herself, body and soul, to mending boys broken by war. She gave all she had and, when the war was over, she made the ultimate sacrifice for her new homeland."

Adam looked from one to the other, wondering what Jessie's last words had been, hoping they had been about him. But she was gone now, and her last words did not matter. His life did not matter. His thoughts turned to Gabby.

"Sir, Miss Zook's brother needs someone." His eyes were pleading. "May I send him to you? Can you help him?"

"I'm sorry, my young friend, but death has been upon me too much the last few days. Miss Zook's life slipped away. And Miss Home—it's happened so quickly. I wanted her to live. I wanted her to love you. You and Miss Home were my remedy to war. Love conquers all, I thought, but evidently not." He shook his gray head. "I must go home." He smiled sadly. "I need my mother."

"You can't desert us," Miss Dix cried. "We need you."

"I'll be back," he replied. "I don't know when. Not long."

Miss Dix reached out to touch Adam. "Send the poor man to me," she said. "I'll take care of him."

"Thank you." He smiled. "Thank you both."

Adam turned to leave, knowing he would never see them again. As he walked back to the Executive Mansion, the clouds parted to reveal the sun. In the middle of the Mall, Adam realized how silent it was for a busy Thursday afternoon. Silence still sounded like death to Adam, but, he decided, death comforted him. It made the pain go away.

Chapter Forty-Nine

Good Friday—the last Friday—arrived with slivers of morning light coming through the curtains into Duff's bedroom, awakening him to sadness and fear. Alethia's withdrawal saddened him; he had hurt her deeply and was sorry for it. He did not know the manner of death Stanton had planned for them, but he knew it would be tonight. A soft rap at the door interrupted his thoughts.

"Come in, Tom Pen," he called out.

The old man came in and shyly deposited the morning newspaper at the foot of the bed.

"Thank you, Tom Pen."

"You're welcome, sir." He looked down.

"You're a good friend to Tad."

"Thank you, sir."

"And a good friend to me."

"Thank you, sir."

Tom Pendel kept his eyes averted as he left the room. He knew Duff was not the real Lincoln, but Duff was not going to dwell on what the servant might think. The dead did not care what the living thought.

Opening the newspaper, Duff noticed one small item on the front page. Rose Greenhow had drowned in late March off the coast of South Carolina when her ship sank, aborting her triumphal return from England where she had been the belle of London society after her book was published. Gold coins sewn into skirt, meant to redeem Southern soldiers from Yankee prisons, had dragged her to the bottom of the ocean.

At ten o'clock, he went to his last Cabinet meeting. Duff was never comfortable maneuvering through the Byzantine debates, walking the tightrope of following Stanton's orders yet maintaining an appearance of independence. From time to time, he relished the chance to defy Stanton or embarrass him in front of Cabinet members.

Looking up at the door after hearing a soft knock, Duff saw General Grant and smiled. He felt at ease with the general, whom he had met several times in the last two years, and went to shake his hand.

"General, good to see you."

"Thank you, Mr. President. Have you heard from Sherman?"

"No. I'd hoped he'd contacted you."

"Not a word."

After his march to the sea, Sherman and his army had turned north to cut a swath through the Carolinas. No one had heard anything from him since.

"I've no doubt he's successfully raising hell," Grant said.

"General," an old, cracked voice called out. "Have you heard from Sherman?"

Duff smiled when Secretary of the Navy Gideon Welles walked in. The old man had been his mainstay and comfort through the years.

Other Cabinet members arrived in quick succession. Secretary of the Interior John Usher: Duff did not like him as well as Caleb Smith, who had died early in the term. Usher had accompanied him to Gettysburg, and Duff had sensed a tinge of irony in Usher's compliments on the address. Perhaps he just had not liked the address—no one much did—and his cynical tone had not meant he knew Duff was an impostor.

Arriving next was Hugh McColloch, who had replaced Salmon Chase, now Chief Justice of the Supreme Court. Duff had found Chase too smug and implacable, but he appreciated McColloch's colorless and efficient qualities.

He also liked the honor, high-mindedness, purity, and dignity of the new postmaster general, William Dennison, who had replaced Montgomery Blair. Duff had admired Blair's openness, but it had disappeared after the incident in which his niece was caught with bottles of quinine sewn into her skirt. Dennison slipped into the room and sat down.

Coming in rapid succession were James Speed, who had replaced the aging Edward Bates as attorney general; Frederick Seward, son of Secretary of State Seward, who was recovering from a carriage accident; and Secretary of Interior James Harlan, whose daughter was marrying Lincoln's son Robert.

Duff regretted the retirement of Bates, a gruff defender of the Constitution; he did not know enough about Speed yet to have an opinion. Sighing, he was relieved Frederick had come for his father, because Seward always scared him with his solemn owl face. Duff was pleased to see Harlan; after all, he was going to be family—what was he thinking, Duff scolded himself. Who was in the Cabinet and who was not was no longer a concern to him, because he was a dead man.

With all the Cabinet members present except Stanton, Duff pulled the cord to call Noah Brooks into the room to take notes. He hoped the meeting would be over before Stanton arrived. This last day would go better without him.

"Now that we're all here—"

"Not all," Brooks interrupted. "Mr. Stanton isn't here."

"We've a quorum," Duff replied. "We must consider reconstruction." He felt he owed it to Lincoln to push his plan as long as he was in the Executive Mansion.

Before Duff could go any further, he heard a coughing at the door. Stanton entered the room. Sighing, Duff sat back and gave up hope to help Lincoln's efforts for an easy transition to one nation. Again he reminded himself: business of state would no longer concern him after tonight.

"Any news of Sherman?" Welles asked.

"No." Stanton sat at the table. "But it's of little consequence. Lee surrendered. The Confederate government is on the run. The war's over."

"But—" Welles began.

"The war's *over*." Stanton slapped his hand on the table.

"There's no need to bang on the table," Vice President Andrew Johnson said, his Tennessee accent dipped in bourbon, as he entered and sat at the table. "You need to learn manners, Stanton." He crossed his arms across his big chest as he stared at the war secretary.

"And you need to learn to stay sober," Stanton said through clenched teeth.

Several Cabinet members shifted uneasily, Duff noticed; he heard some whisper about why Johnson was even there. Lincoln's first vice president, Hannibal Hamlin, had never attended Cabinet meetings.

"Sir," Welles replied, addressing Stanton, "it's of great importance. If General Sydney Johnston vanquishes General Sherman, then all hell will break out. The South will be resuscitated—"

"Mr. Welles," Stanton said impatiently, "you see defeats where there are none. It's foolish to waste our time worrying about something that cannot happen. We've more substantial problems to deal with."

"One of those problems is why you insist on running this meeting," Johnson said, barely below a bellow.

"That's enough," Duff said, interceding. He liked Johnson very much. He might be a drunk, but he was honest to the core.

"Yes, sir." Johnson hung his head. "I know I don't belong here." He recovered his spirit and pointed at Stanton. "But I can still smell a skunk."

Stanton cleared his throat, took a notepad from his pocket, and took over the meeting. Duff clenched his jaw and sat glassy-eyed through several hours.

"Mr. President, that's all I have to report," Stanton finally said, rousing Duff from his stupor.

"Thank you," he replied softly.

Suddenly, the meeting was over. His duties were ended. As the group slowly left the room, Duff felt himself being spun around by Johnson, who gave him a big bear hug.

"I'm sorry I embarrassed you, Mr. President," he blubbered. "I'm on your side, you know. It's just I hate Stanton so much."

"I know, I know." Duff pulled away. "Go drink some coffee. You'll feel better."

As Johnson staggered from the room, Welles came to put a warm, comforting hand on his shoulder.

"It's over, Mr. Lincoln," he said. "I see the weariness in your face. Remember, your second term will have no war. Reconstruction will provoke intense political debate, but it'll be in peace."

"Thank you, sir," Duff said, but still looked down in melancholy.

"Stanton is taking far too many liberties," Welles added in a whisper. "I get nothing clear and explicit from him, a lot of fuss and mystery, shuffling of papers and a far-reaching gaze." He leaned into Duff's ear. "Remember, you're the president. You've the power to remove Stanton from office. Exercise that power."

Tears formed in Duff's eyes, so he nodded, turned away, and walked down the hall to his bedroom, where he put his large hands to his face. By force of will, he commanded his tears to stay. Stanton entered the room and closed the door.

"I've arranged a carriage to take you to the river port."

"Very well." His voice was hollow.

As Stanton walked out, Duff heard voices in the adjoining bedroom. It was Alethia and Mrs. Keckley.

"I feel strange today," she was saying to the dressmaker. "When you return next week, I may have lost weight."

"Oh."

"That means you'll need to go back to my old patterns."

"Of course."

Duff sensed Alethia wanted to say something else to Mrs. Keckley but did not know how.

"Thank you for being a friend." She paused. "A friend is one who accepts you for who you are, and not who you seem to be. You understand what I mean, don't you, Mrs. Keckley."

"Of course, Miss Lincoln."

"You're a very wise person, Mrs. Keckley," Alethia said. "I've been enriched to have known you."

"You're much too kind, Miss Lincoln." Mrs. Keckley added in a whisper, "And may God bless you, whatever happens."

"Thank you," Alethia replied, her voice cracking. "And good-bye."

"Good-bye, miss."

The door opened and shut, and Duff came around the corner to find Alethia sitting on the bed, her hand gently touching her cheek.

"I heard what you said to Mrs. Keckley. It was nice."

Alethia turned her nails into her flesh and pulled down. His larger hand covered hers and pulled it away from her cheek, which was already showing a welt.

"Please, don't. Come with me for a carriage ride. It'll do us good."

Nodding woodenly, Alethia silently followed Duff down the staircase and out the door to the carriage. She brightened sufficiently to wave and smile at pedestrians calling out greetings. Once the carriage had passed from downtown to the countryside, Alethia slumped back in her seat, putting her hands to her forehead.

"Alethia," Duff softly said so the driver could not hear, "I know I've hurt you deeply, for which I'm terribly sorry, and I understand you cannot forgive me. The worst part is that I have to hurt you again, and you'll probably hate me even more." He paused for a response; when none came, Duff continued, "Your friend, Rose Greenhow, is dead."

"What?" Her eyes, filling with tears, snapped to his face.

"She drowned when her ship sank off the coast of South Carolina. She was returning from London."

After moments of searching his face, Alethia collapsed against his shoulder, sobbing. He patted her back and began sputtering words of comfort. Alethia stiffened.

"Don't you dare," she whispered furiously. "How dare you try to console me?"

"I'm sorry," Duff replied.

The carriage continued for miles in silence until they had returned to the city, where they again began waving and calling out to the crowd. After dismounting from the carriage, they entered the Executive Mansion and climbed the staircase. Alethia turned abruptly to glare at him.

"We've only a couple more hours together. Don't speak to me again. After tonight, I'll return to Bladensburg and open my bakery—I hope a better person for the lessons I've learned here. And you, I don't care where you go or what you do as long as you never enter my life again."

Each ate a quiet supper—Duff in his bedroom, Alethia in hers—then began packing. Take nothing to indicate they had been there and leave nothing to indicate the same, Stanton had told them. The silence was killing Duff, until he heard Tad's laughter come down the hall, punctuated by mild admonitions by Tom Pendel. The noise drew Duff to his door.

"Mr. Pendel, thank you for being so kind to Tad."

"It's been a pleasure, sir." He paused awkwardly. "And I hope to continue to do so for the next four years."

"Of course, you will, Tom Pen," Tad interjected brightly, going to Duff's side. "Papa, you're scaring old Tom Pen into thinking he's going to lose his job."

"Please excuse me, Mr. Pendel." Duff smiled and patted Tad's shoulder. "I didn't mean to scare you."

"Don't think a thing about it, sir." Pendel turned to walk haltingly down the hall to the door of the service stairs.

After Pendel disappeared, Tad giggled and put his hand to his mouth. He pushed Duff into the bedroom and shut the door.

"I saved you that time, didn't I, Mr. Papa?" Tad's eyes glistened.

"Yes, you did." Duff tousled Tad's hair. "In a couple of hours your real parents will return, and all will be as it should be."

"Papa did a good job when he picked you to replace him. And when he gets back, I'm going to tell him to fire that Mr. Stanton. I don't like him."

"I don't think many people do like him." He looked toward the door to Alethia's bedroom. "You should say good-bye to Mrs. Mama. She's very sad."

"Yeah, I know. I'm gonna miss her too." He looked up. "Sometime, if you're on a street where Mama, Papa, and me pass, I can't wave to you. You understand why, don't you?"

"I understand. Now go say good-bye to Mrs. Mama."

Duff followed Tad to the door and watched him open it and go to Alethia, who was closing her suitcase on the bed. At first he wanted to hear the tender exchange of farewells, but decided his heart, already strained by exceeding sorrow, could not bear it. Instead, Duff went to the window to watch the sun set over the Potomac, the same time of day he and Alethia first had come to the Executive Mansion.

Robert entered the room and looked down at the floor. "So you're going to the theater tonight?"

"Yes."

"Tomorrow we can have a talk, all right?" He looked into Duff's eyes, then shifted his gaze back to the floor.

"Of course." Duff thought how he would not be the one to talk to Robert. "I don't think I've said this much lately, son, but I'm very proud of you." Duff was proud of Robert, and he was fond of Tad. He wished they had been his sons.

"Thank you, Father." Robert's face brightened.

After a warm hug, Robert disappeared down the hall into his room. Duff leaned against the door and sighed. He heard Tad close Alethia's door and enter his own room. Duff picked up his suitcase and went to her door to knock. Alethia joined him to walk down the service stairs, then his thoughts were drowned out by the crackling of the straw mats. When they opened the door, they saw Adam standing there to take them to their carriage. He looked completely defeated to Duff, and he wanted to say something comforting, but it was futile because they both were dead men. Going through the service drive door, Adam stopped abruptly, his eyes startled as he stared at the carriage driver, a short, muscular man with dark hair. When Duff glanced at Adam, he was inching backward to the door.

"Put the luggage in the back," the driver said.

He and Alethia climbed into the carriage and settled down as it pulled away from the service driveway and into the dark street. Remembering his promise, Duff did not look at her, nor speak to her; instead, he focused on the dark horseman.

"You're not our usual driver, are you?"

The man did not reply.

After several minutes, Duff noticed the carriage turned onto a black, little-used road heading north to the Maryland countryside rather than south to the Potomac. Suddenly, he grasped that this was the time of their deaths. Acting on instinct, Duff quickly turned to Alethia and forced a light kiss on her lips. In the middle of her protest, a shot rang out, and Duff saw a red splotch on her forehead. Looking forward, he heard a loud report, and true silence overwhelmed the carriage.

Chapter Fifty

Darkness covered the city as Stanton's chest heaved in hacking coughs while his carriage clacked up K Street to his home. On the eve of his final triumph over the original ape, he felt heaviness on his lungs.

After the carriage stopped in front of his house, he climbed out and tried to clear his throat as he stood under the gaslight and watched the carriage disappear into the night. When the coughing had stopped, another carriage pulled up and Baker emerged.

"Is it done?"

"Yes."

"Good." He paused. "Are you sure the others will do their jobs?"

"Who knows? I don't trust them."

"Private Christy. Is he still alive?"

"Yes."

"Kill him."

"Yes, sir."

"Do you at least trust the actor?"

"Him more than the others."

"Good."

"You want the power that bad?"

"It took too long," Stanton said in a whisper. "If the war had ended by 1863, I'd let Lincoln return, but the longer it went, the more I knew Lincoln would take revenge."

"That's a lie," Baker replied. "Lincoln would have forgiven you, would forgive you still tonight. It's the power. It's always been the power."

"And what is it for you?" Stanton asked spitefully.

"I'm a simple man," he said. "I'm not a lawyer, like you or Ward Lamon. I'm not smart enough to want more than to be comfortable. And it takes money for that."

"So it's just the money?"

"You're a fool, Mr. Stanton. You think power will make you happy. Power doesn't make you happy."

"Neither does money."

"That's right." Baker smiled. "But it makes being miserable much more fun."

"If you want your money, finish your work," Stanton said.

"Yes, sir."

Baker climbed back into the carriage and rode off into the cold night. Stanton looked up. It was about to rain. He unlocked the door and went inside to find the lights out. Stanton slowly walked upstairs. When he entered his bedroom, Stanton saw his wife sitting by a lamp, reading a book. She was so lovely. Before he could speak, a hacking cough erupted from his throat.

"Your cough sounds bad." Mrs. Stanton looked up from her reading.

"Don't worry about it. I've overcome worse than this."

"How is Mrs. Lincoln?"

"Fine. Fine." Stanton removed his jacket.

"I hope so. She's misunderstood. Losing children is so devastating."

He bent over to kiss her smooth, pale neck with his Cupid's bow lips.

She stiffened. "I don't feel well."

"Please," he whispered. "I need to be close to you tonight." He coughed again.

"You're still too ill," she replied. "You should consult your physician."

"And let my enemies know?"

"They already know."

"Please," he said in a tone so pitiful it caused her to put her book aside.

"Very well."

They turned their backs to each other as they began to undress. Stanton could not keep his mind from wandering back to the events of the night. Most people would accept the fact that the most famous matinee idol of American theater could kill the president.

"Dear, turn off the lamp," she said.

He turned off the gas lamp and unbuttoned the front of his union suit. In case some people wanted a more complex conspiracy theory, Stanton wanted to oblige them with other believable scenarios. As he slipped into bed and slid close to his wife, Stanton decided the surviving Confederate leaders might want revenge. After all, plans to blow up the Executive Mansion had been exposed, and the Lincoln administration had instigated a raid on Richmond to kill Jefferson Davis. He found his wife in her nightgown.

"It's cold tonight," she said.

As he kissed her neck, Stanton thought of another possible plot to muddy the waters. High-level government officials knew Lincoln had turned down loans from the Rothschilds, so the public might believe international bankers wanted him dead.

"On the side, dear," she said. "I can't carry your weight anymore."

Rolling to his side, Stanton put his arms around her waist. A cough erupted, and he had to turn his head. He thought of another plausible conspiracy. Roman Catholics staunchly supported the Confederacy and the institution of slavery. Since most Americans were biased against Catholicism, they could easily be led to believe the Pope had ordered the assassination.

"No kissing. I don't want your cold."

Perspiration rolled down Stanton's forehead as he forced his pelvis into hers. After a few more futile attempts, he rolled away, heaving in frustration.

"Don't worry about it, my dear," she said. "At a certain age, matters of a personal nature lose their importance."

Stanton buttoned the front of his union and sighed.

"Don't dwell on it," she said. "I still love you."

Putting his thick forearm across his face, Stanton felt his eyelids grow heavy. His wife's breath became soft and shallow as her body went limp. He, too, felt himself drifting off, arrested only by a final thought of his official statement about Lincoln's assassination as he stood before the crowds on the street.

"Don't fear. I'm now in control." No, he thought, feeling his limbs grow heavy. That was too self-centered. The people did not want to hear about him; they wanted news about Lincoln.

"He's dead." Too blunt, he decided as he rolled over, becoming more comfortable. His mind had begun to sink into sleep's oblivion when a phrase came to him.

"Now he belongs to the angels."

Stanton shook his head. Angels did not sound appropriate. He thought of another word which pleased him so much he finally fell asleep.

"Now he belongs to the ages."

Chapter Fifty-One

Stepping inside the Executive Mansion service door, Adam slumped against the kitchen wall as he tried to comprehend what was going to happen to the very amiable couple he had known for the last two-and-a-half years. They had been kind to him, and now he mourned their imminent deaths. Adam shook off his melancholia so he could walk into the billiards room with a smile to help the Lincolns move their possessions back upstairs.

"Praise the Lord. No more chamber pots," Mrs. Lincoln said in exultation as she finished packing. "Please take down my French lace curtains, Private Christy."

"Yes, ma'am."

"Who knows what that other woman has done to my room and my finest dresses."

Adam stiffened momentarily, and he noticed that she had noticed.

"I know." She touched his arm. "I'm sure she was a very nice lady. And he was a fine gentleman." Mrs. Lincoln smiled. "Remember, I'm from Kentucky, and we Southern belles must always fuss about something."

"Molly, time to go," Lincoln said.

"Father, we should say good-bye to Mr. Gabby."

"Of course."

Turning the corner of the stack of crates and barrels, Adam and the Lincolns found Gabby lying face down on his pallet.

"Mr. Gabby?" Lincoln said.

"Go away. I'm sad."

"There's no need to be sad, Mr. Gabby," Mrs. Lincoln said. "We all can go back to our normal lives."

"Cordie's dead. Life can't be normal without Cordie."

"As sad as it seems, you will go on without Cordie," Lincoln said. "You will survive, or you too will die. And I don't think your sister would want that to happen."

Mrs. Lincoln gazed up devotedly at him, Adam observed, and he had to turn away because the same fate awaited her tonight. She would lose her husband and would have to struggle to survive, just as Gabby was struggling, and just as he was struggling with Jessie's death. Like Lincoln said, he would learn to live with the grief or allow the grief to kill him.

Kneeling beside Gabby, Mrs. Lincoln patted his shoulder and said, "If all this is too much for you, feel free to stay here a few more days. We won't mind."

When he did not respond, Mrs. Lincoln stood to leave. Adam followed them as they went up the service stairs. On the second floor, Tad bounded from his room to fly into his mother's arms.

"Mama! Papa!" Tad yelled. In a quieter voice he added, "I'm glad you're back!"

As she caressed his tousled brown hair, Mrs. Lincoln whispered, "I can tell you've grown. The woman was good to you."

"Mrs. Mama was great. And Mr. Papa." His face darkened a moment. "I hope you don't mind that I liked them."

Reaching to touch Tad's shoulder, Lincoln replied, "No, I'm glad they took good care of you."

Again, knowing Lincoln was to be assassinated tonight, Adam had to turn his head away so they could not see his eyes clouded with guilt. He knew how it hurt a child to lose a parent. No one would comfort him. No one would listen to him when he said his heart ached. He shook his head. Much more of this emotion, Adam warned himself, and he would go mad.

"Let's play games tonight!" Tad said, beaming.

"We can't, dear," Mrs. Lincoln replied. "Mr. Stanton arranged for us to go the theater to see Miss Laura Keene's farewell performance."

"Oh, him." Tad pulled away from his mother. "Don't go. I don't trust him." He went to his father. "Stay home with me and play games. Then send for that old Mr. Stanton to come here at midnight in his nightshirt. And fire him, right there at midnight in his nightshirt."

Breathing deeply, Adam bit his lip in hopes that Lincoln would do exactly what his son asked. He could save his own life by removing Stanton from all power. His heart raced. The thought of Lincoln firing the war secretary gave him hope again.

"No, son, we have to go."

Tad fell against his father's flat belly and sighed.

"That's all right," Mrs. Lincoln said, turning to her bedroom. "The public expects us to attend. I wonder if I have anything decent to wear."

"Papa?"

"Your mama hasn't been out in one of her fancy dresses in a long time. I can't deny her."

"Mr. Papa had a softer belly than you," Tad said, still leaning against his father. "But he had a soft heart like you." He looked up to smile. "Tell Mama she has to tell me all about the play tomorrow."

Adam watched Tad walk back to his room and, as he shut the door, Adam felt his hope die a second time. Another door swung open, causing Adam and Lincoln to turn their heads. Mrs. Lincoln looked radiant, holding a white dress with little pink flowers.

"I found it in the back of the armoire," she said with delight. "Mrs. Keckley brought it the last week we were here. I never wore it, being in mourning. I'm sure it still fits." Her tiny fingers ran across the top. "I know it's rather low-cut, and shows a modest décolletage, but I feel like celebrating."

"Then celebrate." Lincoln smiled at her. "By the way, Tad wants you to tell him about the play tomorrow morning."

"Oh, I'm going to sleep until noon tomorrow." She paused. "Isn't it odd that in the basement, when I could sleep all day, I awoke early? And you, Father, who usually rise early, slept all day. Perhaps this means we're going to be normal again."

"Yes, normal again," Lincoln softly said.

After she had gone into her room to dress, Lincoln looked at Adam, who sensed the president had noticed his eyes.

"Don't worry," Lincoln said. "I don't blame you." He turned to his bedroom. "Come with me." After they entered the bedroom, Lincoln went to his armoire. "I'm not changing suits. I just want my good hat and overcoat." Putting on the overcoat first, Lincoln looked startled by how large it was on him. "This must belong to the other man. He was larger than me. A dubious distinction, indeed." He looked at Adam. "Did he really fool everyone?"

"I don't know." Adam averted his eyes. "I think he fooled some. Stanton intimidated others into not noticing. A few chose to see only what they wanted to see."

"He was a good man. He treated my son well." Lincoln returned his attention to the coat. "This will be a giveaway." He tossed it on the bed. "I doubt he'll be back to reclaim it."

"No, he won't," Adam said in a subdued tone.

"How did this happen?" Lincoln pulled out a worn stovepipe hat and stuck his finger through a hole.

"The man narrowly missed an assassin's bullet last summer while riding," Adam said.

"Mrs. Lincoln would disapprove if I wore that." He put the hat by the large coat and sat on the bed, motioning to Adam to join him. "You see, when I undertook the labor of running for president and thereby setting in motion the machinery of this war, I knew I'd have to pay the ultimate price for doing the horrible job that had to be done." He leaned toward Adam to whisper, "Thank you for not saying anything to Molly. Let her have these last few hours of happiness."

"See, I didn't gain a pound in that wretched basement." Mrs. Lincoln appeared in the door, preening in her new white dress.

A knock at the door made Adam jump.

"Your carriage has arrived, Mr. President," Tom Pendel said.

"Are you going with us tonight, Private Christy?" Mrs. Lincoln asked.

"No, ma'am. I leave tonight."

"Nonsense," she replied. "We've no ill will against you. In fact, I've grown quite accustomed to you. I'd hate to break in a new adjutant."

Lincoln looked back and forth between his wife and Adam.

"I do believe, Molly, that this young man has a hankering to go home to Ohio, even though it might cause you personal distress."

Chapter Fifty-One

"Oh. Of course. I hadn't thought of that."

Pendel knocked again.

"We must be on our way, Mother," Lincoln said, retrieving his other overcoat and hat from the armoire.

"Good night, Mr. Pendel," Lincoln said.

"Good night, sir; madam."

After they walked down the grand staircase, President and Mrs. Lincoln and Adam went out the door. Adam was taken aback to see the front door guard John Parker standing by the awaiting carriage, already in the early stages of inebriation.

"I don't like that man," Mrs. Lincoln whispered to her husband. "He always reeks of whiskey." She looked up at the cloudy, dark sky. "Oh, dear, it's raining. My white dress will be ruined by the end of the evening."

"Think happy thoughts, Mother," Lincoln said. "The world turns on more than muddy dresses."

They settled into the carriage while Parker staggered to his seat next to the driver. The Lincolns looked back at Adam.

"Good night, Private Christy," Mrs. Lincoln said with a chirp.

"Good-bye, young man."

With his throat choked, all Adam managed was a small wave. And for the second time that night, he watched a couple ride into the dark to their destinies. This time, however, he could not hold back tears. Rushing to the service stairwell, he cried as his feet crackled on the straw mats. At the bottom, he fell against the door, sobbing silently. When he had regained control, Adam opened the door and walked to the billiards room. Inside, he found Gabby curled up on his pallet about to doze off. Adam touched him gently.

"What?" Gabby said, sitting up.

"It's me, Private Christy."

"Oh."

"You have to go."

"But Mrs. Lincoln said I could stay."

"Things have changed." Adam started putting Gabby's clothes together in the middle of one of his quilts. "I know someone who'll help you."

"I remember. The nice young woman Cordie liked."

"No," Adam replied with a steady voice. "Unfortunately, the young woman died. Miss Dorothea Dix will give you a place to stay. Do you know who she is?"

"Yes. The boss lady. Cordie was scared of her."

"Well, she's nice once you get to know her. She'll care for you until a man from New York will come to take care of you."

"New York's good. I know New York. My mother and father died there. New York's a good place to die."

"Don't talk like that," Adam said. "You're not going to die any time soon. I think you're going to live happily for a long time."

"We all have to die sometime. New York is a good place to die."

Adam bowed his head and finished tying Gabby's bundle. He looked up when Gabby began to sniff.

"I smell rain."

"It started drizzling awhile ago."

"I don't like getting wet. It's a long way to the soldiers' hospital, and I'll get wet. I hate getting wet."

His mind racing, Adam finally thought of the hat and coat on Lincoln's bed. They would be too large for Gabby, but they would keep him dry.

"I'll be right back."

"Take your time. It's raining."

As Adam bounded up the matted service stairs, he felt that giving the hat and coat was the least he could do for Gabby after all he had been through because of Stanton's terrible conspiracy. When he opened the door to the second floor, Adam slowed his pace, not wanting to draw attention to himself. He slipped into Lincoln's bedroom, picked up the clothes, and left. Back in the billiards room, he found Gabby still in his corner. Adam smiled at him.

"Here's a hat and coat. Now you won't get wet."

"They're too big." Standing, Gabby inspected them.

"That means you'll have more protection from the rain."

"But I'll look stupid."

"Yes, but you'll be dry."

"It's better to be dry." Gabby inspected the hat and coat more closely. "These are nice." Putting on the coat, Gabby looked down and stroked the fabric. He scrutinized the black stovepipe hat. One of his fingers found the hole. "What's this?"

"A bullet hole," Adam replied. "Mrs. Lincoln didn't want her husband to wear it."

"The president's hat?" Gabby's eyes widened. "Is this the president's coat?"

"Yes."

Gabby carefully put the hat on his gray head.

"Does this mean I'm really the president now?" His eyes revealed deep concentration as he picked up his bundle.

Adam hesitated. He knew the president's double was dead. Lincoln was to be shot soon. How many assassinations would be carried out overnight was uncertain. In this hour of leadership confusion, why not have a leader who was in a permanent state of confusion?

"Yes. You're president."

"I thought so." Gabby nodded with assurance and walked out of his safe place behind the crates and barrels. "My father would have been so proud."

"Good night, Mr. President." Adam gave him his best salute.

Gabby paused long enough to nod seriously before going across the hall, through the kitchen, and to the service entrance door. Adam listened to Gabby opening the door, and expected to hear it slam shut. Then he would be alone to decide his own future. When he did not hear the clang of the door, he frowned. What was happening now? he wondered.

"Who the hell are you?" Adam recognized Baker's voice.

"I'm the president, aren't I?"

Adam held his breath. He did not want Baker to kill Gabby too. No one deserved to die, but Gabby deserved to live more than anyone.

"Get the hell out of here," Baker snapped.

"Yes, sir," Gabby meekly replied.

The door clanged shut, and Adam heard Baker's footsteps through the kitchen, on his way to tie up the last loose end of Stanton's scheme. The future was now, finally, in Adam's hands. He could wait for Baker to enter the door to kill him. He could shoot Baker as he came through the door. Those were not acceptable choices. Pulling out his revolver,

Adam placed the barrel in his mouth, satisfied that, at the end, he was able to control his own destiny.

"What was that?" Cleotis sat up in bed at the muffled gunshot. Cocking his head, he added, "Did you hear that?" He paused. "I think I hear footsteps."

Phebe reached out in the dark, pulled him down to her side, and put her arms around him.

"That's white folks' business."

Bibliography

Donald, David Herbert. *Lincoln*. New York: Simon and Schuster, 1995.

Humes, James C. *The Wit and Wisdom of Abraham Lincoln*. New York: HarperCollins, 1996.

Johnson, Rossiter. *Campfires and Battlefields*. New York: Gallant Books, 1960.

Leech, Margaret. *Reveille in Washington*. New York: Carroll and Graf Publishers, 1986.

Seale, William. *The White House, Volume One*. Washington, D.C.: White House Historical Association, 1986.

Ostendorf, Lloyd, and Walter Olesky, editors. *Lincoln's Unknown Private Life: An Oral History by His Black Housekeeper Mariah Vance 1850-60*. Mamaroneck, NY: Hastings House, 1995.

Internet Sources

John Niven, "Salmon P. Chase," <http://www.Presidents of the United States@Internet Public Library.org.>

Dexter Perkins, "William Henry Seward," http://www.Presidents of the United States@Internet Public Library.org.>

Lydia Perkins, "Edwin M. Stanton," http://www.Stanton.html@pwl.netcom.com.

W.E. Smith, "Montgomery Blair," http://www.Presidents of the United States @ Internet Public Library. org.

Acknowledgments

I wish to express my appreciation to Janet McKinney as editor of my novel for making the process easy and pleasant.

I also want to thank my son Joshua for being my soundingboard and proofreader. He is an avid reader of better authors than I and a student of Civil War history. I appreciate his honesty and support.

In addition I wish to recognize Jeremy McClellan, my niece's husband, for creating my personal computer, which made the process of creating the novel so much easier. He is a kind and intelligent young man.

About The Author

Born in the North Central Texas town of Gainesville, Jerry Cowling grew up with an unusually romantic taste for history, from fantasizing about finding the lost cache of stolen gold hidden by Old West outlaw Sam Bass to empathizing with a Roman child experiencing the eruption of Mount Vesuvius at Pompeii. He graduated from East Texas State University with a degree in journalism and English and spent the next ten years working for newspapers from Kingsport, Tennessee, to Dallas, Killeen, and Temple, Texas. *Lincoln in the Basement* is his first published novel but not the first written. Mr. Cowling has written six novels, one of which was produced on computer disk for a small Florida company. In addition, he has had a play published by Eldridge Publishing Company of Tallahassee, Florida, and has written several others which have received productions and staged readings in Oregon, California, Texas and Florida. He is married with two adult children. In the last few years he has been diagnosed with REM (rapid eye movement) sleep disorder. Doctors only discovered the condition in 1986 with which Mr. Cowling has been afflicted since childhood. He hopes in the future to help bring enlightenment to the public and reassurance to others who have REM sleep disorders by participating in open forums on the subject.